QUEEN OF THE

BOOK II

ORCS

Clan Daughter

MORGAN HOWELL

BALLANTINE BOOKS • NEW YORK

Queen of the Orcs: Clan Daughter is a work of fiction. Names, characters, places, and incidents are the products of the author's imagination or are used fictitiously. Any resemblance to actual events, locales, or persons, living or dead, is entirely coincidental.

A Del Rey Books Mass Market Original

Copyright © 2007 by William H. Hubbell
Excerpt from *Queen of the Orcs: Royal Destiny* copyright © 2007 by William H. Hubbell

Published in the United States by Del Rey Books, an imprint of The Random House Publishing Group, a division of Random House, Inc., New York.

DEL REY is a registered trademark and the Del Rey colophon is a trademark of Random House, Inc.

This book contains an excerpt from the forthcoming mass market edition of *Queen of the Orcs: Royal Destiny* by Morgan Howell. This excerpt has been set for this edition only and may not reflect the final content of the forthcoming edition.

Map illustration: William H. Hubbell

ISBN 978-0-345-49651-5

Printed in the United States of America

www.delreybooks.com

OPM 9 8 7 6 5 4 3 2 1

This book is dedicated to
Mary Jemison, Tenar,
and Carol Hubbell

Your scent lingers,
And we think of you,
Though you have wandered
From sight and touch.
        —Urkzimmuthi Lament

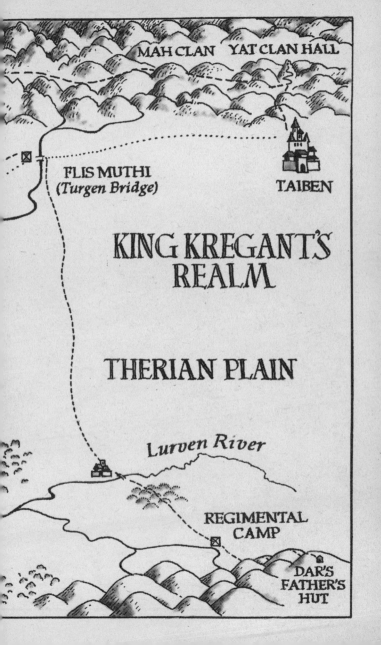

One

♛

Three nights of hard travel had cooled Dar's rage. Considered dispassionately, her prospects looked grim. *One woman and five orcs*, she thought, *deep in enemy territory. I promised to get them home, and I don't know the way.* Nevertheless, Dar didn't regret convincing the orcs to desert. The human king had betrayed them all. The orc regiments had been slaughtered, and the women who served them had perished also. Not even Twea had been spared. Whenever Dar recalled the look on the slain girl's face, her grief returned.

It was late afternoon and Dar was awake, though the orcs still dozed. Sitting upright within a small circle, they resembled idols and seemed as placid. Dar envied the ease with which they slept, while she—despite her exhaustion—napped only fitfully. Dar studied their faces, which no longer seemed bestial or alien. Kovok-mah had saved her life and sheltered her when she was an outcast. Duth-tok, Lama-tok, and Varz-hak were virtual strangers. Kovok-mah's cousin, Zna-yat, had tried to kill her twice.

Gazing at the massive orcs, Dar was still amazed that she was their leader. Yet she had chosen the escape route. It had been her decision to travel at night, "when washavokis cannot see." Female orcs, who were always called "mother," had authority among the urkzimmuthi. As long as Dar's companions regarded her as a mother, she possessed authority also. That was why she led, even if she stumbled in the dark.

Dar and the orcs were still in the hills, though far from the site of the ambush and battle. The steep, wooded slopes made walking difficult, but the rugged terrain provided safety. So far they had encountered no one, for the hills were barren except for tangled trees whose low branches hindered every step. The journey had already taken a toll on Dar. Her legs, arms, and face were crisscrossed with scratches, her bare feet were sore, and her empty belly ached. Her fatigue made the journey seem more daunting, especially considering how ill prepared she was. Their destination, the Urkheit Mountains, lay to the north, but that was all she knew. The orcs were just as ignorant of the way.

Dar's sole consolation was that her branded forehead brought no bounty in King Feistav's realm. *That won't help me if I'm caught with orcs*. Avoiding capture would be difficult. They were surrounded by enemies, so their hope lay in stealth; yet orcs had no aptitude for subterfuge. They were perplexed even by simple stratagems, and Dar had difficulty persuading them to avoid the roadway. If Kovok-mah hadn't followed her, the others might never have. Yet while Kovok-mah supported her decisions, Dar doubted he truly understood them.

Unable to sleep, Dar decided to scout the route ahead. She ascended the slope until she emerged from the trees to stand on a cliff at the hill's summit. The hilltop proved to be the last high ground, giving Dar an unobstructed view of the rolling plain ahead. Haze obscured the more distant features, and Dar saw no trace of the Urkheit Mountains.

The land appeared well populated—a quilt of fields, orchards, and wood lots, all demarcated by dark green hedgerows. A nearby rise was crowned by a low wall that encircled a small village. Dar spotted other dwellings scattered among the fields and orchards and grew apprehensive as she imagined all the hostile eyes the countryside contained. She was trying to plot a safe route through it when Kovok-mah emerged from the trees. "Why did you leave?" he asked in Orcish.

"To study way," replied Dar in the same tongue. Speaking it had become second nature. She gazed at Kovok-mah and read his expression. "Hai, there'll be many washavokis."

"Then there'll be much fighting."

"Thwa," said Dar. "There are too many to fight. We must pass unnoticed."

"So we travel by night?"

"More than that," said Dar. "You must not look like urkzimmuthi."

Kovok-mah curled his lips into a grin. "Have you magic? How will you change us?"

"You'll change yourselves," said Dar. "Leave your iron clothes behind and speak softly or not at all. I've brought cloaks I took from dead washavoki soldiers. From now on, you must wear them."

Kovok-mah looked puzzled. "We'll still be urkzimmuthi."

"In darkness, washavokis may not think so," said Dar. She could tell Kovok-mah was struggling to grasp her idea. "Washavokis don't expect to find urkzimmuthi in their land. They may not understand what they see."

Kovok-mah pondered Dar's words a while before he spoke. "After battle, I said I'd heed your wisdom. I haven't changed my mind."

"Will others heed it also?"

"They'll follow my example."

"Cloaks smell of washavokis," said Dar. "I fear Znayat will object."

"Hai, I think he will."

"Still, he must wear one."

"He swore to follow me, so I can make him do it if that's your desire."

"It is," said Dar, fearing that if her ploy failed and the orcs were attacked, they would sorely miss their armor. She slumped down on a rock, realizing her plan gambled with their lives.

Kovok-mah sensed Dar's turmoil and laid his hand on her shoulder, surprising her with the delicacy of his touch. "I'm pleased you guide us."

Dar sighed. "I'm not used to leading."

"It's natural for mothers to guide sons."

Perhaps among orcs, thought Dar. "Still, it's new to me. I worry about making mistakes."

"When you feel uncertain, remember Muth la guides you."

"Does she?" asked Dar. "I foresaw big battle and Little Bird's death, but I couldn't prevent either. What good are such visions?"

"I'm not fit to answer."

"Muth la is new to me, but not to you," said Dar. "What can you tell me of her ways?"

"She may be preparing you."

"For what?"

"I don't know," said Kovok-mah. "But I think you will when time comes."

"I hope you're right."

"When I have doubts, I follow my chest," said Kovok-mah. "That's why I'll wear washavoki cloak."

"Because of Muth la?"

"Thwa. Because of you. I feel safe with you."

Dar stared up at Kovok-mah, who looked so formidable, and wondered at his words. Insincerity was alien to his thinking. As incredible as it sounded, he was speaking the truth: She made him feel secure. The idea that a woman could do that ran counter to everything Dar had ever been taught. It made her smile, partly because it was so ludicrous and partly because it was so pleasing.

Two

♛

Kovok-mah entered the forest to forage for food while Dar remained to study the territory ahead. When the sun approached the horizon and long blue shadows crept across the land, Dar heard the soft sound of footsteps. The orcs emerged from the trees carrying mushrooms that looked tiny in their large hands. After placing the food before Dar, they marked off Muth la's Embrace using twigs and small rocks. Meanwhile, Dar divided the mushrooms into six piles, then waited for the orcs to join her inside the sacred circle. Once they were all seated, she intoned in Orcish, "Food is Muth la's gift."

"Shashav, Muth la," replied the orcs in unison.

Dar handed out the meager rations. Then she and the orcs ate in silence. Dar doubted the orcs were any more successful at enjoying their meal than she, for the mushrooms were woody and tasteless, intensifying rather than satisfying her hunger. Kovok-mah waited until everyone had finished eating before he spoke. "I've talked with Dargu about what lies ahead."

The other orcs followed his gaze to the darkening land. "Our kind once lived here," said Lama-tok. "That's urkzimmuthi stonework around washavoki houses."

Dar peered at the village on the hill. She had noted its circular wall earlier, but had paid little attention to it. After Lama-tok's remark, she looked at the masonry more carefully, but it was only a gray shadow to her in the failing light.

"There are few trees," said Varz-hak.

"Good," said Zna-yat. "I'm tired of hiding."

"There'll be too many washavokis to fight," said Kovok-mah. "We must pass through this land unnoticed."

"How will that be possible?" asked Duth-tok. "Surely, some will see us."

"We'll cause washavokis to see without understanding," said Kovok-mah. "Instead of wearing death's hard clothes, we'll wrap ourselves in cloaks Dargu brought. We'll travel by night, cover our weapons, and speak not as we walk."

Zna-yat regarded his cousin suspiciously. "You are speaking, yet I hear Dargu's words."

"Hai, and you hear wisdom," said Kovok-mah.

"Wearing washavoki cloaks won't change anything!" said Zna-yat. "If washavokis see us, we should close their eyes with swords."

"That won't get us home," said Dar.

"It's not your home," said Zna-yat. "Why do you want to go there?"

"It's where Muth la sends me," replied Dar.

"I think your words are like those cloaks you wish us to wear," said Zna-yat. "There's something different beneath them."

The orcs had no word for "liar," but Dar understood Zna-yat's accusation. Apparently, Kovok-mah did also. He sprang to his feet. "Such talk shows lack of wisdom."

Dar nervously watched Zna-yat, fearing he would rise and challenge Kovok-mah. Instead, he surprised her by bending his neck in submission. "Then I must learn Dargu's kind of wisdom."

Zna-yat's ambiguous reply didn't calm Dar's apprehension, but it satisfied Kovok-mah. "Good," he said. "Remove your hard clothes. I'll get Dargu's sack of cloaks."

While Kovok-mah went to fetch the cloaks, the orcs began to remove their armor. They wore short tunics beneath their shirts of iron plates, in addition to leggings not unlike those of human soldiers, and heavy sandals. Zna-yat, who was the first to cast his armor aside, walked over to Dar. "My mother's brother's son doesn't understand your washavoki ways," he said in a low voice, "but I do." Then he grabbed Dar's shoulders and pulled her toward him. Bending down, he sniffed her face. Zna-yat's lips formed a partial smile as he released her. "My blood's scent is gone."

Dar kept her expression neutral and said nothing. Instead, she prepared for the night's journey. First, she removed all trace of Muth la's Embrace from the ridge. Then she carefully hid the orcs' discarded armor. Kovok-mah returned with the cloaks and Dar's possessions. These consisted of a few items she had scavenged from the battlefield—a second dagger, a water skin, and the knapsack that had held the cloaks.

When it grew dark, Dar and the orcs headed down the wooded slope. As Dar traveled in the gloom, she pondered what Zna-yat had said. It was clear that his self-imposed truce was over. *But what does he intend to do?* Dar glanced over her shoulder. Zna-yat was only a shadow moving among shadows. If he wished, he could easily kill her in the dark. *What's stopping him?* Dar guessed the answer. *Kovok-mah.*

Dar was certain that Zna-yat didn't fear Kovok-mah. As far as she could tell, orcs were nearly fearless. It seemed more likely that Zna-yat was staying his hand out of consideration for his cousin. *Does that mean I'm safe?* Zna-yat's remark about learning "Dargu's kind of wisdom" provided an ominous hint. Dar reflected upon the nature of "her wisdom." Only human words could describe it. *Guile. Deception. Trickery.* It seemed to Dar that Zna-yat had implied that he wouldn't attack her openly, but would act like a washavoki instead. Yet, the idea that an orc would resort to treachery ran counter to Dar's understanding of orcs. *How well do I know them?*

Sevren and Valamar dismounted, and the two men waited in the dark for the camp to grow quiet. Valamar sneaked in first. When Sevren thought his friend was safe, he led Skymere to the field stables. As he had hoped, the remnant of King Kregant's army was still in disarray. Only a handful of orcs had survived, and the king's human troops were badly battered. When the sentries saw that Sevren was a royal guardsman, none questioned where he'd been.

Sevren tethered his horse, rubbed him down, then watered and fed him before looking for a place to sleep. He was just drifting off when a boot nudged him through his cloak. He looked up and saw Murdant Cron standing above him. "I did na put you on patrol. Where'd you go?"

Sevren said nothing.

"I'll have you flogged, countryman or nay, if you do na answer. Did you loot the slain?"

"You know me," replied Sevren, "so you know the answer."

"I want to hear it from your lips. From the looks of Skymere, you rode far. Did you visit the·battlefield?"

"Aye, I went there. But na to loot. I fulfilled an oath."

"What oath? To whom?"

"I told Dar and Twea they would na be left behind."

"You mean the wee lass and the orc wench?"

"Aye."

"What of your oath to our king? You're his guardsman. He wants you close."

"I know the penalty for leaving camp. I'll take my stripes."

"There's na need for that," said Murdant Cron. "I'll

keep this 'twixt you and me, if you tell me 'twas the last time."

Sevren sighed. "'Twas. She's gone."

"I could've told you she was dead. There was na cause to risk your back."

"Only Twea's dead. I found her where Dar placed her."

"You mean the orc wench lived?"

"Aye. Lived and fled with orcs."

"Then she's a fool. Her company will doom her." Murdant Cron shook his head. "You've always fancied strange women, but she was the strangest yet. That wench brought only trouble."

"Her troubles were na her doing."

"I've heard different tales, but that's all by the way. Forget her, as I'll forget tonight."

"I'll na leave again," said Sevren. "There's na point."

"Good. I want you fit, not flogged. There's like to be more fighting."

"Aye, knowing the king, I'm certain of it."

After a difficult walk down steep slopes, Dar and the orcs reached the edge of the woods. Before them lay a meadow illuminated by a full moon. Even Dar could see well. "Such light will aid our enemies," she said. "Let me check your cloaks."

The orcs halted. Dar covered her brand with a fake bandage, then adjusted the orcs' disguises. She pulled the hoods over their large heads to hide their faces and arranged the cloth to best cover their bulky forms. On men, the garments would have nearly touched the ground; upon the orcs, they ended at midcalf. Only in darkness would anyone be fooled into thinking those who wore them were human.

"You must walk in shadows," Dar said.

"Show us our path," said Kovok-mah, keeping his voice low.

Dar gazed about, trying to get her bearings. The route she had plotted from the hilltop wasn't discernible from her new perspective, and she wasn't certain where she was. Nevertheless, Dar headed toward a hedgerow. "Follow me."

They reached the hedgerow, a boundary formed by tall, thickly tangled shrubs. A narrow footpath ran beside it. From the cliff top, Dar had noted that a network of pathways followed the hedgerows, and she intended to use the paths to avoid the roads. Dar followed the dirt trail until the hedgerow it paralleled intersected with another one. She glanced at the stars to determine where north lay, then chose the path that headed northeast.

Dar's zigzag route took them past meadows, orchards, and newly planted fields. She always walked on the shadowed side of the hedge, and if a path approached a dwelling, she backtracked and found a different one. Such caution made progress slow, but Dar picked up the pace as the night wore on and the entire world seemed asleep.

It was well past midnight when a figure suddenly stepped onto the path from a hedgerow. Dar froze. The figure was a woman dressed in a robe that reached the ground. Dar saw her clearly. She wore a thin metal band upon her head. Thick, dark hair surrounded a face with an exotic cast. It featured pale eyes, a high, broad forehead, and a small chin that was covered with a pattern of dark markings. The woman paced about in a preoccupied manner and appeared not to have seen them. Yet as Dar motioned for the orcs to halt, the woman ceased pacing and stared directly at her.

"Why are we stopping?" whispered Kovok-mah.

Before Dar could reply, the woman spoke. "Naug nav ther?" *Where are you?*

Surprised that the woman addressed her in Orcish, Dar answered in the same tongue. "I don't know."

Kovok-mah spoke as if Dar had responded to his question. "Then shouldn't we proceed?"

Dar turned and whispered. "That woe man sees us!"

"What woe man?" asked Kovok-mah.

Dar turned and pointed. The path was empty. She walked over to where the woman had stood, while scanning about for some sign of her. "She was right here. Didn't you see her? She asked me where I was."

"I saw nothing," said Kovok-mah. "I heard nothing."

"How is that possible?"

"It is Nuf Bahi, when visions come."

Dar realized with chilling certainty that the woman hadn't been flesh-and-blood. *That's why only I saw her.* Dar wished she hadn't. All of her other visions had foretold death, and she feared this one did also. The woman's words seemed particularly foreboding. *I have no idea where I am*, Dar told herself. *I'm lost.* She was seized by an impulse to confess that to the orcs. But when she turned to face them, Zna-yat's expression stopped her. *He's looking for weakness.*

Dar reconsidered what to say. "My eyes see poorly in darkness," she said at last. "Yet Muth la sends me signs."

Three

♛

Each orc responded differently to Dar's vision, and their faces reflected their reactions. Duth-tok was awed. Lama-tok was uneasy. Varz-hak seemed both. Zna-yat had the smug countenance of one who sees through a performer's sleight of hand. Kovok-mah's expression was the most complex. Dar found concern mixed with wonder.

While the orcs didn't hide their emotions, neither did they voice them. Only Kovok-mah spoke. When he did, it was as if Dar had merely stopped to rest. "Are you ready to go?"

Dar took a deep breath. "Hai."

No more visions came that night. Dar continued to lead the orcs, while gripped by the anxiety of the lost. Her only guidance came from the stars, which she followed northward in the hope of reaching mountains. The night grew darker as the moon approached the horizon. As it became more difficult to see, Dar worried less about being seen. Instead, hunger occupied her thoughts. When they had traveled the hills, they had foraged during daylight. That would be too risky where people were about. Somehow, they would have to gather food at night. Nevertheless, Dar didn't bother to search for food in any of the fields they passed, for it was too early in the planting season. The kitchen gardens about the huts were likely yielding their first greens, but the peasants would still be living off last year's harvest. Robbing a larder would be dangerous, and Dar hoped an alternative would present itself.

When the eastern sky began to lighten, finding a place to hide became the most urgent problem. Dar scanned the landscape for a likely spot, but the moon had set and everything appeared as murky grays and blacks. She turned to Kovok-mah. "Washavokis will soon be about," she whispered. "We must rest where they won't find us."

Kovok-mah sniffed the air. "Many washavokis come this way."

Dar pointed toward a dark patch in the distance. "What lies there?"

"Trees," replied Kovok-mah.

"Perhaps that place is good," said Dar. She turned from the path and headed toward the shadowy patch. Struggling though high grass, she thought of her inadequacies. *I see poorly in the dark, and I can barely smell anything, day or night.* It wasn't until Dar was halfway across the meadow that she could make out the trees ahead.

"Help me, Kovok-mah," Dar said. "You must be my eyes and nose. I seek place where washavokis cannot see us, somewhere they seldom come."

"I understand."

When they reached the edge of the trees, Dar asked Kovok-mah what he thought. Kovok-mah paused to look about and sniff. "There is road through trees. I smell newly cut wood. Washavokis visit frequently. Their scent is fresh and strong."

Dawn was approaching, and Dar glanced about with a growing sense of desperation. A thicket of brush caught her eye. She headed toward it, and the orcs followed. Closer up, Dar recognized the arching, thorny canes and dense foliage of wild blackberries. Their berries would still be green, so there was no reason for anyone to brave their thorns.

"We'll be safe in there," said Dar, pointing to the thicket. "If washavokis come nearby, they won't see us."

"What if they do?" asked Duth-tok.

"Be still, and they won't," replied Dar.

"You haven't answered his question," said Zna-yat.

"Any that see us must die," answered Dar. "Yet, once we begin to kill, I fear washavokis will swarm like ants until we're destroyed."

"Dargu speaks wisdom," said Kovok-mah. "It was that way in battle."

The orcs motioned their agreement, even Zna-yat.

When Dar sensed the matter was settled, she began to gingerly pick her way toward the center of the thicket. Despite her care, there was no avoiding the thorns. They stabbed her bare feet, raked her arms and legs, and snagged her shift.

"Stop," said Kovok-mah.

"Why?" asked Dar.

Kovok-mah said nothing, but strode into the brambles and lifted Dar high above them. Then he made his way to the middle of the thicket and cleared an area with his sandaled feet before setting Dar down.

"You didn't need to do that," she said.

"I smelled pain," said Kovok-mah.

The other orcs followed Kovok-mah into the brambles, as seemingly unbothered by the thorns as he. Once they reached the center, they enlarged the cleared space and sat down. The surrounding foliage rose several feet above their heads and screened any view of the woods and meadow. Almost immediately, they closed their eyes and drifted off to sleep. While Dar looked for a spot to sleep also, Kovok-mah removed his cloak and folded it to cushion his broad lap. "Rest here," he said, patting the cloak. "There are no thorns where Little Bird slept."

Dar gave him a dubious look. "I'm bigger than Little Bird."

"Not so much bigger."

Dar stepped back and winced as a thorn entered her heel. When she tried to pull it out, she lost her balance and tumbled onto Kovok-mah's lap.

"Is this not better than lying upon thorns and dirt?" asked Kovok-mah.

"There's not enough room to sleep."

"If you sit properly there is," said Kovok-mah. He grabbed Dar's waist and easily lifted and turned her so she was sitting with her back against his chest.

"I've never slept sitting up," said Dar. "I'll fall on my face."

"I'll hold you so you won't," said Kovok-mah. He wrapped his massive arms about Dar, supporting her torso and providing a place for her to rest her head.

At first, Dar didn't know how to react. If a man had attempted a similar embrace, Dar would have fought free. Yet Kovok-mah's touch felt different. It stirred within Dar childhood memories of being cradled in her mother's arms. She relaxed, and a sleepy calmness stole over her.

"You led us well," said Kovok-mah, his voice so low that it seemed a murmur. "I will watch while you sleep."

Dar closed her eyes, but the scrapes from the thorns still stung. "What does pain smell like?" she asked.

"Somewhat throk, but mulfi."

"I have no idea what you said."

"Throk is strong smell after fire strikes from sky. Mulf is scent of black muck by river."

Dar tried to imagine the combination. "Ugh! Are you sure you want me on your lap?"

Kovok-mah hissed softly, shaking slightly as he laughed. "Scents that reveal feelings are not thought as pleasing or unpleasing."

"So pain doesn't stink?"

"Thwa," said Kovok-mah.

"What else does my scent reveal?"

"That you're brave."

"You can smell bravery?"

"Thwa," replied Kovok-mah, "but I can smell fear. It hasn't stopped you. That is brave."

"I'm not brave," said Dar. "Bravery is lacking fear."

"If that were true, only fools would be brave. You've chosen dangerous path and are wise to be afraid."

"Are you afraid, also?"

"I'm not foolish."

"But I thought urkzimmuthi were fearless."

Kovok-mah hissed again. "That's because you smell poorly."

Dar slept dreamlessly until the sound of voices woke her. She glanced at the sun. It was still morning. Dar looked about. All she saw were motionless orcs and sun-lit leaves. Wrapped in Kovok-mah's arms, she couldn't see if he was awake, though she suspected that he was. The other orcs were. Varz-hak regarded her with a questioning expression. Dar made the sign for "silence."

The voices grew louder until Dar could catch a few words. It seemed that two women were gathering wood and chatting as they worked. Dar struggled to remain calm as the voices sounded ever nearer. Kovok-mah slowly moved his arm to grip his sword. Close by, a twig snapped. Her heart pounding, Dar waited for some clue that they had been spotted. None came. The voices slowly grew fainter as the invisible women departed. Dar relaxed and Kovok-mah released his sword hilt.

Eventually, Dar dozed off only to be awakened again by the sound of more people. She tensely waited for them to depart, but they were joined by others. The wood lot, it proved, was a busy place, and the noise of people coming and going continued throughout the day. Once, a child approached their hiding place so closely that Dar could hear each little footstep in the grass. They seemed only a few paces away. The sounds of activity died down only as sunset approached. By then, keeping still had become exquisite torture. Dar ached all over, and hunger pangs churned her empty stomach.

When darkness finally came, Dar and the orcs left their thorny refuge. Clouds obscured the moon, and the night was darker than the previous one. Dar still led the way, but she relied on Kovok-mah's keen senses in selecting the course. They had frequent whispered consultations, and as the night progressed, Kovok-mah became more adept at finding the stealthiest route. Dar smiled with approval when he skirted a peasant's hut that was still invisible to her. "You're becoming wolf."

Kovok-mah returned Dar's smile, displaying teeth that had faded to nearly white. "I already have wolf's teeth."

Dar immediately wished she had washuthahi seeds to keep her teeth black. "Are my teeth still pretty?" she asked, hoping they were not the same shade as Kovok-mah's.

"Thwa," replied Kovok-mah.

Dar sighed, knowing the word "washavoki" referred to a dog's white teeth.

Kovok-mah understood the cause of Dar's sigh. "You have urkzimmuthi chest," he said. "That is more important than teeth."

Dar and the orcs spent the following day hiding in the dank cellar of a ruined house. There was no food to share and hunger sapped even the orcs' energy. Everyone slumbered until nightfall. Dar awoke, sad from dreaming of Twea and still feeling tired. It was overcast and little moonlight penetrated the clouds. When they began their march, it was so dark that Dar decided to stop slinking about hedgerow pathways and risk traveling on the road. It headed directly northward, and she had confidence that the orcs' keen eyes would spot any humans long before the humans spotted them.

Once on the road, the travelers made better progress, though hunger slowed their pace. They passed fields filled with sprouts and orchards laden with tiny green fruit, but saw nothing fit to eat. Occasionally, they encountered an isolated hut or two. They left the road to avoid those. The travelers were making such a detour when Dar halted. "Kovok-mah," she said, "come with me."

They had been walking through a grove that bordered one side of a peasant holding. Dar led Kovok-mah to the edge of the woods so he could gaze across the fields at the hut. "Look around that hut," said Dar. "Do you see . . ." She paused, trying to think of the Orcish word for "root house." When she couldn't, Dar started over. "I'm looking for house dug into ground—mound of earth with door. Washavokis keep food there."

Kovok-mah gazed into the dark. "I see mound with door." He pointed.

Dar looked where Kovok-mah indicated, but she could barely make out the peasant's hut in the gloom. "I can't see it," she said. "Describe where it is."

"I'll lead you there."

"Thwa," said Dar. "You must not be seen."

Kovok-mah noted that the scent of Dar's fear had grown stronger. "What are you planning to do?"

"We need food. I'm going to get some."

"Why does that make you afraid?"

Dar didn't know the Orcish word for "stealing" or even if the orcs understood the concept. Thus, it took a while for her to explain what she intended to do. When she was finished, Kovok-mah looked concerned. "You say washavokis often do this thing?"

"Hai," said Dar. "If I'm caught, no alarm will go out. No one will track you down."

"Yet you'll be punished," said Kovok-mah.

"Hai."

"What will happen?"

"I don't know," replied Dar, refraining from saying that thieves were often killed or mutilated.

Kovok-mah smelled her apprehension. "This seems very dangerous."

"We haven't eaten for two days. We need food. I see no other choice."

"Please don't go," said Kovok-mah. "My chest is strong in this."

"I must. Now, tell me where mound lies."

After Dar got directions, she warily crept toward the hut. Eventually, she could make out a hump in the ground behind it. When she was in the regiment, she had often encountered such structures on the farms the soldiers plundered. Root houses were stone-lined pits that were roofed over with sod to provide a cool, dry place for storing fruits and vegetables.

When Dar reached the root house, she paused and listened for sounds indicating that she had been detected. When she heard none, she slowly opened its slanting door, fearful that it might creak and betray her presence. The opening was so black that Dar had to find the ladder by feel. After glancing nervously around, she climbed down.

When Dar's feet touched the dirt floor, she could see nothing except a square of night sky above. She shuffled away from the ladder, waving her arms about in cool air that smelled of earth and vegetables on the verge of spoiling. She touched a basket, and her fingers examined its contents. The rough and wrinkled texture of the tubers inside revealed them as tabuc, a root that must be cooked to be edible. Dar continued her search. The next basket smelled vinegary and contained apples. They felt soft and spongy and many were rotten. Dar stuffed a few of the sounder ones into her knapsack.

The next basket was the real prize. Dar recognized its contents on first touch, for goldenroot was a highland staple. It was filling and could be eaten raw. As Dar began to empty the basket, she pondered how much to take. Stuffing her sack would make it more likely that her theft would be noticed, but it would also postpone the need to steal again. Dar decided to risk taking as much as she could.

When the knapsack was filled, Dar lifted it onto her back and hurriedly ascended the ladder. After closing the door behind her, she would have run if she hadn't feared stumbling in the dark. When Dar reached the waiting orcs, she felt waves of exultation and relief. "We must flee," she said. "Come morning, washavokis will look for me."

Four

♛

As dawn approached, Kovok-mah smelled standing water and guided Dar to a swampy spot between two hills. Dar waded into black, shallow water that was choked with reeds. Eventually, she found a spot of ground that was barely above water and called to the orcs to join her. They arrived and marked the Embrace of Muth la by pushing reeds into the wet earth. Dar squatted within the hallowed space, and the orcs joined her. She opened her knapsack. "Food is Muth la's gift."

"Shashav, Muth la," replied the orcs.

Dar handed out round, tawny goldenroots and wrinkled apples. Each time she said "Muth la gives you this food," Dar felt grateful to the Mother of All for providing her the strength to do what was necessary. The roots and apples were past their prime but hunger lent them savor. Dar relished every bite, oblivious of the mosquitoes and mucky ground.

When the meal was finished, Kovok-mah sat down and folded his cloak upon his lap. "Dargu, ground is too wet for you to lie upon."

Dar hesitated, wondering how it would look to the others. Meanwhile, her feet sank deeper into the sodden earth. Dar chose comfort over appearance and climbed upon the folded cloak. She assumed the cross-legged orcish sleeping posture, and leaned her back against Kovok-mah, who gently wrapped his arms about her. As Dar relaxed, she glimpsed Zna-yat. He quickly looked away, but not before Dar caught his disgusted expression.

I risked my life to get him food, Dar thought. *Why does he begrudge me comfort?* Zna-yat's look made Dar recall his veiled threats—threats she had brushed aside during the past two days. It reminded her that she still had cause to worry, and sleep came slowly despite her exhaustion and full belly.

While Dar and the orcs hid and rested, the remnant of King Kregant's army rested also. After several skirmishes, King Feistav had abandoned pursuit. Many of Kregant's men believed they were heading home, but experienced soldiers, such as Sevren and Valamar, suspected not. Rumors were about that the mage would use his arts to reverse the king's fortunes, and those rumors seemed confirmed when some guardsmen were ordered to transform a peasant's abandoned hut into a site suitable for necromancy.

The mage's black tent had been lost in the retreat, and the hut was to be its temporary replacement. The guardsmen labored the entire day under the sorcerer's watchful eye to seal every crack where light might enter. After sunset, they completed the work by blackening the hut's walls and ceiling with a mixture of ash and blood. As the men painted, the mage burned incense that fouled the air. All who breathed it had disturbing dreams that night, especially the two men who fetched the final item the mage required.

Othar waited until the night's darkest hour to return to the hut. Inside, a single oil lamp illuminated the bound child, who shivered in the unnatural cold. The mage closed the door and covered it with a thick curtain before getting to work. Taking a dagger and his iron bowl, he sacrificed the boy and used his blood to paint a protective circle. Once inside the circle, Othar opened a black sack embroidered with spells stitched in black thread.

The bones inside the sack had grown heavier, as if they weren't bones at all but objects crafted from iron or lead. The sorcerer had first noticed the change after the slaughter at the Vale of Pines. Othar didn't understand its cause, but he hoped it foretold a change in his fortunes. He needed a change, for he sensed that the king's anger might overcome his fear. If it did, Othar's life was forfeit for his disastrous counsels.

Despite this, Othar remained devoted to the bones that had placed him in jeopardy. They had become more than tools. The bones had such a hold on him that he was as much their servant as they were his. Without them he was only a sham, for auguring with the bones was the only real magic Othar could perform. Before they came into his possession, Othar's sorcery relied on deception and a knowledge of herbs and poisons. His daunting presence had been all show, for his skills had scarcely exceeded those of a knowledgeable Wise Woman. The bones had changed that. When their unearthly coldness stung Othar's hands, he felt powerful—a true sorcerer at last.

Othar tossed the bones on the earthen floor and studied their portents. Never had the signs been so clear or promising. It occurred to him that the entity behind the bones was pleased by the battle's bloody outcome, and it was rewarding him much the way a sated master throws his slave some meat.

That night, Othar learned much that pleased him. He discovered where rich plunder could be had—enough to appease his greedy king. He saw that the mysterious threat was far away and retreating farther still. Additional study yielded even greater satisfaction. Othar's unknown enemy was moving into peril. The mage read the signs for "betrayal," "bloodshed," and "soon."

*   *   *

Dar carefully rationed the food she stole, and it lasted for three nights of travel. During that time, the small plots bordered by hedgerows gave way to more open holdings. These were separated by woodlands and grew ever larger. Eventually, Dar and the orcs stopped encountering solitary huts. The land's inhabitants lived in compounds that included dwellings of varying sizes, barns, and storehouses surrounded by broad fields and pastures.

With the passage of time and distance, Dar grew accustomed to fear. However, she never lost her awareness of peril, whether she was trekking in the dark or hiding in daylight. She continued to feel lost, for they had yet to glimpse the mountains. Dar also watched Zna-yat carefully. He displayed no hostility toward her, and after a while she began to wonder if she had imagined his disgusted look. Still, Dar made a point of sleeping on the ground.

After the food ran out, Dar resolved to steal some more, though it meant entering one of the compounds. It was well past midnight when she made the attempt. While the orcs hid, she crept toward a stone storehouse nestled among other buildings.

Reaching the compound required crossing a broad field. Dar was close to the first buildings when a dog started barking. She dropped to the ground. Then she waited nervously, prepared to spring up and run for her life. The dog yelped, and the night became silent again. Dar didn't move. A long time passed. Everything remained quiet. After a spell of indecision, Dar began to creep toward the storehouse, her ears straining for the slightest sound. She reached its heavy door without incident and pulled it open just enough to squeeze inside.

The interior of the storehouse had the rich aroma of smoked meats. They were invisible within the pitch-black room. Dar was forced to search for them by shuffling about and waving her arms. When she touched a bin filled with goldenroot, she paused to stuff some in her knapsack. Then she continued groping for the meat that smelled so tantalizing. Dar was still searching when the door flew open and torchlight illuminated her.

The torch was held by a boy who gripped the leash of a muzzled dog. Two grown men, armed with pitchforks, accompanied the boy. He remained put, grinning with excitement, as the two men entered the storehouse. Dar drew both her daggers. The men advanced, backing her into a corner.

"You'll drop those blades if you're wise," said one of the men.

"Stick her!" yelled the boy.

"Patience, young master," said the other man. "Your father said we're to let the thief surrender."

"Best be quick," said his companion.

Dar weighed her chances in a fight, then dropped her daggers.

"Smart lass. Now, kick them away."

Dar complied and one of the men picked them up. Afterward, he ordered her to lie on her stomach. Dar obeyed and felt the prongs of a pitchfork press against her neck as one of the men took her knapsack, then grabbed her left ankle and tied her left wrist to it.

"Get on your feet," said one of Dar's captors. As Dar struggled to an awkward, crouching position—the only stance her bonds permitted—the man addressed the boy. "Tell your father we've caught the thief and shall bring her to the stump."

The boy handed the man the torch, then ran off. "Follow me," said the man. Dar clumsily hobbled out of the storehouse, stopping when the man stopped. "You should've paid heed to the hand," he said.

"What hand?" asked Dar.

The man raised the torch, and its light revealed a hand nailed to the door. Its flesh had weathered until mostly bone remained. "That's to warn thieves. Pity you didn't see it."

The other man prodded Dar with his pitchfork. "Come, lass, let's get this done."

Dar had no choice but to follow the man with the torch, though she didn't need his guidance. Her destination was clearly marked by a small crowd of people, several of whom bore torches also. They stood behind a short, flat-topped stump, talking excitedly. Some children, too impatient to wait for Dar to make her way to them, ran over for a closer look.

"It's a lady," said a small girl. "Will they really chop her hand?"

"Of course," said a boy. "She's a thief."

As Dar approached the stump, she almost cried out in Orcish for help. Then she recalled the slaughter in the rainy courtyard. *It'd be the same here.* If the orcs spared anyone, they'd be hunted down; yet even a massacre would only buy them a small head start. Also, any rescue attempt might cost her more than a hand; she was bound and guarded, easy to strike down. Dar remained silent.

The man with the torch strode ahead and stopped before a man with graying hair who stood foremost in the crowd. "Master," he said, "we caught her in the storehouse with this." He spilled the contents of Dar's knapsack on the ground.

The master called out. "Bring the thief forward."

Several men dragged Dar the rest of the way to the stump and forced her to kneel before it. The stump was obviously where fowl were beheaded, for its blood-darkened top was crisscrossed with ax marks. A large man wearing a bloodstained butcher's smock emerged from the crowd, seized Dar's wrist, and pressed her right arm against the rough, sticky wood. He raised a broad-headed hatchet in his other hand, then shifted his gaze to the master. Dar gazed at him also.

The master's eyes met Dar's. "Fool! Everyone knows the price for thievery."

"I had no choice."

The master's expression became contemptuous. "Too proud to work or too slothful?"

"If you had to choose, would you rather lose a hand or a head?"

"What's this nonsense?"

"Pull the bandage from my brow and see."

The master nodded and the man with the hatchet tore Dar's bandage away to reveal her brand. The sight of it provoked murmurs from the crowd, which hushed when the master spoke again. "I've heard of such marks. Were you slave to goblins?"

"I was," said Dar. "Now the king will reward you for my head." She sighed and laid her neck on the stump.

"Don't you know where you are?"

Dar looked up, feigning puzzlement. "No. I've been lost ever since I ran away."

The master's eyes narrowed. "Then why show your brand?"

"What chance will I have with one hand? I may as well die here."

A woman touched the master's sleeve. "Garl," she said. He turned to her and they had a whispered conversation. Afterward, Garl gazed at Dar. "My wife thinks you'd choose honest work over stealing."

"I would," said Dar.

Garl's wife spoke. "You need not fear the invader or his goblins. This is King Feistav's realm."

Dar forced tears to her eyes. "Oh, praised be Karm!"

Garl's expression remained suspicious. "Faranna," he said to his wife, "she's still a thief."

"If she were to become a bondmaid," said Faranna, "two hands would serve us better than one."

"Perchance," said Garl. "Or they might rob us twice as quick."

"Please, milady," said Dar. "After slaving for goblins, any toil will seem light. Let me serve you."

Faranna smiled. "There are no lords and ladies at Garlsholding. Call me Mistress."

Dar bowed her head. "Yes, Mistress."

"I've agreed to nothing," said Garl.

"Her hand remains forfeit," said Faranna, "if she proves false."

Garl made a show of deliberating before he spoke. "What's your name, girl?"

"Dar."

"You've heard our speech," said Garl. "In return for mercy, will you bond yourself to us?"

"I will, Master."

"Hunda!" called Garl.

The man who had borne the torch stepped forward.

"Unbind the new bondmaid," said Garl. "She'll sleep with Theena." As Hunda went to untie Dar, Garl added, "Bolt her door."

The crowd began to disperse once the excitement was over. Some seemed disappointed by the outcome of events, Garl's son in particular. He walked over to where Dar was being untied and said, "We'll be watching you."

When Dar was free of her bonds, Hunda led her to a barn built of stout timbers. He stuck his torch in the ground, took Dar's elbow, and escorted her into the dark structure. Dar could see little except the shadowy outlines of stalls and the vague forms of the creatures within them. The last stall was larger than the rest, with sides built up to fully enclose it. Its low door was open. "This is where you'll stay," said Hunda. He pushed Dar toward the doorway. "Go in. You're a lucky lass. The master's gentler than I would have been."

As Dar bent down to enter the stall, she heard straw rustling as someone stirred.

"It's too early to rise," said a sleepy voice.

"Aye, it is, Theena," replied Hunda. "The master has a new bondmaid."

Dar entered the stall, and the door closed behind her. The sound of a sliding wooden bolt followed. "Why are we locked in?" asked Theena.

"I was caught in the storehouse," said Dar.

"Stealing?" asked Theena, suddenly sounding wide awake.

"I had no choice."

Dar wished to rest, but was plied with so many questions that she ended up giving an account of her life, beginning in the highlands and ending with her capture that night. It was often fictitious, though she tried to follow the truth whenever possible. Theena was most interested in hearing about orcs, which she called goblins. The region's Goblin Wars were the subject of fearsome legends. "Is it true goblins eat people?" asked Theena.

"I saw it with my own eyes," said Dar, playing for sympathy. "Once, a girl displeased a murdant, so he threw her naked to the goblins."

"What did they do?" asked Theena.

"Pulled her apart like a boiled chicken."

Dar could hear Theena shudder in the dark. "How could you bear it?"

"We would have fled, but we were branded and there were bounties on our heads." Dar groped for Theena's hand and guided it to her forehead. The bondmaid's fingers traced Dar's crown-shaped scar. "The goblins owned me," said Dar. "But now, by Karm's grace, I'm delivered."

"Aye, there are no goblins here," said Theena. "I work hard, but I'm well fed and get clothes each Karmsbirth."

"Do you ever wish to leave?" asked Dar.

"Where would I go?" replied Theena, in a tone that made it clear that the question was unanswerable. "I'm like you. I have no kin."

Dar yawned loudly. "I've been walking all night," she said. "I must rest a bit." She pushed together enough loose straw to cushion the dirt floor before lying down. Though exhausted, Dar couldn't sleep. She wondered what the orcs were thinking. *Do they know I'm a captive or do they think I'm dead? Perhaps they believe I've deserted them. What will they do? Wait for me? Attack? Leave?* The last seemed most likely, making Garlsholding the end of Dar's journey.

Five

♛

Dar managed to get a little sleep before Hunda unbolted the door, roused Theena and her, and told them to milk the goats. Then Dar got her first look at the other bondmaid. She was older than Dar and stocky with a broad face. She wore a calf-length skirt of brown homespun and a loose, sleeveless white blouse that laced up in the front. She was barefoot and her light brown hair was tucked beneath a soiled kerchief.

Theena, whose clothes were worn and patched, was fascinated by Dar's shift. She couldn't help fingering the fabric. "Ooh, it's so fine," she said. "Fit for the mistress."

"A soldier gave it to me. Most like, it came from a dead woman."

Theena jerked her hand away, and changed the subject. "Have you milked goats afore?"

"No. We were too poor to own them."

"Well, it's not hard. I'll show you how."

"When do you eat here?" asked Dar.

"Daymeal's at high sun, but there's porridge after firstwork."

Dar never imagined that her mouth would water at the thought of porridge, but it did. Her stomach grumbled throughout the milking session. After taking the goats to pasture, she finally got to eat.

Dar ate her first meal at Garlsholding in the long stone building where most of the servants slept and all of them dined. A kettle of porridge sat at the end of a long table lined with benches. Wooden bowls and spoons were piled nearby.

Dar was the focus of much curiosity, which Theena happily satisfied while Dar wolfed down her porridge. The bondmaid embellished Dar's already fanciful account, making it sound as if Dar had only narrowly escaped being devoured. Her tales entertained everyone until Hunda stood up. "Time to work," he said. "Dar, go with Theena. But, afore you do, change into these." He handed Dar a small bundle. "Bring me the dress. It's too good for a bondmaid."

Dar did as she was told and returned wearing a worn skirt and blouse similar to Theena's. She gave Hunda the dress, then joined Theena, who handed her a hoe. Shouldering it, Dar followed Theena into the fields.

Kovok-mah crouched motionless at the edge of the woods, watching the compound. As he had expected, the washavokis rose with the sun. Buildings obstructed his view of most of their activities, just as they had the previous evening. Then, his ears had been more useful than his eyes. He had heard the dog barking. Later, he had heard voices, though they were too distant to understand. Kovok-mah had observed torchlight reflected off the buildings, but he hadn't seen Dar since she had sneaked into the compound. *Dargu was afraid when she left*, thought Kovok-mah. *What punishment did she fear?* Having often witnessed the cruelty of washavokis, he feared Dar was dead.

The sun was still low in the sky when washavokis walked into the field. Kovok-mah immediately recognized Dar among them, despite the distance and her different clothing. The way she moved was so familiar that he didn't even have to see her face. Joy filled Kovok-mah's chest when he realized Dar was alive and unhurt.

Kovok-mah watched Dar as she toiled alongside the others. When it became apparent that Dar wasn't being guarded, he grew puzzled. *If she's not prisoner, why is she there?* Kovok-mah continued to observe Dar as he pondered her actions. He couldn't imagine the reason for them, but Dar often did things he didn't understand. Kovok-mah stayed until noon, when Dar and the washavokis returned to the compound. Then he withdrew to where the other orcs were hiding.

Only Zna-yat was awake when Kovok-mah returned. "You've been gone long time," he said. "What did you see?"

"Dargu lives," said Kovok-mah, briefly seeing disappointment in his cousin's face. "I saw her working with washavokis."

"Good," said Zna-yat. "She has returned to her kind."

"I'm not sure of that."

"How can it be otherwise?"

"I think she's doing this to help us."

"How can you be so foolish?" asked Zna-yat. "You seem to forget Dargu is washavoki. You ignore her stink. You touch her. You talk as if she has wisdom."

"She does."

"Because she speaks of Muth la?"

"Mother of All sends her visions."

"Dargu talks of visions because she knows sons can't see them," replied Zna-yat. "Washavokis often speak words that have no meaning."

"You don't understand her."

"It's *you* who doesn't understand. I've watched her magic over you grow ever stronger. It's been painful to witness. Yet now she's gone, and I'm glad."

"My chest says you're wrong," said Kovok-mah.

"Let us depart," said Zna-yat. "Dargu has forsaken us. That was always her plan."

"Thwa! I don't believe it! I'll wait for her."

Zna-yat's face colored, but his voice was even. "Then I'll also wait for Dargu."

After daymeal and a brief rest, Dar returned to work with the other servants. She was conscious of their eyes upon her. *I'm an outsider and a thief.* Hoping to win acceptance, she hoed diligently. It wasn't overtaxing work. Dar had tilled the soil since childhood, and the rhythm of hoeing had a soothing familiarity. As Dar gazed upon the abundant fields and felt warm earth beneath her feet, a sense of peace came over her. For the first time since the soldiers arrived at her father's hut, she was safe. The fear that had been her constant companion was gone. She had food and a place to sleep. All she needed to do was work willingly. Accustomed to toil, Dar thought it was a fair price for serenity.

Dar worked past sunset and was hoeing one last row when she smelled something burning. She looked about and spotted a large bonfire at the far edge of the field. The shadowed woods behind the fire made its flames seem especially bright. Foul, black smoke drifted by.

"Ugh!" said Dar. "What are they burning? Animal carcasses?"

Theena shot Dar a puzzled look. "What are you talking about?"

Dar pointed to the flames, which had grown until they rose above the treetops. "That fire over there."

Theena gazed in the direction Dar pointed. "I see no fire."

"Oh, no," said Dar softly.

"What? What's the matter?" said Theena. "You look like you've seen a spirit."

"I'm just tired," replied Dar. "I'm seeing things."

"We're almost done," said Theena. "You'll rest soon." She resumed hoeing.

Dar resumed work also, but the vision didn't go away. Every time she glanced up, the fire was still burning. Gradually, its flames died down. As they diminished, Dar discerned something within them. There was a blackened post and crumpled against it was a charred form. Dar saw a bent head and torso surrounded by flames. She averted her eyes.

By the time Dar returned to the compound, her serenity was shattered. Dar had been shown something terrible, but she had no idea toward what purpose. All she knew was there was a power abroad that wouldn't let her be.

The following morning, Dar awoke to the sound of the bolt being drawn. Theena yawned close by. "Dar, who's Thwa?"

"Thwa's not a name. It means 'no' in goblin talk."

"Well, you kept repeating it in your sleep. Don't you remember?"

"No, but I remember having nightmares."

Theena gave Dar a sympathetic look. "You're safe here. Soon, such dreams will leave you."

Will they? wondered Dar, but she replied, "I'm sure they will."

Dar helped Theena with firstwork. Afterward, the two women went to the servant hall for porridge. When Dar sat down, an elderly man leaned across the table. "You're not the only one who's seen a goblin. I saw one in the woods close to where you hoed yesterday." He grinned at Dar's stunned reaction, and waited a long moment before he added, "Of course, I was a lad."

Dar struggled to regain her composure. "A lad?"

"Not all the goblins were run off in the wars," said the man, obviously pleased to have an audience. "A few remained. They caught a bull goblin in our very woods."

"What . . . what did they do to him?" asked Dar.

"What you always do with goblins—have a roasting."

"They burned him?" asked Dar, her voice faint.

"Alive," replied the man with a grin. "And, oh, what a stench it made!"

"Gunthar!" said Theena in a scolding tone. "Don't talk of goblins to Dar! Look at her! She's gone all white!"

"I thought the tale would please her," replied Gunthar.

"Well, you thought wrong," said Theena. "Dar has nightmares and she . . ." Theena paused and gave Dar a strange look. ". . . she sees things, too."

"Well, if she sees a goblin, she needn't worry," said Gunthar. "We know what to do."

Six

♛

The next day, Dar worked in a field that bordered the woods. Around midmorning, she thought she heard a low voice coming from the undergrowth. She worked her way toward it. The voice called again. "Dargu."

Dar glanced about to insure that no one was observing her, then entered the woods. Kovok-mah rose from the undergrowth. "Dargu, ma nav fwili sa ther." *Dargu, I am pleased to see you.*

Typically, Kovok-mah's words fell short of expressing his feelings, but Dar appreciated the depths of his joy with one glance at his face. He gazed at her with such intensity that she felt momentarily overwhelmed. Still, she had the composure to reply. "Mer snaf." *I also.*

"What happened to you?" asked Kovok-mah, continuing to speak in Orcish.

Dar replied in the same tongue. "I was caught."

"Did washavokis punish you?"

"Thwa. They showed mercy because they wish me to work for them."

"I'm glad you're safe," said Kovok-mah. He paused a long moment. "What should I do, Dargu?"

"You can't stay here. Washavokis are cruel to urkzimmuthi. I've seen terrible vision."

"Hai, we must go." Kovok-mah's face grew sad, and he was silent a while. "Are you happy with washavokis?"

Dar realized that Kovok-mah was asking if she wished

to remain behind and knew, if she said yes, he would disappear forever. *I could live in peace and safety.* Dar quickly dismissed the idea. *I told Kovok-mah I'd get him home.* "I've been treated well," she said. "But this is no place for me."

The sadness left Kovok-mah's face. "Are you certain?"

"Hai. I'm different from them."

"You're also different from us."

"Hai," said Dar, "but I must follow my chest."

"I'm glad you'll guide us."

Dar heard the sound of a distant bell, then someone was shouting her name. *This is the wrong time to flee,* she thought. *I can't go unprepared.* "I have to go," she said. "I'll join you soon."

"When?"

"As soon as I can. Look for me each evening." Then Dar dashed from the woods and ran over to the servant who had called her name. Before she could explain her absence, the woman pointed to a ragged man on the road. He bore a staff that jangled a bell each time it struck the ground. "A cursed one's coming,"

"Cursed one?" said Dar.

"Someone with the rotting curse. Have you not heard of it? People lose fingers and toes, then hands and feet. Faces, too. The cursed are hideous."

Dar could see that the man's face and hands were wrapped in dirty bandages. "How horrible."

"Run and get some food. Something from the slop pail will do. Leave it by the road so he'll go away."

"Just don't get near him," said Theena.

"Aye, make him keep his distance," said a servant. "Throw rocks if you need to."

"Mind you don't kill him," said another, "because then the curse will pass to you."

"Now hurry," said the first servant. "And come back here when you're done."

Dar ran off on her errand. She was glad to do so, because she wanted a closer look at the cursed one. It seemed a perfect disguise for her and the orcs when they resumed their journey. It would permit her to get food without stealing and insure people kept their distance. As Dar hurried to the kitchen, her mind was already awhirl with plans and focused on the road ahead.

For the rest of the day, Dar learned all she could about the surrounding country. She made her inquiries sound casual—the kind of questions any newcomer might ask. Based on her conversations, she decided a northeastward route to the mountains would be best. Though less direct, it avoided villages and was lightly traveled, for it passed near a ruined goblin city.

Having determined a route, Dar had to obtain rags for disguises, a bell, and her daggers. Doing so required thievery, and getting caught would cost her dearly. The bell came from a harness. Theena's spare skirt and blouse could provide the rags. Dar planned to take them last. She felt guilty about stealing from one with so little, but cloth was scarce and her need was great. The daggers presented the greatest problem, for stealing them would involve the most risk. Yet Dar was unwilling to travel unarmed or face Zna-yat without self-protection. Before Dar could regain her weapons, she had to find out where they were. She pondered the problem late into the night.

The next morning, Dar approached Hunda as he was leaving the servant hall. "May I have a word with you?" she asked.

Hunda halted. "Aye, what is it?"

"Where I come from, only women without virtue go about without daggers."

Hunda looked confused. "What?"

"It marks them as unwilling to defend their honor."

"So? Why tell me this?"

"I'd like my daggers back. I feel naked without them."

Hunda grinned. "You don't look naked."

"Please."

"They're mine now."

"You don't wear them," said Dar.

"And neither will you."

"But you have no need for them."

"I keep them handy," said Hunda. "Be off, and speak no more of this."

Dar left feeling satisfied. As head servant, Hunda slept in a shut bed. It was the only private space within the servant hall, and no servant approached it without his leave. Dar guessed her daggers were there. *If I'm right, I'll take only one. It'll make the theft less obvious.* Even with that precaution, Dar knew she should depart the day of the theft.

At daymeal, Dar surreptitiously studied Hunda's bed. Enclosed by carved wooden screens, it looked like a large box. With the exception of the long dining table and its benches, the bed was the only piece of furniture in the hall. Hunda retired to it after the midday meal, while the other servants napped in more humble places. Most dozed on the benches or the tabletop. Dar joined Theena in the barn, where—too anxious to sleep—she waited for a chance to take her dagger.

Her opportunity came when it was time to resume work. Dar hung back and waited for the servant hall to empty. Then she dashed to the shut bed, and crawled inside, closing the screen behind her. The bed's interior wasn't totally dark, for its screens were perforated to admit air. All of Hunda's possessions were scattered about the enclosed space. Dar tried not to disturb them as she groped about for her daggers. She had just found one of them beneath the mattress when she heard two people enter the hall. Dar peered through the screen and saw that one of them was Hunda.

Perhaps he wants something from here! thought Dar in a rush of panic. If Hunda opened the screen, Dar knew of only one ploy that might save her. She undressed and lay back, expecting discovery any moment. Dar wondered if she could fake desire. From what she knew of men, she doubted much acting would be necessary. *Submission is all they want.* She shuddered at the thought of it.

Through the screen, Dar heard Hunda's voice. "She's not here. Let's check the fields."

When the hall was empty, Dar quickly dressed, took the dagger, and slipped out of the bed. After insuring that no one would see her, she rushed into the barn. She took the bell from its hiding place, then stuffed Theena's spare clothes beneath her own. They made a bulge. *I'll have to hide everything in the woods.* Smoothing her skirt as best she could, she hurried to work.

As Dar neared the field, Theena hurried over to her. "Where were you? Hunda's looking for you."

Before Dar could answer, her anxious look made Theena suspicious. "What's that under your skirt?"

"Nothing."

Theena grabbed at Dar's skirt. Dar jumped out of her reach, but as she did, the stolen garments fell to the ground. Dar picked them up immediately.

"That's mine!" said Theena, sounding both angry and hurt.

"Theena, please understand. I didn't want to take them, but . . ."

"Thief!" shouted Theena. "Dar's stolen again!"

Dar saw the other field hands staring. Then two dashed toward her.

Dar bolted for the woods. As she sped across the wide field, she could hear Theena right behind her. She assumed others were also giving chase. Dar reached the trees and crashed through the undergrowth. A dozen paces into the woods, she halted to lift her skirt and draw her dagger. She turned and brandished it at Theena, who froze at the sight of the weapon. "I'm sorry, Theena," said Dar. Then, seeking to win her sympathy, she added, "I don't want to hurt you, but I escaped with other girls. Young ones who need my care. I have to think of them."

Theena continued to stare at the blade, too frightened to move or make a sound. Dar darted off. She had taken only a few strides when Theena began to call for help.

Escape was Dar's only concern, and she ran heedlessly. When her breath came in ragged gasps, she slowed down and heard the sounds of pursuit. *Of all the ways to flee, this is the worst. They're already chasing me and Kovok-mah won't look for me until evening.* Dar's only recourse was to keep moving and hope the orcs found her before her pursuers did.

The woods were far more extensive than Dar had imagined, and it wasn't long before she was thoroughly lost. She continued wandering, afraid to call to the orcs for help. Toward late afternoon, the trees finally thinned. Dar headed toward the light and spied fields. They belonged to Garlsholding. Men carrying pitchforks seemed on patrol. They were headed in her direction. *I've walked in a circle!* Dar hastily retreated.

Night fell, and a cloudy sky made it especially dark. Dar could see little more than tree trunks. Still, she kept walking until, at last, she spied a pair of yellow eyes in the gloom. "Shashav Muth la! Mer davagitav tha!" she said. *Thank Muth la! I have found you!*

Silence.

Dar felt puzzled and a bit frightened. "Asa nak fa?" *Who is there?*

No reply. The only sounds were quiet footsteps and that of a sword being drawn. "Zna-yat?"

The eyes moved closer.

Dar heard the distant noise of someone running through the woods. The yellow eyes looked away. Dar heard the sword slide into its sheath, then Zna-yat's voice. "Is that Dargu?" he asked in Orcish.

"Hai."

"There were washavokis in woods," said Zna-yat. "I thought you were one of them." He called out. "Kovok-mah! I've found her."

Dar saw green eyes approach, and she moved in their direction. Soon, large hands gently grasped her shoulders. "Dargu, you've returned."

"Hai. I said I would," said Dar, feeling such relief that it nearly eclipsed her shock at having caught an orc in a lie.

Seven

♛

The remainder of the night was a haze of exhaustion. At first, Dar staggered behind Kovok-mah, relying on him to find a way in the dark. When she kept tripping, he lifted her to carry like a child. Dar was too tired to protest. They traveled that way until they left the trees and Kovok-mah set her down. "Which way should we go?" he asked.

Dar could see little in the darkness. "Is there road?"

"Hai," said Kovok-mah, pointing into the gloom.

"We must follow it," said Dar. "When it forks, we will go right. Road will go through hills where we can hide."

Kovok-mah gazed into the night. "Hills are far away."

"You can see them?" asked Dar.

"Hai. Unless we run, golden eye will rise before we reach them."

"I can't run," said Dar.

"I'll run for you," said Kovok-mah. He knelt down. "Climb on my shoulders."

Dar was disconcerted by the idea but realized they wouldn't reach the hills otherwise. She hiked up her skirt and climbed on Kovok-mah's broad shoulders, placing a leg on either side of his neck. He grasped her ankles, then rose. Dar felt as high above the ground as when she rode Thunder. She grasped Kovok-mah's head to keep her balance, taking care not to pull his hair.

"Are you comfortable?" asked Kovok-mah.

"I'll manage," said Dar, not feeling comfortable at all.

Kovok-mah spoke to the other orcs. "We must reach hills while it's still dark. Follow me." With those words, he commenced to run.

Kovok-mah's loping stride had an easy motion, and after a while, Dar grew accustomed to her perch. The road flowed beneath her, a dim, gray ribbon winding through shadows. The countryside was only a murky blur. As Dar sped through the darkness, she was mostly aware of Kovok-mah. Movement united them. She felt the pulse of his blood, the rhythm of his breathing, and the heat of his body as if they were her own. In her exhausted state, she imagined they had become a single creature, running wild in the night.

At last, Dar became aware of black shapes rising in the distance. They entered the hills as the sky lightened in the east. Kovok-mah slowed his pace and left the road to pick his way up a slope and into trees. Dar remained on his shoulders until he gently lifted her from them. She was vaguely aware that the Embrace of Muth la was being marked. When the orcs sat down to sleep, Kovok-mah set her on his lap and folded his arms about her. *He's still warm from running*, thought Dar as she drifted off to sleep.

Dar awoke within a dense stand of undergrowth. It was late afternoon. She was lying on the ground. Zna-yat, Varz-hak, and Lama-tok sat close by, sound asleep. Kovok-mah and Duth-tok were nowhere to be seen. Dar studied Zna-yat's sleeping face in a futile effort to discern what made him different from the others. Recalling the previous night seemed like trying to remember a fading dream. *Did he really draw his sword, or did I only imagine it?* It had been too dark for her to see the weapon. *If he did draw it, what were his intentions?*

Though Dar made an unsettling guess, she was certain of only one thing: Zna-yat had lied to her.

As lies went, Zna-yat's was childishly transparent. He couldn't have mistaken Dar, for he saw clearly in the dark and she had addressed him in Orcish. Dar concluded that Zna-yat was neither accustomed to lying nor good at it. Nevertheless, she was disturbed that he had lied at all, for she had believed that orcs were incapable of such deception. Once again, she was forced to reassess her beliefs. If Zna-yat was capable of lying, then he was capable of treachery. He might not confront her openly; instead, he might choose to use a blade in the dark. That possibility worried Dar, but it didn't terrify her. She had grown used to danger. Zna-yat was just another threat among many. *The trick is never to be alone with him.*

Dar's ruminations were interrupted when Kovok-mah and Duth-tok pushed through the foliage. Each bore handfuls of mushrooms. Dar welcomed the food, but worried about the risks undertaken to gather it. "It's dangerous to seek food in daylight," she said.

"It's safer than taking washavoki food," replied Kovok-mah, giving Dar a meaningful look.

"From now on, I won't need to take it. They'll give it to me." As Dar tore Theena's skirt and blouse into rags, she explained how they would disguise themselves as cursed ones and how she would collect offerings along the way. When she finished, the two orcs looked confused.

"Dargu, you have strange ideas," said Duth-tok.

"This will work," said Dar.

"Are washavokis so foolish?" asked Kovok-mah.

"Hai," said Dar.

Kovok-mah curled his lips into a grin. "Then we are fortunate, indeed." He regarded the rags and wrinkled his nose. "I'd like to wash those before we wrap ourselves with them."

"That is wise," said Dar. "Zna-yat will complain less."

"You understand him well," said Kovok-mah.

Dar doubted it. "Where will you wash them?"

"There is stream nearby."

"I'll help you," said Dar.

Dar still had hopes that she had misread Zna-yat, and she wanted Kovok-mah's impressions on the matter. However, when Duth-tok accompanied them, she chose to postpone that discussion. Kovok-mah led the way along slopes that were so heavily wooded that Dar soon stopped worrying about being spotted. A short walk brought them to a stream that tumbled down a hillside. Its clear water flowed cold and swift over bare rocks. Kovok-mah knelt down and began scrubbing the rags. Duth-tok and Dar helped.

Dar did her best to wash the rags, but it soon became obvious that the orcs wished to cleanse away scents that she couldn't detect. As they persisted in scrubbing cloth that seemed clean, Dar thought uneasily about her own odor. She didn't need an orc's nose to know both she and her clothes could stand washing. Dar excused herself and walked upstream to scrub her garments and bathe. She removed her clothes and tended to them first, scrubbing and rinsing them repeatedly. Afterward, she bathed. The icy water quickly chilled her, and Dar was soon shivering violently. Yet, she continued scrubbing as if she could somehow cleanse all the washavoki from her.

Dusk found Dar walking down the road disguised as a cursed one. The bell atop her newly made staff jangled with each step. Dar's brand was covered with a rag. Against her nose pressed another, which she had smeared with clay the color of dried blood. Rags were also wrapped around both her hands, so that one appeared entirely fingerless and the other seemed to be missing two. After dark, the orcs would venture forth in similar disguises, but only Dar's could withstand scrutiny in daylight. Thus, only she could get food.

After sneaking about for so many days, it took some time for Dar to get used to walking openly on the road. It helped that there was little traffic. The hills were sparsely populated, and Dar walked a long while before she encountered a small holding. It lay at the end of a dirt path leading into a hollow. Dar walked toward it, striking the ground with her staff to announce her approach. She still was a fair distance from the buildings when a stone flew over her head. Dar stopped walking and saw that the stone thrower was a boy. He was accompanied by a woman. The boy stooped to gather more rocks, but he didn't throw them.

"Stay away," the woman shouted. "I'll leave you bread."

Dar bowed and began backing down the path, keeping an eye on the boy. As she retreated, the woman advanced until she reached the road. There, she laid a blue-green object on the ground, then hurried away. Dar waited to examine the offering until the woman was gone. It was half a loaf of bread, covered with mold. As Dar bent to pick it up, a stone hit the ground in front of her. A second struck nearby. Dar grabbed the bread and hurried off.

Returning to where the orcs were hiding, Dar served the moldy bread with the mushrooms. By the time the meal was finished, it was dark enough for the orcs to leave the woods. The waning moon cast little light, and the bell warned off anyone who was curious about the travelers on the road. Thus they passed uneventfully beyond the hills into country where small peasant holdings alternated with wild lands.

Dar spent the day sleeping in the woods until it was time to get food. She visited several holdings, and the evening meal was more ample, though less edible. Dar felt awkward proclaiming that such garbage was Muth la's gift, but the orcs didn't complain.

When it grew dark, Dar and the orcs continued their journey. The moon had yet to rise, and Dar could see little more than the pale dirt of the roadway. No light shone from any hut's window and the landscape was wrapped in shadow. Thus, when Dar turned a bend and saw the fire, it immediately caught her attention. She halted. "Do you see anything unusual ahead?" she asked Kovok-mah.

He peered down the roadway. "Thwa."

Dar sighed and resumed walking. "I thought so."

The vision persisted. It burned on the roadside, and Dar could avoid it only by making a detour. There seemed little point in doing that, so she said nothing and continued onward. The blaze didn't seem illusory. As Dar neared it, she felt heat. The flames lit the road, creating long shadows behind the travelers.

Dar felt Kovok-mah touch her shoulder. "You see something," he said.

"Hai," whispered Dar. "It's a . . ."

"Don't tell me!" said Kovok-mah. "Muth la is revealing this to you alone."

Eventually, they were so close to the fire that Dar broke out into a sweat. Against her will, her eyes were drawn to the blaze and the crumpled figure it contained. As Dar began to weep, the flames faded into cool darkness.

After the vision departed, Dar had the impression that she had undergone a trial. Almost immediately, the sadness and fear that had oppressed her were replaced by calmness. She interpreted this change as evidence that she had passed the test. Dar's new tranquillity persisted through the night and into the following morning. When they stopped to rest at dawn, Dar fell asleep easily. She awoke totally refreshed in the late afternoon and glanced about. Kovok-mah was gone. *He's probably foraging*, she thought, wishing that he hadn't left.

Dar waited for Kovok-mah to return, and when he didn't, she decided to scout the road ahead. The farther she traveled from Garlsholding, the less sure she was of the way. Dar covered her brand, then ventured out as an ordinary traveler in hopes of encountering someone who could give directions.

The early-summer sun lingered in the sky, and the tops of the trees that flanked the road glowed green-gold in its light. The winding road appeared little used, and Dar encountered no one. She walked until the sun sank lower and the empty lane was shadowed. Dar was about to turn back when she heard someone running toward her from the direction she had just come. Worried that she was being chased, Dar was about to hide when she heard the runner break out laughing. The joyful sound put her at ease, and she decided to speak to whoever approached.

Soon, a young man dressed in hunting clothes appeared. When he spotted Dar he let out a gleeful whoop and sped toward her. "We caught one!" he shouted. "We caught one!"

"Caught what?" asked Dar.

The man stopped, eager to tell his story. "We was huntin' boars with the hounds when we saw it walkin' through the woods. We loosed the pack on it. Killed five dogs and nearly killed Tarl and Gam afore Sav clubbed it. What a fight!"

"What are you talking about?" asked Dar with a rising sense of dread. "What did you catch?"

"A bull goblin! The first one round here since Grandpa was a boy."

"Did you kill it?"

The young man grinned. "Not yet. I'm gettin' folks so we can roast it proper."

"I'd like to see that," said Dar. "Where is it?"

"Up the road a jog. We dragged it there and tied it to a tree."

Dar hesitated only a second. Then she thrust her dagger into the man's chest. The move was one Sevren had taught her—a quick uppercut under the ribs and into the heart. The man stared at Dar with a look of surprise, mouthed some soundless words, and collapsed. Dar watched him die. The guilt she felt for his slaying was more than balanced by her concern for Kovok-mah. The orc was innocent. The man was not. Suddenly, Dar's visions of fires made terrible sense. All she could hope was that they didn't show the inevitable.

Dar grabbed the man's ankles and dragged his corpse into the undergrowth. After hastily covering traces of the slaying with dirt and leaves, she dashed up the road. Dar had no way of knowing if the man had told others of the orc's capture. Thus, she had no idea what she would find. The image of a mob hurrying to burn Kovok-mah alive lent speed to her steps.

Dar heard the men before she saw them. She didn't know how many hunters there were, but she heard more than two voices. Knowing that she would be outnumbered, she devised a ploy to put the men off guard. Dar left the road and entered the woods, taking a circuitous route toward the noise. Eventually, she caught a glimpse of men upon the road. Dar ripped open the front of her blouse, then ran noisily toward them, bawling as she did. As she neared the road, she could see an orc's broad back. His arms were pulled backward around a tree trunk and his wrists were tied.

Three men stared at Dar with astonishment as she emerged from the trees. They held stout spears. Two more men lay on the ground nearby, seriously wounded.

Several massive hunting dogs, black and fierce-looking, milled about. "Help!" Dar cried. "A goblin attacked me!" She dashed past the tree, halted, and whirled about. "That's the one!"

It was Zna-yat who was tied to the tree. His clothes were torn, he was mauled in several places, and his head was covered in blood. Yet he was conscious and vainly straining against the ropes. Dry brush and branches were piled about his feet. He looked as shocked to see Dar as she was surprised to see him.

"It'll not hurt ye now," said a man who fixed his eyes on Dar's breasts. "Stay with us and watch it burn."

"I must revenge myself on it," said Dar, drawing her dagger.

Zna-yat grew agitated at the sight of the weapon, causing two of the unwounded hunters to break out laughing. The third seemed less amused and grabbed Dar's wrist. "Don't spoil our fun."

Dar lowered her voice to an intimate tone. "I just want a little piece of him. A finger, perhaps, so I can remember your bravery." She moved closer and added in a breathy whisper. "You'll be glad you let me."

The man grinned. "Take your finger, then."

Dar walked over to Zna-yat and whispered in Orcish. "I'll cut ropes. Shout like it hurts." She stepped behind the tree, where the orc's wrists were bound with several coils of thick rope. As soon as Dar started to saw at them, Zna-yat bellowed. The men grinned and hooted. The rope, however, didn't cut quickly, and one of the hunters soon became curious. "What's taking so long?" he asked, walking to where Dar was still sawing at Zna-yat's bonds.

When Dar moved to block his view, he strode closer and saw her cutting the rope. "Hey!" he shouted, grabbing for his knife.

Dar slashed his throat. After that, chaos ensued.

Blood sprayed from the man's neck. At the sight of it, the dogs sprang at Dar. Zna-yat broke free and grabbed a stout branch at his feet. A dog slammed into Dar, knocking her down. Another bit her ankle and tugged. Dar stabbed the first dog as it went for her throat. Someone screamed. Dar stabbed the dog again. Her dagger slipped between its ribs. Someone moaned. The dog pulled away, twisting the weapon from Dar's grasp. A second scream. Dar kicked at the dog biting her ankle. The dog held fast. The pain was excruciating. Someone kicked her. Dar rolled. A spearhead penetrated deep into the earth, just inches from her nose. There was a sickening crunch. Someone fell upon Dar, knocking her breathless. A dog yelped, then whimpered. There was another yelp and teeth no long gripped Dar's ankle. Then there was silence.

Dar pushed a corpse off her and gazed upon a scene of carnage. Clearly, Zna-yat had used surprise to his advantage. All the men were dead. Two had their skulls caved in. The man who had lain upon Dar had a spear protruding from his back. Three dead dogs lay close by. Zna-yat stood above her, his forearm bleeding from a fresh slash. He seemed dazed. Dar slowly got to her feet. Her ankle was bloody and throbbing painfully, but she could put weight on it.

"Did any washavokis escape?" asked Dar.

"What?" asked Zna-yat.

"Are all washavokis who saw you dead?"

"Thwa. One ran down road after I was bound."

"I killed that one," said Dar.

Zna-yat stared at Dar in amazement.

"We'll be safe if we hide these dead washavokis and their dogs," said Dar.

Zna-yat seemed distracted. He didn't reply.

Dar grabbed the ankles of the nearest man and strained to drag him into the undergrowth. "Help me!"

Zna-yat finally spoke. "I'll do this." He lifted the corpse easily and carried it off.

While Zna-yat disposed of the bodies, Dar retrieved her dagger, then limped about erasing signs of the struggle as best she could. A lot of blood had soaked into the dirt road—too much to eliminate completely. As Dar worked to conceal the gore from the struggle, its reality hit home. She began to shake from horror. *I had to do it,* she told herself. *Now it's over. It's over. We're alive. They didn't burn him.*

When Zna-yat returned from hiding the last of the dogs, Dar was also done with her task. "We should return to others," she said.

Zna-yat grabbed Dar and swung her over his shoulder, just as he had the corpses. "I'll carry you."

"Put me down," said Dar. "I can walk,"

"Thwa," replied Zna-yat, striding toward where he had hidden the bodies.

"You're going in wrong direction," said Dar.

"I must get my weapons," replied Zna-yat. Since Dar was slung over Zna-yat's shoulder, she couldn't see his face, but he sounded disturbed. His grip was firm and inescapable. Dar's dagger was pressed against his torso, beyond reach. Dar realized the irony of her situation; she had risked her life so that she would end up alone with Zna-yat and completely within his power.

Eight

♛

Zna-yat carried Dar only a short distance before he set her down in a small clearing. There was evidence of struggle everywhere. Dead dogs lay about, one severed in half. Blood was splattered on the trampled weeds. A matted trail marked where Zna-yat had been dragged away. As Dar surveyed the scene, Zna-yat searched the weeds. He found his dagger and sheathed it, but when he discovered his sword he didn't put it away. Instead, he turned to face Dar. He still seemed agitated, and the blade trembled slightly in his hand. "I smell your fear," he said.

Dar said nothing, but she placed her hand upon the hilt of her dagger.

Zna-yat moved closer. "You're wise to fear me."

Dar wondered how fast she could run with an injured ankle. *I can't outrun an orc*, she thought, recalling her ride on Kovok-mah's shoulders. Nevertheless, she prepared to throw her dagger and try. For the moment, however, she remained perfectly still.

"After I was caught, you were safe," said Zna-yat. "Why did you come?"

"I've had visions of urkzimmuthi burning."

Zna-yat said nothing. He simply stared at Dar as a mournful sound rose from deep in his throat. It grew louder, and Zna-yat's trembling became more noticeable. He dropped his sword at Dar's feet, then fell to his hands and knees. It took a while before he regained the composure to speak. "Muth la has entered my chest," he said.

"I've awakened from evil dream and see with open eyes. You're wise and good. I've been foolish and wicked. I'm ashamed of your fear." He lowered his head. "Bite my neck."

Dar knew that a bent neck was a sign of surrender among orcs, but she had never heard of one orc biting another. It seemed drastic, and she hesitated.

Zna-yat didn't move. "Please, Mother, leave your mark."

Dar remained uncertain. "What does bite mean?"

"My life will become yours."

"That would be great gift," said Dar. "Why would I deserve it?"

"I was caught because hate made me careless. I had only one thought—to slay you. I planned to hide your body and say nothing. You saw evil in my chest and repaid it with courage."

"Why did you hate me so?" asked Dar.

"I thought washavoki had no place with urkzimmuthi. I didn't understand."

"Understand what?"

"When I threw you into river, washavoki died. Your life was Muth la's gift. Now you serve her. Please, Dargu, allow me to undo my evil. Your bite would bless me."

Dar overcame feelings of awkwardness to kneel down and bite Zna-yat's neck hard enough to leave a mark. As she did so, he sighed as if a great weight had been lifted from his shoulders. Zna-yat rose, and Dar had never witnessed such a dramatic transformation. His blood-covered face bore the reverent and peaceful look of one absolved. "Shashav, Dargu," he said. "Shashav, Muth la."

Kovok-mah was visibly upset when Zna-yat returned carrying Dar. "Both of you are wounded!" he cried. "What has happened?"

"We have fought washavokis and their dogs," said Dar. "All of them are dead. We will be safe awhile."

"Are you badly hurt?" asked Kovok-mah.

"Dargu's ankle was bitten," replied Zna-yat.

"It hurts, but bone isn't broken," said Dar. "Zna-yat's wounds are greater."

"Thwa," said Zna-yat. "They are small."

Kovok-mah examined Dar's ankle. It was still bleeding and had begun to swell. "Zna-yat was wise to carry you," he said. He scrutinized his cousin's face. "Something else has happened."

"Hai," replied Zna-yat. "Dargu has bitten my neck."

Kovok-mah appeared dumbfounded, and Dar couldn't tell at first whether he was pleased or dismayed. She glanced at the others. They looked equally astonished. Witnessing the orcs' reactions made Dar appreciate the momentousness of Zna-yat's announcement.

As surprise slowly faded from Kovok-mah's face, his lips curled into a broad smile. "I'm much amazed."

Zna-yat grinned back. "No less than I."

Dar broke the silence that followed. "Kovok-mah, do you have magic for Zna-yat's wounds?"

"I'll need to find proper herbs," he replied.

"You should do it quickly," said Dar. "We must be far from here by morning."

While Kovok-mah left to find the plants he needed, the other orcs washed the blood from Dar's and Zna-yat's wounds. As they worked, Dar gave an account of the brush with the hunters, but she didn't speak of what transpired between her and Zna-yat. When she finished, Zna-yat added, "I was captured because I tried to slay Dargu."

His frankness surprised Dar, but not the orcs. "I've smelled your anger for long time," said Duth-tok. "I'm glad you're free of it at last."

"Hai," said Lama-tok. "Now there'll be harmony."

"Even sons can see this is Muth la's work," said Varz-hak. "You were wise to bare your neck. Dargu will make good use of it."

"I know this now," said Zna-yat, bowing his head toward Dar.

As Dar listened to this talk, she realized how isolated she had been. No one had spoken to her about Zna-yat's hatred, not even Kovok-mah. She still didn't fully under-stand the consequences of biting Zna-yat's neck. *I lead them, but we seldom speak. I know nothing about their lives, except that Kovok-mah is fond of goats.* She re-solved to change that.

Kovok-mah returned, carrying several different plants. "Muth la has provided. I've found what I need."

"Tend Zna-yat first," said Dar. "He has more wounds."

"Thwa," said Zna-yat.

"I'll decide," said Kovok-mah. "Even mothers obey healers." He counted out five small green berries and handed them to Dar. Then he gave a larger number to Zna-yat. "Chew these very well," he said, "then swallow them."

Dar popped the berries into her mouth and bit down. Their bitterness nearly made her gag. Dar forced herself to chew. By the time she swallowed, Kovok-mah was holding her ankle as he chewed a mouthful of herbs and spit greenish saliva into her wound. It burned and tingled at first; then numbness followed. Afterward, Kovok-mah swabbed the tooth punctures with a mashed leaf. Before he turned his attention to Zna-yat, he asked Dar about the route they would take that night.

"Why do you need to know that?" asked Dar.

Kovok-mah handed Dar a large, fuzzy leaf. "You'll sleep after you chew this."

"I can't sleep. Not tonight," said Dar. "We must leave here."

"I'll carry you while you sleep," said Kovok-mah.

"Thwa," said Dar. "If we meet washavokis, I must speak with them."

"I'm healer," said Kovok-mah, "and I think sleep is best for you."

"You must heed Dargu," said Zna-yat. "Carry her, but don't give her leaf."

"Nayimgat not only gives sleep," said Kovok-mah, "it also heals."

"I'll chew some tomorrow," said Dar. "Tonight, I'll need my wits."

Kovok-mah didn't argue further. Instead, he put fresh herbs in his mouth and turned to treat Zna-yat's wounds. Once all of them were cleansed and numbed, and the dog bites were swabbed, he sewed up the gash in Zna-yat's arm. By the time he was finished, it was night.

Soon, Dar was being carried down the dark, empty road. She could only hope that they hadn't gone astray. Asking directions was out of the question. Sooner or later, the slain hunters would be discovered, and Dar wanted no one recalling travelers on the road. Thus, while she and the orcs disguised themselves as cursed ones, they muffled the bell and moved as quickly and silently as possible.

They encountered no one. As the night progressed, Dar grew less anxious. The herbs dulled the pain in her ankle, and being carried had a lulling effect. Resting her head upon Kovok-mah's shoulder, Dar gazed into the night through half-closed eyes. When she spotted the fire, she was unsure if she was dreaming or having another vision. Its flames burned behind them, not by the road ahead. They grew ever smaller as Kovok-mah bore her away. Eventually, the blaze seemed little different from the stars that filled the sky, and just as distant.

Nine

♛

When dawn approached, the orcs hid in a wood. Since Dar had been prevented from begging, there was nothing to eat. For her, at least, hunger became irrelevant after Kovok-mah had her chew the healing leaf that caused her to sleep. When she awoke, it was night. The orcs sat motionless about her. Kovok-mah's eyes glowed pale green in the starlight. The other orcs slept. "Why didn't you wake me?" Dar asked. "We must begin our journey."

"It's too late to travel," said Kovok-mah. "Golden eye will rise soon."

"You mean we wasted whole night?"

"We wasted nothing," said Kovok-mah. "You needed to rest."

Dar felt her ankle. It was no longer hot and swollen. She flexed her foot. There was less pain. She smiled. "So, even mothers obey healers?"

"Wise ones do," replied Kovok-mah.

"And you give nayimgat leaves to those who don't."

"If they're fierce or stubborn, it's good magic."

"Then why would you give it to me?" teased Dar.

"Because you're both," replied Kovok-mah.

Dar wondered if those traits had scents and, if they did, what they smelled like. She didn't bother to ask. When orcs spoke of scents, she felt like a blind person hearing about rainbows.

"When morning comes and washavokis wake," said Dar, "I'll try to get food."

"That won't be necessary," said Kovok-mah. "We gathered much food yesterday."

"So, you took risks while I slept."

"Not so many," said Kovok-mah. "Few washavokis live here. Our ancestors once farmed this land and their crops now grow wild." Kovok-mah gestured to a large pile of tubers, roots, and fleshy leaf stalks.

"It looks like you feasted," said Dar.

"Not yet," said Kovok-mah. "Mothers own food."

"You've been waiting for me to serve it?"

"That is proper way."

The prospect of ample food and a day of rest filled Dar with a sense of well-being. It surpassed the peace she had felt at Garlsholding, for it was more than the absence of fear. As a bondmaid, no one cared about her. The orcs clearly did. Relaxed, and still sleepy, Dar yawned.

"Ground is cold in morning," said Kovok-mah, folding his cloak to cushion his lap.

Dar took the hint and climbed upon it. He wrapped his arms about her. "Ground is cold," she said. "I'm glad you're so warm."

The food that the orcs had gathered was new to Dar. Thung was a succulent leaf stalk filled with thick sap that reminded Dar a little of broth. Brak was a tuber with crunchy yellow flesh that had a nutty flavor. The pashi roots were bland, but filling. The meal was satisfyingly ample. It also reminded the orcs of home and turned their thoughts in its direction.

"Air was clear yesterday," said Duth-tok. "I saw Blath Urkmuthi."

"Did mountains look close?" asked Dar.

"Thwa, but it was good to see them," said Duth-tok.

Lama-tok sighed. "I long to work their bones again."

"Hai," said Duth-tok. "Kip and bakt fit hand better than sword."

"What's 'kip' and 'bakt'?" asked Dar.

"Tools to shape stone," said Duth-tok. He made the motions of striking a chisel with a hammer. "Hit kip with bakt."

"You worked stone?" asked Dar.

"Hai," said Lama-tok. "Tok clan is famed for it."

"Lama and I built Zna-yat's vathem," said Duth-tok.

Dar turned to Zna-yat. "What's that? House?"

Zna-yat smiled. "House for mice, perhaps. Vathem is wall to make even ground on slope. There are many vathems around our homes. Mountainsides look like this." He traced imaginary terraces in the air.

"You farm?" said Dar. "I thought you were soldier."

"Killing isn't proper work," said Zna-yat. "At home, I grow brak and pashi. Kovok-mah raises goats and makes hard milk. Varz-hak makes sand ice."

"Sand ice? What's that?" asked Dar.

"Special wisdom of Hak clan," said Varz-hak. "We have way to melt sand. When it cools, it is clear and hard like ice, but not cold."

"You can see through little door of sand ice," said Kovok-mah, "but rain and wind do not come in."

Dar imagined shutters that wouldn't darken a hut. "That would be useful."

"Hai," said Varz-hak. "Even washavokis desire them. I also make sand ice vessels to store things. You can see what's inside."

"If you drop them, they break," said Kovok-mah. He laughed. "Hak clan wise to make things everyone wants and everyone breaks."

"You have such useful skills," said Dar. "Why do you fight?"

"Sons must protect mothers," said Kovok-mah.

"How does fighting for washavoki king protect mothers?" asked Dar.

"I don't know," said Kovok-mah. "That is queen's wisdom."

"Perhaps," said Zna-yat, "if we do not fight for washavoki king, washavokis will attack urkzimmuthi land."

"Perhaps you're right," said Dar, thinking Zna-yat had a better grasp of human ruthlessness than the others.

"Long ago," said Kovok-mah, "urkzimmuthi did not fight. We made no weapons. None wore death's hard clothes."

"Those were lessons washavokis taught our ancestors," said Zna-yat.

No wonder you hate them, thought Dar. "They were cruel lessons," she said.

"Hai," said Zna-yat, "but you'll teach us different ones."

"I have no lessons for you," said Dar.

"You will," said Zna-yat.

Once again, Dar marveled at Zna-yat's conversion. *Two days ago, he was plotting my death. Now he talks as if I have a special destiny.* Though the idea made Dar uncomfortable, she appreciated how Zna-yat's transformation affected the others. It put them at ease, and they were talkative for the first time. For a while, the conversation centered on the orcs' occupations. Then Dar changed the subject to a more personal one, for she was curious to know if the orcs were married. She found it difficult to express the question in a way they understood. "Oh," said Lama-tok after Dar's third attempt, "Dargu asks if we have muthvashi."

"Only young sons fight," said Kovok-mah. "Those with muthvashi stay home."

"So none of you have muthvashi?" asked Dar.

"Thwa," said Kovok-mah.

"I think Duth-tok will soon," said Lama-tok. "Our muthuri has wise nose."

"What does that mean?" said Dar.

Kovok-mah smiled at Dar's confusion. "When muthuri considers who should be her son's muthvashi, she's wise to heed her nose."

"Why is that?" asked Dar.

"When two care for one another, it's easy to detect," said Kovok-mah.

"It can be smelled?"

"Hai," said Duth-tok. "Scent is pleasing."

"I thought such smells were neither pleasing nor unpleasing," said Dar.

Duth-tok smiled. "When scent comes from mother you care for, it's *very* pleasing."

Dar wondered if it was the fragrance of love or desire. The question seemed too intimate to ask. Instead, she asked a different one. "What is this scent called?"

"Atur," said Duth-tok. "How I miss it!"

Dar's first leisure in many months had a celebratory air, as if she, too, were nearing home. She repaired her torn blouse, but otherwise spent the time resting or conversing. What Dar relished most was her newfound sense of belonging. She felt bound to her comrades, not just by need and common purpose, but also by mutual affection.

When darkness fell, Dar and the orcs put on their disguises and resumed their journey. Dar's ankle was tender, but she was able to walk. There was no need for her to seek offerings along the way, so they traveled without interruption. The land grew drier. Scrubland replaced forests. As the holdings they passed became smaller and more isolated, Dar worried less that the orcs would be overwhelmed if they were recognized. When dawn approached, they left the road and slept in a clump of brush.

The following night was similar to the previous one, except the food ran out. The travelers slept through the day until the sun was low. Then Dar went out to approach holdings where she was given food to go away. Often, stones were thrown as she departed. It was dark before she had collected enough scraps for a meager dinner.

As the travelers continued northward, the land rose imperceptibly and grew more arid as it did until it was nearly desert. When the moon rose and cast shadows, Dar discerned the traces of ancient channels on the barren plain. Though weathered to little more than a grid of shallow depressions, they were impressive in scope. Kovok-mah noticed Dar gazing at them. "Long ago, urkzimmuthi dug those to bring water from faraway river."

"This place was once called Greenplain," said Zna-yat.

"What happened?" asked Dar.

"Washavokis came," replied Zna-yat.

The following day, Dar began approaching holdings early. She needed more time to collect food owing to the distance between settlements and because the offerings reflected the peasants' poverty. By late afternoon, Dar had only a few moldy roots when she approached another holding. It looked deserted except for one hut where smoke issued from the eaves. Dar almost passed it by, but hunger spurred her to seek an offering. Striking her staff smartly on the ground to jangle its bell, she approached the hut, keeping a wary eye for thrown rocks.

Usually, people appeared long before she reached the nearest building, but this time no one came out. Dar continued up the path toward the hut. She was very close before its door opened and a man emerged. He looked ancient, with a long white beard and skin as wrinkled as dried fruit, but he moved vigorously. He bore no food. "I fear not the cursed," he said.

"It's more worthy to give from charity than fear," said Dar.

The man smiled. "You have a fair tongue, so I'll give

you something better than food." He bounded to where Dar stood and snatched the bandage wrapped about her face. His smile broadened into a grin. "See, I've restored your nose. Shall I return your missing fingers next?"

Dar stood silent and red-faced.

"Your toes gave you away," said the man. "The cursed lose those first."

Dar began to back toward the road, wondering if she would have to defend herself.

"Don't go," said the man. "I've been expecting you."

"What?" said Dar.

"The feathers foretold deception," replied the man. "It's your defining trait."

Dar wondered if the man was crazy.

The old man ignored Dar's suspicious look. "Sup with me. It can't be pleasant to brave scorn and stones for scraps."

"Thank you, but I must go."

"Back to the others?"

"Others?" said Dar. "There are no others."

"Aye, that's the deception again," said the man, his eyes crinkling with amusement. He looked at Dar's small, rag-wrapped bundle of roots. "That won't feed six."

Dar backed farther away, trying not to look surprised.

"Ther nat suthi na breeth," said the man. *You are wise to be cautious.*

Dar halted.

"Washavokis are cruel and treacherous," said the man. "Only they would brand a mother. Kramav thwa ma. Ma nat urkzimmuthi." *Fear me not. I am urkzimmuthi.*

"Tha gavat thwa urkzimmuthi," replied Dar. *You do not seem urkzimmuthi.*

The man smiled and parted the hairs of his beard to give Dar a glimpse of black lines tattooed beneath it. "I was born washavoki, but this is my urkzimmuthi clan tattoo. My clan name is Velasa-pah."

"The first part means 'one who sees,'" said Dar. "That seems appropriate. The urkzimmuthi call me 'weasel.'"

Velasa-pah nodded. "I think 'Dargu' is a fitting name for you."

"You talk as if you know me," said Dar, feeling both mystified and wary. "I've no idea who you are."

"I'm a relic," said Velasa-pah. "When I was young, this land was green and the urkzimmuthi lived in peace."

Dar stared at the old man in disbelief. "That was many ages ago!"

"Muth la has preserved my life. Come inside. We'll consult the feathers."

Velasa-pah turned and walked toward the hut, clearly expecting Dar to follow. She hesitated and watched him. He didn't look dangerous. Indeed, Dar wondered why he had seemed vigorous before, for his gait faltered. Velasa-pah paused at the entrance to his hut. "Come," he said, "I've been waiting a long time."

Dar felt compelled to obey. She entered the hut. A kettle bubbled over a small fire, filling the air with a savory aroma. "That's muthtufa," said Velasa-pah, gesturing at the pot. "Good urkzimmuthi stew. Your friends will enjoy it." He pointed to a large sack nearby. "There's enough brak and pashi in there to get you to Blath Urkmuthi." He smiled at Dar's puzzled look. "As I said— you were expected."

Dar glanced about the hut. Though its exterior walls had been square, its interior ones were circular. A row of stones was set into the ground at the hut's entrance to complete the circle formed by the walls. "We're within the Embrace of Muth la," she said.

"Aye," replied Velasa-pah. "All urkzimmuthi dwellings contain one."

Dar noted that pegs were set into the walls and a wide variety of herbs hung from them along with numerous sacks and pouches. "Do you do magic?"

"I have some skill," said Velasa-pah. He hobbled over to the wall and removed a sack. It looked antique, and the designs embroidered upon its worn cloth had faded until they were nearly invisible. Moving slowly, as if the effort pained him, Velasa-pah lowered himself to the earthen floor. "Come, Dargu. Sit beside me. Let's see what guidance the feathers have for you."

Dar sat down, and the old man opened the sack with palsied fingers. Feathers of different colors fluttered to the floor. Once they settled, Velasa-pah leaned over and blew upon them. The feathers moved, but it seemed to Dar that it wasn't Velasa-pah's wheezing breath that had rearranged their pattern. After they settled for a second time, the old man silently studied them. A long time passed before he spoke. "Visit Tarathank."

"Where's that?" asked Dar.

"It's the urkzimmuthi ruin that lies close to this road. Washavokis avoid it."

Dar recalled the tales she had heard at Garlsholding of a haunted goblin city. "I've heard of that place," she said, "but I don't know where it lies."

"The road splits north of here. You must look carefully, for the western fork is never used and hard to spot. Follow it to the city."

"Is that all I need do?" asked Dar.

Velasa-pah peered at the feathers longer and his expression grew sad. "Follow your chest."

"What?" said Dar.

"Your chest understands what your mind cannot. Heed its wisdom. It won't always be easy."

"All right," said Dar, thinking this advice was vague at best.

"There is a man who listens to bones," said Velasa-pah. "He is your enemy, but the bones are a greater enemy." Velasa-pah gazed at the feathers a while longer, then shook his head. "Perhaps you should blow upon them," he said. "Blow gently."

Dar leaned over and blew. The feathers crumbed into dust.

"So it ends," said Velasa-pah. "I'm going to rest now, so you must wait for supper. Get your friends. This food is Muth la's gift. It should be served by a mother." Velasa-pah lay down and closed his eyes. "Vata, Dargu," he murmured. *Good-bye, Dargu.*

Dar rose. She looked outside and was surprised to see that it was dark. She glanced at Velasa-pah. He was already asleep. "Vata, Velasa-pah," she whispered, then hurried into the night.

When Dar returned with the orcs, the fire beneath the kettle had died to embers and she could see little by its faint light. The kettle and the sack of food were where Dar had last seen them, but the hut was empty otherwise. There was no sign of Velasa-pah and the walls were bare. Kovok-mah looked about. "Dargu, if I did not see this food, I would think you had another vision. This place has been empty long time."

Zna-yat skirted a pile of dust to examine the kettle. "I can't believe some washavoki made muthtufa."

"He claimed he was urkzimmuthi," said Dar. "Said his name was Velasa-pah."

Zna-yat looked amused. "Velasa-pah? Well, that washavoki knew some tales."

"Who is Velasa-pah?" asked Dar.

"Great wizard who died long ago," said Zna-yat. "His clan is lost, victims of washavokis."

Ten

♛

Dar and the orcs traveled two nights to reach Tarathank. As they neared the mountains, the land turned green again, but few people tilled its soil. Holdings became solitary huts, surrounded by a sea of tall grass. On the last night of their journey, the travelers passed no dwellings at all. By then, the ancient road was so overgrown that it seemed little different from the surrounding prairie. Only the orcs' keen vision allowed them to follow it at night.

As far as Dar's companions knew, no orc had visited the city for generations. Yet it loomed large in orcish tales. It was the queen's city, home to the Pah clan, from which a long line of monarchs arose. Other clans lived there too, so Tarathank was called the City of Matriarchs. It had been the center of orcish civilization, a place of marvels. As Kovok-mah and the others spoke of it, their voices reflected awe and excitement.

The orcs could see the ruins long before they reached them, but Dar got her first glimpse of Tarathank only when dawn lit the plain. The city was distant, but prominent, for it sprawled over the only hilltop. Every town Dar had ever seen possessed a defensive wall, but the crumbled structure that encircled the city could not have served a military function. It was a negligible barrier, dwarfed by the ruins it enclosed. A roadway zigzagged up the hillside to its entrance. Surveying the landscape, Dar said, "There's no one to see us. Let's go on."

The immense ruin seemed closer than it actually was, and the travelers didn't reach Tarathank until midmorning. Its entrance had been a delicate, gateless archway. Though broken, it still looked elegant. Beyond the ruined arch, Dar saw a city ravaged by war. Its defenselessness made its destruction seem all the more wanton. Most of the buildings near the low wall were burned and reduced to rubble. Only farther in was the demolition less complete.

The travelers entered Tarathank and walked its silent streets, where they found time and nature had continued the destruction wrought by war. Weeds and trees pushed up between paving stones and filled the interiors of roofless buildings. Vines shrouded most of the structures. The vegetation didn't seem wholly out of place, for the city's builders preferred natural forms. The ruined structures favored curves and arches over right angles. Even the stones within the walls were not rectangular, but varied in shape and size. Doorways, window frames, and pillars were carved with flowing botanic lines. Thus, even buildings several stories high seemed to have grown from the earth.

Tarathank was the first city Dar had ever entered, and even in decay it awed her. The orcs were similarly impressed. Everyone walked quietly, feeling that the city's grandeur and tragedy required it. When Dar finally spoke, she thought her voice sounded unnaturally loud. "We should find place to rest."

After wandering the winding streets, they encountered a vine-covered building that still had its roof. It was modestly sized compared with its neighbors, but it seemed grand to Dar. Like the other structures on the street, it was a home.

From her conversations, Dar knew orc dwellings housed extended families, and the size of the house reflected that. All the females who once had lived there would have been blood relations—mothers and daughters, spanning several generations. When sons married, they left to join their wives, but daughters always remained under the same roof. As Dar passed the numerous rooms in the abandoned house, she gained a sense of the collective power of mothers. Husbands would come as outsiders to live among females united by blood and a lifetime of association. Dar thought, *No wonder they treat mothers with respect.*

Though the house was structurally intact, it had been looted and vandalized. Most of the rooms were bare except for dried leaves that had drifted in through smashed windows. Occasionally, they encountered bits of moldy cloth or pieces of splintered furniture, but little remained that spoke of the lives spent within the rooms. Dar spied pieces of sand ice lying on the leaf-littered floor beneath a window. She picked up a shard to examine it. It did seem like warm ice. Dar gazed through the pale green fragment, trying to imagine it filling the window.

As Dar explored with the orcs, a pattern to the house became apparent. A main passageway snaked through the structure connecting a series of large, circular rooms, each featuring a hearth. Smaller rooms branched off from those. Kovok-mah explained that a room with a hearth was called a "hanmuthi"—*fire of mother*—and it was the center of a family's daily life. The adjoining rooms were primarily used for sleeping. On the house's second floor, they found a hanmuthi that was particularly grand. Its floor was mostly clear of litter and a series of large windows admitted ample light and air. Above the hearth was a hole in the ceiling surrounded by the remnants of a metal chimney.

"This is good place to rest," said Dar, who had grown accustomed to making decisions.

Usually, the orcs set up camp by marking off the Embrace of Muth la. This time, they behaved differently.

Duth-tok and Lama-tok wandered into one of the small adjoining rooms and Varz-hak and Zna-yat entered another. Dar was left standing with Kovok-mah. "Should we not mark circle?" she asked.

"Walls of hanmuthi form Muth la's Embrace," said Kovok-mah.

"So we can sleep anywhere?"

"Hai. Everywhere is within sacred circle."

Dar glanced at the empty chambers, feeling reluctant to enter any of them. "I'm not used to sleeping alone," she said.

"This is fearful journey," said Kovok-mah. "Your nearness brings me comfort."

"Then let us rest together."

An adjoining room lit by windows attracted Dar. She entered it, and Kovok-mah followed. Upon its walls was a relief showing children running unclothed through a field of flowers. Someone had gouged their faces, reducing them to shallow craters in the limestone. Yet, even in its marred state, the relief was a beautiful work of art. The flowers were carved with delicate detail and the running children seemed alive and joyful. Only the claws on their fingers and toes marked them as urkzimmuthi.

Dar noticed a line of curious marks beneath the relief. "What are those?" she asked.

"Words," said Kovok-mah, pointing to them as he read.

> "Laughter echoes not
> In soft spring fields.
> Flowers always return.
> Children visit only once."

Dar had heard of reading, but had never seen anyone do it. She was unsure which astonished her more—that Kovok-mah had read those lines or that they had moved him so deeply. His eyes were mournful as his fingers caressed the exquisitely worked forms.

"I think urkzimmuthi are like these children," he said. "When we depart, no one will recall our faces."

"Why do you speak of departing?" asked Dar.

"This empty place shows how we've dwindled. When we are gone, who will remember us? To washavokis, we are only monsters."

Dar thought of Leela, who had killed herself rather than face orcs, and guiltily recalled the gruesome tales she had told Theena. Beholding Kovok-mah's sorrow made Dar want to ease it. "Thwa, Thwa," she said softly. "You are gentle and good. I am washavoki and . . ."

"Thwa! You are not."

"I am. My teeth are white like dog's."

"So? Now mine are also."

"I smell."

"I like your scent."

"Look at me! What do you see?"

"Dargu, why do you speak like this? You are mother . . . seer . . . guide. Your chest is not washavoki, and chest is most important."

"My chest wishes you were not sad," said Dar.

Kovok-mah smiled wanly. "Then I must strive to be happy."

Dar dreamed of Velasa-pah. He sat silently upon the floor of the room where she and Kovok-mah slept, watching her with an expectant look on his face. When Dar asked what he wanted, he crumbled to dust. The image was so disturbing that it woke her.

Dar was sitting in Kovok-mah's lap. She had grown accustomed to the orcish upright sleeping position, but it was comfortable only because Kovok-mah supported her. Dozing folded in his arms was preferable to lying on the ground, and Kovok-mah liked her to do so. It calmed him. Dar recalled a doll of twisted straw that one of her little half sisters took to bed, and imagined she served a similar function. The idea made her smile.

Vines draped over the room's shattered windows, dimming the light and keeping the room cool in the afternoon's heat. Dar was still tired and wished to sleep some more, but she kept thinking of Velasa-pah. She had never seen deep magic before, but felt certain she had witnessed it in his stone hut. While what happened there might be explained away, instinct told Dar that would be foolhardy. Velasa-pah's advice, like her visions, shouldn't be ignored. Yet what he had told her seemed of little use. She knew of no man who listened to bones. The feelings that stirred within her chest were unsettled and often contradictory, hardly guidance at all. *Well, at least I'm in Tarathank.* Dar wondered why she was directed to the ruined city. *Perhaps I'm supposed to find something.* She couldn't imagine what it could be.

Realizing she wouldn't sleep, Dar rose carefully so as not to disturb Kovok-mah. Her bare feet made no noise as she walked over to the window and peered out. The overgrown city looked like a forest of bizarrely shaped trees. It was eerily quiet. No birds called, and the air was still. Judging from the low angle of the sun, it was late afternoon.

Dar turned about and saw that Kovok-mah was watching her. "I'm sorry if I woke you," she said.

"I've been awake awhile. You seem restless."

"I was thinking of Velasa-pah. Zna-yat said he's mentioned in old tales. Who was he?"

"Muth la made urkzimmuthi first," said Kovok-mah, "and for long time we knew no washavokis. When they first appeared, we called them 'urkzimdi'—second children. In those days, some urkzimdi were reborn into clans. One was Velasa-pah. He became great wizard, though great was his sorrow."

"Why?"

"It can be painful to see future."

"I know," said Dar, thinking of her own visions. "What happened to him?"

"He foresaw destruction of Tarathank, but queen didn't understand war. It was his fate to see all he loved perish."

"Yet, he lived."

"Thwa. All urkzimmuthi perished in Tarathank."

"But he was washavoki."

"He was not," said Kovok-mah. "He had been reborn."

"How?"

"I don't know. It doesn't happen anymore."

Dar thought of the lonely old man in the stone hut. "That's sad tale," she said. Yet she hoped it was true, for the one she imagined was even sadder.

"Tales told here lack happy endings," said Kovok-mah.

"Yet we were supposed to come to this place," said Dar. "I don't know why." She sighed. "I fear we must stay awhile."

Dar's decision to linger in Tarathank didn't disappoint the other orcs. Rather, it gave them a chance to pursue their interests. The following day, Zna-yat found an iron kettle that still held liquid. After scouring the rust from its interior, he searched long-abandoned gardens for culinary herbs. By the time Lama-tok and Duth-tok returned from studying the city's stonework, Zna-yat had a stew cooking on the hearth. Varz-hak came back a little later with a collection of glass shards in colors he had never seen before.

Only Kovok-mah had no personal project. Instead, he

accompanied Dar as she wandered about the city. She was looking for something, but she had no clue as to what it was. Kovok-mah tried to be cheerful as they poked about the deserted buildings, but being an orc, he was unable to disguise his feelings. The ruins depressed him, and Dar knew it.

The only discovery that lifted Kovok-mah's spirits was a bathing pool located in a nearby courtyard. A steady stream of water poured into it from a stone spout set high in the wall above. The tiny waterfall made a soothing sound. Moreover, the constant flow of water prevented leaves from accumulating, and the pool was the first they had encountered that wasn't choked with muck and weeds. When Dar was ready to depart, she saw that Kovok-mah was reluctant to leave, so they stayed a while longer and watched the falling water.

After dinner, all the orcs but Kovok-mah were brimming with talk of things that had fired their imagination. Zna-yat had encountered two herbs that were new to him. Varz-hak passed around his collection of shards so that everyone could hold them up to the light. Duth-tok and Lama-tok waxed eloquent on stonework and prevailed on Dar to visit a wall they particularly admired.

Dar returned at dusk to find Kovok-mah gone, and his absence made her feel that she had neglected him that evening. She had been caught up in the other orcs' enthusiasms while he sat silent and alone. When the orcs retired to sleep and Kovok-mah hadn't returned, Dar decided to find him. She suspected that he had gone to the pool. It wasn't distant. If she hurried, there would be enough light for her to find the way.

Dar left the building and made her way through the street. So many plants grew between the paving stones that it resembled a meadow. The house that contained the pool was huge and burned. In the twilight, its entrance was a black hole. Dar nearly turned back, but recalling

Kovok-mah's sadness made her press onward. She felt her way through the passage until she saw a dim light ahead. She moved toward it, heard the sound of falling water, and entered the courtyard.

Kovok-mah stood waist-deep in the pool, facing away. Water cascaded over him, and he seemed unaware of Dar's approach. She halted at the pool's edge. Kovok-mah was ten paces away, motionless. The water flowing over his skin made it look as if it had turned to silver. Dar was transfixed by Kovok-mah's beauty. He seemed the embodiment of strength and power. Dar knew he possessed a gentle spirit—a spirit that made her feel secure. Gazing at Kovok-mah, Dar envisioned his arms about her as she slept. *He'll be fresh and clean tonight. I should be also.*

The idea of bathing with Kovok-mah made Dar both nervous and excited. The mere sight of him awakened a need she had long denied—a desire for tenderness and intimacy. Kovok-mah remained absolutely still, as if waiting passively. *This will be my choice*, Dar thought, *not his.* She wavered a moment, uncertain what she wanted. Then Dar shed her clothes and entered the water. It was warm, yet goose bumps rose on her flesh. *What am I doing here?* she asked herself. *Bathing.* Dar knew that wasn't true. Still facing away, Kovok-mah stepped back from the stream of water, then froze. *He knows I'm here, but I can still leave. He won't turn around.* Dar moved closer, instead. Soon, she was near enough to touch him. Kovok-mah remained motionless. Dar reached out her hand, then hesitated.

The warm, moist air bore a scent that Dar had never experienced. It was at the farthest reach of her perception—elusive, yet primal and compelling. Dar breathed deeply. Her senses heightened, and she felt energized. She brushed her hands over Kovok-mah's broad back. His skin was cool, but she felt the heat beneath it. The scent intensified. Dar's head swam with its fragrance.

Kovok-mah turned, his eyes radiating warmth. "Dargu," he said, tenderly voicing her name as both plea and promise. He didn't ask her why she was there or what she wanted. Dar realized why. *He can smell what I'm feeling!* She sensed that he understood those feelings better than she did. Her thoughts were ambivalent, yet her essence bespoke yearning. She surrendered to that yearning.

"I'm here," Dar whispered, "because I followed my chest." Standing on her tiptoes, she kissed Kovok-mah. She could only reach his breastbone.

"What was that?"

"It was gesture," said Dar. "It means . . ." She paused, groping for a neutral word, but the Orcish language wasn't suited for equivocation. ". . . it means I show love."

"I don't know this gesture."

"Then show me your own," said Dar. "I am mother. Treat me as one."

Kovok-mah placed his powerful hands upon Dar's shoulders and gently drew her toward him. His fingers drifted over her skin as lightly as a breeze. The same hands that had crushed a man's throat with a single squeeze caressed her with exquisite delicacy, awakening her body. There was no urgency in his touch, only gentleness and reverence. When Kovok-mah lifted Dar from the water, she was uncertain what he would do, but she was unafraid.

Kovok-mah carried Dar to a mossy spot and set her down. Dar lay on her back as Kovok-mah settled beside her. She glanced below his waist and, to her relief, saw that he was no larger there than a man. Kovok-mah caught her looking and smiled. "Dargu, we are not blessed."

"I don't understand."

"We may not thrimuk, but I may give love."

He won't tup me, thought Dar, uncertain if she was more relieved or disappointed. Then Kovok-mah's lips drew her attention. He didn't exactly kiss her neck—the tip of his tongue was more active than in a human kiss—but the sensation was distinctly pleasurable. It became even more pleasurable as his lips traced a trail to her breasts. They lingered there. He sucked in her nipples and caressed them with his tongue. Dar felt a warm glow spread through her body. Then gentle fingertips replaced Kovok-mah's tongue as his lips traveled down her belly.

Dar was surprised when she guessed where Kovok-mah was headed. She had never heard of a man doing such a thing. *He's not a man*. Then she felt Kovok-mah's tongue between her legs. She had never experienced such pleasure in her life. Warm, tingling ripples washed from the center of her body. All her senses became more intense. Kovok-mah continued licking and the ripples became waves. Soon, Dar was arching her body against his face. The waves grew stronger. Their intensity became overwhelming. Dar writhed. She cried out in ecstasy. The feeling slowly subsided, leaving Dar limp and blissful.

Kovok-mah lay back and gently pulled Dar on top of him. As their bodies pressed together, Dar sighed with contentment. She kissed Kovok-mah's chest, then slid along him until she reached his lips. "This is called 'kiss,' " she whispered. She kissed his mouth.

Kovok-mah smiled. "I like this kiss."

Dar kissed him again.

"Are you happy?" asked Kovok-mah.

"Can't you smell it?"

"There is no scent for happiness."

"But there's one for love."

"Hai," said Kovok-mah, "but love and happiness are different things."

"Tonight, they're not," said Dar.

Eleven

♛

Life had taught Dar to associate passion with abuse and surrender with degradation. Once she had learned that lesson, she fought all desire, even in herself. If Kovok-mah had been a man, if he had pressed his attentions, or if Dar hadn't felt in control, their union by the pool never would have happened and the feelings it released in Dar would have remained suppressed. Lying naked with Kovok-mah, Dar wasn't inclined toward contemplation. The newness and wonder of her experience precluded that. Yet she was aware that something unexpected and special had happened. She sensed it would cause complications, but she pushed those concerns aside and savored the moment.

Before Dar and Kovok-mah left the moonlit courtyard, they bathed again, washing one another with playfulness and sensuality. Afterward, Kovok-mah led Dar through the dark back to their room. She snuggled within Kovok-mah's arms to sleep, but found herself wide awake instead. Her head was awhirl with questions and one of them dealt with language. *Kovok-mah called what we did "ura zul"—"giving love."* Dar wondered if "zul" truly meant "love," and if the word was as imprecise as the human expression. Men both "loved ale" and "loved women." Tupping was called "making love," though love often had nothing to do with it. Was "zul" similarly vague? Dar had told Kovok-mah "Mer valav zul"—"I show love"—but she was uncertain what she had actually communicated. More important, she was uncertain what she had truly meant.

Do I really love an orc? Having never loved a man, she had no standard to compare her feelings. The only man she had ever kissed had been Sevren. That impulse had felt natural. So did the desire aroused by Kovok-mah and the intimacies that followed. Yet a disturbing thought arose that those urges weren't natural at all. *Have I done something wrong?* For a while, joy and shame warred in Dar's mind. *Velasa-pah told me to follow my chest. That's exactly what I did.* Dar knew that the same women who would be outraged and disgusted by what she had done also tupped soldiers for a few roots or a pillaged dress. *I've sided with the orcs*, she concluded. *It's what they think that matters now.*

Dar returned to the essential question: What were her feelings toward Kovok-mah? After some introspection, she came up with a list of things that she knew were true. *I enjoy his company. I care about his feelings. I trust him. I like the way he treats me.* Dar liked him touching her, and she had especially liked what he had done by the pool. *Maybe that's love. I guess I'll find out soon enough.*

The next morning, Dar quickly discovered that the other orcs had "wise noses." Kovok-mah's and her scent declared their attraction as clearly as if they had made a formal announcement. No one said anything, but the orcs didn't hide their reactions. Lama-tok and Varz-hak looked surprised. Duth-tok seemed pleased. Zna-yat appeared neither; he looked concerned. Dar was taken aback that her innermost feelings were so readily discernible. She sniffed the air trying to catch the elusive scent she had detected in the pool, but her sense of smell was inadequate to the task.

Zna-yat's reaction bothered Dar, and she sought an

opportunity to speak with him privately. It came soon after she announced that they would leave Tarathank that night. Zna-yat went to search for additional food, and Dar followed him. She approached the orc as he foraged in an overgrown courtyard. "Was this once garden?" asked Dar, trying to sound conversational.

Zna-yat looked up. "Hai, very long ago."

Dar walked over to him. "Have you found anything to eat?"

"Very little. Weeds crowd good plants out."

"I suppose you can smell good plants."

"Hai."

"You once said you could smell my fear," said Dar. "What did you smell this morning?"

"You're asking me to be impolite," said Zna-yat.

"Why?"

"No one mentions obvious scents."

"Scents aren't obvious to me. Please tell me what you've noticed."

Zna-yat bowed his head. "I smelled atur about you. Duth-tok spoke of this scent."

"It marks love, doesn't it?"

"Hai."

"And Kovok-mah has this scent also?"

"For many days."

"I think I smelled it last night," said Dar. "Before then . . . Well, I had no idea."

"Mothers ignore this scent when it doesn't please them," said Zna-yat. "I thought you were doing same."

"Kovok-mah never said anything."

"It wouldn't have been proper for him to speak."

"But *you* knew how he felt," said Dar.

"Hai."

"I feel stupid," said Dar.

"I'm stupid one," said Zna-yat. He bowed his head. "Forgive me, Dargu. I didn't understand."

"You looked concerned this morning. Why?"

"I think Muth la has chosen difficult path for you."

Dar sighed. "Perhaps so. How does one become blessed?"

Zna-yat seemed flustered by Dar's question. "Blessed?"

"Hai. I think that was word."

"For couple to become blessed, both his and her muthuri must approve."

Dar blushed. So *"blessed" must mean "married,"* she thought, wondering what Zna-yat surmised from her question. She was too embarrassed to ask and turned to leave. "Thank you, Zna-yat, you've been helpful."

"I'm honored to aid you however I can."

Zna-yat watched Dar push her way through the weeds that had long ago conquered the garden. Soon she was gone, and only her scent remained. The fragrance of atur hung heavily in the still air, leaving no doubts about Dar's feelings. Zna-yat pitied her.

It was late afternoon before Zna-yat managed to get Kovok-mah alone. Once he did, he hustled his puzzled cousin into a chamber where they wouldn't be overheard. "Dargu spoke to me this morning," he said, watching Kovok-mah's face closely. "She wanted to know about blessing."

Kovok-mah's expression turned uneasy. "What did you tell her?"

"That muthuris must approve," replied Zna-yat. "I want to know what made her ask that question."

"I acted properly."

"My neck bears Dargu's mark, which makes her nearer to me than kin. So, I ask you again—why this talk of blessing?"

"I said we couldn't thrimuk because we weren't blessed."

"So, you planted seed in her chest," said Zna-yat. "Did you not think it might grow?"

"She came to me. How could I deny her?"

"Yet you'll have to deny her eventually. Your muthuri has wise nose, and she won't be pleased by what it smells. You cannot oppose her. There'll be no blessing. You must have known that."

"Hai," said Kovok-mah. "I was both happy and sad. Soon, I'll be only sad."

"And Dargu will be likewise. You've been unkind."

"I followed my chest."

"I understand," said Zna-yat. "Your muthuri will not."

"I don't blame her. I scarcely understand it myself," mused Kovok-mah. "At first, Dargu was just some amusing washavoki. Different, but strange like all washavokis."

"Muth la guides Dargu," said Zna-yat. "Perhaps Muth la guided you as well."

"Hai. This is Muth la's doing. That's why Dargu fills my chest. She smells strange, she's not pretty, and yet . . . and yet . . ." Kovok-mah's voice trailed off. He looked miserable.

"It's too late to undo last night," said Zna-yat. "Whatever sorrow it will bring has already been unloosed."

"Should I tell Dargu what awaits her?"

"Thwa," said Zna-yat. "Let her be content awhile."

Twelve

♛

Dar felt that she had been sent to Tarathank to fall in love with Kovok-mah. Believing that she had, there was no reason to linger in the city, so she told the orcs they would depart that night. Yet, when evening approached, Dar regretted her decision to leave. Her newfound passion imbued the ruins with an aura of romance, transforming everything. Overgrown streets became picturesque, and deserted buildings felt tranquil. The idea that she would never visit the pool again seemed unbearable.

Zna-yat was preparing the final meal before departure when Dar grabbed Kovok-mah's hand. "Come," she said, tugging at him. Kovok-mah rose and followed her. In the hallway Dar whispered, "Let's bathe before we go." It was more a demand than a suggestion, and Dar was confident that Kovok-mah wouldn't refuse. As she hurried to the pool, she felt gripped by aching need.

At the courtyard, Dar shed her clothes and ran naked into the water. There, she impatiently waited for Kovok-mah to join her. When he entered the pool, she flung her arms about his torso and planted kisses on his chest. Kovok-mah sensed a desperate edge to Dar's desire, and he sought to ease it. He lifted and held her so that they were face-to-face. "Dargu," he said softly, "there's no need to hurry."

"But we must leave soon."

"Everyone will be patient."

"Do you think they know why we left?" asked Dar, blushing at the thought.

"This path is new only to us," said Kovok-mah. "Many have traveled it since Muth la made world. Everyone understands." He smiled. "I have time to give you kiss." Kovok-mah puckered his lips and gave Dar a noisy peck on the nose.

Dar giggled. "You're silly."

Kovok-mah proceeded as slowly and tenderly as he had the previous night. After he brought Dar to climax, she moved to lie on top of him in a state of contentment. Kovok-mah said nothing, but gently caressed her back. After a while, Dar lifted her head from his chest. "Am I very different from urkzimmuthi mothers?"

Kovok-mah had been expecting that question. "You are like them in many ways."

"How am I different?"

"Your claws are flat, your eyes are different color, your nose is round, and your body is . . ." Kovok-mah searched for a proper description. "It is like youngling's."

"How?"

"You are light . . . delicate."

"Are my breasts like urkzimmuthi mother's?"

"Hai."

Dar's eyes narrowed. "How do you know?"

"Urkzimmuthi mothers don't cover breasts, except when it's cold."

"Am I too short?"

"Some mothers are your size."

Knowing that Kovok-mah would answer truthfully, Dar had difficulty asking the next question. "Am I ugly?"

"It doesn't matter to me."

"So I am."

"Dargu, sight of you brings me joy. I care not what others think."

Dar kissed Kovok-mah. "Then, I don't care either." And, for the moment, she truly meant it.

Dar's hair was still damp when she led the orcs from Tarathank. The surrounding prairie spread in all directions, gray under a rising moon. The Blath Urkmuthi—*Cloak of Mothers*—formed black silhouettes on the near horizon. Dar didn't try to follow the overgrown road. Instead, she pushed through the tall grass, taking the most direct route to the mountains. The stay in the city had interrupted the cycle of traveling by night and sleeping by day, and Dar was tired even before they started. It was still night when she called a halt to sleep.

When the sun rose on the empty countryside, Dar decided that it would be safe to journey by day. The mountains were close, and there was little chance the orcs would encounter a force they couldn't overcome. "Throw away your rags," she said, tossing her fake bandages upon the ground. "We'll travel openly."

For the orcs, abandoning their disguises marked an occasion for celebration. Zna-yat grinned at Dar as he ground his rags into the dirt. "We've escaped death because of you," he said. Then Zna-yat bowed his head to Dar, and the other orcs did also.

"Dargu said we'd become wolves," said Varz-hak, "and we have." He leaned back and howled. Lama-tok joined in.

"We should call her 'wolf,' not 'weasel,' " said Lama-tok.

Kovok-mah smiled. "She's too tiny to be wolf."

Dar responded by grabbing Kovok-mah's neck and pulling his head down to kiss his lips. Duth-tok, who had never seen a kiss before, laughed. "This weasel is so fierce that she bites Kovok-mah's face."

"That was 'kiss,' not bite," said Kovok-mah.

"I think she's tasting him," said Lama-tok.

Dar licked her lips. "He's sweet and juicy."

All the orcs hissed with laughter, except Kovok-mah, who looked discomforted. "Did I say something wrong?" asked Dar. The question made the orcs hiss louder.

"Sons cannot be sweet and juicy," said Kovok-mah in a low voice, "only mothers."

Dar turned bright red.

Upon the road, the presence of the other orcs inhibited Dar, and she was more reserved around Kovok-mah. Yet restraint only increased her yearning. The feeling she identified as love seemed like a form of hunger that was never satisfied. Kovok-mah's nearness didn't ease it. Rather, it had the opposite effect. Dar assumed her scent made her feelings obvious, but Kovok-mah made no advances. The lack of aggression, which had initially put Dar at ease, began to make her insecure.

When Kovok-mah's passivity began to feel like rejection, Dar learned how quickly love became unhappiness. *He's changed his mind. He's ashamed of giving love to an ugly washavoki.* That idea made her miserable and withered her confidence. She became unsure how to behave around him and too embarrassed to ask. Dar responded to her unhappiness by pushing herself physically. She set a pace that was punishing—though only to herself—in an effort to purge her misery through exhaustion.

By hard walking, the travelers reached the foothills of the Blath Urkmuthi in two days. These rose abruptly from the plain like a rocky coastline on an ocean of grass. The irregular wall of stone that towered behind them was a bleak and imposing barrier. No vegetation softened its crags, whose bare limestone resembled the folds of a crumpled cloak. Dar ascended a stony hill to get an unobstructed view. When she reached its summit, she didn't like what she saw. The way looked hard and unforgiving. "I hoped for something better," she said.

"This is no evil place," Zna-yat replied. "These mountains sheltered our foremothers when washavokis fell upon us."

"How far is your home from here?"

"One moon's walk at least."

The news disheartened Dar. All her efforts had been toward reaching the mountains, and she had come to think of them as her destination. Instead, they were only another obstacle. "How can we pass through them?" she asked.

"It is said there are secret paths," said Zna-yat.

"Secret? Then, what good are they?"

"You'll find way."

Zna-yat's lack of concern annoyed Dar. She was worried about the journey, and it felt like only she bore that burden. Dar was tempted to tell that to Zna-yat, but decided there was little point; he would agree to whatever she said, but his faith would remain undiminished. Instead, she asked him to tell her what he knew about the Blath Urkmuthi.

Dar learned that the mountains were inhospitable and mostly uninhabited. However, their harshness had made them a haven when the washavokis invaded. The surviving orcs retreated to the heights to launch attempts to retake their lands. At Garlsholding, they spoke of these forays as "the Goblin Wars." They had lasted for decades and were savagely fought. In the end, the orcs won back no territory; all they acquired was an evil reputation.

During the Goblin Wars, orcs lived throughout the mountain range, though the most habitable portion lay to the east. The climate was milder there, for the highlands were less elevated. After the fighting ceased, the orcs abandoned the harsh western heights to settle north of King Kregant's realm.

Zna-yat recounted the hard times after the invasion—how refugees from cities tried to farm stony mountain hollows. He spoke of slow starvation in winter and sudden butcheries when summer brought washavoki raids. Zna-yat recounted how the urkzimmuthi in the east gradually recovered, although they never equaled their former glory. It was a long story, but Dar learned nothing that would aid in choosing a route. The old pathways had been made for fleeing washavokis, and even if they still existed, they were not meant to be found. Eyeing the sack of food, Dar wondered how long it would last.

Since the orcs expected her to lead the way, Dar studied the lofty wall of rock before them. She assumed that any eastward pathway would lie within the interior of the range, and she looked for a means to get there. A cleft to the west appeared to be a pass. Dar pointed it out to Zna-yat. "That seems good way," she said. "You have sharp eyes. What do you think?"

Zna-yat gazed at the cleft. It resembled a gap in the cliffs, though it could be a dead end. It was located atop a steep slope of jumbled boulders. "Climb will be long and hard," he said.

"Hai," said Dar. "I think urkzimmuthi would choose such path to flee washavokis. Pursuit would be difficult."

"That sounds like wisdom."

There was still enough daylight to go farther, and Dar was anxious to continue. She pointed out the way and told the orcs to gather firewood as they walked. "We'll have fire tonight," she said. "Washavokis are far behind, and it will be cold in mountains."

By the time the sun had set, the travelers were high above the plain but only partway to the cleft. It had been an exhausting and perilous climb, where the sound of constant wind was broken by the occasional crack and rumble of falling rock. Once, when they huddled behind a boulder as stones shot past, they found an orc's bleached skull. Despite the danger of sleeping on the slope, Dar was too spent to continue in the dark. Her feet, though hardened from weeks of walking, were sore from clambering over rough rock, and every muscle ached.

The travelers set up camp by a huge boulder that offered shelter from falling rocks, but none from the wind. The ground about it was so steep and uneven, they had difficulty marking the Embrace of Muth la. When Zna-yat finally succeeded in lighting a fire, it blazed brightly and streamed sparks into the windy dark. Though the fire comforted Dar, what she really wanted was Kovok-mah's arms about her. Yet he sat immobile, his eyes on the flames.

Zna-yat roasted their ration of pashi over the flames. Mothers owned the food, but sons often cooked it, and Dar was glad that Zna-yat had taken over the task. When he was done, she served the roots, which were more flavorful when roasted. After eating, Dar climbed onto Kovok-mah's lap. Only then did he hold her.

Dar rose with the sun, stiff from the previous day's exertions. She led the way into the cleft, reaching it by late morning. It was choked with fallen rock. As Dar clambered over loose stone and boulders, she spied scattered bones along with rusted weapons. Eventually the footing grew less precarious. A final turn revealed a narrow alpine valley and, beyond it, another ridge. The valley was a desolate place of scattered boulders and windblown grass. The travelers entered it and headed eastward.

The way seemed easy at first, but over time the incessant wind took its toll. Dar couldn't get warm, and she was thoroughly chilled by the time they encountered abandoned dwellings. Their roofs had caved in long ago, and all that remained were shallow pits surrounded by the tumbled stones. Their circular design marked them as orcish structures. Nearby were rows of stone wind-breaks to shelter garden plots that had reverted to turf. Gazing upon the ruins, Dar pitied the orcs who had once lived in them.

Around noon, the travelers entered a winding canyon in the far ridge. The footing was treacherous and it was late when Dar and the orcs exited and found themselves high on a mountainside with a commanding view of the country beyond. A range of snow-covered peaks lay to the north. The area between the overlook and the distant range was only slightly less mountainous. It consisted of a confusing series of ridges and valleys that reminded Dar of a rutted road. She turned to Zna-yat. "Do urkzim-muthi still live there?"

"None I've heard about."

Dar wasn't surprised, for the rugged terrain below looked almost as barren as the valley they had left behind. Here and there, Dar spotted green. But bare rock dominated. Dar imagined the orc refugees' discouragement when they first gazed upon the scene. It was a bleak place, and the travelers' prospects seemed equally bleak. *Even wolves can starve,* thought Dar.

Thirteen

♛

The way down the mountainside was neither easy nor evident, and Dar was forced to turn back several times when she encountered a sheer drop. Night caught the travelers high upon precarious slopes. The orcs huddled on a narrow ledge while Dar passed out the food. They seemed exhausted. After eating, the orcs quickly went to sleep, while Dar worried she had led them astray.

They reached a narrow, twisting valley by the end of the next day. It was a stark place, supporting only hardy vegetation. There was coarse grass, scrubby brush, and an occasional stunted tree. Sometimes the travelers encountered ruined dwellings, but whatever crops had grown there had vanished without hands to tend them.

The terrain—not Dar—determined which way they went. High ridges restricted travel, often forcing her to walk in the wrong direction. The alternative was to climb over a ridge into another valley that twisted also. In such a maze, it was impossible to tell how much progress was made. The orcs turned inward and marched silently. As cold, hunger, and fatigue wore down Dar, her misgivings intensified. The orcs' silence seemed a sign that they had misgivings also. *This journey was my idea*, Dar thought. *I said I'd lead them home.* She regretted making such a rash promise.

After two days of wandering within the maze of valleys, Dar's spirits were at a new low. At dusk she pointed to a ruined house whose tumbled stones still marked Muth la's Embrace. "We'll stay here."

The orcs quietly entered the ruin and Dar opened the bag of food. There were only five pashi roots left. "Food is Muth la's gift," she said.

"Shashav, Muth la," replied the orcs.

Dar handed Kovok-mah a root. "Muth la gives you this food." As she spoke those words, Dar felt the food was Muth la's final gift—a gift she didn't deserve. A tear rolled down her cold cheek. Dar wiped it away and handed out the remaining roots. When they were gone, she rose and wandered empty-handed into the dark. She didn't care where she was headed, as long as the orcs didn't see her tears. A line of rubble loomed ahead. Dar climbed over the stones, then slumped against them. As silent tears flowed, she heard someone approach. Dar dried her eyes as Kovok-mah stepped over her hiding place. "Go away," she said.

Kovok-mah silently laid five pieces of pashi root by Dar's feet. The sight of them almost made Dar break out sobbing. "I don't deserve these!"

"This food was Muth la's gift," said Kovok-mah, "and we may give to whomever we please. Will you eat with us?"

"I wish to be alone."

"Then I must go," said Kovok-mah. "Yet my chest desires something."

"What?"

"Your happiness."

"You might as well wish for more food," said Dar. "There's none of that either."

"Please, Dargu. May I stay?"

"Why would you bother?"

"I think you understand."

"I don't," said Dar. "All I know is that love is like food. It fills you for a while, but soon you're empty."

"That's not what I smell."

"Don't tell me there's scent for emptiness, too!"

"I smell atur."

"Well, I can't smell it. I don't know how you feel. You don't speak to me. You don't touch me."

"I hold you at night."

"But only at night."

"I behave properly," said Kovok-mah.

"I don't know what that means! All I know is that I feel alone."

"But wind carries my feelings."

"What good is that to me? I can't smell them," said Dar. She seized Kovok-mah's hand and pressed it against her face. "Touch carries your feelings. Words, also. Wind does not."

Kovok-mah shook his head. "I've been foolish. I sing to mother who cannot hear." He paused. "This speaking . . . this touching . . . seems strange to me."

"Just say what you feel."

"That is seldom done, but I'll try. Touching will be difficult."

"You had no problem by the pool."

"I had permission then."

"You don't need permission."

Kovok-mah looked shocked. "Would you have me act like some washavoki?"

Dar realized that was exactly what she was asking. "Thwa," she said. "I must act like urkzimmuthi mother, but I don't know how."

Kovok-mah simply gazed at her. Even in the darkness, she could tell he was uncomfortable. Kovok-mah's silence made Dar equally uncomfortable. *Why won't he show me what to do?* she wondered. Then she had an insight. *He needs permission.* "Sit beside me," Dar said. Kovok-mah complied. "Pretend I am mother."

"You *are* mother," said Kovok-mah.

"Pretend I'm urkzimmuthi mother who smells atur."

"Does this scent please you?"

"Hai."

"Then you will touch this son whose atur pleases you."

"What if I don't?" asked Dar. "What will son do?"

"Nothing."

"What if I, also, smell of atur?"

"Still nothing."

"Why?" asked Dar.

"Sons who touch mothers without their leave offend Muth la. She will not welcome his spirit when he dies, and it will wander, lost forever."

Dar envisioned Murdant Kol trudging the Dark Path for eternity. The idea was fiercely satisfying. "But if son and mother both have atur, why would she not touch him?"

"Mother's muthuri may object," said Kovok-mah, "or perhaps son's muthuri."

"They must approve?"

"Hai."

Dar was glad there was no one to tell them how to behave. Through further questions, she discovered that, from a human perspective, the roles of orc males and females were reversed. It was mothers who made advances, while sons were expected to be demure. Understanding a mother's role was one thing; acting it out was quite another. Dar had no experience with the subtleties of romance, even with her own kind. Expressing her feelings to an orc seemed doubly difficult. Yet she had to try. Rising to her knees, she sniffed Kovok-mah's neck. "Perhaps I smell atur," she said. "I can't really say."

"It's there, Dargu."

"Touch me," said Dar. Saying the words felt awkward, like she was begging or, even worse, demanding.

"Mothers do not speak, Dargu."

"What do they do?"

Kovok-mah showed her. Among humans, the gesture would have been brazen and slutty; yet Kovok-mah assured her that it was both proper and polite. Dar tried it, and Kovok-mah tenderly brushed her face with his clawed fingers. "Dargu, I . . ." He paused, unsure how to put his feelings into words. "Dargu, my chest is filled with you." Then he gave Dar a clumsy kiss.

When Dar and Kovok-mah returned to the circle, a fire was blazing and the orcs were awake. Dar was acutely aware that they could smell what she was feeling. Kovok-mah sat down and she climbed upon his lap. Then, although it felt awkward, she took Kovok-mah's hand and guided it to her breast. The orcs acted like it was an everyday occurrence.

Zna-yat smiled. "So, Kovok-mah has not displeased you."

"Thwa," replied Dar. "I'm displeased with myself. I've led poorly."

"I think not," said Zna-yat. The others gestured their agreement.

"We may die," said Dar.

"Perhaps," replied Duth-tok, "but no washavoki will slay us."

"You've done well," said Varz-hak.

"They speak wisdom," said Zna-yat. "You've shown us Muth la's path, however it ends." He bowed his head and made the sign of the Tree.

Dar was comforted, despite the orcs' fatalism. The Cloak of Mothers would be a far better resting place than the Vale of Pines. Yet Dar couldn't help thinking they would be dead all the same.

Fourteen

♛

The following day, Dar woke in better spirits. She guided the orcs by plodding along, choosing whatever path felt best to her. For all practical purposes, they were lost, although neither she nor the orcs ever had more than a vague idea where their destination lay. By late afternoon, they were deep into the maze of ridges and valleys. By then, finding food seemed as important as finding a way home. Though they foraged as they walked, the results were scant. Dar wondered if starving orcs had scoured the land so thoroughly that nothing edible survived. Despite all their efforts, she and the orcs were reduced to eating woody mushrooms that served mostly as an exercise in chewing.

The next day was like the previous one, except everyone was far hungrier. Walking on an empty stomach was tiring, so Dar halted the march early, attempting to substitute rest for nourishment. The trek resumed next morning. In the afternoon, they entered the broadest valley they had yet encountered. There, they discovered a shallow river. Dar turned to Zna-yat, who knew the most about the Blath Urkmuthi. "Have you heard of this river?" she asked.

"Thwa," he replied. "No one visits this land. Its lore is forgotten."

Dar decided to follow the river downstream. After she and the orcs had walked a while, they passed a place where debris partly blocked the channel. Lama-tok stopped and stared at it. "Dargu, I see something interesting."

Dar walked back to where he stood. "What is it?"

Lama-tok pointed to the stones that had trapped the debris. "That is bridge."

Dar saw Lama-tok was right. The river was spanned by a straight and even line of stones that obviously had been placed there. Only the pile of branches and logs on the upstream side had obscured their symmetric pattern. Sometimes a single large boulder formed a stepping-stone. More frequently, several stones were fitted carefully together. "Another ruin," said Dar. They had encountered several that day.

"This one has been repaired recently," said Lama-tok, pointing to one of the stepping-stones. To Dar's eyes, its unmortared stonework looked little different from that of the others; however, she didn't doubt the former mason. She scanned the countryside and thought she saw a hint of a path. *Either few travel here, or they don't wish to be detected.*

The other orcs gathered round. Duth-tok agreed with his brother that some of the stonework was new. "No more than one winter old."

"Who would have done this?' asked Dar.

"Urkzimmuthi fitted those stones," said Lama-tok.

Dar turned to Zna-yat. "You said this land was abandoned."

"That is what tales say," he replied. "If urkzimmuthi still live here, no one speaks of them." He looked warily about and the other orcs did the same. No one told Dar they were concerned for her safety, but their actions spoke for them. *The Goblin Wars were fought here,* she thought, recalling Zna-yat's stories of washavoki raids. *Hatred is bound to linger.*

"Dargu," said Zna-yat. "Which way should we go?"

Dar considered the possibilities. *We can try to find*

whoever made the trail, she thought, *or we can flee*. The latter choice was more appealing, but Dar felt it was the wrong one. *If Muth la is truly directing my path, I'll be safe*. She pointed to the faint pathway. "We'll go that way."

Kovok-mah said nothing, but he was visibly worried by Dar's choice. When she began to lead the way, he stayed close by her side. Dar was only a short distance from the river when the trail disappeared. She halted and peered around for some clue that orcs had passed there. Nothing appeared disturbed. She turned to her companions. "I cannot find way."

"Do you wish to find strange urkzimmuthi?" asked Zna-yat.

"Hai."

"Trail is marked with scent," he said. "I can follow it."

As Zna-yat moved in front, Dar saw Kovok-mah shoot him an angry look. *Kovok-mah smelled the trail, too*. As Dar had this thought, she felt Kovok-mah's hand gently stroke her back. "I'll be all right," she said, knowing that Kovok-mah also smelled her fear.

After Zna-yat took the lead, Dar expected to encounter orcs quickly. She got that impression because he moved so surely, pausing only infrequently to sniff the air. Yet, when the sun set, the travelers had gone far without discovering the trail makers. Before it became too dark for her to see, Dar called a halt. "Gather much wood," she said. "Tonight, we'll build big fire to show we aren't hiding. If urkzimmuthi come, be peaceful."

The travelers had found no food, so the fire was their only comfort after a hard day. They sat around it in the dark, warming themselves but not resting. Knowing that orcs preferred to attack at night, Dar snuggled by Kovok-mah but didn't encumber his sword arm. She watched the flames, feeling tired but anxious, while Kovok-mah gently stroked her back. Suddenly, his fingers froze.

Dar looked about, but could see nothing beyond the circle of firelight. All the orcs seemed tense, and their eyes were turned in one direction. Dar gazed where they were looking. She saw nothing and heard nothing for a long while. Then pairs of yellow eyes appeared in the dark. Dar counted them. Three . . . seven . . . eleven. Still, there was no sound.

An orc stepped into the firelight. He was oddly dressed, but Dar's attention was focused on his drawn sword. It was huge and ancient-looking. Kovok-mah also kept his eye on the weapon as he rose slowly. The other orcs did the same. They kept their blades sheathed as Dar had instructed them, but each grasped his sword hilt. Dar rose along with the orcs, and as she did, the stranger's eyes glared at her. "Why is this washavoki alive?" he asked in strangely accented Orcish.

Zna-yat replied evenly. "This mother guides us."

"Fool!" said the stranger. "It is no mother."

Zna-yat maintained his calm demeanor. "You lack understanding."

"It is *you* who lacks understanding," replied the sword-wielding orc. "This washavoki must die. I will kill it now."

Zna-yat whipped out his sword. "Try, and you will die."

Dar noted that the stranger's rusty sword was shaking and concluded that he wasn't used to fighting. Following her instincts, Dar stepped between him and Zna-yat. "Muth la wants no sons to die."

The stranger stared at Dar with astonishment. "It spoke tongue of mothers!"

The stranger's companions emerged from the darkness. Like him, they had weapons ready, though many carried only clubs. "How can it know of Muth la?" asked one.

"Muth la speaks to those who listen," said Dar, "though she says more to some than to others."

"To this mother, Muth la says much," said Kovok-mah.

"Matriarch's law is all washavokis die," said the stranger.

"If she has wisdom to make laws," said Dar, "then she has wisdom to change them. Take me to her so we might speak together. I will abide by her ruling and these sons will also."

"Our Mother will keep your skull," said the stranger. He sneered. "This washavoki smells of fear."

"Hai," said Dar. "I don't fear your matriarch's wisdom, but I fear your foolishness. Now show me way."

The stranger hesitated, looking confused and uncertain. At last, he gestured to Dar and her companions. "Come," he said.

Dar dreaded hiking the trail at night, but she felt she had to. She wanted to prevent a confrontation, and leaving immediately accomplished that. Still, she was well aware that she had undertaken a desperate gamble. Unless the clan's matriarch changed the law, Dar was going to her death. Her companions could not protect her. She had staked all her hopes on the open-mindedness of a single orc. If that orc thought like most washavokis, Dar was doomed.

Fifteen

♛

Dar's journey in the dark was neither short nor easy. Her escort set a punishing pace over rocky ground, and Dar's feet were bleeding by the time he halted in front of a high ridge. Dar could barely make out the low, stone structure nestled in a shadowed hollow. Though it was fairly large, its turf roof caused it to blend into the landscape. Dar assumed it was a hall. The building was dark until someone emerged from a door, briefly revealing a firelit interior.

Dar's first impression was that a tall, stocky woman approached. She was dressed like the orc males, with cloth wrapped around her waist to make a skirt that extended below the knees. A short cape covered her shoulders; otherwise, her torso was bare. When she came closer, Dar saw her features more clearly.

Dar gasped. She had seen a similar face before—in her vision by the hedgerow. *That was no woman who spoke to me. She was an orc!* Dar saw how she had mistaken her for a human, for orc females looked different from the males. The mother before her had a smooth forehead, even teeth, and a robust body with nearly human proportions. While her face was more delicate than a male's, its features were orcish. Beneath a prominent brow was a nose that had a thin ridge and a broad base. Her small chin featured a tattooed design that extended to the bottom lip.

The mother barely glanced at Dar. Instead, her attention was on Dar's guide. "Why have you brought this animal here?" she asked in a voice that revealed authority and annoyance.

"It wishes to speak with Our Mother," replied the orc. Dar thought he sounded meek.

"How could you know that?"

"Because I asked him to bring me here," said Dar.

"It speaks!" said the mother with surprise. Then she turned to the guide. "Still, husband, you should have killed it."

"It had sons protecting it. They looked skilled in fighting."

"I wanted no one to die," said Dar. "That's why I came."

"It's *you* who will die, washavoki," said the mother. "It's our law."

"I wish to speak to your matriarch about this law," said Dar. "I will abide by her decision."

"Thwa," said the mother. She addressed her husband. "Kill it."

As soon as the mother uttered those words, Zna-yat, Kovok-mah, and the others drew their swords. "Stop!" Dar yelled. Her protectors froze. They were just an instant from launching their attack. "Muth la does not want urkzimmuthi to slay one another."

The mother looked aghast at the scene before her. Her spouse's sword was still halfway in its scabbard, while Zna-yat's blade pressed against his neck. "Why do these sons obey you?" she asked.

"I am mother," said Dar.

"Muth la guides her," said Zna-yat. "We heed her wisdom."

"No one fight," said the mother. "I'll return." Then she reentered the hall.

As Dar waited anxiously, she tried to recall everything she knew about orcish courtesy and regretted that she hadn't paid more attention to the subject. What little she had learned would soon be vital. Dar wondered how much would be applicable.

Before the mother returned, Dar noticed a small stone structure standing apart in the shadows. One side was open to display its contents—neatly stacked human skulls. The topmost layer was higher than Dar's head, and she guessed there were hundreds, maybe thousands, of them. While Dar gazed at the gruesome repository, the mother emerged from the building. "Only washavoki will come inside," she said.

Dar entered the building. Beyond the door were steps descending to a short hallway. She followed the mother into a circular room that was mostly underground. It was a hanmuthi—*hearth of mother*—like the one in the house at Tarathank, though its dimensions were more modest. A fire burned in a central hearth, illuminating stone walls pierced by low, arched doorways that led to small chambers. There was no metal chimney, only a smoke hole in the sooty ceiling. The doorways framed the faces of children and a few adult sons. Only mothers sat in the hanmuthi's central room. Over two dozen were seated on the stone floor. One sat on a wooden stool. Her breasts were withered, her hair was white, and her face was wrinkled, but she looked vigorous and strong. Her pale yellow eyes gazed at Dar with authority.

Dar assumed the seated mother was the clan's matriarch. She bowed her head and made the sign of the Tree.

The matriarch said nothing.

"Are not guests greeted here?" asked Dar.

"When mice come to take my pashi, I don't greet them," said the matriarch. "I kill them."

"I'm not here to take anything."

"You're here to kill my children. That's what washavokis do."

"Twice, I've prevented their deaths," said Dar. "You

know this. I'm here seeking wisdom. It's proper to greet me."

The matriarch made a show of considering Dar's response. At length she spoke. "I am Muth-pah."

Dar knew that all clan matriarchs took the name "Muth." The important thing was to be greeted. It was a vital first step, and Dar relaxed a bit once Muth-pah gave her name. She bowed again. "I am Dargu."

"So weasel, not mouse, comes to my hall. Why?"

"I followed my chest."

"Then you have little sense."

"Velasa-pah told me to do thus," said Dar, hoping the name would give her some advantage. "He said it would be hard."

Muth-pah shot Dar a startled look. "Velasa-pah?"

"Hai."

"Speak of him."

"I met him near Tarathank," said Dar. "He lived alone and was very old. He said he was born washavoki, but had Pah clan tattoo. Then he made magic using feathers. After we spoke, I never saw him again. If he had not given me food, I would have said he was vision."

"You have visions?" asked Muth-pah.

"Hai."

Muth-pah silently studied Dar a while before declining her head. "Sit, Mother," she said. "Are you hungry?"

Then Dar knew she would live.

Dar awoke to the hushed sounds of the household rising. Sitting in Kovok-mah's lap and enveloped by his arms, Dar feigned sleep. She wanted to sort out her impressions of the previous night before facing so many strangers.

Most of what had happened after Muth-pah called her "Mother" had been dictated by customs Dar only partly understood. First, Dar's companions had been

brought into the hall for a lengthy round of introductions. Dar's empty stomach had grumbled while every
adult member of the household addressed every guest
and was addressed in return according to complicated
rules of precedence. Dar tried to recall all the faces and
names, but it was difficult. All the mothers' names had
ended with "pah," which was their clan. A few of the
sons had been members of the Pah clan also, but most of
the males had possessed different clan names, indicating
they were wedded to Pah clan mothers. The son who
had threatened Dar at the campsite had been named
Thak-goth.

The introductions had been followed by an even more
lengthy discussion of kinship. The apparent objective
had been to discover some tie between the household and
the guests. This task had been especially difficult due to
the clan's isolation. Dar had thought she would die of
hunger before Varz-hak established some tenuous con-
nection to Duth-smat, the husband of one of Muth-pah's
granddaughters. Duth-smat was related to the entire
household by marriage and Varz-hak had easily established his kinship to Kovok-mah, Zna-yat, and the two
Tok brothers. Thus, everyone—except Dar—had been
proven to be related.

Once the matter of kinship had been settled, food was
brought out at last. Muth-pah served it in a formal meal
where the guests ate while everyone else watched. Their
attention had been focused on Dar, making her extremely self-conscious. During the meal, a sleeping
chamber had been prepared. Like those in Tarathank, it
connected directly to the hánmuthi. When her guests had
eaten, Muth-pah rose to address them. "Share our hall as
you have shared our food. Rest from your journey."

That had been the signal for the household to retire.
As sons had cleared away the meal, everyone else went to
their sleeping chambers. The room for Dar and her com-

panions was small, and if the orcs hadn't slept upright, it would have been too cramped to accommodate them. Dar had climbed onto Kovok-mah's lap. Knowing she was being watched, she had guided his hand to her breast to demonstrate her status as a mother.

While Dar recalled those events, the hall grew quieter as it emptied. After a while, she began to hear excited whispers that sounded very close. Dar cracked one eyelid and saw that the doorway was filled with children. One tiny mother wasn't fooled by Dar's squinting. "Washavoki is awake!" she said in a loud voice.

Dar opened her eyes and curled her lips into a smile. The children, who looked very young, shrank back while continuing to stare at her with a mixture of fright and fascination. They closely resembled human young, reminding Dar of the carvings of the playing children in Tarathank. Like those children, they were unclothed, despite the chilly air.

A mother shouted "Lanut Muth Dargui!"—*Let Weasel Mother be!*—and the children scampered from the room. Then the same mother disregarded her own directive and knelt before the low doorway. "Day's greeting, Dargu," she said. The accent of her Orcish sounded musical to Dar's ears but made it difficult to understand.

"Tava," replied Dar.

The mother smiled. "I'm Mi-pah. Our Mother says I'm your sapaha."

"I don't know that word," said Dar.

"I will answer questions and show you what you wish to see."

My guide, thought Dar, and regarded the mother more closely. She was as tall as Dar, yet lacked a chin tattoo and breasts. *She's only a girl!* Dar wondered why Muth-pah had chosen her. She could think of several reasons but was uncertain which was the most likely. "Are you sapaha for these sons, also?"

"Only you," said Mi-pah. "Come."

Though disconcerted to receive direction from someone Twea's age, Dar felt she should obey. Besides, Mi-pah didn't seem like a child. She displayed the confidence of an adult. In fact, she seemed more confident than any woman Dar had known.

Dar rose from Kovok-mah's lap. He had remained silent and still throughout Dar's conversation with Mi-pah. Dar found that puzzling, for she was certain he was awake. As she followed Mi-pah out of the hall, Dar glanced back and saw that Kovok-mah was already on his feet. *He's been acting differently ever since we got here. So have the others.* Dar guessed the change reflected a deference to the Pah clan mothers—deference that apparently extended to one as young as Mi-pah. *They're real urkzimmuthi mothers. I'm only a washavoki woman.*

When Dar exited the hall, she saw the stone structure filled with skulls and felt compelled to take a closer look. Mi-pah followed. Most of the skulls appeared ancient. The bottom ones had crumbled into shards. Only the upper layers were intact. Three skulls in the uppermost layer still had flakes of dried flesh and patches of hair.

"I was six winters old when we put those there," said Mi-pah. "One had long hair like yours."

A woman! Dar shuddered.

"You're first live washavoki I've seen."

"So what do you think?" asked Dar, trying to sound casual.

"You look like ugly youngling," said Mi-pah. "You smell strange, too."

"Bad?"

"Thwa, just strange," said Mi-pah. "Come."

Mi-pah led Dar along a well-worn pathway that followed a stream and ended where a low stone dam created a pool in a sunny spot. "This is summer bathing place," said Mi-pah. She unwrapped her skirt and entered the water. "Come."

As Dar undressed, Mi-pah exhibited a frank interest in her body. She was particularly surprised when Dar removed her loose blouse. "You're blooded!" she exclaimed, gazing at Dar's breasts.

"Blooded?"

"You receive Muth la's Gift each moon," said Mi-pah, sounding uncertain as to whether she was making a statement or asking a question.

"Hai. I receive Gift."

Mi-pah pointed to Dar's brand. "Is that your clan mark?"

"Thwa, I have no clan."

"No clan?" said Mi-pah, who seemed to have difficulty grasping the idea. "But you would be all alone."

"I am."

As Dar entered the water, which was warmer than she expected, Mi-pah scooped something that resembled grease from a pot by the edge of the pool. When she spread it on her skin, it made tiny bubbles that the water washed away. "What's that?" asked Dar.

"Depyata," replied Mi-pah. She spread some on Dar's arm. It felt slippery. "It's for cleaning skin."

"It's better than sand," said Dar.

"Hai," said Mi-pah, who moved so she was behind Dar. "I'll wash your back."

Dar didn't know how to respond, but Mi-pah's firm yet gentle touch felt good. Dar soon relaxed as the orc worked silently. After a while, Mi-pah asked, "Are you fully grown?"

"Hai."

"Is Kovok-mah your husband?"

Dar, certain that every mother in the hall would soon learn her answer, responded carefully. "We're not blessed."

"Will your muthuri speak with his?" asked Mi-pah.

"I don't know your customs."

"Yet sons obey you," replied Mi-pah. "Why?"

"Sons respect mothers."

Mi-pah finished rinsing Dar's back and moved so they were face-to-face. "But you're washavoki."

"Muth-pah called me mother."

"But why do sons obey you?"

"They believe Muth la guides me," said Dar. "I have visions."

"What kind of visions?"

"I don't know if I should speak of them."

"I'm mother," replied Mi-pah. "It's fitting."

As Dar bathed, she described her visions—Twea's spirit on the Dark Path, the battle in the Vale of Pines, the orc mother by the hedge, and the reoccurring visions of the burning urkzimmuthi. She spoke of being saved from drowning by a tree and how she came to be called "Muth Velavash." Dar gave only the facts of those events without venturing to interpret them. Mi-pah listened with rapt attention until Dar began to describe her encounter with Velasa-pah. "Don't speak of him!" Mi-pah cried out. "That matter is for Muth-pah."

"Is he reason why Muth-pah spared me?"

"I think so," said Mi-pah. Afterward, she fell silent.

Dar was relieved that Mi-pah didn't question her further, for she couldn't imagine describing her life in the highlands or the army without appearing degraded in the young mother's eyes. She rinsed the last of the depyata from her skin and left the pool to dry in the sun. Mi-pah joined her. "Were you told to ask those questions?" asked Dar.

"Hai."

"Are you finished?"

"Hai, but I have my own question."

"What is it?" asked Dar.

"May I touch your claws?"

Dar smiled. "Of course."

Mi-pah's fascination with Dar's fingernails and toe-nails was the first hint that she was still a child. Her examination of Dar's toes was so intense, it made Dar giggle. The sound startled Mi-pah, which caused her to hiss with laughter.

When Dar was dry, she dressed. She donned her undergarment and skirt but not her blouse. Using the laces from its front, she hung it about her shoulders so it resembled the capes that the blooded mothers wore. Though it was chilly to go bare-breasted, Dar felt it wise to emphasize her femininity. Thus attired, she asked Mi-pah to show her around.

The clan had dwelt within the folds of a southern-facing ridge for generations, and over the long course of years, they had made many painstaking improvements. The bathing pool was only one of them. Mi-pah showed Dar terraced fields upon the ridges that were invisible to anyone below. Storehouses and animal pens were similarly hidden. Care had been taken to screen pathways from view.

Dar was surprised that mothers and children worked in the terraced fields, for Zna-yat had said males did the farming. "Where are sons?" she asked.

"They watch western pass and guard against washavokis."

"For what purpose?" asked Dar. "Washavokis live far away. I have traveled through land near Bath Urkmuthi. It is empty."

"It's our clan's fate to do this," replied Mi-pah.

"Why?"

"Only blooded mothers know."

So that's it, thought Dar. Mi-pah's my sapaha because she's old enough to ask Muth-pah's questions, but not old enough to answer mine.

Sixteen

♛

By the time Dar and Mi-pah returned to the hall, the midday meal was nearly ready. It consisted of a pot of stew with the same savory aroma of the one Velasa-pah had prepared. The hall's single hanmuthi wasn't large enough to accommodate the entire clan in one sitting, so the mothers ate first. Muth-pah commenced the mothers' meal by thanking Muth la. That was the sole formality. The mothers served themselves and their children, then sat about chatting.

This casual behavior surprised Dar. "I always said 'Muth la gives you this food' while serving," she said to Mi-pah.

"That's because you served sons," replied Mi-pah. "It's *our* food."

Dar seized the opportunity to ask another mother a question that had long puzzled her. "Why do we own food?"

Mi-pah regarded Dar as she might an infant. "Everyone knows that."

"I don't."

"Because Muth la rules world through mothers. Children enter life through us. Food comes from our breasts. We're Muth la's eyes and hands. We speak her words. Our gifts are her gifts."

"That makes sense," said Dar.

"Is it not same among washavokis?"

"Thwa. Sons rule because they're strong."

"If that were wisdom, then bears would rule world," said Mi-pah. "No wonder washavokis are evil."

Someone called to Mi-pah, who rose and joined a group of mothers at the other side of the room. Dar was left alone, an outsider amid the everyday life of the clan. She envied the mothers about her. They seemed dignified, vibrant, and comfortable in their authority. Mi-pah was already deep in animated conversation. From the way the mothers kept glancing in her direction, Dar was certain they were talking about her. Muth-pah joined the group and spoke with Mi-pah. After a while, Muth-pah rose and walked over to Dar. "Tava, Dargu," she said.

Dar bent her neck respectfully. "Tava, Mother," she said, using the honorific form of address.

"You understand courtesy," said Muth-pah. "And you have bathed. Many live in this hall. You should do it often."

"I will, Mother," Dar replied, "though I won't be staying long. I promised sons I would take them home."

"Do you know way?"

"Thwa. I hope you can tell me."

"Way to next hall is hidden. You'll need sapaha."

"Would one of your clan do this?"

"We'll speak of it after Bah Niti," said Muth-pah.

Dar tried to hide her disappointment, for the moon was in its last quarter and Bah Niti—*Hidden Moon*—wouldn't occur for five more days. "What should I do until then?"

"Be useful. It's said each mouth brings two hands," replied Muth-pah. "Your sons are already on patrol."

"I can work in fields," said Dar.

"Good," said Muth-pah as she rose. "We'll speak again."

Dar watched Muth-pah cross the room and join another group of mothers. After Muth-pah spoke, a mother turned to look at Dar. She was the one who had ordered Thak-goth to kill her. She seemed amused.

Dar finished her meal alone, trying to be philosophical about her isolation. *I'm a clanless, ignorant outsider, but despite that, they call me "Mother."* Dar didn't sense hostility. Rather, she felt the sting of being different. *"Weasel Mother" was what Mi-pah called me.* That recollection led to an unsettling notion. *This could be a foretaste of the rest of my life.* Once Dar reached Kovokmah's homeland, her brand would prevent her from ever leaving. Dar realized she could easily end up as a lonely oddity—*a weasel mother.*

Dar lingered after eating, hoping to serve Kovok-mah and the others. When only elderly and half-grown sons appeared for the meal, she realized her companions were still on patrol. Just then, the mother who had stared at Dar approached with Mi-pah in tow. "Our Mother says you wish to work in fields."

"I'd like to be useful," replied Dar.

The mother turned to Mi-pah. "Mi, take two tivs and go with Dargu to high field. Hren is planting pashi."

"Hai, Mother," said Mi-pah. "Come, Dargu."

Mi-pah led Dar to a storeroom. There, she handed Dar a tiv, which turned out to be a short-handled digging tool with a flat iron head. *Planting pashi will be stoop work*, thought Dar as she followed Mi-pah outside.

The high field was long and narrow, covering the top of a winding ridge. A low stone wall kept its soil from washing away. Dar guessed that the field's rich loam had been carried by the orcs up the same steep path that she and Mi-pah had ascended, for the rest of the ridge was rocky and barren. A small group of mothers, some who looked Mi-pah's age, were bent over and swinging tivs.

"Hren-pah! Weasel Mother and I are here to help."

An older mother, who was thick-limbed and a head

taller than Dar, approached. She gave Dar a quick lesson on how to plant pashi, then handed her a bag of root cuttings. Afterward, Dar joined the mothers who spanned the field in a single line and went to work. The soil wasn't hard to dig, but the tiv was a heavy tool meant for stronger arms, and using it required bending over. Dar's back soon ached. She said nothing, taking her cues from the other mothers. Even the youngest worked without complaint. It was heavy labor and it went on until sundown, when Hren-pah called a halt at last.

On the way down to the bathing pool, Hren-pah spoke to Dar for the first time since she had shown her how to plant. "You look like youngling, but you work hard."

Dar curled her lips into a smile. "Shashav, Hren-pah."

The mothers, who had labored silently throughout planting, began to chat. As Dar listened to their conversations, she noted that the blooded mothers dropped the "pah" when they addressed one another. Much of their talk concerned a mother named Fre and her recent journey to find a husband. "I heard Thak-goth's sister's son desired her," said a mother.

"And she desired him," said another.

"It made no difference," said Hren-pah. "His muthuri would not give blessing. Fre must look elsewhere."

"Poor Fre!" said the first mother.

"It's sad," agreed Hren-pah. "Fre loved unwisely." She gave Dar a meaningful look.

After bathing, Dar returned with the mothers to the hall for the evening meal. Discovering that Kovok-mah and the others were still absent, she asked Hren-pah when the patrol would return. "Not until Bah Niti," she replied, "unless they catch washavoki."

"You were first they caught in six winters," added another mother, "so don't expect your velazul early."

Dar blushed. "Velazul" translated as "lover," though she didn't understand its connotation among the orcs. Since there was no one she felt comfortable asking, she had no way of telling if the mother was voicing understanding or disapproval.

Once the sons were fed, the household prepared for sleep. Families gathered in their sleeping chambers and Dar retreated to her empty room. As the fire in the hearth died down and the hanmuthi grew dark, she witnessed intimacy between mothers and their spouses. The feelings it stirred made her turn away. Without Kovok-mah to hold her, Dar was forced to lie upon the floor. Its hardness aggravated her aching back, making it difficult to sleep. Loneliness compounded the problem. Dar missed Kovok-mah. As she dwelled upon his absence, Dar realized how much she had come to care for him. That made the mothers' talk at the bathing pool especially worrisome. *If they thought Fre loved unwisely, what would they say of me?*

Seventeen

♛

After Dar spent the following day planting pashi, she bathed with the mothers who had worked alongside her. Three were blooded—Hren, Twu, and Dree. Two were younglings—Ji and Wra. Ji, who had developed breasts, was anticipating receiving the Gift and could hardly wait. "Muthuri thinks I'll be tattooed by fall," she said. "I hope she's right."

"You've grown fast, Ji," said Twu-pah. "I was fifteen winters before I was marked."

"But you were blessed next summer," said Ji-pah.

"I was lucky," said Twu-pah. "How many sons visit here? Look at Fre."

"Thirty winters and still not blessed," said Hren-pah.

"We're too distant from other halls," said Twu-pah. "Muthuris don't want their sons to move here, so they withhold their blessing."

"That son named Zna-yat called our clan lost," said Dree-pah.

"Then he speaks foolishly," said Hren-pah. "*His* clan is lost, not ours. We've stayed true."

"Yet what has it gained us?" asked Dree-pah. She sighed. "Every hall lies eastward. Zna-yat lives so far away, we might as well be lost."

Twu-pah sniffed and grinned. "Do I smell atur?"

Dree-pah splashed her.

"Use more depyata, Dree," said Twu-pah. "Perhaps you can wash it off."

"No wonder Muth-pah sent those sons on patrol," said Hren-pah. "They'll leave soon, and who needs heavy chests about the hall."

"It's not only me who smells of atur," said Dree-pah. "Dargu does too."

"Kovok-mah, also," said Twu-pah. "Why does he love you, Dargu?"

Dar blushed. "I thought it was impolite to speak of such things."

"Among sons that's true," said Hren-pah, "but we're all mothers here."

"So why *does* he love you?" asked Twu-pah.

"I don't know," said Dar.

"Because he lacks sense," said Hren-pah.

"I think not," said Dree-pah. "Dargu bit Zna-yat's neck. He says Muth la has bestowed her powers. They attract sons."

"And hardship," added Hren-pah.

The mother's talk reinforced Dar's impression that life in the settlement was out of kilter. Sons who should be involved in everyday clan life spent their time guarding against a nonexistent enemy. Even as an outsider, it was clear to Dar that the sons' absence put a strain on everyone. The hall needed expansion, planting went too slowly, and mothers had difficulty finding mates. The Goblin Wars were long over, but their shadow still darkened lives.

Dar settled into a routine as she waited for the patrol to return. She worked in the fields, bathed with the mothers, ate with them, and slept alone. She participated in clan life, yet was excluded in subtle ways. Conversations stopped when she approached. Mothers were polite, but guarded when they spoke to her. Dar came to sense that everyone knew something important was about to happen; something that involved her.

The patrol was expected to return in time for Bah Niti, which would be marked by a feast. On that day, no mothers worked in the fields. Many, Dar included, gathered wood for a series of bonfires. Others worked on preparing a special meal. All day long, Dar sensed growing excitement, especially among those mothers whose spouses were away. There was no midday meal, and everyone worked into late afternoon. Afterward, the bathing pool was crowded. As Dar washed, she was certain that she detected the scent of atur in the air. *It must be strong, if even I can smell it.* She was also aware that the scent might be her own, for she longed to be with Kovok-mah again.

It was dusk when the sons tramped up the valley, weary from their long patrol. Dar fought the urge to dash up to Kovok-mah. Instead, she watched the other mothers for cues on how to behave. They had gathered outside the entrance to the hall, where they gave no voice to their excitement. This puzzled Dar until she realized the wind bore their feelings to those returning.

When the patrol arrived, the mothers greeted them, and Dar observed the breast-touching gesture many times. It seemed more a means to communicate desire than to initiate it, and both sons and mothers behaved decorously afterward. When Kovok-mah approached, Dar imitated the other mothers. Before, she had always worn a blouse, and she was unprepared for the surge of desire his touch aroused. The air filled with an intoxicating fragrance, and her body became alert to every sensation. After Kovok-mah's hand drifted away, she felt unable to speak.

Kovok-mah smiled. "Dargu, it's pleasing to see you dressed like other mothers." He reached out and softly ran his fingers over Dar's cheek. "You've been much in my chest."

Dar pressed her lips to his palm and kissed it. "Let's go where we can be alone," she said.

Then Dar heard Muth-pah's voice. "Dargu will enter darkness tonight."

Kovok-mah's hand instantly fell from Dar's cheek. He bowed his head. "I'm sorry, Mother. I didn't know."

Muth-pah strode away before Dar could ask what she was talking about. Instead, she questioned Kovok-mah. "Why did you apologize? What is this darkness?" She reached out to grasp his hand, but he jerked it away.

"I'm sorry, Dargu, but we must stay apart."

"Why? What's happened?"

"Only mothers can enter darkness. This mystery is hidden from sons. Tonight, you are thwada."

"Thwada? What does that mean?"

"Someone untouchable," replied Kovok-mah, already retreating. "Someone dangerous."

Once again, Dar was left alone, but this time she intended to do something about it. She sought out Muth-pah, gave a perfunctory bow, and vented her frustration. "What did you say to Kovok-mah? Why am I thwada?"

Muth-pah seemed unperturbed. "Tomorrow you can be with your velazul. Not tonight."

"Why?"

"You will enter darkness. You cannot eat or be with son until you return."

"What if I refuse to do it?"

"Do you want sapaha to lead you through mountains?" asked Muth-pah. "If so, you will come with me tonight."

Muth-pah's manner disturbed Dar, but she realized there was no choice but to give in. "What is this darkness?"

"Place where visions come," said Muth-pah. "We'll go there together. Tonight, you'll serve at feast. Later, you'll understand everything."

On the day of Bah Niti, no one ate until the feast, which wouldn't begin until all daylight left the moonless sky. Already hungry, Dar was annoyed that she would have to fast. Hunger made her irritable, and her irritation increased when she discovered that all the sons scrupulously avoided her. Everyone knew that she was thwada, and even mothers kept their distance. Dar's only satisfaction was that Muth-pah was also thwada.

The feast took place outdoors. The Embrace of Muth la was marked in an open space using piles of wood that would later be lit to create a ring of bonfires. The entire clan gathered within the ring and waited for darkness. A lone fire burned within the center of the circle. There, mothers stirred a huge pot of savory stew. When the wind blew its aroma in Dar's direction, her mouth watered. She sat beside Muth-pah and the two were an island of solemnity within the festive gathering. Dar was surprised by how openly couples displayed their passion. Dar found it hard to watch, for the sight aroused thoughts of Kovok-mah.

When the night sky filled with stars, the bonfires were lit. Then Muth-pah and Dar served the feast. After that was done, the matriarch led Dar away from the circle of light. As Dar followed her into the dark, she still had no idea where she was going or what she would do there. The two walked awhile until they reached a fold in the ridge's rocky wall. No starlight entered there, and it appeared absolutely black except for the dull red light of a fire's embers. Muth-pah halted at the shadow's edge and began undressing. "Take off clothes," she said.

When Dar was naked, Muth-pah took her hand and led her into the darkness. At first, Dar could see nothing except the embers and was dependent on the matriarch's guidance. As Dar moved farther into the gloom, her eyes adjusted. She saw that the embers' glow reflected off the sides of a fissure within the ridge's stony wall. Whether by artifice or natural forces, the opening resembled the entrance to a womb. Just outside were two copper vessels the size and shape of small cauldrons and a small wooden bowl. Muth-pah handed Dar the bowl. "Drink this."

Dar sipped the liquid. It was earthy and bitter.

"Drink it all," said Muth-pah. She watched Dar empty the bowl before grabbing one of the copper vessels. "Now you must be cleansed," she said, pouring herb-scented water over Dar's head and body. Then she had Dar do the same for her.

Afterward, Muth-pah told Dar to enter the fissure, which was the opening of a narrow, low-ceilinged cave. The embers of several fires were beacons leading the way deeper into the rock. Muth-pah told Dar to follow them. After Dar passed each beacon, Muth-pah extinguished it with water from the other copper vessel. Thus, as Dar traveled deeper into the cave, darkness closed in behind her and the air, which was already hot and pungent with smoke, grew steamy.

The tunnel made a sharp turn and terminated in a rounded chamber with a ceiling so low that Dar had to squat to enter it. A cavity in its floor held more embers. "Sit," said Muth-pah. Dar sat cross-legged. Muth-pah did the same, then poured the remaining contents of the vessel on the embers. Total darkness arrived with a loud hiss.

"I feel dizzy," said Dar.

"Your spirit is leaving your body," replied Muth-pah.

Dar touched herself for reassurance, but her fingers were numb. She felt that the floor was dissolving and she would soon fall. Dar tried to fight that sensation by speaking. "Tell me why I'm here. What am I supposed to do?"

"You said you spoke to Velasa-pah. Perhaps you will again."

"I think he's dead."

"He is. That's why you're here. Only spirits can speak to spirits."

"Then won't I be dead also?"

"You may return," said Muth-pah, "if Muth la wills it."

"Thwa," said Dar. "I can't do this." She tried to rise, but her body wouldn't respond. It was so numb that the only evidence that she still had a body was a pain below her breast. It felt hot and cold at once. The pain spread, and, in her mind's eye, Dar saw a hole growing in her chest. As it did, her essence streamed out into the black void. As her being dissipated, Dar perceived there was something else within her. She didn't know what it was; yet she knew it was precious. "Must save . . ." she mumbled. Then, there was only the void.

Eighteen

♛

Someone was pouring water over Dar's body. It felt good, despite its chill. Dar opened her eyes. She was lying outside the cave beneath a dawn sky. Muth-pah bent over her holding a copper vessel. "Tava, Dargu," she said. "You've returned."

Dar looked about with confusion. "What happened? I don't remember anything, except . . ." Dar felt her chest for a wound, but her flesh was whole. "I thought I died."

"Death tasted you," said Muth-pah, "but it did not swallow. You passed test."

"What test?"

"It is said washavokis often spoke words that had no sense."

"Such words are called 'lies.' Did you think I said them?"

"When you spoke of Velasa-pah, I had to know if you spoke these 'lies.' I had to know if he sent you here."

"He didn't," said Dar.

"He told you to follow your chest. That's why you came."

Dar had no recollection of divulging Velasa-pah's advice to Muth-pah. "So that's why you spared my life," Dar said. "To question me in darkness."

"Once, Pah clan was queen's clan. When queen ignored Velasa-pah's warnings, she sealed clan's fate. That is why we linger here, forgotten. Our doom was to guard against washavokis and wait."

"Wait for what?"

Muth-pah gazed at Dar thoughtfully, apparently weighing what to say. It was a while before she answered. "Muth la gives wisdom, but she's seldom generous. I've learned less than I hoped and don't understand everything I've learned. But I know this: World has changed." Muth-pah clasped Dar's hand and bowed to her. "Shashav, Dargu."

"I don't recall saying anything. All I remember is pain."

"If you remember it, then it was vision from Muth la," replied the matriarch. "Heed its message."

Dar said nothing. While all her visions were frightening and enigmatic, this one was particularly so. It seemed a glimpse of her dissolution. Dar rose, dressed, and followed Muth-pah to the hall. There, she realized the import of her visit into darkness, for the entire clan was waiting outside the hall for her and Muth-pah's return. An expectant hush fell over them. Then the matriarch spoke. "World has changed. So says Velasa-pah." A murmur arose from the crowd, then died away. "No more will sons deliver death. Tonight, we will burn skulls in ceremony, then turn our eyes eastward."

It occurred to Dar that Velasa-pah had sent her to inform his clan that the Goblin Wars were finally over. *That knowledge could have been the precious thing inside me*, she thought. *The news of it could be what streamed from my chest.* Dar willingly embraced this interpretation of her experience. It seemed confirmed by the joy caused by Muth-pah's announcement. Both mothers and sons beamed as they realized that the arduous and futile patrols were a thing of the past.

As Dar watched the clan disperse, exultant with the news, she felt tired and woozy. It was a while before she noticed Kovok-mah, waiting for her like a proper son. With faltering steps, she walked over to grab his hand

and brush it against her breast. "I'm very tired," she said, "yet I want to be alone with you."

Four days later, Dar and her party departed the Pah clan settlement. Within that short time span, Muth-pah's announcement had altered everything. Sons worked the fields with such vigor and enthusiasm that the planting was done early. With more hands available for every task, more could be accomplished. Work began on expanding the hall, and hope pervaded the talk at meals. Life had so improved that Thak-goth thought his sister would change her mind and bless the union of her son and Fre-pah. Thus, he offered to serve as sapaha to Dar and her companions so he might accompany Fre-pah and her muthuri to the Goth clan settlement.

Fre-pah behaved as though the blessing was assured, and her optimism set the tone for the journey. Dar felt lighthearted also. She was no longer lost or ragged. For the first time, she walked with sandals on her feet. The footwear was a parting gift from Muth-pah, along with an outfit of urkzimmuthi clothing. Dar wore a newly made neva, a length of woolen cloth that was wrapped around the waist to form a skirt, and kefs, a pair of short capes. One was worn on top of the other in warm weather. When it was cold, one cape covered the chest. Thus attired, Dar felt more like an urkzimmuthi mother.

The hidden trail to Goth clan territory wound through a network of valleys, and the way was often hard. The travelers passed abandoned halls and spent nights in some of them, but it was nine days before they encountered any orcs. These were three Goth clan mothers who were collecting herbs. They knew Fre-pah and her muthuri, but Dar amazed them.

"Dargu is like Velasa-pah," said Thak-goth. "Muth la guides her." Afterward, the mothers treated Dar with respect but curiosity.

Later that afternoon, Dar spied terraced fields and a collection of stone halls. Thak-goth led them toward the one where his sister had her hanmuthi, which was one of several within her muthuri's hall. Recalling her first meeting with Muth-pah, Dar was slightly nervous as she neared the building, but not nearly as nervous as Fre-pah. As the time approached to speak to her velazul's muthuri, optimism deserted her.

Thak-goth's muthuri, Tho-goth, was the ranking mother in the hall, so she was the one who greeted the visitors. They found her seated on a stool in the rearmost hanmuthi. Since only strangers were formally greeted, Tho-goth nodded to the two Pah clan mothers, then addressed Dar. "I've received news of you. It's said you can speak, but I know not how to greet you."

Tara-pah, Fre-pah's muthuri, spoke up. "This mother has Muth-pah's blessing."

"I know not which is stranger," said Tho-goth, "that you name washavoki 'mother' or that Muth-pah blessed it." Then Tho-goth's curiosity got the better of her manners, and she rose to examine Dar more closely. "I've never seen washavoki before." She sniffed Dar and appeared surprised.

Tara-pah spoke again. "This mother has led these sons through many perils. She also entered darkness to guide our clan. Much has changed since she came. Sons have put aside weapons to work alongside mothers."

"I'm amazed," said Tho-goth. "This is pleasing news." She declined her head toward Dar. "Greetings, Mother. I'm Tho-goth."

Dar bowed and stated her name. Afterward, her companions were greeted. A meal followed where the conversation began with news of Tho-goth's relatives at the Pah clan hall and ended with an account of Dar's adventures. Those astounded Tho-goth. "Dargu, I must take you to Muth-goth tomorrow. She'll be most interested, and I'm certain she'll find sapaha for you and these sons."

Tara-pah waited until the meal was over before bringing up the subject of Fre-pah's blessing. She suggested the matter should be reconsidered in light of changes wrought by Dar's revelation. "Life used to be hard for husbands of Pah clan mothers," she concluded, "but future will be different."

Tho-goth considered Tara-pah's arguments, then frowned. "You speak wisdom, but I doubt my daughter will agree. Thak-goth doesn't understand his sister. She wants her son close, whether he's content or not. Yet we can speak with her. Perchance she'll change her mind."

Dar watched hope depart from Fre-pah's face, and her heart went out to her. Later that night, when Dar lay against Kovok-mah's chest to sleep, she heard an unfamiliar sound coming from the adjacent chamber. It was low-pitched and repetitive, like muffled whimpering. "What do I hear?" whispered Dar.

"Fre-pah is sad," whispered Kovok-mah as he embraced Dar a little closer. "She will not be blessed."

"What will she do?"

"Return home, never to see her velazul again."

Fre-pah, her muthuri, and Thak-goth departed for home early the following morning. Dar remained and was presented to the Goth matriarch later that day. Muth-goth was the most elderly orc Dar had ever seen, and the only frail one. Her flesh hung from her large frame and her face was a cobweb of wrinkles surrounded by wispy white hair. After formal greetings, the matriarch rose with difficulty from her stool and hobbled toward Dar. She halted a hand's length away and squinted at her with frank curiosity. "I've already heard much about you," Muth-goth said. Her lips curled into a grin. "You're no washavoki! Your teeth are black."

"I chew washuthahi seeds, Mother," replied Dar.

"It helps," said Muth-goth as she continued her examination. "But not much. Still, it's better to be wise than pretty. Are you wise?"

"I doubt it," said Dar.

Muth-goth grinned again. "Wise answer." She turned to the others. "I wish to be alone with Dargu."

When the room cleared, Muth-goth sat upon her stool and invited Dar to sit at her feet. "Muth la speaks to urkzimmuthi mothers," said Muth-goth, "but only to very few. Is it common for washavoki mothers to receive visions?"

"Thwa," said Dar. "I've never heard of it."

"Some say visions are gifts. Others claim they are burdens. Whatever they are, they're rare," said Muth-goth. "I once had visions. Speak to me of yours."

Dar recounted everything, and Muth-goth listened without comment until Dar had finished speaking. By then, her expression was troubled. "So you encountered Velasa-pah. This is news, indeed."

"Who is he, Mother? Those in Pah clan would say little, even after I returned from darkness."

"They keep his tale deep in their chests, for his fate and theirs are intermingled. Yours, too, I think."

"How?"

Muth-goth merely smiled. "So, Dargu, why do you think Muth la has given you visions?"

Despite having her own question evaded, Dar answered the matriarch's. "I'm not sure," she replied. "I understand some visions, but most make no sense to me."

"Ones that make no sense are most important," said Muth-goth. "They show things that have yet to happen."

"How can they guide me if I don't understand them?"

"Did your vision of burning tell you what to do when you saw Zna-yat bound to tree?"

"Thwa," replied Dar. "I followed my chest."

"That's Muth la's way," said Muth-goth. "She shows where path will fork, but you must choose which course to take."

"Then what's point of visions? What good are they?"

Muth-goth hissed. "Do you think I know Muth la's mind? I'm old and have seen much, but I'm child next to World's Mother. All I know is this—Muth la sends visions to suit her purposes, not yours."

Dar sighed. "I suspected as much."

"Yet good will come from them if you act wisely."

Dar bowed her head. "Hai, Mother." Still, she couldn't help wondering, *Good for whom?*

The following day, Dar and her companions departed, guided by the sapaha that Muth-goth had provided. As her journey's end grew closer, Dar worried about her reception at Kovok-mah's hall. *What muthuri would want a washavoki for her son?* When Dar imagined how perverse her passion would seem, she felt her situation was hopeless. Dar brooded over the matter until it occurred to her that Kovok-mah's muthuri was Zna-yat's aunt. *Perhaps he can tell me what to expect.* When they stopped to rest, Dar pulled Zna-yat aside for a private conversation. "Zna-yat, I need guidance."

"You are mother. It's not my place to advise you."

"Yet you must. You have knowledge I need."

Zna-yat bowed. "How can I help you?"

"You know that Kovok-mah fills my chest. When I enter hall of his muthuri, what will happen?"

"Dargu, don't enter that hall."

"Why?"

"Dargu, you're wise. You know why."

"Kovok-mah's muthuri will disapprove."

"She'll know his feelings, but she won't understand them," said Zna-yat. "I think she'll be angry."

Dar let out a wrenching sigh. "Then there's no hope for me. No place for me either."

"You've bitten my neck, Dargu. There'll always be place for you in my muthuri's hall."

It took only a moment for Dar to realize that living in Zna-yat's hall was her only option, and she was grateful for the offer. Before, she had assumed that she would stay with Kovok-mah. Yet his muthuri had no reason to take her in, and she would quickly discover one to turn her away. Dar's future seemed set, and it didn't look promising.

Toward late afternoon, the travelers entered another empty valley. Dar spotted a suitable campsite and called an early halt to the day's march. After eating, she led Kovok-mah away. They didn't return until morning.

Zna-yat took Dar aside soon after her arrival. "Dargu," he whispered. "You are not blessed."

"We acted properly," said Dar. "We gave each other love, nothing more." Yet Dar wished they hadn't acted properly. She would have gladly consummated her love if Kovok-mah had been willing, but honor restrained him. Thus, despite a night of passion, she felt denied. By the concern in Zna-yat's face, Dar sensed that he surmised her true desire. "I won't be foolish," she added.

"Mothers who thrimuk before they are blessed become thwada for rest of life," said Zna-yat.

"I know," said Dar. Still, she couldn't help thinking that, once Kovok-mah departed, she might as well be untouchable.

"My chest is heavy for you," said Zna-yat. "Joy too easily becomes sorrow. Kovok-mah feared this in Tarathank. He dreaded end of this journey."

"If he knew it would end this way, why did he ever give me love?"

"You came to him and requested what his chest desired most," replied Zna-yat. "He thought it was Muth la's doing."

Dar sighed, thinking how Muth la had her own purposes. "He was probably right."

Zna-yat pondered Dar's dilemma a while before he spoke again. "Kovok-mah's muthuri must not learn about you too soon."

"Why?" asked Dar. "What difference will it make?"

"It will allow you to seek counsel," said Zna-yat. "Yat clan is queen clan, and its mothers are subtle thinkers. They may see path for you."

"It's not Kovok-mah's nature to speak words without meaning. How can he hide his love?"

"I'll advise him to avoid speaking of you," replied Zna-yat, "and to dwell outside his muthuri's hall. If he spends summer among his goats, she may not suspect his feelings."

Once again, Dar saw how Zna-yat was different from the others. He grasped the uses of deception. In contrast, the essence of Kovok-mah was honesty, and Dar couldn't envision him hiding his emotions. Even if he could, she couldn't imagine how she would ever become acceptable to Kovok-mah's muthuri. *I'm washavoki. Kovok-mah's silence won't alter that.* Still, it seemed her only hope. "I'll tell him to follow your plan," Dar said, "though I doubt it will change anything."

"Perhaps it won't, Dargu," said Zna-yat. "Yet it will gain you time, and Kovok-mah may see you as long as his muthuri doesn't forbid it."

"And if she does forbid it?"

"You will be apart forever."

Dar gathered the orcs together, and Zna-yat laid out his plan in full. It was a simple one: They would split up upon reaching familiar territory. Zna-yat and Dar would proceed to the Yat clan hall. Kovok-mah would journey with the others and arrive home last. All promised to mention Dar as seldom as possible and never to call her mother or refer to her by name. In that way, Zna-yat hoped that Kovok-mah's muthuri wouldn't connect Dar to the scent of love lingering about her son.

Dar endorsed Zna-yat's scheme, although she was ambivalent about it. On one hand, it offered hope—however slender—of rejoining Kovok-mah. On the other hand, it hastened the day of their separation.

As the travelers trekked eastward, the terrain became more hospitable. Trees softened the mountainsides and the trail became easy. It was both the most pleasant time in Dar's life and the most melancholy, for her present contentment made the future seem all the more bleak. She set a leisurely pace and would have stretched out the journey longer if the orcs—with the exception of Kovok-mah—had not been eager to return home.

After ten days of travel, they reached known territory and their sapaha headed home. The travelers followed a path that increasingly showed signs of use and encountered a broad stream spanned by a small stone footbridge. On the other side, the path diverged. Kovok-mah approached Dar. "This stream flows into river crossed by Flis Muthi."

"One washavokis call Turgen?"

"Hai," replied Kovok-mah. He paused, reluctant to continue. "It is here we must part."

"Not yet," said Dar. "My chest is breaking."

"Your chest is big, Dargu. It's too strong to break."

"I wish it would," said Dar. She sighed. "Yet it won't. Let us speak awhile before you go."

"I'll speak as long as you want."

"Then you'll have to speak forever," said Dar. "Come." She took Kovok-mah's hand, and led him down the stream's sandy bank. There, Dar kicked off her sandals to wade into the water. It flowed clear and cool around her legs. Kovok-mah joined her. Dar smiled. "Remember when you made me bathe?"

"You were frightened," said Kovok-mah. "Yet even then, you were fierce."

"You said Weasel was good name for me."

"It still is."

"You also said I smelled."

Kovok-mah enfolded Dar within his arms and breathed deeply. "I lacked wisdom then. Your scent is beautiful."

As Kovok-mah held Dar, she felt him trembling. Tears welled in her eyes. She didn't want to cry, and the effort to suppress her sobs made her tremble also. "Dargu," whispered Kovok-mah. "Muth la doesn't speak to sons, but I know this—she brought us together and she'll do so again."

Dar wished she was as equally certain, but none of her visions foretold such happiness. Nevertheless, she couldn't bear to disagree. "Hai," she said. "I'll feel your arms again. But not soon enough. You should go now."

Kovok-mah released Dar. She stood still and stared into the distance, unable to watch him go. Yet she listened for each footstep as he walked away. Dar remained in the river until her feet were numb. All the while, she wished it hadn't mattered that she and Kovok-mah weren't blessed. *If he were washavoki, this would have ended differently. We'd have run off together.* Yet Dar knew Kovok-mah would never dishonor her, not even to make her happy.

Nineteen

♛

When Dar climbed up the bank, Zna-yat was waiting for her. He held out Dar's old washavoki clothing. Dar understood his hint. "Why shouldn't I dress as mother?"

"News travels quickly among urkzimmuthi. Kath-mah not only has wise nose, she is wise in other ways."

"Kath-mah?" said Dar. "Do you mean Kovok-mah's muthuri?"

"Hai. When she smells his atur, she will seek to learn what mothers he has been with."

"Won't she just ask?"

"That's not done," replied Zna-yat. "She'll wait for him to speak of his velazul. Meanwhile, she'll try to guess."

"I see," said Dar. "I'm glad you understand Kath-mah so well." She eyed her old garments with distaste. "I'll be less glad to wear those again."

After Dar changed, she followed Zna-yat on a path that headed downstream. The stream soon joined a river and they passed several empty fishing camps. They walked until sunset, then camped in one. Though Zna-yat offered to hold Dar, he looked relieved when she chose to sleep on the ground.

The following day, Dar and Zna-yat encountered an orc settlement. They stopped for directions and Zna-yat explained that they were survivors of a battle. "This washavoki saved my life," he said, pointing to Dar. "Now it flees with me."

The orcs looked at Dar curiously. "It looks too small to save you."

"It's small, but cruel," replied Zna-yat.

"Don't you fear it?" asked one of the orcs.

"Thwa, it has grown peaceful."

"Are you sure?" asked another orc, eyeing Dar's dagger.

Zna-yat made a gesture that was the equivalent of a shrug. "Well, peaceful for washavoki."

Throughout the exchange, Dar pretended she couldn't understand Orcish. She didn't speak until the settlement was out of sight. Then she hissed. "So I'm cruel but peaceful? I thought urkzimmuthi did not speak words without meaning."

"Your power must be hidden," replied Zna-yat, "so I said little. But what I said made sense."

"I've killed, so I guess I'm cruel," said Dar, "but I don't feel peaceful."

Dar and Zna-yat traveled openly, but unobtrusively, for five days. When they approached the valley of the Yat clan, Dar donned her urkzimmuthi clothing. "I am mother, and that's how I'll enter your hall."

Zna-yat bowed. "It could not be otherwise."

The Yat clan's valley twisted, so the clan hall was long hidden. At first, Dar saw only meadows containing sheep, goats, and small huts where shepherds dwelled in the summer. Soon, Zna-yat began to encounter kinfolk upon the road. Each time, he stopped to tell his story. All were amazed that he had returned alive, for news of the deadly battle had preceded him. They were equally amazed by Dar and by the way Zna-yat introduced her. He told everyone that she was a mother who had saved his life and guided him through many dangers. The encounters grew ever more frequent, so the final part of Dar's journey was drawn out, and she realized that news of her arrival would reach the hall long before she did.

At last, Dar rounded a bend and beheld a small mountain at the valley's end. Terraces covered its sides like green shingles, and the Yat clan hall crowned its top. Even from a distance, it looked large and impressive. It reminded Dar of Tarathank, not the homey dwellings of Muth-pah and Muth-goth. "*That's* your hall?" she said in an awed voice.

"Hai. Queen lived there," said Zna-yat. "One day, she will again."

Dar didn't know the Orcish word for "palace," but the hall seemed one to her. That impression increased as she and Zna-yat neared it. Upon reaching the mountain, the road zigzagged among the terraced fields until it reached the summit, which was entirely covered by the great stone building. It seemed to have grown there, with vaulted roofs that mimicked the curves of weathered rock. Like Tarathank, it lacked military structures. It was a home, albeit one the size of a small town, not a fortification. Dar was both puzzled and fascinated by the way its arched windows reflected the light. "Why do windows sparkle?" she asked.

"They're covered with sand ice," replied Zna-yat, "so rooms are filled with light, yet warm. You'll like it here, Dargu."

Dar gestured agreement, though she actually doubted it. Having spent her life in a one-room hut, she suspected she would feel out of place in such a grand hall. She trudged up the road with growing apprehension until she reached the hall's arched entrance. It contained a pair of large doors with elaborate, decorative hinges. Two sons who wore no armor and bore no weapons opened it on their approach. A young mother stood inside the doorway and addressed Zna-yat in Orcish. "Brother! I thought I'd never see you again!"

"I'm here due to this mother," replied Zna-yat, bowing toward Dar.

"Our muthuri wishes to greet this one," said Zna-yat's sister. "Lead it . . . Lead *her* to our hanmuthi."

Dar said nothing. She followed Zna-yat and his sister down a long hallway, which was illuminated from above by sand ice skylights. The hall curved like a wiggling snake, and Dar assumed each turn marked the outer wall of a different hanmuthi. That meant the hanmuthi of Zna-yat's muthuri was the fourth one inside the hall. Its entrance was a stone archway carved to resemble trees with interlocking branches. The stonework, though impressive, lacked the finesse of the carvings in Tarathank.

A short hallway led to a circular room with a raised hearth in its center and a copper chimney that extended from the ceiling. Arches pierced the room's outer wall. Most of these were doorways to adjoining chambers, but three were windows with panes of sand ice. The windows amazed Dar so much, she didn't notice the mother seated on a carved wooden stool until she spoke. "Greetings," said the mother in the human tongue. "I am Zor-yat. Zna-yat is my son."

Dar bowed. "Mer nav Dargu," she said. "Mer pahav Pahmuthi." *I am Dargu. I speak Orcish.*

"You speak it well," replied Zor-yat in Orcish. She continued in the same language. "I hear you saved my son."

"Hai. I believe it was Muth la's will."

"Perhaps it was," said Zor-yat. "Yet it was your deed." She bowed. "You'll always have place here."

Dar bowed more deeply than Zor-yat. "Shashav, Mother."

Zor-yat nodded toward Zna-yat's sister. "This is Nir-yat, who is yet unblessed. She'll make you welcome."

The introduction was evidently the signal for Nir-yat to lead Dar away, which she did. Dar followed her through one of the doorways and down a long hallway to a small, unfurnished chamber. One wall featured a window similar to the ones in the hanmuthi, but smaller. "We'll share this chamber," said Nir-yat, who didn't look happy about it.

"It's so beautiful!" said Dar, trying to appear appreciative. Being far from the hearth, the room was chilly despite the sunlight streaming in from the window. Already, she was tempted to adjust her kefs so one of the capes covered her chest. Yet because Nir-yat remained bare-breasted, Dar did also. She continued to praise the room. "I've never seen such floor," she said, pointing to the mosaics that decorated it and marked Muth la's Embrace. "It's like walking on flowers." As Dar stepped over to examine the window, two sons entered the room. One bore a wooden chest under each arm. The second carried a rolled-up mat and iron cube with perforated sides, metal feet, and an insulated handle. Embers glowed inside it, warming the room.

"Muthuri says your kind sleeps lying down," said Nir-yat. "She has ordered thing called 'bed' to be made for you. It will arrive before night."

"Your muthuri is both wise and gracious," replied Dar.

"Perhaps you wish to bathe now."

Dar nearly smiled at Nir-yat's transparency. *Poor thing*, she thought, *stuck with a smelly washavoki.* "Hai. I'd like that very much."

While Dar washed, Zor-yat interrogated her son. "You left to slay washavokis," she said. "Now you bring one to our hall. Why?"

Though Zna-yat towered over his muthuri, her scornful gaze intimidated him. "She's here by Muth la's will."

"Muth la's will! What do *you* know of such matters?"

"Twice I tried to kill Dargu. Once, I threw her in river and watched her sink. Yet tree pulled her from water."

"Not every tree is Muth la."

"I came to think this also," replied Zna-yat, "so I sought her death again. Yet Dargu foresaw my own death and prevented it. She slew washavokis so I might live."

"It slew its own kind?"

"*Her* own kind, Muthuri. Take care how you speak. Dargu has bitten my neck."

"Why didn't you tell me this before?"

"Because I can serve both you and her. She's not our enemy."

"Have you learned nothing about washavokis?"

"Dargu is different. Muth la sends her visions. I think Dargu was sent to aid us. Already, she has led sons through many dangers and risked her life on our behalf. She also spoke with Velasa-pah and entered darkness to guide Muth-pah."

Zor-yat started at the mention of Velasa-pah, but she regained her composure before her son noticed. "Guiding Muth-pah accomplished nothing. Her clan is lost and will remain so."

"Dargu caused them to change their ways," replied Zna-yat. "Doesn't that show Muth la's hand at work?"

"You speak of matters beyond your knowledge. Keep silent, lest your foolish tales stir up trouble."

Zna-yat bowed his head submissively.

"Everything you say surprises me," said Zor-yat. She took her time before making a judgment. "Perhaps you've acted wisely," she said at last. "This washavoki has bitten your neck, so I'll honor your obligation. I don't yet know what honor Dargu merits. Maybe none."

"Much," said Zna-yat.

Zor-yat curled back her lips. "You grow bold in her behalf." She flashed her son a knowing look. "Already, you keep things from me."

Zna-yat looked away.

"Soon, I'll bring Dargu before my sister," said Zor-yat. "Afterward, we'll decide this washavoki's fate."

Knowing that he had made Dar's case as forcefully as he dared, Zna-yat bowed to his muthuri and left the room.

Twenty

♛

Dar gazed listlessly out the window of her room, wondering what her place would be in the community beyond it. *If I'm to have one.* All Dar knew was that whoever was making that decision was taking her time. Already Dar had been waiting for two days.

Nir-yat interrupted Dar's musings with yet another question. "How did you learn speech of mothers?"

"One son taught me."

"Why?"

"Because I asked him."

"But why would he agree?"

"I think I amused him," said Dar. She smiled. "He said I was fierce."

Nir-yat's expression underwent a subtle transformation. "Who was this son?"

"Someone from another clan," said Dar, suspecting her scent had betrayed her feelings. "We have parted."

Nir-yat didn't press the matter, but Dar worried that she already had revealed too much. "What's going to happen to me?" she asked.

"I don't know. Muth-yat will decide."

"Do you know when?"

"Whenever she's ready. Meanwhile, I'll keep you company."

To learn everything you can, thought Dar. She had quickly figured out that Nir-yat was a spy, though not a skilled one. Like most orcs Dar had encountered, the young mother asked questions directly, and Dar supposed Nir-yat wouldn't deny that she passed on the answers. Dar's situation was complicated by the fact that Nir-yat was her only source of information, for the two were kept isolated. Normally, sleeping chambers adjoined the hanmuthi and meals were eaten communally; yet Dar and Nir-yat seldom left their room. Even when they bathed, they used a basin, not the communal pool.

Through conversations with Nir-yat, Dar began to form a picture of life in the Yat clan hall. Much of it was similar to that in any orc settlement. The principal difference was the Yat clan was the governing clan. Matriarchs of the other clans met in the hall to receive guidance from the queen. They still did, although the queen resided in Taiben, recovering from a mysterious malady. Dar was surprised to learn the queen lived among the washavokis. Although Kovok-mah had said she received "strong healing magic" from them, Dar had assumed it was a cure, not ongoing treatment. Since the queen's relocation, edicts arrived via sons who served in the orc regiments.

Dar was also surprised to learn the queen was Zoryat's sister, as was Muth-yat, the Yat clan matriarch. From her travels, Dar assumed that the oldest mothers always held the highest standing, and she didn't expect mothers in their middle years to rule a clan. Nir-yat explained why they did, but her explanation was sketchy. It involved something called "Fathma," which Dar imagined was an attribute similar to charisma.

The Yat clan had other halls besides the one Dar was staying in. All the eastern clans were large and spread out. Only the "lost" Pah clan occupied a single hall. Nir-yat spoke of them dismissively as an expiring relic fixated on the past. "They still believe Velasa-pah's prophecies," she said. "Though none have ever come to pass."

"What prophecies are those?" asked Dar.

Nir-yat hissed. "Predictions history proved wrong. Only lorekeepers remember them now."

As her isolation dragged on, Dar became convinced that Muth-yat would see her only when she felt adequately informed. Thus, Dar answered all questions truthfully—if not always completely—and volunteered additional information. Yet she chose not to reveal her feelings for Kovok-mah, or even mention him, until she knew how those feelings would be received.

In time, Nir-yat's disdain dissipated. Dar's accounts of hardship and peril fascinated the young mother, who never tired of hearing about her brother's rescue. On the fourth morning, Nir-yat gently stroked Dar's scarred ankle during a retelling of the fight with Zna-yat's captors. In a voice filled with compassion, Nir-yat said, "How could washavokis treat one mother so?" At that moment, Dar realized she had won Nir-yat over. Later, Nir-yat left and didn't return until late afternoon.

Shortly afterward, Dar was called before Muth-yat. The matriarch was seated in a room of special magnificence. It was circular, like a hanmuthi, but there was no hearth in its center. Instead, there was an elevated stone seat. Though it lacked a back or arms, its size and the richness of its carvings convinced Dar that it was a throne. All the arches in the room's wall contained windows, which offered a view of the surrounding mountains.

Muth-yat was seated on a stool at the throne's base. Zor-yat sat close by. Dar could tell the two mothers were sisters; both possessed similar features and imposing bearings. After Dar's escort left the room, the matriarch nodded her head. "I am Muth-yat."

Dar bowed deeply. "I'm Dargu."

"I know of your deeds and how you came to bite my sister's son's neck," said Muth-yat. "Now, we shall speak of deeper things." With that, she launched her interrogation. Nir-yat had told Muth-yat everything, so the matriarch's questions were very specific. Most of them concerned four events: Dar's dream of the mage trying to find her as she hid beneath a veil of leaves; her vision of the urkzimmuthi mother by the hedge; her encounter with Velasa-pah; and the time Dar entered darkness with Muth-pah. Both the matriarch and her sister grilled Dar until the sun set and the room grew dark. Finally, the questioning was over. Muth-yat clapped her hands and a son entered the room. "Dargu is finished here," she said. "Take her back to her room."

Dar bowed and left no wiser about her fate.

After Dar departed, Zor-yat turned to her sister. "What do you think?"

"Washavokis often speak words without meaning, tales they call 'lies,'" said Muth-yat, "but I don't believe Dargu spoke them."

"Are you sure?" asked Zor-yat. "How could she have met Velasa-pah? That sounds like lie."

"It's too improbable to be good lie, and washavokis are skillful at creating such tales."

"So if she met him, does that mean his prophecy is coming true?"

"Velasa-pah spoke to Dargu about mage, not fate of clans," said Muth-yat. "Besides, nothing in his prophecy has ever come to pass, nor is anything likely to."

"Your words put me at ease. Still, I think Dargu is hiding something."

"I agree," said Muth-yat, "and it's something important."

"Do you think it's meaning of her visions?"

"Thwa. She doesn't understand them," said Muth-yat. "She doesn't even know she saw our queen."

"When our sister asked 'Where are you?' do you think she was speaking to Dargu?"

"Most likely. Otherwise, why would Dargu have visions of mage?"

"I see your meaning," said Zor-yat. "Mage holds our queen, and Velasa-pah said mage was Dargu's enemy."

"Hai, but Dargu didn't understand," said Muth-yat. "She doesn't know mage listens to bones."

"Velasa-pah said bones were her greater enemy," said Zor-yat.

"I think he meant bones could detect her."

"Detect her doing what?"

"I'm not yet sure," replied the matriarch. "I'm certain of only one thing: If mage is Dargu's enemy, then she's our friend. I think Muth la has sent us Dargu to be our tool. We must take care how we use her."

"Do you have plan?"

"Not yet. I need to think some more. Meanwhile, honor Dargu and keep her close. We can use her only once. When Dargu entered darkness, she foresaw her death."

Twenty-one

♛

Dar learned of Muth-yat's decision through indirect ways, starting the following morning. Zor-yat arrived in Dar's chamber, her lips curled into a smile. "Dargu," she said, "your chamber is ready at last! Let me show you."

Zor-yat led Dar back to the hanmuthi. "Now that we have three unblessed mothers, I had to rearrange things." She showed Dar a large, elegant chamber adjoining the hanmuthi. A mother was already in it. "This is Thir-yat, Nir-yat's younger sister," said Zor-yat. "Thir-yat, this is Dargu, who has bitten your brother's neck."

Thir-yat bowed politely, and Dar returned the bow.

Two sons appeared bearing furnishings from Dar's old room. As soon as Dar's chest was set down, Zor-yat opened it. It contained only a dagger, for Dar had discarded all her washavoki clothing. "This will not do!" exclaimed Zor-yat in a surprised tone. "You need more clothes." She regarded Dar's outfit, as if she had noticed it for the first time. "That's very quaint, but styles are different here. I know mother who does fine work. I'll send for her. Tonight, you must be properly dressed."

Zor-yat breezed out of the room as Nir-yat entered it. "Is this for us? Window chamber?"

"Hai," said Thir-yat, grinning. "Muthuri said it's because of Dargu."

Nir-yat smiled. "Shashav, Dargu."

Dar felt relieved. Sharing a chamber off the hanmuthi

meant inclusion in daily life. She especially appreciated how Zor-yat's choice of rooms insured that Thir-yat and Nir-yat would be satisfied with the arrangement. Zor-yat had put on a gracious performance, yet Dar suspected it was a performance all the same. It seemed more likely that Zor-yat had been waiting for Muth-yat's decision, not for the room to be readied. Once again, Dar had witnessed an orc twisting the truth, and it made her uneasy.

"There's to be feast tonight," said Thir-yat, "to celebrate Zna's return and honor Dargu's deeds."

As Thir-yat spoke, a gray-haired mother appeared in the doorway. She bowed to Dar. "Mother," she said, "I'm Thorma-yat. Zor-yat asked me to prepare your clothes." Thorma-yat frowned. "You have strange body. This will be difficult."

Thorma-yat asked Dar to undress, then measured her using different-colored strings, which she knotted to record each dimension. Afterward, she produced a bag of fabric swatches and asked, "What cloth do you favor?"

It was the first time Dar had ever been asked such a question. Before, her wishes had never mattered. Dar felt deeply moved as she fingered the colorful fabrics. Nir-yat noticed. "Your eyes grow wet. Are you hurt?"

"Thwa. It means I'm happy," said Dar. "These are so beautiful and soft."

"I'll be happy when you choose one," said Thorma-yat. "There is much work ahead and little time."

Dar selected indigo cloth for her neva and a sky blue fabric for her kefs. After Thorma-yat hurried off, Nir-yat offered to give Dar a tour of the hall. Dar gladly accepted. The hall proved a thriving place, more like a small city than a dwelling. There were walled gardens, sacred places, stables, workshops, communal baths, numerous hanmuthis, even more storerooms, and a huge kitchen that served the entire hall.

Later, Nir-yat showed Dar the terraced fields that covered the mountainside. Many of the fields contained plants with tiny yellow blossoms that swayed in the breeze. Dar wondered which field Zna-yat had worked, surrounded by its wall built by Lama-tok and Duth-tok. Thinking of her traveling companions made Dar long to see them. *Life was simpler on the road.* She recalled falling asleep in Kovok-mah's arms so vividly that she almost felt his touch. Dar shook the image from her mind, then noticed Nir-yat watching her. "What were you thinking about?" asked the mother in her customary directness.

"How pretty crops look."

Nir-yat shot her a strange look. "You must love flowers very much."

Orcs had no midday meal on feast days, so by the time Dar bathed and dressed in her new clothes, she was ravenous. She was also jittery. The occasion would mark her formal introduction to Zor-yat's extensive family—three generations of orcs with whom Dar expected to spend the rest of her life. Knowing her reception would foreshadow that life, Dar's trepidations returned in force. She began to pace anxiously about the room.

"Don't worry, Dargu," said Nir-yat. "Muthuri is pleased with you."

"And your clothes look nice," added Thir-yat.

Indeed, Thorma-yat had performed a miracle within the time allotted, and Dar's new kefs and neva fit perfectly. "You're right, Thir-yat," Dar said, "I've never worn anything so lovely." She popped a washuthahi seed into her mouth to insure that her teeth were properly blackened and continued to wait.

When the sun began to set, sons brought food from the central kitchen. They set a cauldron upon the hearth and arranged platters of delicacies about it. The hanmuthi filled with savory aromas as both sexes of Zor-yat's family assembled for the feast. Zor-yat sat upon her stool while everyone else sat on cushions. Nir-yat, Thir-yat, and Dar were seated on her right side. Zor-yat's husband, Dna-tok, sat on her left, along with Zna-yat, her only unblessed son. Zor-yat's three blessed daughters, with their spouses and children, completed the circle about the hearth. In all, twenty-three individuals gazed at Dar.

Zor-yat rose. "Long has there been empty spot within this circle. Long did I believe Zna-yat had rejoined Muth la. Yet here he sits, having passed through many perils. He returned with tales of mother who saved him. That mother is Dargu."

Zor-yat bowed to Dar. "Shashav, Dargu."

After Dar returned the bow, Zor-yat spoke again. "All alive are Muth la's children. Think this as you regard Dargu. I see one who is guided by Muth la. She deserves our honor and friendship. Join me and welcome her."

Everyone in the room bowed to Dar. "Welcome, Dargu."

Dar bowed. "Shashav."

Zor-yat walked over to the cauldron, and intoned the words that blessed the feast. "Food is Muth la's gift."

The room echoed with the response. "Shashav, Muth la."

Youngling sons quickly distributed metal plates and small wooden drinking bowls. Then Zor-yat personally served everyone stew. She was followed by the blooded mothers, who passed out the other delicacies and poured herb-scented water into drinking bowls. Dar was invited to join in these tasks. Once everyone was served, the feasting began.

The room quieted as everyone satisfied their hunger

with food Dar thought was superior to any prepared for King Kregant. Scent was an important element of every dish, and all the food was spiced. The aromas tended to be subtle, though perhaps not to the orcs' keen noses. Dar marveled at the wide variety of flavors and relished everything.

When the eating slowed, Zna-yat launched into an account of his rescue. He showed a skill for drama, and soon had everyone spellbound. After he finished speaking, Zor-yat brought out a large silver urn. It turned out to be a drinking vessel that was passed among the adults. Each drank deeply when it was his or her turn. Dar did the same when the vessel reached her. The dark liquid it contained had the spicy sweetness of washuthahi seeds and warmed her stomach like brandy.

By the second time the vessel reached Dar, she was already feeling the draught's effects. Every sensation was pleasantly heightened, and she felt relaxed and happy. The third time she drank from the silver vessel, the room seemed to dance and the voices about her blended into incoherent music. In a state of bliss, Dar failed to notice that the orcs were less affected by the drink. Yet even they were in a buoyant mood. Nir-yat beamed as she shook Dar's shoulder. "Dargu, I must tell you something," she said, slurring her words slightly.

"What?"

"Dargu, I was like my brother. At first, you displeased me. But now . . . But now I'm so, so glad you're here."

Thir-yat chimed in. "Dargu, you're no . . ." She erupted in a fit of hissy orcish giggles. "Dargu, you're no washavoki. Your teeth are pretty."

"Hai," said Dar, grinning to show them off. "So are my new clothes. I wish Kovok-mah could see them."

"Muthuri's brother's son?" asked Nir-yat.

"Hai," said Dar, her caution gone. "He said my teeth were pretty, too." Then she added, "He liked my scent."

"*He* taught you how to speak?" asked Nir-yat.

"Hai," said Dar, "I miss him so."

Nir-yat leaned close to Dar and breathed in deeply. "Hai," she whispered. "I can tell."

Twenty-two

♛

Dar awoke next morning with a throbbing head. She had no memory of her indiscretion, but Nir-yat did. Nir-yat kept that information to herself, for she saw Dar's feelings as understandable, though unfortunate. She couldn't imagine Kovok-mah returning Dar's affection.

Dar moaned. "Oh, my head."

"You drank too much falfhissi," said Nir-yat.

The word meant "laughing water," though Dar didn't feel much like laughing. She moaned again.

"Cold bath will help," said Nir-yat. "Then it's off to work."

Dar expected to work, but not so soon. On her way to the bath, she learned she was to be a cook. Every mother acquired a skill, and Zor-yat had determined that Dar would be taught to prepare food. It seemed an unlikely choice. Dar's sense of smell was inferior to an orc's, yet it would be crucial in spicing dishes. Nevertheless, a muthuri was rarely questioned in her hanmuthi, and Dar felt that she was in no position to do so. If Zor-yat wanted her to cook, she would learn to cook.

Nir-yat left Dar in the charge of a rotund mother named Gar-yat. "So, Zor-yat wants you to cook," she said, her expression reflecting her low opinion of the idea. She sniffed. "You smell of falfhissi."

"We had feast last night," replied Dar.

"I know," said Gar-yat. "I helped prepare it." She handed Dar some washuthahi seeds. "These will help with your head. Until it clears, you can peel pashi." Gar-yat led Dar over to a bin filled with pashi roots, stopping to get a knife along the way. A son was sitting on a bench close by, peeling roots and tossing them into a bowl.

"Tathug-hak," said Gar-yat, "here is Dargu, Zor-yat's washavoki mother. She's peeling pashi today."

Tathug-hak bowed politely, but said nothing. Dar sat next to him and began to work. As she peeled, she pondered the words of Gar-yat's introduction, for they seemed to define her. "Washavoki" meant she was an outsider. "Mother" meant she was due respect. Dar was uncertain what it meant to be "*Zor-yat's* washavoki mother," but she felt it was a significant distinction. Everyone seemed to know of Dar, and she suspected that was Zor-yat's doing. Zor-yat had also chosen Dar's training without consultation. *Is she my protector or my keeper? What are her plans for me?* She recalled Zna-yat's statement that the Yat clan mothers were subtle thinkers, and she believed him. Already, Dar felt caught in an invisible web, gently constrained for some unknown purpose.

Dar continued to work in the kitchen every day. There, Gar-yat endeavored to teach her. The subject was extensive, and while Dar's poor sense of smell made her an inept pupil, Gar-yat persisted. Dar found her training interesting, but frustrating. Sometimes, she prepared dishes that tasted fine to her but were deemed inedible. Nevertheless, Dar worked diligently and tried to devise ways to use spices that relied on measurement rather than smell or taste.

She ate in the hanmuthi, where meals often included visitors. Unblessed sons and mothers frequently visited other halls as part of courtship. Since Dar ate with Nir-yat and Thir-yat, she met all the sons who dined with them. Three weeks after Dar's arrival, a son joined the midday meal. Nir-yat introduced him. "Dargu, this is Kathog-mah."

After Dar acknowledged his bow, Kathog-mah asked, "Are you washavoki who traveled with my cousin?"

"Who's your cousin?' asked Dar, feigning ignorance.

"Kovok-mah."

"Hai. We journeyed together," said Dar, keeping her voice and expression neutral. "How is he?"

"He's become strange. He lives with his goats."

"It was hard journey," replied Dar. "Perhaps his strangeness is to be expected."

"It made Dargu strange," said Nir-yat, flashing Dar an unsettling look.

Kathog-mah hissed. "But Dargu is washavoki, and all washavokis are strange."

"Well, I would not want to live with smelly goats," said Thir-yat.

"Kovok-mah claims he likes their scent," said Kathog-mah.

For some reason Dar didn't understand, the remark made Nir-yat hiss with laughter.

The following afternoon, Dar sought out Zna-yat. He was cultivating weeds when she arrived. When he saw her, he set aside his hoe and bowed. "Tava, Dargu. I'm surprised to see you."

"Do you know Kovok-mah has returned?"

"Hai. Kathog-mah told me."

"He's following our plan," said Dar. "He's not living in his muthuri's hall."

"So I heard."

"Zna-yat, I want to see him."

"Please pardon me, Dargu," said Zna-yat. "It's not my place to speak, yet my chest says I must. It's too soon to see Kovok-mah."

"You don't understand! I need to see him!"

"I do understand, but I think you should wait."

"I bit your neck!"

Zna-yat bowed low. "And I will obey you." He sighed. "Mah clan hall is two days journey. We can leave tomorrow, if that's your wish."

"It is," said Dar, already excited by the prospect. "But what should I tell Zor-yat?"

"That we visit Kovok-mah."

Dar didn't want to do that, but she realized lying would be unwise. Lying was something washavokis did. For a moment, she considered canceling the journey or confiding in Zor-yat about her feelings, but she rejected both options. "It will be short visit," she said. "Besides, unblessed mothers travel often."

"Hai. To visit relatives or find husband."

"Zor-yat knows I traveled with Kovok-mah. She won't think it strange that I wish to see him."

"Perhaps," replied Zna-yat.

"I'll speak to her tonight," said Dar. After briefly discussing the route with Zna-yat, Dar left, giddy with anticipation. When she returned to the kitchen, she was met by Gar-yat. "Matriarch wishes to see you. She waits in Great Chamber."

Dar hurried to the Great Chamber and found Muth-yat seated on the stool by the throne. The matriarch rose before Dar could bow. "Dargu, come walk with me."

Dar silently followed Muth-yat through numerous rooms and hallways until they came to a neglected courtyard. A low dome occupied its center. The dome's stonework looked more ancient than any Dar had seen about the hall. Muth-yat pushed her way through tall weeds to the structure and swung open its weathered door. She had Dar descend a short flight of steps before closing the door and following her. Dar gazed about the room, where the only light came from a central hole in the vaulted ceiling. Its stone floor was littered with dry leaves, and a large, circular flagstone lay at its center. Muth-yat sat cross-legged among the leaves. "Sit by me," she said.

Dar obeyed.

"This is sacred place," said Muth-yat. "Here, Fathma returned to urkzimmuthi."

"I haven't heard that tale," said Dar.

"And you won't hear it now. I brought you here for another reason. Muth la is strong here. Do you feel her presence?"

"I think so."

"You and I are alike. We both are mothers. We both have visions." Muth-yat paused. "I had vision concerning you."

Dar feared her feelings for Kovok-mah had been revealed. Nervously she asked, "Will you speak of it?"

"You appeared before me and asked, 'Why am I not born?' I have learned vision's meaning by consulting ancient texts."

"Will you tell me?"

"When your kind first appeared, we called them urkzimdi—second children. We welcomed them as younger siblings. Some dwelled with us and seemed to have spirits that were part urkzimdi and part urkzimmuthi. Velasa-pah was one. Dargu, I believe you—like him—have mixed spirit."

"My chest feels mixed," replied Dar.

"Do you like washavoki part?" asked Muth-yat.

"Thwa."

"In this, you are also like Velasa-pah. That is why he was reborn."

"I don't understand how rebirth is possible," said Dar.

"When you were baby, your body was different, yet you were Dargu. If you lose arm or leg, your body would be different, yet you'd remain Dargu. When you die, your spirit leaves body. Body may look unchanged, but it won't be Dargu. It's spirit that defines your being, not body. Velasa-pah used magic to purge washavoki from his mixed spirit so only urkzimmuthi remained. Others have also undergone that rite. I have studied this ancient magic. One can be reborn."

Dar's heart leaped at this unexpected news. "So I could become urkzimmuthi?"

"Hai," replied Muth-yat, "if you underwent this magic."

"Would I look like urkzimmuthi?"

"You would remain ugly, but you would receive Yat clan tattoo, so all would know your nature."

"Then I desire to be reborn."

"I must warn you. This magic is trying. Birth is never easy."

"I'm used to hardship."

"There is danger, also," said Muth-yat. "Not all babies live."

"If Muth la wanted me to die, I'd be dead already."

"Then, if you desire to undergo this magic, I encourage you. So does Zor-yat."

"Velasa-pah told me to follow my chest," said Dar. "I will do so. I will be reborn."

"Then this is what you must do," said Muth-yat. "Tell no one. Eat nothing. Enter this place tonight as moon rises. Wear no clothing. Then it will begin."

"Is that all?" asked Dar.

"That's all you may know. You should leave now."

Muth-yat remained seated as Dar left the building to tell Zna-yat that she had changed her mind about seeing Kovok-mah. Dar didn't explain why, and he didn't ask. Afterward, she wandered among the terraced fields in a state approaching ecstasy. The world was full of promise. Dar felt she finally understood the point of all her hardship. For the first time, Muth la's purposes and her own seemed in perfect harmony.

Twenty-three

♛

Dar didn't return to the hanmuthi. When dusk came, she went back to the overgrown courtyard to wait for night and the moon to rise. It reminded her of Tarathank, for nature was reclaiming it. The flowers of luxuriant weeds perfumed the air. Dar thought she caught a whiff of her atur mingled with their fragrance.

The sky darkened. Stars appeared. Dar waited. At last, the moon rose over the horizon. Dar made her way to the dome's doorway, removed her clothes, and descended the stairs. The room was nearly pitch black, but after her eyes adjusted, she could make out changes since her previous visit. The leaves were gone, and the circular flagstone had been moved aside to reveal an opening in the floor. It was wide enough for Dar to fall into and filled to the top with water. In the dim light, she was unable to tell whether it was a shallow basin or a deep well.

The door slammed shut and the room was plunged into near-total darkness. Dar heard a sound like a bolt siding into place. "Tava!" she called. "Who's there?" Silence. Dar waited for someone to explain what was happening. She heard a faint sound coming from above and looked upward. A blue-black patch of sky was visible through the hole in the room's ceiling. As Dar gazed at it, the patch disappeared. The darkness became absolute.

Dar tried to be calm, but her situation unnerved her. Although she knew rebirth would be trying, she had expected to know what she would face. The mystery of her situation was more frightening than the darkness. It was impossible not to conceive sinister explanations for what had happened. *Does anyone know I'm here, besides Muth-yat?* For all Dar knew, she had been entombed. "Thwa," she said aloud. "This is magic, not murder." Yet doubt remained.

Dar lay down and tried to rest, but it was impossible to get comfortable. She sat up and thought of Kovok-mah. She imagined his reaction when he learned of her transformation and indulged in pleasant fantasies. Her thoughts wandered. Dar relived her past and envisioned her future. She nodded off and dreamed. She woke and waited for something to happen. Nothing did.

Dar felt the need to relieve herself, but doing it in a sacred space seemed wrong. "I should wait," she told herself. *For how much longer?* Already she had no idea how long she had been in darkness. After a while, her bladder ached. The need for relief became increasingly urgent. Dar began to crawl about the room on her hands and knees, stopping frequently to feel her surroundings. Eventually, she discovered a hole near the wall. It was the width of her outstretched fingers. She investigated it and decided it could serve as a toilet. Afterward, she speculated whether that was its intended function. If it was, it might mean that she would remain in the room a long time.

Later, Dar became thirsty. She groped about until she found the pool in the room's center. She hunched down until her lips touched liquid, then drank. The tepid water had an earthy aftertaste. She drank only a little, then crawled away. She was frightened of the pool. It was invisible. Perhaps it was also deep. Dar envisioned blundering into it and drowning. "How could that possibly happen?" she asked. Her mind readily conjured up the answer. *I'll lose my wits and stagger about in the dark.* It didn't seem far-fetched. Dar crawled in the dark until she touched a wall. Then she pressed against it for dear life.

Time passed. Dar slept and woke, drank from the pool and used the hole. Dar grew hungry, than ravenous. For a long while—perhaps days, she had no way of telling—she thought of little else but food. Then hunger deserted her and Dar began to forget her empty body. It was already invisible.

In the perfect darkness time lost meaning. Dreams and waking thoughts became indistinguishable. Dar believed she was on the Dark Path, a spirit returning to Karm or Muth la, she couldn't remember which. Later, she alternately shivered with cold and burned with fever. Finally, Dar collapsed and became one with the unthinking dark.

The flame was tiny, yet to Dar it seemed extremely bright. She stared at it without emotion or comprehension. It simply was. Voices spoke. They were unintelligible. Hands lifted her, so she was upright on her knees. Someone held a bowl to her lips and tilted it so sweet white liquid entered her mouth. Dar swallowed some. The rest dribbled down her chin and chest. Dar drank some more. Her head cleared slightly, though she would have fallen if the hands had let go.

The tiny flame moved, and as it did, more flames appeared. The darkness fell back further. Dar saw the room was filled with mothers. They were chanting, but Dar was too groggy to catch the words. One mother stepped forward to straddle the opening in the floor. She pulled her neva up to her waist, then squatted. A second mother drew a blade across the squatting mother's thighs. Bloody lines appeared, looking black in the dim light. Blood flowed into the water.

Dar was lifted up. Her feet touched the bloody water. Then she was slowly lowered into it. Dar remained still and silent, watching passively as the water overflowed and spread over the stone floor. When the water reached Dar's waist, she was eye-to-eye with the squatting mother. Her face was familiar. Then the hands let go, and Dar slipped beneath the water.

It was blood-warm. Too weak to struggle, Dar sank. The sinking seemed endless. She looked upward. Small flames danced far away. The water colored them red. Dar's lungs began to ache. She breathed in. Water filled and dissolved her.

Dar became aware that someone was holding her. She opened her eyes and beheld Zor-yat. Torches had replaced the tiny flames, and the room was brightly lit. Mothers circled around the pair, wiping the pinkish liquid from Dar's body while Zor-yat cradled her.

"Her eyes are open," said Zor-yat to the assembled mothers. "Dargu-yat," she cooed, "I'm your muthuri."

A white cloth was brought, and Zor-yat wrapped Dar in it. Then she rose, lifting Dar effortlessly. "This is my child," said Zor-yat in a loud voice. "Tell clan that new mother has been born. Her name is Dargu-yat." Then Zor-yat carried Dar through the hall as the mothers followed, singing thanks to Muth la. Dar wept like a baby, but she wept for joy.

Dar spent three days in Zor-yat's sleeping chamber recovering her strength. Her muthuri fed her milk and dressed her in new clothes. During those first days, only immediate family visited. They greeted her as if she were a newborn, giving their familiar names and calling her "little sister." Later, the entire clan paid their respects. Each visitor precisely described his or her relationship, often using terms Dar had never heard before. After they left, Zor-yat explained what the terms meant, though Dar doubted she would ever get them straight.

The magic hadn't altered Dar's body. She looked no

different. Her vision and her sense of smell were no keener. Yet she was certain she had become urkzimmuthi, for that was the way she was treated. In this respect, the magic's power changed everything. When Dar moved back to her room, Nir-yat and Thir-yat were her older sisters. They spoke to her with less respect but more affection, and no topic was too personal.

"Some newborn," said Nir-yat with a smile. "With tits like those, you'll be blooded before next moon."

"Lucky you," said Thir-yat. "It was fourteen winters before I received Muth la's Gift."

Dar, who had never considered her period a "gift," was puzzled. "Why am I lucky?"

"You'll be grown-up," said Nir-yat.

"And get your tattoo," added Thir-yat.

"Will it hurt?" asked Dar.

"Muthuri says it's no worse than childbirth," said Nir-yat.

"Neither is it better," said Thir-yat. "Ayee! How my face swelled up!"

Nir-yat hissed. "She looked like berry."

"Now I'm sweet and juicy," said Thir-yat.

"In your dreams," retorted Nir-yat. "No son has given you love."

"That's what *you* think," replied Thir-yat. "Remember this spring, when we visited Muthuri's brother?"

"Hai," said Nir-yat, "and I saw you leave with that son. But I smelled no atur afterward."

"He wasn't pleasing," replied Thir-yat.

"Then it wasn't love-giving," replied Nir-yat. She turned to Dar. "Don't worry, Dargu. Son wasn't Kovok-mah."

"What about our cousin?" asked Thir-yat.

"Tell me more about tattoos," said Dar quickly. She reached out and touched the design on Nir-yat's chin. The black markings were slightly raised. Each clan had a distinctive tattoo that its sons and mothers received when they reached adulthood.

"Muthuri will take you to latath after you receive Gift," said Nir-yat. "Latath will make clan mark. It takes whole day. You must show strength to prove your fitness. Lie still and don't cry out."

"Jvar-yat is latath here," said Thir-yat. "She's very skilled."

Dar looked at her sisters' chins and appreciated Jvar-yat's handiwork. The tattoos were a pattern of swirls falling from a line that marked the edge of the lower lip. They reminded Dar of waterfalls. Despite the intricacy of their pattern, both tattoos were perfectly identical.

Dar received her clan tattoo a week after she was reborn. The procedure was part ceremony, with Muth-yat, Zor-yat, and her family chanting prayers for a long and happy life. Dar lay outdoors on a wooden bench, as Jvar-yat bestowed the mark of the Yat clan using thorns dipped in a black paste. Dar's lip and chin were pricked over a thousand times, and each time stung. By sunset, her lower face felt on fire.

That night, Dar sucked a liquid meal through a hollow tube, for her face was too swollen to take nourishment otherwise. While she lay awake in the dark, Nir-yat tried to comfort her. "You'll be glad you're marked," she whispered, "when you see your velazul."

"Wnnph," replied Dar.

"I know your feelings. We'll visit him."

"Kumm?"

"We'll talk soon."

Twenty-four

♛

When Dar's face was no longer swollen, she wanted to see it. Orcs disdained mirrors, so Dar sought out a pool to view her tattoo. She found one in a sunny courtyard. The pool was in a basin carved from black basalt, which made it more reflective. Dar leaned over the basin's edge and was shocked by what she saw.

The face peering back was ugly. All its proportions seemed off—the brow was too delicate, the bridge of the nose wasn't sharp, and the chin was rounded. Worst were the brown eyes; they resembled those of rats. Dar touched her cheek to confirm that the grotesque thing reflected in the water was truly her. It was. Only her black teeth looked right. They were enhanced by her beautiful tattoo. Dar traced its lines with her fingers, imagining Kovok-mah doing the same. *He loves me despite my looks.* Still, she was glad for her pretty new feature.

"I thought I'd find you here," said a voice.

Dar turned and saw Nir-yat. "After I was tattooed, I came here often," said Nir-yat. She sniffed the air and smiled "Are you thinking of your velazul?"

Dar's first impulse was to deny that she had a lover, but she checked herself. Instead, she asked, "How did you know?"

"I have nose. Besides, you told me."

"I did?"

"Falfhissi loosens tongues," said Nir-yat.

"So Muthuri knows, too?"

"I doubt it, little sister."

"I should speak to her," said Dar. "I wish to become blessed."

"You're rushing matters. Is Kovok-mah your first ve-lazul?"

Dar recalled her suitors in the highlands. None would qualify as a lover. The only man she had ever kissed had been Sevren, and that had been just once. "Hai," she said. "Kovok-mah is first."

"Did he give you love?"

"Hai."

"That's no reason to think of blessing," said Nir-yat. "Don't talk to Muthuri yet. See Kovok-mah, instead. I visit his hall often. I'll take you with me."

"When?"

"As soon as you like."

"Tomorrow?"

Nir-yat hissed softly. "My, you *are* eager."

The following day, Dar and Nir-yat left to visit the Mah clan hall. Such visits were common and no one seemed surprised when Nir-yat announced that she was bringing her new sister along. After packing some extra clothes and a few provisions, the two departed in the morning.

Once on the road, Nir-yat plied Dar with all manner of gossip. Dar heard about the queen's mysterious illness that only the washavoki mage could treat and how her long absence cast a pall over the entire clan. She learned why the queen backed her elder sister in the contentious election for Yat clan matriarch. Dar was told who chewed too much washuthahi; who was happy with their spouse and who wasn't; which sons went off to kill for the queen and which sons died for her; who was giving love to whom; and who was honored and who was in dis-repute. Dar learned the story of Harz-yat, a mother who became thwada and lived alone for fifty winters. Dar found out that Jvar-yat honed her skills by tattooing piglets sedated with falfhissi. She also learned that when Gar-yat refused to bless her son's velazul, he joined the orc regiment and died in battle.

Nir-yat did more than gossip. At times, she spoke to Dar as an older sister. "Kovok-mah's your first velazul," she said. "It's too early to think about getting blessed."

"Only Kovok-mah will ever care for me," said Dar. "Without him, I'll spend my life alone."

"You don't know future."

"I know my chest is empty without him."

"So enjoy his company, and keep his muthuri out of it."

"But . . ."

"That way, you can see him. Once Kath-mah's involved, she'll decide that."

"Why would she forbid it? I'm urkzimmuthi now."

"Muthuris want granddaughters," replied Nir-yat.

Dar's face fell. "I hadn't thought of that."

"Perhaps it's no problem," said Nir-yat. "I know nothing about magic. Maybe if you're reborn, you can have children."

Dar doubted it. In fact, the idea that she could get pregnant unsettled her.

"Don't be glum, Dargu. Muthuris look other way until things get serious. While flowers bloom, think not of winter."

Dar resolved to follow her sister's advice, and found it easy on a journey where anticipation heightened the pleasure of hiking. Their way wound between green mountains with peaks colored by the reds and golds of autumn. The brisk air was perfect for walking, and the pair traveled far before stopping for the night. They stayed in a hall of a distant relative. She had heard of Dar's rebirth and was pleased to meet her. That evening,

Dar told her tale, holding everyone spellbound. Once again, she was encouraged by her unquestioning acceptance.

Dar and Nir-yat reached Mah clan territory the next afternoon. It covered the southern side of a mountain furrowed by a network of ridges. The ridgetops were covered with terraced fields, and the hollows were used to pasture sheep and goats.

"Listen," said Nir-yat when they neared the mountainside. "Hear different tones of bells?"

Dar cocked her ear. "I think so."

"Each tone marks different flock." Nir-yat listened intently. "That's cousin Kovok's bell." She pointed toward a hollow to the left. "He's grazing his goats there today."

Dar rushed in its direction. "Let's go!"

Nir-yat hurried to keep up, grinning as she went. The ground grew steep, forcing Dar to slow down. Soon, she was panting. "Only goats belong here."

"And sons who herd them," said Nir-yat. She gazed up the grassy hollow and spotted something. "Hide, Dargu! Quick!" After Dar scurried behind a bush, Nir-yat called out. "Tava, Cousin Kovok!"

From her hiding place, Dar heard footsteps. Then Kovok-mah answered. "Tava, father's sister's daughter. Why have you journeyed here?"

"Muthuri has new daughter."

"Yet another? Muth la has blessed her."

"I've brought her here to show you."

"That's long journey for one so young."

Nir-yat grinned. "She's big for her age. Will you see her? She's behind bush."

Unable to contain herself any longer, Dar stepped from her hiding place. Kovok-mah froze. "Dargu?"

"I'm Dargu-yat, now. I've been reborn."

Kovok-mah bounded down the slope, halting just before Dar. "How's that possible?"

"Magic," said Dar as she grasped Kovok-mah's hand and brushed it across the front of her kef. "I've become urkzimmuthi."

Kovok-mah reached out and traced the lines of Dar's tattoo, but not in the way she had imagined. He seemed unable to believe his eyes and compelled to confirm such a miracle by touch. "Surely, this is Muth la's doing," he said in an awed voice.

"Hai," said Dar.

Before she could say more, Kovok-mah embraced her, lifted her up, and breathed in deeply. Dar threw her arms about his neck as he savored her scent.

"Dargu. Dargu. Dargu," he said in a low voice that mingled joy and wonder. "You've changed, yet you're same. I don't understand."

"You've always understood," replied Dar. "You saw urkzimmuthi in me before anyone else. If it wasn't there, magic would have failed."

Kovok-mah smiled. "I'm glad I was so wise." Still holding Dar's torso with one arm, he swung his other arm beneath her knees and lifted them so she was cradled in a nearly horizontal position. Dar giggled as he began to plant orcish kisses all over her face and neck.

This prelude to giving love was interrupted by Niryat. "Cousin Kovok," she said, "Dargu walked two days to see you. She can manage to walk to your hut. I'll watch your goats."

Kovok-mah set Dar on her feet, bowed to his cousin, and led Dar to his hut. It was located in a small hollow with steep sides that formed a natural corral. A high fence of interwoven branches enclosed the hollow's entrance and a wooden shelter for the goats lay at its rear. Kovok-mah's hut was next to it—a tiny, windowless stone structure with a hide flap for a door. It didn't look much larger than the reed shelter he carried on his back when he fought for the king. The goats seemed to have better accommodations.

Dar strode across the muddy ground and entered the hut. The opening was so low she had to stoop, and its interior was spare. A mat of woven reeds on the earthen floor, some pegs in the wall, and a small fireplace were the sole amenities. When Kovok-mah entered, their two bodies nearly filled it. Dar barely noticed. She was with her love, and only that mattered.

The sun was low by the time the two lovers had spent their passion. Dar dressed and gazed about the shadowed hollow. Goats had stripped all its greenery. The air smelled of them and their manure. "*This* is where you live?"

"Hai."

"All alone?"

"I have my goats."

"Who serves you food?"

"I must serve myself."

"I'll stay and serve you."

"This place is unfit for mother," replied Kovok-mah.

"I've slept in worse places."

"But you're urkzimmuthi now," said Kovok-mah. "Our mothers live in halls. Did you see any at our camps? Even in Taiben, there are none."

"I doesn't matter," said Dar, "as long as you're here."

"It matters, Dargu-yat, because it will matter to my muthuri."

The resignation in Kovok-mah's voice disquieted Dar. It reminded her of when she had warned him of the ambush in the Vale of Pines. *He knows there's trouble ahead and feels powerless before it.*

*   *   *

Nir-yat proved an inept goat herder. When Kovok-mah found her, his goats were scattered over the mountainside. Nevertheless, he thanked her before he hurried off to round them up. Dar watched him scramble up the slope, captivated by his grace and power. "You must have had good time," said Nir-yat. "Your atur overpowers smell of goats."

Dar smiled. "Thank you for watching them."

"You're welcome," said Nir-yat. "Though, if I'd known they were so stubborn, I would have thought twice. It was like herd of muthuris. Which reminds me—you should bathe before you meet our aunt."

On the way to the hall, they stopped by a stream. As Dar scrubbed away her scent in icy water, Nir-yat spoke of their destination. The Mah clan occupied many halls, which were scattered over the mountain. The one Kath-mah lived in had only one hanmuthi. "We'll be greeted by Ter-mah," said Nir-yat. "She's Kath-mah's younger sister."

"If Kath-mah is eldest, why isn't it her hanmuthi?"

"Kath-mah has two sons, but Ter-mah has two daughters," replied Nir-yat, as if that explained everything.

It was dusk when Dar and Nir-yat entered the modest hall where Kovok-mah's parents lived. Ter-mah was seated in the hanmuthi to formally greet them. "Sister's husband's sister's daughters, welcome." Nir-yat and Dar bowed and returned the greeting. Then Dar's formal introductions began. These were in order of precedence. She was first greeted by Ter-mah's daughters, followed by Kath-mah, who had green eyes like her son. Dar then greeted those whose standing was lower than hers: Ter-mah's husband, then Ter-mah's daughters' husbands, followed by Javak-yat, who was Kath-mah's husband, and finally Ter-yat's daughters' children. When the introductions were completed, Ter-mah fed the visitors.

After the meal, Dar and Nir-yat retreated to the chamber of Kath-mah and her husband. Their aunt and uncle were eager for news, especially of Dar's rebirth. Javak-yat seemed pleased to have a new niece, but Kath-mah's reaction was more complex. She turned to her husband. "Your sisters certainly have Muth la's favor," she said. "Zeta-yat became queen. Zoy-yat became matriarch. And Zor-yat, who already had five daughters, now has six!"

"Muth la favored you also, Mother," said Dar. "Very few survived battle, but your son was spared."

Kath-mah snorted. "Spared? Small difference it makes. I never see him."

"We seldom see his brother, either," said Javak-yat to his wife. "That doesn't mean he's lost to us."

"Kadat lives in his wife's hall!" retorted Kath-mah. "He already has daughter. Kovok lives with goats!"

"War is hard," said Dar. "Even sons who live may have wounded spirits. Give him time to heal."

"Dargu-yat," said Javak-yat, "you were with our son. Will you speak of him?"

Dar's emotions ambushed her. She felt the urge to pour out her feelings to Kovok-mah's parents, but she didn't dare. Instead, she was stammering about his bravery when Nir-yat interrupted. "War was hard on my sister also. It pains her to speak of it."

"Pardon me, Dargu-yat," said Javak-yat. "I didn't realize what I was asking."

Dar nodded politely. "You are as thoughtful as your son."

Kath-mah looked at Dar quizzically; then her expression turned irritated. "Well, war may have brought you pain, Dargu-yat, but it made you urkzimmuthi mother. Kovok became goat."

*   *   *

The next morning, Javak-yat left to tend his cheese-making. Kath-mah remained in the hanmuthi to host a "samuth." Dar broke down the word into "see" and "mother," which described a samuth's function perfectly. Unblessed sons came by to introduce themselves, flirt, and hopefully impress an unblessed mother. Nir-yat had been to many samuths and knew all the sons who dropped by. She was in her element—perfectly comfortable and totally in command. Dar found her playful, witty, and sometimes rather lewd.

If it hadn't been for Dar's presence, only Nir-yat's favorites would have bothered to show up. Word was out, however, that a new unblessed mother was at the samuth. Almost every unblessed son in the surrounding settlement dropped by. Dar evoked the same reactions in every one—curiosity and disappointment. The encounters were often difficult because orcs didn't resort to polite pretense in awkward situations. Many sons thought Dar was interesting, but all found her ugly and communicated that impression—sometimes tactfully and sometimes not. The samuth lasted through the midday meal and late into the afternoon. Throughout, Dar yearned for Kovok-mah, yet dreaded he might appear. He did not.

After the last visitor departed, Nir-yat whispered to Dar, "Your first samuth is always hard. Every son comes. Next time, only those who like you will."

"Then I'll have no visitors," Dar whispered back.

"Don't believe that! Sons are drawn by more than looks. Jvar-yat is as ugly as goat; yet she's blessed."

Dar smiled, though she wondered if Nir-yat's reference to a goat was intentional.

Twenty-five

♛

Dar and Nir-yat left the following morning accompanied by two mothers who wished to visit the Yat clan hall. The company caused Dar to forgo visiting Kovokmah again, for she feared word might reach Kath-mah's ears. Already, Dar feared Kovok-mah's muthuri would be a barrier to her happiness. That concern increased Dar's despondency over leaving.

The weather mirrored Dar's mood. Dank fog obscured the road and hid the mountains. Cold drizzle arrived by late morning. Everyone walked silently, which suited Dar, who had no desire to chat. The four spent the night huddled beneath a ledge, unable to light a fire. The next day, drizzle turned to steady rain. Dar was thoroughly bedraggled when she reached home.

Warmth and food eased Dar's body, but not her mind. The brief reunion with Kovok-mah only increased her pain over their separation. Her yearning seemed as physical as thirst or hunger, and just as necessary to satisfy. Yet Dar knew there was little chance of that happening soon.

Dar hid her feelings as best she could, assured by the knowledge that there is no scent for unhappiness. Each day, she worked hard in the kitchen, in hope that keeping busy would ease her heartache. Her cooking improved, but not her spirits. She thought no one had noticed her mood until she was summoned to speak with the matriarch.

When Dar entered the Great Chamber, she found Muth-yat alone, peering out a window. The sky was gray and the brown peaks had their first dusting of snow. The matriarch turned and smiled. "Dargu-yat, I'm pleased to see you." She walked over and touched Dar's tattoo. "Jvar-yat did fine work."

Dar returned Muth-yat's smile before bowing. "I'm much pleased with it, Mother."

"As you should be. Are you also pleased to be urkzim-muthi?"

"Very much."

"I understand why, for I have lived among washa-vokis," said Muth-yat. "When my muthuri was queen, I often visited them. Old washavoki king ruled then. He was different from his son."

"So I've heard," said Dar.

"Washavokis have no Fathma," said Muth-yat. "That's why son is king now, even though he's cruel and has strange desires."

"He favors killing," said Dar. "I've seen that myself."

"Without Fathma, we might have queens equally cruel and strange."

"I've heard of Fathma," said Dar, "but I'm not sure what it is."

"Fathma is special spirit," said Muth-yat. "Muth la created it long ago and gave it to first queen. It bestowed wisdom, compassion, and fortitude. Before queen died, she passed Fathma to mother most fit to rule. If old washavoki king had possessed Fathma, he wouldn't have passed it to his unworthy son, and washavokis would have better king now."

"So Fathma doesn't pass from mother to daughter?" asked Dar.

"Sometimes it does, but often it doesn't. Muth la guides queen before she dies."

"When you took me to place where I was reborn, you

mentioned Fathma. You said it returned to urkzimmuthi there."

"I'm pleased you remember," said Muth-yat. "Fathma is passed when queen approaches death. When washavokis destroyed Tarathank, they killed queen and everyone around her. Fathma was lost, and there was no queen. Chaos followed. Many died and much was lost."

"How did Fathma return?" asked Dar.

"Child was born who possessed it. She grew up to be queen." Muth-yat grasped Dar's hand and leaned closer. "If urkzimmuthi lose Fathma again, evil times will return. I tell you this because it's my greatest fear." Muth-yat's face grew grim. "When Fathma passed to my sister, she became queen. Now she lives among washavokis in Taiben. There are no urkzimmuthi mothers there, only sons. She is sick. She may die."

Dar had seen the mage who was "treating" the orc queen's illness. He didn't seem capable of charity. *More likely, he's making her sick.* "Sons should take queen from that place," Dar said.

"I agree," said Muth-yat. "Yet sons obey queen, not me."

"Does she want to stay?"

"She says she does."

"Why?"

"I don't know."

Though Dar felt uneasy giving advice, she thought she must speak up. "I think you should visit queen and find out."

"Mage has forbidden it."

"Urkzimmuthi do not obey mage."

"Queen does," said Muth-yat. "Mothers are turned away. None have seen her for five winters. Dargu, I think mage has used magic to gain power over queen."

Dar thought it was possible, but she was puzzled why Muth-yat confided in her. Such matters seemed to concern the Council of Matriarchs, not someone like her. Then Dar realized where the talk was heading, and the thought twisted her stomach.

Muth-yat smelled Dar's fear, but continued anyway. "Dargu-yat, you're urkzimmuthi mother and daughter of queen's sister. Yet washavokis are fools. They will not see this. You could go to Taiben. You could see queen and learn what has happened to her."

As Muth-yat waited for a reply, she smelled Dar's fear grow stronger. "Mother," said Dar in a shaky voice. "You're wise to say washavokis will not see me as urkzim-muthi. They'll treat me like mother of their kind. This mark on my forehead means anyone who kills me will receive gift. Though I fear death, I fear something else even more. I will have urkzimmuthi spirit, but be compelled to live like washavoki." Tears began to flow down Dar's face. "It's horrible life, with no dignity or peace. Our speech lacks words for cruelties washavokis inflict on mothers."

Dar fell to her knees before Muth-yat. "Please, Mother, don't ask me to go. My chest will break."

Muth-yat stroked Dar's hair as she would a child's. "Dargu-yat, Dargu-yat," she murmured. "I won't ask you to go against your chest. You're my sister's daughter. Stay in our hall and be happy. I'll find another way."

Dar wiped her tears, feeling both relieved and ashamed. "Shashav, Mother."

Muth-yat smiled. "Go back to kitchen. Think no more of queens or mages."

Muth-yat had returned to the window when her sister entered the chamber. "Snows are coming," said Zor-yat. "Dargu should leave while road is clear."

"Dargu isn't leaving," said Muth-yat.

"What?"

"She's afraid," replied Muth-yat. "I don't blame her. You know how washavokis treat mothers."

"Dargu was washavoki. She's used to it."

"She's urkzimmuthi now."

"Which means she must obey you," retorted Zor-yat.

"I believe she must go willingly. Otherwise, fear will lead to her death."

"So what? She's going to die anyway."

"If she's to achieve our goal, her chest must be behind it," replied Muth-yat.

"But you said it's not," said Zor-yat, showing her irritation. "All our efforts have been pointless. *And* she's living in *my* hanmuthi, not yours. I have to call her daughter and eat her terrible cooking."

Muth-yat smiled. "Gar-yat says it's improving."

"Then serve it in *your* hanmuthi!" Zor-yat sighed. "Sister, we've spoken like washavokis and what have our meaningless words gained us? Welcoming Dargu hasn't worked."

"Not yet," replied the matriarch. "But we haven't learned Dargu's secret. When we do, things may change."

"Time's running out," said Zor-yat. "I hear our sister calls for more sons to kill for washavoki king."

"Hai. She wants them in Taiben before winter."

"More sons to die! What madness!"

"Yet, we must obey," said Muth-yat. "Zor, discover Dargu's secret. When sons leave for Taiben, I want Dargu with them."

Twenty-six

♛

Dar was stirring a pot of stew when she glanced up. Washavoki soldiers encircled her. They held out bowls, expecting to be served. "Go away," she told them. "I'm urkzimmuthi now."

The soldiers moved closer. "You're no piss eye," said one.

"I am. I've been reborn." Dar held up a hand to show them her claws, but her nails were flat. She stared at them, puzzled.

"You don't scare us."

A soldier thrust his bowl at Dar's face. "Fill it."

Dar looked about, but saw only washavokis. After she ladled stew into the soldier's bowl, others held out theirs. Dar served the men, all the while wondering how they got there. They crowded closer, jostling her. Dar ladled stew as quickly as she could, but the mob never seemed to thin. Then a soldier pushed his way through the others, shouting in a gurgling voice. "You stole my dagger." Dar knew it would be Muut even before she saw him. He glared at her with dead eyes, his crushed throat a dark purple. "You're a thief!"

"You no longer needed it," said Dar.

"Give it back!" Muut lunged, and Dar threw stew in his face.

"Serve the man," said a steely voice, "and this time, mind you get it in his bowl."

As Dar dipped her ladle in the pot, Muut disappeared.

In his place stood Murdant Kol. He smiled coldly. "You're still my woman," he said, holding out a bowl. "Do as you're told."

Dar started to obey, but when she lifted the ladle, Murdant Kol's bowl uncoiled like a snake and became a whip.

Dar woke with a start, moist with sweat. Moonlight streamed though the window, illuminating Nir-yat and Thir-yat, who were sound asleep. Dar gradually calmed down, but not completely. Her dream left a lingering disquiet that she couldn't shake. It was the feeling that, despite all that had happened, she still belonged to the regiment.

After a long while, Dar drifted off to uneasy dreams. She couldn't remember them the following morning, but they heightened her need to see Kovok-mah. When snow covered the pastures, Kovok-mah would winter with his muthuri. Dar craved one more chance to have him to herself. Spurred by that thought, Dar went to tell Zor-yat that she would be visiting the Mah clan again. Zor-yat looked surprised. "Nir said nothing of this."

"She doesn't know," said Dar. "I'm going alone."

"You know way?"

"Hai, Muthuri."

Zor-yat appeared intrigued. "You're going to see some son, aren't you?"

Dar didn't reply.

"Come, Dargu. It's not my brother's company you seek. Nor Kath-mah's."

"It's their son's," replied Dar in a low voice. "We care for each other."

Zor-yat smiled. "Of course! You traveled together." She made a show of sniffing the air. "My nose has been unwise. Most unwise!" Her eyes narrowed. "How long have you had kept this secret?"

Dar felt as though a weight had been lifted from her chest. "Ever since I arrived."

"I see," said Zor-yat, annoyed that she hadn't noticed before. Yet, on reflection, she realized why she had ignored the signs; it never occurred to her that a son could have feelings for a washavoki.

"Muthuri, I wish to be blessed."

"Blessed! This *is* serious! Have either of you spoken to Kath-mah?"

"Not yet."

Zor-yat's expression grew thoughtful. "I think that was wise. Kath-mah can be difficult. It's best I talk to her first, muthuri to muthuri."

"You'd do that?"

"Of course. You're my daughter, and Kovok-mah is fine choice."

Dar's face lit up. "I can't wait to tell Kovok!"

"Oh, you shouldn't see him until I speak with his muthuri. Then he can visit you here. That's more proper."

Dar's excitement dampened, and it showed. Zor-yat hugged her. "Waiting is hard when feelings are strong."

"Hai, Muthuri."

"Then I'll leave today to speak to Kath-mah. If things go well, your velazul will be here soon."

Two evenings later, Zor-yat arrived in the hall where Kath-mah lived. Everyone was surprised to see her, for she rarely visited. As Zor-yat shook the sleet from her cloak, Kath-mah's sister greeted her. "Welcome, sister's husband's sister. Your errand must be urgent to travel in such weather."

Zor-yat smiled ruefully. "What we muthuris do for our children! I'm nearly frozen." She bowed her head to Kath-mah. "Brother's wife, it's good to see you." After Kath-mah returned her greeting, Zor-yat asked, "Where's your son?"

Kath-mah wrinkled her nose. "Still with his goats."

Zor-yat was pleased to hear this, but she said, "How unfortunate, since my errand concerns him."

"How?" asked Kath-mah.

Zor-yat regarded her brother. "Will you leave us, Javak? This is muthuri talk."

Kath-mah escorted her visitor into her chamber, where the two huddled together. "What is this matter, Zor-yat?"

"After my daughter visited here, she told me of her interest in your son. She's quite serious about him."

Kath-mah beamed. "Nir-yat and my Kovok? It would be perfect match!"

"Not Nir-yat. Dargu-yat."

Kath-mah's expression darkened. "Your washavoki daughter?"

"She's not washavoki. She's been reborn."

"Her spirit has been reborn," retorted Kath-mah, "but not her body. You can't breed sheep and goats."

"Nevertheless, your son's drawn to her. He's been her velazul for several moons."

"How do you know this?"

"Dargu told me. She visits him at his goat hut."

"And she wants my blessing?"

"Dargu-yat will never bear daughters nor have her own hanmuthi, but her sisters will take care of her. If you give your blessing, Kovok-mah will have pleasant life."

"Pleasant? Ha! Ask your brother how it is to have no daughters! My nieces are above me. Someday their daughters will be also."

"So what should I tell Dargu?" asked Zor-yat.

"Tell her that Kovok is forbidden to see her."

"I'm not surprised by your answer, but I fear its consequences."

"What consequences?"

"Those reborn have special gifts. Like Velasa-pah,

Dargu-yat has magic powers. How else could one so ugly attract your son? If you tear him from her, she will break his chest."

"So what am I to do?"

"Send your son to Taiben, and Dargu will forget him. By his return, she'll have different velazul."

"Are you sure?"

"She's my daughter. I understand her ways."

Kath-mah frowned. "You've brought ill tidings. All my choices are hard ones."

"This can end well," said Zor-yat. "Think on what I've said. If you send Kovok-mah to Taiben, let us know so Dargu can begin to forget him."

Dar's mood swung between optimism and despair during Zor-yat's absence. She hadn't felt so powerless since being branded and sent to the regiment. Her fate seemed completely out of her control; all she could do was wait for Kath-mah's decision.

At times, Dar was almost giddy with the prospect of being blessed. Other times, she tried to steel herself for the worst and imagine how she would cope without Kovok-mah. She felt that unique circumstances had brought them together and the love that resulted could never be duplicated. Dar's first samuth seemed proof. *If Kath-mah doesn't bless us, I'll spend my life alone.* Dar had heard of women who dedicated their lives to Karm, living apart to pray and toil until they walked the Dark Path. Once, Dar had envied such a life, but it seemed dreary after Kovok-mah had awakened her need for intimacy. She didn't want to grow old without love.

The fourth day after Zor-yat's departure, Dar was so anxious that Gar-yat sent her from the kitchen rather than have her ruin another dish. Dar spent the afternoon outside the gate, watching the road for her muthuri. It was nearly dark when Dar spied Zor-yat walking alone, her cloak whipped by the wind. Dar raced down the zig-zagged roadway and met her at the base of the mountain. "What news, Muthuri?"

"It's better than I hoped, Dargu."

"Will she bless me?"

"Not yet," replied Zor-yat. "But she'll allow Kovok-mah to see you. Don't be discouraged. This is hopeful."

"But I desire more than hope."

"My news surprised Kath-mah, and she needs time to think. When she does, I expect she'll see wisdom in this match. Look for Kovok-mah. He should visit soon."

Dar hugged Zor-yat. "Shashav, Muthuri."

Zor-yat continued up the hill, glad that her hood and the darkness hid her face. Her deed felt unnatural, and she worried her expression might betray her. *Meaningless words leave foul taste.* Yet Zor-yat believed that if her ploy worked, Muth la would forgive her.

Twenty-seven

♛

Zor-yat's news briefly raised Dar's spirits, but only a visit from Kovok-mah could provide real assurance. Dar waited for one ever more anxiously. Her mood soon infected the entire hanmuthi, so all her sisters began to watch the road for travelers. Five days after Zor-yat's return, Nir-yat appeared in the kitchen. Dar was elated until she saw Nir-yat's subdued expression. "Dargu, Javak-yat is here with news."

Dar felt a cold sensation in her stomach. "What is it?"

"It's best you hear from him."

Dar hurried to the hanmuthi. She found Javak-yat seated with his sister and drinking hot herb water. Expecting the worst, Dar interrupted their conversation. "Uncle, where's Kovok-mah?"

Javak-yat appeared surprised by Dar's urgency. "He's gone to Taiben."

"Taiben?"

"Hai. All clans must send sons to kill for washavoki king. Our queen . . ."

"This is my fault," said Dar. "You sent him away because of me." She burst out sobbing.

Javak-yat stared at Dar in astonishment. "Sister, why is your new daughter making such strange noises?"

"I think she's sick," replied Zor-yat, regarding Dar sternly. "Dargu, go rest in your chamber."

Javak-yat watched Dar hurry away, then gave his sister a suspicious look. "Why did you visit Kath-mah?"

"Muthuri business," said Zor-yat. "If Kath-mah didn't tell you, I won't either."

Nir-yat was waiting in the chamber when Dar rushed in and collapsed on her bed. Though as astonished as her uncle by Dar's tears, she sensed their nature and cause. "I'm sorry, Dargu."

By force of will, Dar stifled her sobs, but nothing could stifle her despair. "Kath-mah doesn't understand," she said.

"Understand what?"

"She has sent Kovok to his death."

"No muthuri would do that."

"No muthuri has seen what I have. Washavoki king cares not how many sons are slaughtered."

"Our queen would never allow . . ."

"She doesn't understand either." Dar turned her face to the wall.

After a while, Dar heard Nir-yat leave the room. Dar lay on her bed, consumed by misery. Before, she had worried that Kovok-mah would be forbidden to see her. Javak-yat's news made her fear that Kovok-mah would die. His death seemed likely—even inevitable—and Dar felt responsible. *He barely escaped the first time*, she thought, recalling the final battle's carnage. In her mind's eye, each slain orc became Kovok-mah.

Dar was still on her bed, when she heard Zor-yat's voice. "Dargu, this is not your fault. All clans must send sons to Taiben."

Dar turned to face her muthuri. "Kovok just returned from battle. Why must he kill again?"

"Only unblessed sons are called. After this summer, few remain."

"He would have been safe if Kath-mah had blessed us."

"Blessings take time," said Zor-yat. "She'll do it when he returns."

"Did your brother say that?"

"Hai, but you're not supposed to know. Don't speak to him of it."

"So, I'm not reason why Kovok's gone."

"Of course not. Our queen is reason. It's her command. Be patient. You'll be blessed."

"Thwa, I won't," said Dar, her voice dull. "I know it in my chest."

"Why do you say that?"

"Because Kovok won't return."

"Have you had vision?" ask Zor-yat, sounding concerned.

"Thwa, but I've seen war."

"Queen's command has brought sorrow to many mothers, not just you."

Dar was silent, but her eyes welled with tears. Zor-yat, having lived among washavokis, understood what they signified. She searched Dar's face for other hints of what she was thinking. Meanwhile, Dar was engaged in an inner struggle and oblivious to the scrutiny. She might obtain her heart's desire, but only if she took a deadly risk.

Zor-yat patiently waited. She had said all that she could. Only time would tell if her words had the desired effect. After a while, she detected the scent of fear. It gradually grew stronger until it filled the room. Then Dar spoke. "Muth-yat was right."

Zor-yat feigned puzzlement. "Right about what?"

"I must go to Taiben."

"Taiben? Whatever for?"

"To see our queen and discover why she commands sons to kill. If I succeed, I may save Kovok-mah."

"How will you do this?"

"I'm not sure, but my chest tells me I must try."

After Dar spoke with Zor-yat, she was sent to see Muth-yat. The matriarch was pleased by Dar's decision.

"I'm certain Muth la has guided you," she said. "Zor-yat must be proud. You are worthy daughter."

Dar acknowledged the praise with a bow. Then Muth-yat surprised her by having washavoki clothes brought in. "You'll need these for your journey." It was obvious that the shabby cloak and shift had been carefully selected, for they were typical of the clothing worn by women in the regiment. Dar thought they were too clean, but otherwise perfect.

"Dargu," said Muth-yat. "I have no idea what you'll find and can give you little advice or help. I'll tell sons of our clan to aid you, but rely on your own wisdom. When in doubt, follow your chest."

Dar thanked the matriarch and an awkward silence followed until Muth-yat told Dar to prepare for her journey. Dar left carrying the bundle of clothes and wondering if she had been manipulated. Nevertheless, she was resolved to go to Taiben. Only there could she expose King Kregant's treachery, and only there would she be with Kovok-mah.

Dar didn't directly return to Zor-yat's hanmuthi. Instead she went outside to soil her washavoki clothing. The terraced fields looked as desolate as the mountains beyond. Dar shivered, more at the prospect of the days ahead than from the cold. Tossing the clothes on the ground, she began to step on them.

Zna-yat approached. "I hear we're going to Taiben."

Dar stopped grinding her shift into the dirt. "Our clan sent you to kill?"

"Thwa. Have you forgotten that you bit my neck?"

"You need not come."

"If you think that, you're mistaken. My life is tied to yours."

"I won't need your protection. Kovok-mah will be there."

"How can you be sure?"

"Why wouldn't he be?"

"Never before have sons been called to Taiben this time of year," replied Zna-yat. "Washavokis like to kill when it's warm. Something strange is happening."

"What?"

"I have no idea, but I think you shouldn't go."

"I have to, Zna-yat. Only I can do what must be done."

"Our muthuri and her sister are behind this, aren't they?"

"Hai. Do you question their wisdom?"

"They are wise," said Zna-yat. "Yet, what is best for clan may not be best for you."

"I'm frightened, but I've made up my mind. Don't frighten me more."

Zna-yat bowed his head and said no more, though Dar sensed he wished to. He left soon afterward, and Dar finished soiling her garments alone.

Zna-yat had to obtain armor and a reed shelter, and this delayed Dar's departure a day. She imagined that the journey to Taiben would be a long one and was surprised to learn they would reach King Kregant's capital in two days if the weather held. It was frigid and the sky threatened snow when they set out in the early morning. Zna-yat walked beside Dar, swathed in iron, his breath whitening his helmet as it froze. Seven other orcs accompanied him as part of the clan's quota for the army. Good-byes had been said inside the warm hall, but Niryat and Thir-yat waved at Dar from a window. Dar waved back for as long as she could see them.

The road was called the New Road, though it had been built in King Kregant's grandfather's time. Constructed to encourage trade, the route cut through a steep ridge that had formerly kept the orcs isolated. The road was less traveled than in earlier days, but it remained in good shape. A messenger on horseback could travel between Taiben and the Yat clan hall in a single day, although it had been years since one had done so. During the current king's reign, mainly orc soldiers used the road. Far more went to Taiben than returned.

Owing to the cold, Dar still wore orcish clothing. Her kefs and neva were made of thick, warm wool, as was her hooded cloak. Dar's boots had belonged to an orc child and had bulbous toes to accommodate claws. Thus outfitted, Dar was comfortable as she solemnly marched with her kin. There was no banter, for everyone's thoughts dwelled on battle. While only Dar and Zna-yat had witnessed war, the others had heard grim tales.

The party camped for the night inside the passage cut into the ridge. Although it was the highest point on the road, its walls offered shelter from the wind. Within its confines, Dar slept bundled in her cloak. As evening approached on the following day, they spied Taiben from a hilltop and stopped to gaze at the city. It crowned the only high place on the plain below. The city's walls seemed to squeeze its buildings into a confusing jumble. The royal palace dominated the cityscape—a fortress within a fortress—with high walls that sprouted towers.

Zna-yat pointed to the orc garrison. It lay outside the city, enclosed by a separate wall that Dar had expected to be circular. It was not. "Where is Embrace of Muth la?" she asked.

"Each barracks is one," replied Zna-yat.

Dar noted that almost all the buildings within the garrison's walls were circular. There were many dozens, packed close together in long rows. "And washavoki soldiers move among them?"

"Hai, but they dwell in Taiben. Only washavoki mothers live in camp."

Trapped inside, Dar thought. She studied the gated garrison. Human soldiers paced atop its walls. Even from a distance, it resembled a prison.

Twenty-eight

♛

Dar arrived at the garrison on Zna-yat's back, hidden in his rolled-up shelter. Unable to see, she relied on other senses to tell her what was happening. Dar assumed they were at the gate when Zna-yat halted and she heard a human voice. "What clan you?" it asked in abominable Orcish.

"Yat," replied Zna-yat.

"More come?" asked the voice.

"Thwa," replied Zna-yat.

"Follow this one. It show house," said the voice before switching to human speech. "Murdant, take the piss eyes to barracks seventeen. Have women bring them supper."

"Aye, sir," said a second voice.

Dar heard hinges creak; then Zna-yat began to move again. He walked awhile before lifting the shelter from his shoulders. Dar remained within her hiding place while the orcs settled in. Then she heard Zna-yat's voice boom out. "Gather round! I have brought someone with me." The shelter was unrolled. Dar sat up, still dressed in her orcish clothes, and gazed about the room. Over two dozen astonished orcs stared at her. Dar rose to greet them and assert her authority. "I am Dargu-yat," she said in Orcish, "reborn urkzimmuthi by ancient magic. My muthuri is Zor-yat, sister of queen."

Zna-yat spoke next. "I am Zna-yat, her brother." He gestured toward his companions. "These sons are Dargu-yat's clan kin."

Whether it was Dar's bearing, the tattoo on her chin, her fluent Orcish, the presence of her kin, or a combination of all these things, the strangers treated her with deference. They bowed and returned the greetings. These formalities were interrupted when Zna-yat, who had been keeping watch, warned that washavokis were approaching. Dar hid just before the hide flap on the doorway moved aside and two women entered the barracks to serve porridge to the new arrivals. After the women left, Dar emerged from hiding to explain her actions. "I hid because washavokis lack sense," she said. "They wouldn't understand I'm urkzimmuthi. They would try to prevent me from seeing my aunt, though it's Muth la's will that we speak together."

An orc bowed low to Dar. "Pardon me, Dargu-yat, but our queen will only speak to sons."

"Her sisters think evil magic forces her to say that. I was sent to discover if that is so."

"How will you do that?" asked another orc.

"I don't know yet."

"We know one thing," said Zna-yat. "No washavoki should see Dargu-yat."

"But they're everywhere," said an orc.

"Do they come inside this room?" asked Dar.

"Only woe mans. They bring food and firewood."

"Set guard," said Dar. "Warn me whenever they approach."

An orc wearing a leader's cape bowed to Dar, then posted a sentry by the doorway.

I should be safe within here, thought Dar as she gazed about. The building's single room was just large enough to accommodate three dozen orcs and their equipment. Though built by men, it resembled a hanmuthi. Circular walls marked the Embrace of Muth la, and a hearth was in its center. Because orcs slept sitting upright, the barracks was only twelve paces in diameter, and its occupants' massive bodies filled most of it. It would be a small refuge.

Outside were numerous other barracks, enough to accommodate many hundreds of orcs. Surrounding the barracks were high walls with a stout gate and washavoki soldiers. Dar's impression that the camp was a prison returned, and she regretted coming. Her task seemed overwhelming. *I was such a fool. How will I ever see the queen?* Even finding Kovok-mah seemed daunting. For all Dar knew, soldiers would capture her the instant she left the barracks. She felt trapped and teetered on the brink of panic.

Zna-yat must have smelled her fear, for he moved close to her. "Dargu, all sons here will help you."

Zna-yat's words reminded Dar that she need not do everything herself. *I'm a mother. I can lead, and I'm surrounded by strength and loyalty.* Bearing that in mind made her prospects seem less bleak. "Tomorrow, spread word among urkzimmuthi that I am here," she told Zna-yat. "Also find Kovok-mah."

"I'll do these things," said Zna-yat. "Now are you glad I came?"

Dar smiled slightly, exposing teeth that had begun to fade to white. "I was wise to bite your neck."

The following morning, Dar spoke with Magtha-jan. He wore a leader's cape because he had fought before. "Did you fight this summer?" asked Dar. "Were you at battle in valley of pines?"

Magtha-jan grimaced. "Hai, I was there."

"I was also."

Magtha-jan stared at Dar with the amazement of sudden recognition. "You were Muth Velavash! You blessed sons before battles."

"I did."

"Did you bless sons before battle in valley of pines?"

"Hai. Afterward, I led them home."

Magtha-jan made the sign of the Tree. "Mother, I'm glad Muth la sent you. I want to return home and kill no more."

"Magtha-jan, I don't know where my path will lead. Yet I hope your wish can be fulfilled."

Through her conversation Dar learned what happened after she deserted. Magtha-jan described how he survived the ambush and fought his way to the valley's entrance. There, he helped King Kregant's men repulse a series of attacks that left both sides mauled. Eventually, the enemy withdrew, and Kregant's remaining forces retreated. Magtha-jan had believed they were marching home until the army changed course and the orcs were ordered to attack a "washavoki holy place." Despite their small numbers, they took it easily. After soldiers "filled many wagons," the army headed homeward.

When Magtha-jan arrived at Taiben, he wasn't sent home. Instead, the queen ordered all orcs to remain at the garrison. It was nearly empty at first, because so few had survived the campaign. Since then, the garrison had been filling up as the clans sent sons to replenish the empty ranks. New regiments were forming, and some shieldrons had already seen action. Magtha-jan knew that they had killed some washavokis, but nothing else.

Dar learned little about the doings of the king's human soldiers, because Magtha-jan avoided washavokis whenever possible. Within the garrison, his sole contact was with the branded women who served food and brought fuel. Magtha-jan said orcs occasionally entered the palace to receive orders from their queen, but he had never done so. Few made those visits, which were both rare and brief. Otherwise, no orc set foot inside Taiben. Neither did they leave the garrison except to fight.

After speaking with Magtha-jan, Dar worried the

orcs would be less useful than she had hoped. King Kregant seemed careful to isolate them from their queen and also from himself. He was aided by the orcs' disdain for washavokis. Once again, her task seemed impossible.

"I've found Kovok-mah," said Zna-yat when he returned.

Dar's heart leaped at the news. "Where? Did you speak with him?"

"Only briefly. I told him you were here. He asks if you will see him."

"Hai! Hai! Hai! I'll go right now."

"That would be unsafe. There are washavokis everywhere."

"Then how can we meet?"

"He said wait until night. After washavokis lock woe mans in hall, most of them leave. There is empty barracks nearby. He'll be there."

After Zna-yat pointed out the barracks, there was nothing for Dar to do but wait. She was alone all afternoon while the orcs had weapon practice. Most of the newcomers had never wielded a sword or battle-ax and had to learn the skill. Dar hid among the piled shelters while they were gone and watched from the same place as terrified women served the evening porridge. They all appeared recently branded, and Dar recognized none of them. Dar ate after they left, then continued to wait for dark.

When twilight left the sky, Dar crept from the barracks. The moon had yet to rise. Dar had changed into her washavoki shift, hidden her dagger under it, and reluctantly abandoned her warm orcish boots. As the cold ground chilled Dar's bare feet, she peered about to get her bearings. The barracks were rows of black shapes, barely distinguishable in the darkness. Dar cautiously made her way toward the one where Kovok-mah waited.

The silent garrison seemed deserted until Dar spied movement on the surrounding wall. *A guard*, she thought, wondering why one was needed. *What's he guarding against? Attack? Escape? Both?* Whatever his purpose, he was alone and didn't seem a threat.

Dar reached the empty barracks. Its doorless opening was a patch of black. She stepped into the dark room and saw the pale light of two green eyes. She moved toward them. "Kovok?" she whispered.

"Hai."

Dar reached out and touched iron. Kovok-mah was in armor. She groped for his hand and grabbed it to pull it toward her breast. His arm wouldn't budge. "Kovok?"

"You shouldn't be here"

The coldness in his voice surprised Dar. "You asked me to come."

"You shouldn't be in Taiben. You must leave."

"Since when do sons tell mothers what to do?" asked Dar, trying to sound playful.

"That's my muthuri's wisdom."

"Do you mean same muthuri who will bless us?"

"Why do you speak foolishly?" said Kovok-mah. "She will never bless us."

"That's not what I heard."

"Did my muthuri speak to you?"

"Thwa, but . . ."

"Well, she spoke to me. She said giving love clouds judgment. That's why only muthuris decide who shall be blessed."

Dar pulled again at Kovok-mah's hand. It remained rigid. "Touch me."

"It's forbidden."

"Why?"

"Muthuri said so."

It irritated Dar that she couldn't see Kovok-mah,

while he could see her. She felt he was hiding. "I'm here because of you!"

"I didn't ask you to come. Leave and forget me."

"It's not that simple. I can't forget you."

"Muthuri says you will."

"She's wrong."

"Dargu-yat, you're urkzimmuthi mother now. How can you doubt Muthuri's wisdom?"

Dar felt betrayed. *One word from his muthuri, and he forsakes me. How could he change so quickly?* Then a terrible insight came. "You expected this! You *knew* we'd never be blessed!"

"Dargu-yat, please forget me."

"You *knew*! You *knew*!" Dar struck at the green eyes and hit the jaw below them. Kovok-mah remained still. She hit him again.

Dar was torn between rage and heartbreak. "Kusk washavoki!" she screamed. It was the foulest name she could think of. Then she rushed into the night, her vision blurred by tears. She ran heedlessly until someone stepped from the shadows and blocked her path. Before Dar could dart in another direction, a sword point pressed against her throat.

"Well, what do we have here?" said the soldier. "A birdie tryin' ta fly away?"

Twenty-nine

♛

Fear flushed Dar's mind of anger and sorrow. She knew what happened to women who deserted.

"Ye were daft ta think ye'd make it," said the soldier.

"I wasn't running away," said Dar. "He said if I met him, he'd give me shoes."

The soldier glanced down at Dar's bare feet. "Who?"

"I don't know his name. I just arrived."

Without lowering his sword, Dar's captor stepped closer to peer at her forehead. "That brand's not new."

"The orcs brought me. I've been their captive ever since the ambush. Look at my chin. That's how they mark women."

"Ye been with *orcs*?"

"Yes, and believe me, it's better here."

"Where ye must tup fer shoes?"

"He didn't mention tupping."

The soldier laughed. "Then ye're a greater fool than I thought."

Dar expected the man would try to rape her. Her mind raced, thinking what she might do. Having lost her bearings, she didn't know where to run, and trying to reach her dagger would be suicide. Only when he pulled up her shift could she attempt to stab him. *If I called for help, would the orcs reach me in time?* Unsure, Dar waited for the man to make the first move. Then he surprised her by sheathing his sword. "I'll take ye back ta yer barracks. If no one sees us, I'll not turn ye in."

"Thank you," muttered Dar.

"Don't do this again. More like that man had a prick waitin' than a pair o' slippers. And there's a murdant here who looks fer reasons ta flog women. Come on. Walk in front o' me."

"I don't know which way to go."

"Fer Karm's sake!" said the soldier, wrenching Dar's shoulder so she pointed toward the gate. "Move!"

As Dar began to walk, the soldier asked "What's yer name, birdie?"

"Leela."

"Well, Leela, I'm Five Fingers." The soldier poked Dar's back with the stump of his right wrist. "That's all I got. That's why I'm stuck here."

Dar halted before a rectangular stone building with high, narrow slits for windows and a heavy door that was barred on the outside. Five Fingers peered about before lifting the iron bar with his good hand. He pulled the door slightly open, then whispered to Dar. "Get inside, Leela. Hurry!"

Dar slipped past the door, and it shut behind her. As she gazed about, she heard the bar fall into place. Except for the embers of a dying fire, the room was pitch black. The air smelled of smoke, a latrine, and washavokis. Someone was weeping softly. The only other sounds were snoring and sleepers stirring in the straw, which lay thick around Dar's feet. It felt gritty and trampled. Beneath the straw was stone. Dar lowered herself to the floor and began to grope about. She moved only slightly before encountering a body. She drew back from it and encountered another.

Dar lay down. By then she had begun to shake. Her world had changed in an instant, stripping her of everything she had gained. It took awhile before the waves of fear and despair receded, and Dar felt calm enough to assess her predicament. Having grown accustomed to orcish honesty, what surprised her most was that either Zor-yat or Kath-mah had lied. Dar found it easier to believe Kovok-mah's muthuri was the culprit. Dar had never liked her. *She lied to Muthuri to avoid a scene, then used what she learned against me.* If Zor-yat had lied, the implications were far more upsetting. Dar didn't dwell on them, for she had a more immediate problem: Soldiers would arrive at dawn. *The orcs don't know I'm here. If Teeg or Kol finds me, I'll never leave this place alive.*

Dar took her dagger from its hiding place and tied its cord around her waist. It was her only preparation for the morning, and a desperate one. She couldn't survive a confrontation, only sell her life as dearly as possible. Dar regretted not practicing with the weapon, but she regretted other things more. *Sons will die because I failed. I let down Muth-yat, Muthuri, and all the urkzimmuthi.* As upset as she was with Kovok-mah, she couldn't bear the thought of him in battle. Yet there was nothing Dar could do except wait and hope for a miracle.

The moon rose. Light filtered through slits that served as both windows and chimneys. Dar saw the floor was covered with sleeping women, enough to serve several regiments. Embers smoked upon a hearth at the far wall. There the bodies were thickest. Only the floor about the open latrine was completely bare. The weeping had ceased, and the silent room resembled the aftermath of a massacre. Recalling Twea and her other slain comrades, Dar thought the women were as good as dead. *Just like me.*

Dar was still awake when someone pounded on the door at first light. A burly woman rose. "Kitchen duty!" she shouted, then called out names. Women groaned and rose. "Fire duty!" More names were rattled off. "The rest of ye, off yer arses."

"But, Marta, there's naught to do," said someone.

"Move the wood pile to the other end of the camp."

"But, we just finished moving it yesterday."

"Then move it again," said Marta. "Idle girls get flogged."

All the women rose. Dar mingled among them, trying to be inconspicuous. The door opened and some soldiers entered the building. Dar moved away from them. She noticed a woman who was throwing up, her face hidden as she knelt over the latrine. Dar rushed beside her and pretended to be sick also. The soldiers passed close by, selecting women for some work detail. Dar continued to make retching sounds until they left. Then she raised her head from the malodorous hole.

The woman next to her finished being sick and sat upright. "Dar?" she said in an incredulous voice.

Dar turned and her heart sank. "Hello, Neena."

Neena seemed about to say something, but started retching again. When the fit passed, she moaned. "I've been this way for two moons. Karm help me."

Dar regarded her former nemesis, trying to gauge her intentions. She saw no enmity; Neena only looked sick and forlorn.

"Dar, what happened to you? I thought you were dead. Who did that to your face?"

"Orcs."

"How cruel!"

"At least I'm alive," said Dar.

"We're the only ones who are."

Dar felt a surge of hope. "All the soldiers were killed?"

Neena's expression turned bitter. "Oh they did fine! We're the only *women* left." She sighed heavily. "I guess you did whatever was necessary. I did too. Can you forgive me?"

"Sure."

"At least you're not pregnant."

"Kol's child?"

Neena made a face. "Teeg's. Kol tossed me to him like a bone to a dog."

"How are that pair?" asked Dar, trying to keep her voice neutral.

"Kol's still riding high, but Teeg . . ." Neena smiled grimly. "He's dead."

"How?"

"He'd drink anything, even if it tasted off." Neena gave Dar a meaningful look. "Taren showed me a few tricks. There's a leaf . . ."

"Why are you telling me this?"

"We're going to be friends," said Neena. "I'm sharing my secret so you'll know you can trust me. Now, why did you come back?"

Dar doubted Neena's motives, but took care not to show it. "The orcs brought me."

"Your piss eye lover tire of you?"

"Yeah, and I don't want another."

"What's it like to tup one?"

"Not what you'd think. He was gentle and . . ."

"And what?" asked Neena, watching Dar with an intrigued expression.

"It doesn't matter now. When's your baby due?"

"Not soon enough to escape Frey's fate."

"She ended up in a loving home," said Dar.

"No, she didn't. Kol drowned her. He laughed when he told me."

"Kusk washavoki! Fas Muth la tak mat fath!" *Washavoki filth! May Muth la kill his soul!*

Neena stared at Dar with astonishment. "What did you just say?"

"May Karm slay his filthy soul!"

"He doesn't have one," said Neena. "I learned *that*

the hard way. Come on, we have to leave. The barracks is nearly empty."

Dar followed Neena as she hurried outside. There Neena spied Dar's dagger. "Get rid of that right now! If a soldier sees it, you'll be flogged for sure!"

Dar snapped the cord that tied the dagger to her waist and glanced around for a place to hide her weapon. "Shield me while I bury it," she said. Dar half expected Neena to decline the risk, but Neena covered her while she used her blade to dig a shallow hole.

After Dar buried her dagger, Neena exhaled with relief. "That was close," she said. "A flogging's bad enough. But worse, Kol would learn you're here. He hates you, Dar! And this time, you have no orc to save you."

Dar declined to tell Neena about Zna-yat and the others. *That will be my secret.* "How can I avoid him?"

"He doesn't come here often," said Neena. "Life in camp is different from on the march. Discipline is strict, and soldiers don't bother us as long as we look busy." Dar and Neena joined the procession of women headed for a huge stack of firewood. Throughout the morning, they moved logs from one side of the camp to the other. Whenever they could talk, they did.

Neena had wintered in Taiben the previous year, and she told Dar what to expect. The soldiers oversaw the women during the day, but didn't mingle otherwise. "The Queen's Man hates round bellies," said Neena, "so he locks us in at night. Tupping can get you flogged." Neena thought Dar could avoid Kol's notice, but only for a while. "Your brand's old, for one thing, and old hands are put in charge of scabheads. That means dealing with the murdants."

The more Dar learned, the more certain seemed her doom. She considered hiding among the orcs, but that would be a temporary solution. For the first time since anyone could remember, orc troops were being used in winter. Sooner or later they would take to the field, and Dar would have nowhere to hide.

"I know a safe place for you," said Neena as they hauled another load of logs.

"Where?"

"Taiben."

Dar snorted. "Sure. I'll leave right away."

"You have a contact—that guardsman who got you work in the king's kitchen tent."

"He might be dead."

"And he might not."

"It doesn't matter either way. He'll never know I'm here."

"I know someone who could pass a message."

"Neena, why are you doing this?"

"I hate Kol as much as he hates you. I'd love to spite him."

"And helping me will do that?"

Neena grinned. "Yes! I'll hide from him what he wants most."

Thirty

♛

Dar wondered if a miracle had occurred. Neena's help was as unexpected as her change of heart. *Has she really changed?* It seemed possible. *She could have turned me in and I'd have never known.* That seemed better proof of Neena's trustworthiness than her admission that she had poisoned Teeg. Also, it was easy to believe that spite motivated Neena. It fit her character.

Nevertheless, Dar was cautious—especially with Neena's messenger. He was a soldier who appeared alongside Dar as she carried firewood. "Heared ye have a message," he said in a low voice. "Keep walkin' and say it."

Dar glanced at him. His greasy face had a shifty look, but he was her only hope. "It's for a guardsman. Can you get it to him?"

The soldier's face wrinkled with contempt. "A pretty boy? Aye, I know where they drink."

"He's a murdant. Blond and big. When last I saw him, he had a short beard. His name is Cron."

"And what am I ta say?"

"Ask him to tell his countryman that Twea's mother is here and needs to go to Taiben."

"That's a riddle, not a message. Who's this countryman?"

"Cron will know. You need not."

"Have it yer way," said the soldier. He turned and strolled away.

When escaping camp seemed a possibility, Dar's fear of being recognized heightened. Only action lessened her anxiety. Though it might be days before her message achieved results—if it ever did—Dar made what preparations she could. When it was time to serve the orcs, Dar served Zna-yat's barracks. Once the food was delivered, she convinced the scabheads that she didn't need their help. After they left, Dar said in Orcish, "Food is Muth la's gift. Tonight, you'll serve yourselves. I must speak with my brother concerning our queen." Then she and Zna-yat had a private talk.

"Why didn't you return?" asked Zna-yat.

"Have you spoken to Kovok-mah?"

"Hai. He said you ran away."

"Did he tell you why?"

"Hai, Dargu. My chest is heavy."

"Mine, also. But I've found way to see our queen. I must stay with washavokis awhile."

"Is that safe?"

"Nothing's safe. Yet I think it's my path."

Zna-yat bowed. "How can I help?"

"Wait for my message. It may come from washavoki."

"From woe man?"

"Probably hairy-faced one."

"I'll wait and do whatever you say."

Dar began to rise, then halted. "Zna, it may be that I'll never see you again. If that's so, remember this . . ." Dar stroked Zna-yat's face as her eyes welled with tears. ". . . I was glad and proud to be your sister."

Dar lay upon the straw-covered floor of the women's barracks. Though she was tired from a day of hauling and stacking wood, she was too jumpy to fall asleep easily. Being with the women made her vulnerable, but if Sevren was to help her, she must remain where he could find her. Despite that rationale, she felt reckless. *Maybe Sevren's dead or living elsewhere. If not, he probably has a woman.* Dar was surprised that hadn't occurred to her before. *Anyway, why would he want to help me? Because I kissed him once?* Dar felt naive. *I did my best to discourage him.* A disturbing question arose. *If he does help me, what will he expect in return?* The answer was all too easy to imagine. *Sevren's no Murdant Kol,* Dar told herself. *He wouldn't force me.* Yet doubt remained. *How can I be certain?* Dar realized she was certain of nothing. As in the game of knockem, she had cast the bones. Only time would show how they would fall.

The following day was filled with drudgery and anxiety, but uneventful. Dar kept aloof and tried to be inconspicuous, though she feared her tattoo drew attention. She didn't serve the orcs that night. Instead she cleaned huge cooking pots, glad they hid her face as she scrubbed their insides.

Dar's third morning in the women's barracks began like the previous ones. Someone pounded on the door. Marta rose and called out names for kitchen and fire duty and told the remaining women to move the woodpile again. When the door opened, a murdant was waiting outside. Behind him were three guardsmen wearing blue and scarlet, one mounted on a horse.

"Listen up!" said the murdant. "Here's a treat fer lucky bitches. These guardsmen got a stable ta be mucked. Indoors work with nice warm horseshit. Step lively if yer chosen."

The guardsman on horseback was Murdant Cron, and he began pointing at different women, seemingly at random. He would utter, "That one," and the murdant from the camp would have her come forward. After a dozen selections, Dar began to fear that she wouldn't be chosen. *Perhaps he doesn't see me!* Then Murdant Cron pointed at her. "That one." As Dar hurried to join the

women standing behind the horse, Neena whispered,
"Good luck!"

Murdant Cron chose five more women to clean the
stables, then handed a bag to the murdant from the
camp. It looked like it contained bottles. "For your
help," he said.

The murdant peeked inside the bag and grinned. "Always happy ta oblige tha guard. They're yers fer tha day."

Murdant Cron addressed the assembled women.
"Follow me." Then he led the procession to the gate. He
gave the soldiers guarding it another bag. While they
opened the gate, he spoke to the women. "Stick close together, and do na try anything foolish. Outside these
walls there's a bounty on your heads." Then he rode
through the open gate. The branded women followed,
while the two guardsmen walked on either side like herd
dogs minding a flock.

Zna-yat watched Dar leave. He had been sitting inside
an empty barracks to watch the women's building ever
since Dar had spoken to him. Zna-yat wore full battle
armor and his broadsword lay unsheathed upon his lap.
He looked menacing, and anyone who spied him kept
their distance. For the first time in his life, Zna-yat
wished he understood the washavoki tongue, for it
would have helped him understand what he had just witnessed.

Dargu didn't look fearful, Zna-yat thought. *Perhaps
she planned this.* He recalled the blue and scarlet washavokis. *Dargu and Tahwee spent time among them.* Zna-
yat thought they might be somehow different from other
washavokis. *My cousin will know.* Zna-yat rose to find
him.

Kovok-mah stood alone in the practice field, hewing a
tree stump with his sword. Each blow resounded

throughout the garrison. He was about to strike again when he heard someone say, "You must be very angry at that stump."

Kovok-mah pivoted. "Father's sister's son, what brings you here?"

"Washavokis have taken Dargu-yat away."

Kovok-mah hit the tree stump with such force that it split in two. "This is my fault! She came because of me! She thought we were to be blessed."

Zna-yat regarded his cousin curiously. "Why would she think that?"

"I don't know." Kovok-mah slumped as though his armor had suddenly grown heavier. "I called her foolish."

"Dargu-yat is never that. I think she wanted washavokis to take her. They wore blue and red."

"Those soldiers guard washavoki king. Why would Dargu wish to go with them?"

"She wants to see our queen. You're not sole reason why Dargu came to Taiben. My muthuri played her part."

"It doesn't matter," said Kovok-mah. "Dargu's words still pain my ears. She called me . . ." His expression grew even more miserable. "I'll seek battle. Kill many."

"Because you desire to be killed yourself? Remember when we spoke in Tarathank? You knew this day was coming."

Kovok-mah hung his head. "Dargu said same thing."

"In Tarathank, you said your feelings were Muth la's doing. I believe you showed wisdom. Show it again. Muth la did not change your chest so you would seek death."

"Since when do you know Muth la's will?"

"I know Dargu-yat walks Muth la's path. I think you and I were meant to follow."

"How?"

"Remain here and find out."

*　　*　　*

Neena was hauling wood when she felt a hand grab her breast. She spun around to face the soldier who had carried Dar's message. He smiled lewdly. "I saw yer bitch friend leave. I want my pay."

"Keep your hands off me!" hissed Neena. "We could be seen!"

"I heared men at the gate got brandy. All I'm gettin' is a tup."

"Where would I get brandy? That was the guardsman's doing."

"I spent half the night findin' that pretty boy. All *they* did was open the gate."

"And if we get caught, *I'll* be flogged."

"Stiff-neck rules! Runnin' errands ta get what I used ta have fer free!"

Neena forced a seductive smile. "You'll be glad you delivered that message."

"Then, hurry up and make me glad. There's an empty barracks . . ."

"First, you must do something else."

"Ye didn't say nothin' 'bout somethin' else!"

"I just want to know her message."

"Maybe I fergot it."

Neena moved closer and spoke in a low, sultry voice. "I'll make you very, *very* glad you remembered."

"Tell yer countryman that Tweet's ma wants ta go ta Taiben. That's what she said."

"Who was the message to?"

"Some murdant. Cron. Say, what's this all about?"

"That's my business."

"Karm's arse! That's what *she* said, too! All ye bitches are sly. And I swear, Neena, ye're the worst! Why would ye risk a floggin' fer a friend?"

"What friend?" asked Neena. Then she smiled. "Where's that empty barracks?"

Thirty-one

♛

The garrison lay within sight of Taiben's gate, but not near it. Dar and the other women traveled over flat, open ground before ascending the steep road that entered the walled city. The massive gate was open, but guarded, and there was a line of travelers waiting to gain entrance. Murdant Cron led his charges directly to the gate, where the guards admitted them immediately.

The only other city Dar had seen was Tarathank, and King Kregant's capital differed from it in almost every way. Foremost, Taiben was alive. Its cobbled streets were filled with people, overwhelming Dar with their bustle, noise, and smell. The buildings were similarly chaotic. They seemed to have sprouted like mushrooms on a rotten log, the newer ones crowding the older. More than a few looked on the verge of tumbling down.

Once inside the city's walls, Murdant Cron picked up his pace, and the women hurried after him. They crowded close together, afraid of being snatched so their branded heads could be exchanged for coins. Dar spied a few men who seemed capable of the deed. After a short trip through packed and winding streets, Dar saw another wall with iron-studded gates. The gates were shut and flanked by guards. The procession halted before them.

"Guardsman Murdant Cron here, with a detail of stable muckers."

The guards opened the gates, and Dar and the others

passed through a short tunnel into a paved courtyard. It was flanked on three sides by an assortment of buildings—barracks, storehouses, workshops, and stables—crammed together like those in the city. The palace lay at the far side of the courtyard, high and capped with towers. Its lower portion was unadorned stone, pierced by narrow slits, but the higher levels sported balconies, terraces, and windows.

The long building that housed the stables dominated one side of the courtyard and featured many large doors. One was open, and Murdant Cron led the women through it. The murdant hadn't given any sign that he recognized Dar, nor did he while assigning the women their jobs. He marched them past the rows of stalls, splitting off groups of two or three. This process continued until only Dar was left. "Follow me," said Cron as he entered a room piled with hay. Sevren was sitting on a bale. "I hope she's worth the trouble," said Cron.

Sevren rose, his attention fixed on Dar. His eloquence had deserted him, leaving him speechless. Cron addressed Dar instead. "Well, lassie, why'd you come back?"

"Orcs brought me."

"And why would they do that?" asked Cron. "Our Majesty provides them with women."

Dar was unsure how to respond, so she remained silent.

"Back in base camp, they called you orc wench," said Cron. He spoke to Sevren as though resuming an argument. "Maybe she's a camp follower."

"Orcs don't keep whores," said Dar.

"Then why'd you come?"

"Out of loyalty."

"To whom? Our king? Your regiment? Sevren?" Cron put a sarcastic twist on the last choice.

"My comrades," said Dar, instantly wishing she had held her tongue.

Cron smiled and gave Sevren a vindicated look. "I take it you mean the orcs. Then why do you wish to leave them?"

"To save my life. A murdant I once spurned serves in the garrison. He swore to kill me, and he meant it. He's tried before."

Sevren spoke for the first time. "Dar speaks truly. I know of the man. Murdant Kol's notorious."

"Fond of the whip, I've heard," said Cron. "But Sevren, this is different from last time. You know that." He turned to Dar. "I'm a murdant in the royal guard. My duty is to my king, and you're his property. My men can na pluck a woman from his regiments, even if she claims she's threatened."

"I can still serve the king," said Dar. "I can cook."

"He has lots of cooks already."

"I cook orcish food and the orc queen is the king's guest. I can prepare her favorite dishes."

Cron shrugged. "I'll speak to Davot. Who knows? Maybe he can use you. But do na get your hopes up." Then he left the room.

"Do na mind Cron," said Sevren. "He's worried, but he got you here. It was his idea to bring you with a pack, so you wouldn't be noticed."

"Still, he doesn't approve."

"He thinks I'm being foolish. Perhaps I am." Sevren approached Dar, giving the impression that he was about to embrace her. When Dar stiffened, he restrained himself. "What's that on your chin?"

"My clan tattoo. I'm Dargu-yat now, with an orc family. Mother. Father. Sisters and brothers."

"Husband?"

"No."

Sevren appeared relieved. He reached out and tenderly brushed his fingers over the lines on Dar's chin. It seemed a ploy to touch her. "I'm glad you're here," he said.

"And sad also. It was pleasant to think you were happy and free."

"I was both awhile."

"But you came back."

"I had to." Dar decided to gamble on telling the truth. "The orc queen's my mother's sister. I need to know she's well."

Sevren seemed amused. "You don't look like royalty."

The remark annoyed Dar. "No. I don't."

Hearing the edge in Dar's voice, Sevren sensed his error. "I only meant your clothes and lack of shoes seem less than regal."

Dar said nothing, and Sevren sought to change the subject. "I kept my vow and searched for you and Twea after the battle. I found Twea's resting place and knew you had survived. Ever since, I've wondered how you fared."

"I told the orcs I'd get them home, and I did. We made our way to the Urkheit Mountains, then traveled eastward to their homeland."

"*You* led them?"

Dar smiled wryly at Sevren's surprise. "Orcs are different from men. They listen to women."

"Well, they were wise to listen to you," replied Sevren. "How does it feel to be back?"

"Even worse than I imagined."

"I hoped you had come back for me."

Sevren's directness surprised Dar, and she took care how she replied. "Ever since the battle, I've been a leaf in the wind. Now, I've been blown here."

Sevren stared at the floor. " 'Twas a fool's hope."

"I never forgot your kindness to Twea and me," said Dar. "That's why I sent that message."

"Then I'll content myself with your good opinion."

Dar smiled, more comfortable with Sevren's eloquence than his sincerity. "And what of you since the battle?"

Sevren's face darkened and he lowered his voice to a whisper. "All's gone ill. I feel tainted as a guardsman, for the king used his orcs to plunder Karm's temple."

"I heard."

"The shrine lay in Feistav's kingdom, but that's na excuse—the goddess rules all the world. Men blame the orcs, but 'twas men that gave the orders and men who profited. But na me," Sevren added quickly. "I stayed apart and took nothing holy. That dress I gave you has been my only pay."

"I guess most were less pious."

"Aye. And their sacrilege has caused na end of trouble. Folk are stirred up. Kregant's using orcs against his own people."

"Why would he risk sacking a temple?"

"Some say greed, and they're part right. But I think it was mainly Blood Crow's doing."

"The mage?"

"Aye. After he consults his magic bones and says what must be done, Kregant heels like his dog."

With a sudden chill, Dar remembered Velasa-pah's words. *There is a man who listens to bones. He is your enemy, but the bones are a greater enemy.*

Sevren watched Dar's reaction with concern. "You've gone white."

Before Dar could reply, Cron returned with Davot, who smiled upon seeing Dar. "I remember ye," he said. "How fares yer wee friend?"

"Dead," said Dar.

Davot looked upset. "Oh dear! I'm so sorry. So sorry." He paused and collected his composure. "Murdant Cron says ye cook orc food."

"I was taught in their royal kitchen."

"Really? How strange. How fortunate. The orcish queen's been off her food," said Davot. "It's a worry. Aye, for sure. The king's mage is displeased." Davot shuddered slightly. "*Most* displeased. Perhaps orc dishes would improve her appetite."

"So, you want her?" asked Cron.

"I'll give the lass a try." Davot looked at Dar. "What's yer name again?"

"Dar."

"Well, Dar, ye can sleep in the kitchen with the scrub-maid."

"Thank you."

"Then I guess it's settled," said Cron. "How can His Majesty mind? Dar's still serving orcs."

Davot led Dar to a chimney-covered building connected to the palace. When he opened its door, warm air, savory aromas, and wood smoke flowed from a cavernous room. The kitchen's far wall was lined with fireplaces large enough for several people to stand inside. In one, a huge boar slowly turned on a spit cranked by two women. In addition to the fireplaces, there were brick ovens and metal stoves, but the floor space was taken up mostly by tables. There, men were busy preparing elaborate dishes while women did more menial tasks.

"Here we cook for the entire palace," said Davot. "Everything from porridge to peacocks."

"And muthtufa, kambek, and roast pashi?" asked Dar.

"Never heard of those."

"They're all orc dishes."

"I see," said Davot, already distracted. The kitchen was his domain and all its activity his responsibility. Gazing about the room, Davot saw tasks he wanted done or done differently. He walked into the thick of things, giving orders while Dar trailed behind. Caught up in the demands of the moment, Davot seemed to forget why Dar was there. It was a while before he spoke to her again. "What do ye need to get started?"

"A pot and ingredients," said Dar. "But I only know their Orcish names. I think that . . ."

"Weena!" bellowed Davot. A large, middle-aged woman hurried over. "Weena, this is Dar. She's going to cook for the orc."

"A *girl's* to cook?"

"Only for the orc," said Davot. "Get her what she needs." Then he turned his attention elsewhere.

Weena's gaze fixed on Dar's brand. "I've heard of girls like you. Maybe you've cooked for orcs and soldiers, but this is a proper kitchen."

"But one that can't cook proper orcish food," replied Dar. "That's why Davot brought me here."

Weena scowled. "He said I'm to help you, and I will. But don't put on airs. You'll work like the other girls when you're not cooking." Then Weena took Dar through the storerooms. There Dar was able to find a number of items she could use. "Whiteroot" turned out to be pashi, "groundnut" was brak, and some of the kitchen's spices were also used by orcs. Dar assembled the ingredients to make brak fried in seasoned oil. She cooked it in one of the fireplaces where she also roasted pashi.

At dinnertime, a server took the food Dar had prepared, releasing her for other tasks. Wearing a blue smock over her shift, she helped carry food to the banquet hall. She used a servant passageway, part of a network of narrow corridors and stairs that allowed the help to move through the castle unseen. The passageway was dimly lit, so when Dar emerged into the banquet hall, it seemed ablaze with light. She placed a large silver tray of wine-poached fruit on the serving station, then gazed about in wonder.

The great, ornate hall was filled with people and noisy with their talk. It seemed a place where a bit of gossip or a change in the seating could alter lives. Everyone appeared to be testing the wind while eating and drinking. In the charged atmosphere, Dar was of no consequence and, hence, invisible.

The head table was on a platform at the hall's end. All who sat there faced the rest of the room. King Kregant was enthroned at the table's center, flanked by his queen and the black-robed mage. A boy, eight winters old at most, was seated next to the queen. A dozen men, all richly dressed, dined with them. The main floor of the hall contained three long tables that were perpendicular to the head one. They were filled with persons who dressed less richly and who dined on plainer fare. Blue-clad servers scurried about the room, pouring wine and bringing food. One of them noticed Dar gawking and hit her with his serving spoon. "Off with ye! There's more food to be got!" Dar headed toward the door but stopped to stare again once the server turned away.

Dar focused on the most dismal element in the splendid scene—the mage. *This is my enemy*, she thought. Even from across the room, the withered sorcerer looked menacing. His presence clearly dampened the spirits of those about him. The king looked subdued and his queen appeared frightened. Dar lingered until the mage looked up, as if disturbed by a sudden noise, and turned his gaze in her direction. Then Dar quickly retreated down the dark passageway.

Thirty-two

♛

When Dar returned to the kitchen, Weena made her clean pots. While Dar scrubbed, the kitchen grew calmer and less crowded. The cooks disappeared after the final courses went up. Soon serving platters were brought down for washing. Leftovers were set aside for later use or given to the staff for dinner. Dar ate, then resumed washing. As cleanup proceeded, the help was gradually dismissed until only Dar and the scrubmaid remained. Bea, the scrubmaid, was a ragged woman who possessed the earnest cheerfulness of a half-wit. She grinned as she helped Dar upend the great pots so they could dry. "Weenee says ye'll sleep with me."

Dar didn't relish the idea, for Bea smelled. "You needn't share your bed. I'll find my own place to sleep."

"I don't mind. Really! Toaty sleeps with me. He eats rats."

Dar hoped Toaty was a cat. She heard a pan fall over. "Is that Toaty?"

"Toaty's here," said Bea, pointing to a gray tom rubbing against her leg.

Dar peered about the kitchen. All but one lamp had been extinguished for the night. The only other light came from embers in the fireplaces. Much of the room was wrapped in shadow, and one of the shadows was moving. At the sight of it, Bea retreated to a corner. Dar remained put. "Who's there?" she called out.

"Just me."

"Sevren? What are you doing here?"

The shadow resolved into the figure of the guardsman. He held out a pair of shoes. "I want to give you these."

"Why?"

"The palace floors get cold."

"And what do you want in return?"

"I did na come to barter. These are a gift."

Dar hesitated, then took the shoes. They were new. "Thanks."

Sevren smiled. "Try them on, they will na bite."

Dar slipped on the shoes. They fit and their leather was soft.

"You do na trust men," said Sevren.

"I find it hard after what I've been through."

"It's a skill that can be learned if you have the right teacher. You trusted me enough to send that message."

"Yes."

"Where are you sleeping?" asked Sevren.

"The scrubmaid has a mattress. We'll share it."

"She need na bother. I spoke to Davot. You do na have to sleep here."

"Are you offering me your bed? No thanks."

"You can have it to yourself."

"No!"

"Why na trust me one more time? You'll be safe."

"I'm safe here."

"If you change your mind, the guards' quarters are in the courtyard, right next door. My room's on the second floor."

"I won't." Then Dar felt she sounded ungrateful. Sevren made her uneasy, but not in a frightening way. *He's never given me cause to doubt him.* "You were kind to think of me." Dar gave Sevren's lips an impulsive peck. Then she quickly retreated, the kiss surprising her as much as it did Sevren.

*　　*　　*

Queen Girta knocked on her husband's door, knowing the king was drunk. He could become violent, but drink also loosened his tongue. Girta risked his wrath only because she was desperate. "Enter," said the king. His eyes narrowed when he saw his wife. "Wha'ya want?"

Girta assumed her most timid manner. "Milord, 'tis rumored that Othar had another child taken to the tower."

"So?"

"Lady Rowena's son is missing," said Girta. She watched her husband's face grow pale, and horror came over her. *He knows what happened!* Girta summoned her nerve and spoke again. "Do you think Othar . . . Could he have . . ."

"How should I know?" snapped Kregant.

"But, milord, he's *your* mage."

"Mine?" The king laughed bitterly. "You're queen. Ask him yourself."

"I can't. He terrifies me."

Kregant refilled his wine goblet, then emptied it like a thirsty man. He gazed at his wife with eyes that had difficulty focusing. "Used to think he was my servant. Clever with herbs. Nothing more. Then . . ." His face contorted with despair. "Those cursed bones!"

"They changed him," said Girta in a quiet voice. "Not just his face. There's a chill about him—a wind from the Dark Path."

"Think I haven't noticed? I wear furs to dinner. The man's ice cold, if he's still a man."

"Get rid of him!"

Kregant shivered. "Can't."

"Because he poisoned your father for you?" That was only a guess on Girta's part, and she wanted to hear how her husband would reply.

Kregant was too drunk to perceive the snare. "Too late for blackmail. I'm king now."

"Then why can't you be rid of him?"

"Too dangerous. He could join my enemies."

"Not if he's dead."

King Kregant refilled his goblet. "Bones would warn him. B'sides, I need him. There's danger. My foe's returned."

"What foe?"

Kregant gazed at his wife stupidly. "Foe? Not sure yet. Othar's searching. But he needs blood. So much blood." The king's head slumped on his chest as he passed out.

Girta regarded her unconscious husband with disgust. She had never loved him, but royal marriages had nothing to do with love. The match had benefited Girta's father and given her a crown. When she married, Girta had believed a crown was more than a weight upon the head. She had since learned differently. Girta's son was the sole unblemished part of her life. She loved him fiercely, and any foe of the king also threatened the prince. Thus, while Girta was certain that a man she loathed and feared had killed her best friend's son, she hoped the boy's death had not been in vain. If the mage's sorcery had exposed an enemy, the prince would be safer. That hope shed some light on the king's dilemma; even demons have their uses.

Thirty-three

♛

Dar was asleep at the edge of Bea's mattress when Davot shook her awake. He was grinning. "Every bite!" he said. "She ate every bite of what ye cooked!"

Dar blinked sleepily. It wasn't yet dawn. "That's good."

"Didn't touch the venison pie, the poached fruit, nothing from the king's banquet. But she liked yer food. Praised it. I should be jealous."

"It was nothing special."

"Maybe so, but it's official now—ye'll cook for the orc and serve her, too."

"Serve the queen? I'd have to bathe first."

"Aye, I know all about that. We have a room for washing. Fresh robes, too. She's been here awhile, ye know."

Dar saw an opportunity and seized it. "I'll like to have more orcish spices. It'd help me cook."

Davot looked dubious. "And how would I get those?"

"There's an orc in camp who would fetch them if I spoke to him."

"Orcs can't come to the city without the king's leave."

"We could meet outside the gate. I'd need an escort, though."

Davot smiled knowingly. "Sevren, perhaps?"

"He'd do."

"I'll arrange it. Meanwhile, think of what ye'll make for dinner."

Davot hurried off. Dar rose, put on her new shoes, and breakfasted on leftover bread. While she ate, she pondered where events were taking her. She had the unsettling feeling that her arrival in Taiben had been foreordained. *Why else would Velasa-pah warn me about the mage?* Dar was still uncertain why he warned her about the bones. *I've heard stories of magic tokens. How can such things be an enemy?* Dar knew nothing of deep magic. The idea that it might be used against her was terrifying.

Sevren arrived while Dar was making muthtufa. By then it was midmorning. "Davot said you had an errand."

"Can you go to the orc garrison?"

"A guardsman can go anywhere on the king's business."

"This is the king's business. I need you to get a message to an orc."

Sevren looked uneasy. "What should I say?"

"The orc's name is Zna-yat, and he's in barracks seventeen. He doesn't speak our tongue, so you'll have to memorize what to say."

Sevren looked even more uneasy. "I don't fancy saying things I do na understand. What if I insult him?"

"Zna-yat is expecting my message. He'll do nothing to displease me."

Sevren grinned. "And snapping my neck would displease you?"

Dar ignored the jest. "Say 'Dargu-yat vak pah ala Zna-yat.' That means 'Dar has a message for Zna-yat.'"

Sevren repeated the phrase until Dar was satisfied. Then she said, "When an orc speaks to you, ask him if he's Zna-yat. Say 'Na tha Zna-yat?' 'Hai' means 'yes.' 'Thwa' means 'no.'"

"What if he says no?' "

"Then repeat my first message until Zna-yat shows up. Then say 'Sutat. Tha pahat ta Dargu-yat.' That means 'Come. You speak with Dargu-yat.' It would be a good idea to bow before you say it. Take him to wherever you think we should meet, then say, 'Geemat.' That means 'wait.' Then get me."

"I take it bowing again wouldn't hurt."

"Politeness never does."

Sevren gave a mock bow and asked Dar to repeat all the phrases he must learn. After he memorized everything, he departed and didn't return until the afternoon. By then, the muthtufa was simmering. Dar left it in the care of a kitchen maid, and Sevren led her to the meeting place. It was beyond the gate but still in view of the guards. The approach to the city had been cleared of any cover for an enemy, leaving only a tiny guardhouse between the city and the camp. Thus, Dar felt conspicuous as she met Zna-yat. He bowed, then grinned. "Dargu, already you have taught courtesy to washavokis," he said in Orcish.

Dar answered in the same tongue. "Only this one."

"What do you wish of me?"

"I'll need spices from clan hall. More importantly, tell matriarch that I'll see our queen tonight and every night thereafter. When you return, I may have more messages." Dar handed Zna-yat a metal token that Sevren had given her. "Washavoki king gives these to urkzimmuthi who carry his messages. When you return, you'll need it to contact me."

Zna-yat bowed low. "Great is your wisdom, Mother. Tell me what spices you desire and what I must do when I return with them."

After Dar had concluded her business, Sevren escorted her back to the kitchen. "I've seen hardened soldiers tremble before orcs," he said. "I'll confess, I was a tad shaky myself. But you . . . I could hear the respect when that orc spoke, though I did na understand a word."

"He honors me because I bit his neck."

"You what?"

"It's a long story."

Sevren regarded Dar with awe. "I think it's *you* I should be bowing to, na the orc."

Dar felt nervous and excited as dinner approached. She didn't know what to expect, but she was certain the night would be eventful. Davot brought the woman who would show the way to the queen's chamber. He also inspected the muthtufa Dar had prepared. Davot didn't taste the stew, but poured the contents of a vial into it and stirred thoroughly. "That's healing magic," he said, "so don't ye taste that dish again."

"Who prepared that magic?"

"The mage."

"Does the queen know it's in her food?"

"I'm a cook. Magic's not my concern. Yers neither."

Davot hurried off to supervise the banquet's preparation, leaving Dar with Fertha, the queen's former serving woman. Fertha was more than happy to relinquish her duties. "It's a long climb ta the chamber," she said. "Ye have ta light yer own torches on the way and wash and change afore ye serve. There's a place outside her door fer that."

"What can you tell me about the queen?"

"It's an orc, so what's there ta tell? I'd rather serve hounds, but I guess yer used ta them."

Dar colored, but replied evenly. "I am. When should I serve her dinner?"

"Not afore the king dines. That wouldn't be proper. When his banquet starts, I'll show ye the way."

A short while later, Dar climbed a narrow spiral stairway lugging a hamper containing the queen's dinner. Fertha led the way. The queen's chamber was on the sixth floor. Once Fertha reached it, she took Dar down a

long passage to a small room. A torch on the wall illuminated a copper basin filled with water, some blue
robes hanging on hooks, and two doorways. "The door
ta the left goes ta the orc's room. Ye've served orcs afore,
so ye know 'bout the bathing and the robes. Ye can wait
here while she eats, then bring the dishes down. Put out
the torches as ye go." After those instructions, Fertha
hurried off.

The bathwater was scented with flowers rather than
herbs. It was cold, but Dar scrubbed herself thoroughly.
When she was done, she donned one of the blue serving
robes, took a deep breath, and entered the orc queen's
room.

The door opened noiselessly and Dar had left her
shoes in the outer chamber. Thus she caught the queen
unawares. She was gazing out a window at the Urkheit
Mountains. Although it was dusk, no lamp or torch illuminated the chamber. Even so, Dar could see it was
richly decorated, though as sparsely furnished as any
hanmuthi. A stool, a sleeping mat, and a pair of chests
were the sole furniture. A circle painted on the floor
marked Muth la's Embrace. The queen sat in its center
on the stool, facing away from Dar. She wore a long robe
similar to those noble women wore in court. A thin gold
band encircled her head.

Dar set the hamper on the floor, then bowed very low.
"Tava, Muth Mauk." *Greetings, Great Mother.*

The queen continued to gaze out the window, but answered in a dull voice. "Ga pahak Pahmuthi." *It speaks
Orcish.*

"Mer nav urkzimmuthi." *I am orcish.*

Upon hearing Dar's reply, the queen turned around,
causing Dar to gasp with astonishment. "Muth Mauk,"
she said in Orcish, "I've seen you before."

The queen replied in the same tongue. "My mind is
filled with mist. I don't recall."

"I had vision of you. It was Nuf Bahi, and I was beginning journey. You asked where I was."

The queen rose unsteadily. She reminded Dar of Zor-yat and Muth-yat, but she looked gaunt and confused. She shuffled over to Dar and touched her chin. "You don't look urkzimmuthi, but that mark . . ."

"I was reborn. I'm Dargu-yat. Zor-yat is my muthuri."

Dar expected the queen to react to her sister's name, but she only looked troubled. "Mist," said the queen in a distracted voice. "Everything is mist."

"Zor-yat is your sister."

"Sister? I have sister?"

"You have two. They're worried about you. Don't you remember them?"

"I smell muthtufa," said the queen. "I remember that." She moved toward the hamper.

Dar snatched it up, then bowed very low. "Don't eat it, Mother. Have boiled roots instead."

The queen's expression turned petulant. "Why?"

"I think it's poisoned. That may be why your head is filled with mist."

"Poisoned?" The queen seemed straining to recall something. After a long silence, she asked, "Are you really urkzimmuthi?"

"Hai, Mother. Magic has made me so."

The queen's eyes narrowed. "Whose magic?"

"Your sisters' magic. Zor-yat and Muth-yat."

"Why are you here?"

With sudden and startling clarity, Dar knew the answer. "Muth la has sent me to save you."

Thirty-four

♛

The kitchen was dark when Dar returned from Muth Mauk's chamber. She poured the untouched muthtufa into slop pails, wondering if it would poison the royal swine. After cleaning up, she crawled onto Bea's mattress, but sleep didn't come. Instead, Dar pondered what to do. Her conversation with the lonely queen had been disheartening. Mostly, Muth Mauk had rambled incoherently. She seemed thoroughly addled, though there were glimmers of awareness. At those times, she appeared to struggle against the potion that ensnared her mind. Those brief moments seemed all the more poignant after derangement returned.

Due to the queen's confusion, Dar learned little by talking to her. Muth Mauk was vague about how she came to the palace or why she remained, though she appeared afraid to leave. She seemed to believe the king was fighting for the orcs, not the other way around. Dar worried that the queen's wits were irreparably damaged, but hoped that Muth Mauk's mind would clear if she ceased taking the potion. Dar had already devised a scheme to insure that the queen's food would be free of it.

Murdant Kol kept a room in Taiben. As Neena gazed about it, she was oppressed by its austerity. The dark, paneled walls lacked decoration, and the minimal furniture—a bed, a table, two stools, and a chest—was plainly made. She felt that the abode perfectly reflected the severity of its occupant, who watched her from across the table. His cold blue eyes held a trace of amusement. "Well, Neena, you got your request. You're in the city. Just remember—only your head needs to return to camp."

"A severed head speaks not."

"I've always thought that was its virtue."

"You'll want to hear my tale."

"I doubt it. I've no use for women's gossip."

"Dar lives," said Neena. "I've seen her." She noted with satisfaction that Murdant Kol's face tightened, though he tried to keep his expression neutral. "She made a fool of you. She's still doing it."

"Tell me where she is."

"I want something in return."

"What?"

"I'm with child, and I don't want to end up like Loral. I'll speak if I can stay in Taiben."

Kol smiled. "Is that all?"

"That's enough for me. Arrange it so I never go on another march, I'll tell you where Dar's hiding."

"That's easily done."

"Swear then. Swear by Karm as the High Murdant."

"I swear by Karm that if you reveal Dar's whereabouts you'll live out your days in Taiben. I swear this as High Murdant." Kol made the sign of the Balance to seal his oath.

Neena was satisfied. "The orcs brought Dar to camp seven days ago. She managed to get a message to a guardsman, some murdant named Cron. It was 'Tell your countryman Twea's mother wants to go to Taiben.' The next day, a murdant took a bunch of women to clean the royal stables. Dar went with them, but she didn't return."

"Is that all?" asked Kol. "She might be anywhere."

"Dar's branded, so she can't leave the city. Now that you know she's here, she won't be hard to find."

Kol nodded. "You're right. So, Neena, would you like to work in the palace? I have connections. You could be a maid. After what you've been through, it'd be easy work."

"I'd like that."

"Then it's settled. I'll speak to my friend tomorrow." Kol rose, opened the chest, and took out a bottle and a goblet. "This calls for a celebration. We both got what we wanted." He sat down and poured a generous drink. "I'm afraid I only have one goblet. You can drink first. As I recall, you weren't fond of Dar either."

Neena grinned. "I hold no grudges. After all, she's helped me become a maid." Neena raised the goblet. "To Dar." Then she drained it in three gulps. The brandy was sweet with a hint of bitterness, and Neena enjoyed the way it warmed her stomach. Kol took the goblet and refilled it, but left it untouched. Instead of toasting, he watched Neena with a smile she found unnerving. "Aren't you going to drink?" she asked.

"I'm more discriminating than Teeg," said Kol.

The reference to Teeg alarmed Neena. As she tried to think of an innocent response, the warm sensation in her stomach became a burning. It grew ever more intense until she moaned and doubled over in pain. The room seemed to spin, and Neena tumbled from the stool. Lying on the floor, she couldn't move. Neena saw only Kol's boots as he rose and walked over to her. With his foot, he rolled her so she faced upward.

Neena could barely make her mouth work. "Wh . . . ?"

"Why? Did you really think I hadn't guessed? I merely saved the brandy you poisoned and bided my time."

"Bu . . ."

"But I swore an oath?" Kol grinned. "I've kept it. You're living out your days in Taiben."

Neena's mouth quivered, but she was unable to make

another sound. Kol watched the color drain from her face, which soon froze in an expression of pain and surprise. Then he drew his sword and dragged Neena's body into the alley.

The following day, Dar made muthtufa again, but this time she made two pots of it. One she cooked in the fireplace Davot had assigned her. She simmered the other inside an oven. No one in the busy kitchen paid notice. When dinner approached, Davot poured the vial of potion into the muthtufa simmering in the fireplace, and after he left, Dar exchanged the pot with the one in the oven.

When Dar brought up dinner that night, the queen seemed little changed. If anything, she looked more haggard. However, after Muth Mauk ate, her eyes were clearer. "I think sun is rising," she said. "Mist is burning off." She smiled at Dar for the first time. "Zor-yat was always cleverest. And you say you are her daughter? Tell me how this is so."

Dar described her rebirth, but the queen's attention seemed to wander. She was staring out the window when the tale was finished. A long while passed before she spoke. "It's hard for me to think. Perhaps it will be easier tomorrow. For now, I'm still uncertain."

"Uncertain about what, Mother?"

"Many things." The queen smiled. "Call me Auntie and speak to me of home. It's good to hear speech of mothers again."

By the time Dar returned to the kitchen, she felt encouraged. The poison's hold on the queen seemed to be loosening. *Perhaps, in a few more nights, I can tell her what the king has done.* Dar thought it was too early to reveal the king's treachery, for she doubted that Muth Mauk was yet capable of discretion. Discretion would be vital if Dar was to rescue her. How that might be accomplished was as uncertain as the queen's health. Dar was sure of only one thing: Any mistake would be fatal.

As Dar cleaned up, the daytime watch of the royal guard went off duty. Sevren retired to his room, but many of his comrades went to taverns. Murdant Kol headed for the same taverns, though he seldom drank. Having collected Neena's bounty, he intended to spend it on drinks for guardsmen, buying their goodwill while loosening their tongues. In time, he would discover the identity of Cron's countryman. That would set him on Dar's trail. The city was big, but Dar couldn't leave it. Sooner or later, he would find her. Kol's step quickened. The hunt was on.

Thirty-five

♛

Dar's main concern was the orc queen's health. Everything depended on it. As long as poison clouded the queen's mind, Dar was imprisoned, for she had resolved not to leave without Muth Mauk. The queen's mental state improved each day, but there were other changes. As her wits sharpened, her body shriveled. Dar feared the poison was a blaze that destroyed while retreating. Muth Mauk noticed Dar's concern and sought to reassure her. "Think of me as drying fruit," she said with a smile. "I lessen, yet what remains is stronger." Regardless, Dar thought the queen looked frail.

While Dar fretted, the rest of her life fell into a routine. When Dar wasn't cooking or serving the queen, she helped Bea scrub and wash. She preferred the half-wit's cheerful company to that of the other servants, who sneered at her brand and treated her haughtily. Sevren often visited after he went off duty, appearing while Dar was cleaning up. He always brought candied fruit for Bea, who savored the treat while he talked with Dar.

Though Sevren was concerned about Dar's safety, he came for other reasons. Dar couldn't smell love like other urkzimmuthi mothers, but she saw it in Sevren's actions. Her presence subdued him. He was nervous and happy in her company and almost orcish in his respectfulness. Nevertheless, he was bold enough to repeat his offer to share his room. Each time Dar declined, he accepted her decision. One evening, he brought Dar a blue shift like those serving women wore. Dar accepted it because it helped her blend in with the other servants, and because—as with the shoes—there were no conditions attached.

Dar knew she was being courted, and while she didn't encourage Sevren, she didn't discourage him either. She might need his help, and his company was pleasant. All Dar's highland suitors had been arrogant and randy, but Sevren was neither. Yet, despite Sevren's courteous attentions, Dar still pined for Kovok-mah. She had already forgiven him, realizing that he must obey his muthuri. The finality of their separation made Dar's heart ache. To distract herself from unhappiness, Dar focused on aiding the queen.

On the eighth night Dar served her, Muth Mauk was waiting by the doorway. One glance at the queen's shrewd face told Dar that the monarch's mind was restored. Muth Mauk looked at the hamper. "Is that muthtufa I smell?"

"Hai, Auntie. It's been simmering all day." The queen sat down, and Dar gave her some of the stew. "Food is Muth la's gift."

"Shashav Muth la," said the queen. She tasted the muthtufa and made a wry face. "Your spirit is urkzim-muthi, but your tongue and nose remain washavoki. Your cooking shows it."

Dar bowed. "I'm unskilled."

"Hai, but Muth la didn't send you here to cook. I remember little of our first meeting, but I recall this: You said you came to save me."

"I did, Auntie."

"Tell me your story, Dargu-yat. Leave nothing out. I must know everything."

Dar spoke of her childhood and how she ended up in the regiment. She told of her abuse by men and of finding refuge with Kovok-mah. She recounted her first visions, Zna-yat's attempt to drown her, and her rescue by a tree. Dar relived the battle at the Vale of Pines and the rage it brought. She told of her journey with the orcs and how she came to bite Zna-yat's neck. She described every detail of her encounter with Velasa-pah, but hesitated to speak of the pool at Tarathank until the queen gently encouraged her. It was late night by the time Dar finished her account.

Muth Mauk's yellow eyes fixed on Dar with penetrating intensity. "Dargu-yat, I believe Muth la prepared your path, but it was you who chose to walk it. That's her way. One must choose goodness. I'm proud you're my niece."

"Shashav, Auntie."

"Now it's *my* time to make choice: If you can lead me from this place, I'll go with you."

The following day, a city watchman arrived with a message for Davot. "There's two piss eyes at the gate with somethin' fer ye," he said. "They want a girl to fetch it." Davot called for Dar and sent her with the watchman to see the orcs. Dar would have preferred Sevren as her escort, but declined to ask for him in the presence of the watchman. It would arouse his curiosity, for serving girls did as they were told.

The watchman accompanied Dar outside the city gate where the orcs were waiting. One of them was Zna-yat. The other one was Kovok-mah. The mere sight of him evoked painful feelings. Dar thought Kovok-mah looked as uncomfortable as she felt. She spoke to Zna-yat in Orcish. "Why is he here?"

"He can speak to washavokis, I cannot."

Dar spoke to Kovok-mah in Orcish. "Tell washavoki that Zna-yat wants to show me what he brought."

As Kovok-mah did this, Dar whispered to Zna-yat.
" me spices as we talk."

Zna-yat opened his sack and began pointing to the different herbs. "What message do you have for me?"

"Black Washavoki poisoned queen. Her thoughts were not clear, but I have healed her. I will take her from city."

"When?"

"I don't know. Soon, I hope. All I can say is watch city at night. When queen appears, sons must protect her."

"But we're locked behind walls."

"Tell washavoki soldiers you have sickness. Say you must stay outside walls or sickness will spread."

As Dar had hoped, Zna-yat grasped the purpose of the deception. "And when I see queen?"

"Have weapons hidden on you. Slay camp guards and open gate. Sons must be ready."

"They will be." Zna-yat regarded Dar with brotherly concern. "Dargu, you have big chest."

Dar smiled wryly. "You mean you smell my fear? Close your bundle. I must go."

The watchman, who had kept his distance from the orcs, joined Dar after she shouldered the sack of spices. "Never heard anyone speak piss eye talk afore." He stared at her brand. "Ye from the regiments?"

"I've served there."

"And now ye're in the palace." The watchmen grinned. "Who'd ye tup fer that?"

Dar fixed the watchman with a cool glance. "Someone bigger than you."

Dar no longer worried about the queen's mind, but she remained troubled by the queen's health, which hadn't improved. Muth Mauk's best hope lay in seeing the Yat clan's healer, a mother renowned for her skill. To do so, she had to escape Taiben, and accomplishing that became Dar's chief concern. The problem gnawed at her. She could sneak the queen down the servant passageway at night, but both the palace and city gates would be shut and guarded. Dar could think of no way around those obstacles.

Distracted by her dilemma, Dar burned the queen's stew before she could divide it and hide one portion. As she hastily prepared a second batch, Davot appeared earlier than usual with the mage's potion. "The stew's not ready!" Dar cried out.

"No matter," replied Davot as he removed the stopper from the glass vial. "Cooking doesn't harm the magic."

Dar grabbed a spoon from the boiling stew and brushed it against Davot's bare arm as he reached out to pour the potion. When the spoon burned him, Davot dropped the vial. It shattered on the stone hearth. "Oh, Master! I'm sorry! Please forgive my clumsiness!" Dar winced and steeled herself for a beating, but Davot didn't strike her. Instead, he stared at the spilled potion, his face white with terror.

"Karm save me!" he said. "That was the last of it! I'll have to . . ." He stopped and his face grew calmer. "No, *ye'll* have to get more potion."

Dar suddenly understood Davot's terror. She asked where she had to go, dreading the answer. "You must visit the mage," replied Davot. "He'll be in his tower."

"What should I tell him? Or will he know? It's said he reads minds."

"I've heard that, too. Say the vial was dropped, but do not say by whom."

Dar realized that if the sorcerer could see her thoughts he would not only know that Davot had dropped the vial, but that Dar had caused him to do so. The mage would also know why. *How stupid of me!* she thought. *I could have let the queen go hungry. Now I've ruined everything!* Yet she saw no choice but to obey Davot and take her chances, poor as they might be.

Davot was anxious for Dar to leave and watched fretfully while she finished making the stew. After Dar added the last ingredients, he gave directions to the mage's tower and sent her off. As she left, Dar sneaked a charred stick from a fireplace. Once she was out of sight, she used it to obscure her tattoo with soot and smudged her face as well. Then Dar climbed the stairs of the servant passageway and exited on the seventh floor into a hallway with bricked-up windows. A single torch dimly illuminated the iron door at its end. Dar approached the door with trepidation. There were no guards. Fear protected the sorcerer's tower.

Dar used the door's knocker. Its sharp sound echoed loudly. Davot had told Dar to expect no reply. When the echoes died into silence, she pulled open the door and began to climb the stone stairs. The darkness seemed thicker inside the tower, more like smoke than the absence of light. As she ascended, the air grew colder until her breath showed. Dar was breathing rapidly by the time she reached a second iron door. "Enter," said a voice.

Dar opened the door and stepped into a room. Though filled with lit candles, it was little brighter than the stairwell. The pale light glinted off polished wood and golden-threaded tapestries, but the rich furnishings only emphasized the gloom. The mage sat in a chair as elaborate as a throne, reading a dusty scroll. He looked up "Well?"

Dar bowed her head. She tried to fake terror and found it came naturally. "Sire, I was sent from the kitchen to get healing magic for the queen."

"Look me in the eye!" barked the sorcerer.

Dar obeyed. The mage's face was young, yet withered as if twisted by a blast of malice. His dark eyes peered at Dar, seemingly lifeless but not sightless. Dar feared they were holes through which her spirit might tumble and be lost forever. "There was a vial ready for this night," said the mage in an icy voice. "Tell me, girl, what happened to it?"

"It was dropped."

When the mage spoke again, his voice was quieter and more menacing. "By whom?"

Dar tried to swallow, but her throat was dry. "A maid. I don't know her name. They beat her senseless and sent me in her stead." Dar waited for the mage to read the truth and inflict some terrible punishment. Nevertheless, she continued to meet his gaze.

A thin smile came to Othar's lips. "Whoever beat that maid did her a favor. Come with me. You can help me make new magic."

"I help the likes of Your Lordship?"

Othar grinned maliciously. "Aye. Like the stick helps the fire. Come." The mage rose, seized a candelabra, and opened a door to another room. "Follow me. Touch nothing."

Dar entered the windowless room. It smelled of blood and was even colder and darker than the outer one. There, the numerous candles in the candelabra cast only a pale, watery light, devoid of warmth. Dar peered about the chamber. The walls were lined with shelves, which held numerous vessels and boxes. There was a stone table with a fire bowl carved in its surface. As Dar's eyes grew accustomed to the darkness, she noticed a rusty circle painted on the floor and saw a black stone pedestal standing in the darkest part of the room. A black cloth bag lay upon it. Dar sensed that whatever the bag contained was the source of the room's oppressive atmosphere. *The bones?* She stepped toward the bag for a closer look.

The mage seized her arm. "What's in that bag can burn your dirty face worse than hot iron. Would you like to look like me?" The mage studied her, not loosening his hold. "We've met before."

Dar lowered her eyes. "I bring food to the banquet hall."

"And what's a branded girl doing in the palace?"

"I . . . I have a lover, sire. He got me a place."

Othar pulled Dar to the stone table and stretched her arm over an iron bowl. He took a bone knife and pierced one of Dar's veins. Dar looked away as her blood flowed into the bowl. "A slut's blood will do for this magic," said Othar. "You're lucky I only need a little." To Dar, it seemed forever before the mage released her arm. "Sit down," he said. "Wait while I finish this."

Dar shivered on the stone floor as the mage added ingredients to her blood. He lit a fire and cooked the mixture awhile, poured it through a cloth into an iron beaker, and used the beaker to fill a series of vials, one of which he handed to Dar. It was already cold to the touch. "Take this to the kitchen," said the mage. "And tell Davot that if anyone breaks another vial, he's to roast their heart and serve it to me personally."

Dar bowed very low. "Yes, sire." Then she hurried away. She relaxed only when she left the tower. Then she felt elated, for she was certain of two important things: The bones were in the black cloth sack, and the mage couldn't read minds.

When Davot emptied the vial into the queen's supper that evening, he had no idea that it contained water tinted with a bit of Dar's blood. He was too relieved to notice any difference. "Cook their heart he said? Oh dear! I daresay he'd make me cook my own." He gazed at the large purple mark around Dar's punctured vein. "Ye're a brave lass, ye are indeed. Not everyone returns from the tower."

Thirty-six

♛

Muth Mauk detected the trace of Dar's blood in her stew and had Dar recount her encounter with the mage. Afterward, the queen told how the mage had ensnared her while she was visiting old King Kregant. "I fell ill, along with everyone in my party. Black Washavoki was great healer. No evil marred his face then. He gave magic to all, but only I lived. Any mother who visited me sickened and died. To spare others, I came to this room. Then old king died and mist filled my head. I could not tell dreams from waking life. Black Washavoki gave me words, and I spoke them." Muth Mauk looked distressed. "Thus I brought evil upon sons and mothers."

"Evildoers may twist goodness to their purposes. Auntie, don't blame yourself."

"I must oppose that evil I caused. Dargu, when can we leave?"

"I don't know. I have yet to find way."

"You must hurry."

Muth Mauk's urgency was a weight on Dar's chest. *How can I overcome iron gates, stone walls, and deep magic? I've raised false hopes.* Yet she didn't voice her doubts to the queen, or lie. "I'll try," Dar said.

As Othar sat in the dark, a thought came. *You should have killed the girl.* The mage spoke to the darkness. "I would have, but I needed her to deliver the vial." *Was that wise?* Othar thought perhaps he should ask the bones. Yet, that would require another sacrifice, and he doubted it would be worthwhile. The bones had grown vague again. When thrown, they had always moved as if blown by unworldly winds, but lately the winds had become swirling eddies that left confusion in their wake. The mage felt he was in the center of a storm or—more likely—a struggle. Though much that the bones said was unintelligible, one message was clear: A threat was close. Very close.

"Yes, I should have killed the girl," said the mage. "Tomorrow, I will. I'll send for her and finish the job." Othar smiled. He hadn't killed a woman for a while. It would be pleasant.

It was very late when Dar returned to the kitchen, and the lamp had burned out. The only light in the cavernous room came from embers in the fireplaces and pale moonlight outside the windows. Dar set the hamper down, too tired to clean up, and groped her way toward Bea's mattress. A faint noise stopped her.

"Sevren?"

Silence.

It must be Toaty, Dar thought. She reached the mattress, sat down carefully so as not to wake Bea, and took off her shoes. She was about to lie down when she touched something wet and sticky on the mattress. Dar examined her hand by the dim light cast from a nearby fireplace. *Blood!* Dar shook the motionless scrubmaid. "Bea? Bea!" Her body was already cold.

Dar heard footsteps. A man's form was briefly silhouetted against the windows. He was near. "Your friend wasn't very clever, but she was talkative."

"Kol?"

"Still recognize my voice? I'm touched." Dar started to rise when a lash whistled through the air and cracked above her head. "Sit down!" Dar slumped on the mat-

tress. "I missed on purpose, so don't do anything foolish."

Dar wished that she had her buried dagger or even a
kitchen knife, but the knives were stored on the other
side of the room. Playing for time, she asked. "How did
you find me?"

Kol chuckled. "Never trust a woman."

"Neena?"

"She set me on your trail. The guardsmen were tight-
lipped, but the watchman gave you away. The rest was
easy."

"What do you want?"

"To do my duty." The whip whistled in the gloom, invisible. Another loud crack. Dar flinched and Kol
laughed. "You're a deserter. The scabheads need an example."

"Then why flog me here?"

Another crack made Dar cower. Kol's voice seemed to
purr. "I'll only start here. Wound you. Blind you. I'll finish you in camp in a way that will leave an impression."

Dar glanced about for some kind of weapon. A meat
spit lay upon two brackets in the closest fireplace. A few
hours earlier, it had skewered an entire boar. Its sharp
point could easily pierce a man. As Dar prepared to
lunge for it, she thought of something to distract her foe.
"Hurt me, and the orcs will tear you to pieces."

Murdant Kol was silent, and in the stillness Dar
bounded for the fireplace. She made three long strides before the whip's thongs wrapped around her ankle, biting
her flesh and tripping her. Dar fell short of the spit. Hot
ash and embers scorched her outstretched hands. Kol
tugged at the whip to free it for another blow, but its
thongs still gripped Dar's ankle. He bent forward to grab
the coils and Dar saw his face for the first time. His eyes
had a maniacal gleam. She threw ashes in them.

Kol bellowed with rage and pain as dust and sparks

obscured his face. He dropped his whip and it released Dar. She scurried under the tables. For the first time, she had the advantage. Darkness hid her, and she knew where to go. Kol blundered about while Dar quietly crawled to the door closest to Sevren's lodgings. When she reached it, she bolted outside. Dar heard Kol cursing from across the room.

Dar ran to the building next door. Knowing only that Sevren lived on the second floor, she bounded up the stairs into a dark hallway lined with doors. "Sevren!" she shouted. "Sevren!" Several doors opened and men peered out. One rushed toward her. "Dar!"

"Kol's after me!"

Sevren pulled Dar toward his doorway. "Lads," he shouted, "let no stranger pass. Better yet, chase him off." When Dar was in his room, Sevren shut the door. "Quiet," he whispered as he grabbed his sword. Then Sevren blew out the candle and stood motionless, poised to attack. Outside the door, booted feet clumped on wooden floorboards. The sound gradually died away.

A long while passed before a voice called through the closed door. "Sevren, he got away."

Sevren lowered his sword, walked over to the bed where Dar sat, and leaned his weapon against the wall.

"Hold me," said Dar, voicing the words like a gentle command. Sevren sat on the bed and wrapped his arms around her. Dar was trembling slightly. "Thank you," she whispered.

"Sons protect mothers," said Sevren.

"Where'd you learn that?"

"I've been talking to a sand ice merchant who visits orcs often. He speaks their tongue and prefers their company."

"Why would you do that?"

"I have this problem. You see, I love an orc woman. I must learn how to behave."

"And what did he tell you?"

"That I should bathe often. In truth, it's caused no harm."

Dar sniffed.

"Do you smell my atur?" asked Sevren.

"No. I can't smell love."

"Then why did you ask me to hold you?"

Dar changed the subject. "Why do you love me?"

"I do na know. It must be Muth la's doing."

"Don't joke about Muth la!"

"Then mayhap it's Karm's doing. Mayhap Muth la and Karm are the same—something too great for minds to grasp. I understand nothing except how I feel."

Dar grew quiet in Sevren's arms, and it was a while before she spoke again. "Sevren, do you love me enough to save me? To save me, knowing you'll lose me forever?"

"That's a bitter bargain."

"I can't stay here. Kol will make trouble."

"He'll na harm you. I'll see to that."

"The mage is my greater enemy. What Kol has done will give me away."

"Why would Blood Crow care about you?"

"I came here to take the orc queen home."

Sevren sighed. "I see." He was silent awhile. "Dar, I'd risk my life to save you, gladly too. But the orc queen's another matter. It means going against the king."

"I won't leave without her. I made a promise I cannot break."

"Will you die to keep it?"

"Yes. And I'll die soon. Tomorrow, most likely."

"Dar . . ." Sevren's voice trailed off.

"Are there ways out of the palace and city besides guarded gates?"

"Aye, there are sally ports and other secret ways. Kol probably escaped through one tonight."

"Do you know them?"

"Of course. I'm a guardsman. But showing them is treason."

"No one need know," said Dar. "The queen and I won't be missed till dinnertime. By then, we'll be long gone."

"But the mage . . ."

"He can't read minds. That's only show. I know because I lied to his face and fooled him. And think of this: If the queen escapes, the king will lose his orc army."

Sevren's frown faded. "Then who'll plunder temples for him? He'll be hard put to find the men for such work."

"So, will you help me?"

"Aye." Sevren smiled ruefully. "Valamar was right about you."

"How?"

"He said you'd bring trouble."

"I won't. At least, not to you. Just get me outside the walls, and the orcs will do the rest." Dar kissed Sevren's cheek. "Fu nat gatash min. You are worthy son."

"When do you want to leave?"

"Tonight."

Dar and Sevren waited until the moon had set before sneaking back into the kitchen. Dar put on her shoes and grabbed her old shift before leading Sevren to the queen's chamber. The queen was asleep, sitting upright. Dar gently touched her shoulder. "Muth Mauk, mer nav Darguyat." Then she switched to the human tongue for Sevren's benefit. "This washavoki is friend. He will help us leave. We must be quiet and walk where washavokis will not see us."

Muth Mauk rose and surprised Dar by asking if the shift was for her. Dar thought she would have to explain the purpose of a disguise, but it proved unnecessary. The queen donned Dar's old shift, then hid her gold band within its folds. She was so withered, Dar's clothes fit loosely. After the queen changed, Dar covered her tattoo with a mixture of flour and soot. She had already covered her own.

At Sevren's insistence, Dar wore his dagger. Otherwise, she carried nothing for the journey. Haste was more important than food, water, or warm clothes. If she could reach the orcs, they would be provided. If she couldn't, they would be unneeded.

Thirty-seven

♛

The orc queen moved like an old woman, gripping Dar for support as she slowly descended the stairs. Every step took effort. Dar refrained from urging her to hurry, for she knew the queen was doing her utmost. Muth Mauk's weakness had been less evident when she was confined to her chamber. Yet once her life depended on speed, the effects of her poisoning were starkly apparent. Dar feared it would be dawn before they reached the city walls.

Upon reaching level footing, Muth Mauk was able to move slightly faster. Sevren led her and Dar to the stables by a route that hugged the shadows. Eventually, they sneaked in a side door. The stables were dark, but Sevren knew the way. He entered a stall and moved boxes to uncover a small hole in the wall. "I'm afraid we'll have to crawl. Can you manage, Your Majesty?"

"Hai," mumbled the queen.

Sevren bowed to Muth Mauk, then entered the hole. Dar heard him crawl a short distance then whisper, "The way's clear."

Dar and the queen followed and were soon outside the palace walls, standing in a stable yard. Sevren led them into shadows before hiding the hole's entrances. "Only guardsmen and their ladies know that way," he said.

While Dar wondered how many women had followed Sevren through the hole, he entered a shed and returned with a two-wheeled manure cart. Then he bowed low to the queen. "This stinks, but it can carry you through the streets."

The queen smiled. "Tonight, it is better to be fast than fragrant."

Sevren lifted Muth Mauk into the cart, threw some hay over her, grabbed the cart's handles, and began to push it as fast as he could without making a racket. Dar trotted alongside. As Sevren hurried through the winding streets, he looked anxiously at the sky. "Folk will be stirring soon."

Eventually he reached an opening in the city's thick outer wall. It was a narrow tunnel that was the same size as a doorway. A lit torch was set into its wall. Sevren approached it indirectly. "Someone's inside," he whispered. "Stay out of sight. Dar, I need the dagger." Dar gave it to him, and Sevren hid the weapon in his jerkin before striding into the opening.

Braced against the wall, Dar could hear Sevren's voice. "Yo there, watchman, King's Guard here. Did someone pass this way tonight?"

"A murdant, sometime after midnight."

"Why did you na stop him?"

"I knew him. He's from the regiments."

"That's na excuse."

"Don't be tight-arsed. Since when do . . ." The man's voice was cut short by a grunt followed by the sound of a body hitting the ground. The torch in the tunnel went out, and Sevren appeared. He handed Dar the dagger. "The way's clear."

Sevren had already opened the door at the tunnel's far end. Dar spied the watchman's corpse there. "You should leave now," she said. "You've risked enough."

Sevren hesitated.

"Go," said Dar tenderly. "Ride south this spring. Buy your farm and forget me. I was just passing through." She embraced Sevren and kissed him on the lips. When

Dar led the queen outside the city's walls, Sevren closed the door behind them.

There was a hint of morning in the sky, but the landscape was still dark and empty. Dar could make out the walls of the garrison and the hills beyond them, but little else. If Zna-yat was watching for her, he was too distant for her to spot. "Only little way farther," said Dar.

"Good," said Muth Mauk.

After the queen traveled a short distance, her breathing became labored. Soon, each breath was a rattling gasp. By then, the eastern sky was pink. Dar realized they could be seen from the city walls and their only hope lay in rescue by the orcs. She scanned the garrison for some sign of them but saw none. Suddenly Muth Mauk froze. "What is it?" asked Dar.

"Washavokis!"

Dar gazed about but saw nothing. "Are you sure?"

"They come from little building. Five are running. Another comes on horse."

Dar heard hoofbeats and spied a man on horseback. He was still far off, but moving to circle around them and cut off retreat to the city. Apparently, he was unaware that the queen could barely walk. Dar assumed the horseman was Murdant Kol. Whether he had spotted her by dumb luck or by patient waiting made no difference, her fate was sealed. She halted and the hoofbeats slowed. Soon, Dar could make out soldiers on the road. They were jogging toward her. "Don't be afraid, Auntie. They only want me. They'll take you back to your room."

"Thwa. I won't return."

"You must. You're our great mother."

Muth Mauk didn't reply.

Dar watched the soldiers advance with a sense of dread and resignation. When the men were thirty paces away, they drew their swords. "Halt!" shouted one.

Dar wondered why he shouted, since both she and the queen hadn't moved. Then Sevren sped past her, sword raised. He plunged into the advancing soldiers, blade swinging. Two fell almost immediately, and the deadliness of Sevren's attack seemed to cow the remaining three. They fought so timidly that Sevren had the upper hand, despite being outnumbered. Another soldier fell, a leg nearly severed. The fourth soldier ran, spurring the remaining man to fight with desperate vigor.

Dar heard rapid hoofbeats and turned to see Murdant Kol riding Thunder and swirling his whip above his head. Bearing down upon them on his huge horse, he seemed unstoppable. Dar thought to warn Sevren, but realized that it would distract him in the midst of combat. Soon Kol would be within striking distance. *I must do something!* With no time to reflect, Dar acted on impulse. She drew the dagger Sevren had given her and threw it.

Kol was moving so swiftly that Dar had no idea if she hit him. She narrowly avoided being trampled. Then the whip fell from Kol's hand as Thunder veered away from Sevren. The horse slowed and Dar saw the murdant pull the bloody dagger from his shoulder. He tossed it on the ground and reached for his sword. The blade was only partway drawn when Kol sheathed it. The action made Dar guess that Kol's wound affected his sword arm. Instead of attacking, he spurred his mount toward the garrison. Sevren's opponent glanced toward the retreating horsemen. It proved a fatal mistake.

Sevren was wiping the blood from his sword when Dar ran over to him. "Are you hurt?" she asked.

"One cut. 'Tis na deep."

"Go! Go quickly before you're seen!"

Sevren gazed up at the ramparts. "Too late for that."

"Oh, Sevren, you were safe. Why did you . . ."

"I could na watch you die."

"But Kol will bring more soldiers," said Dar, realizing Sevren's sacrifice would buy them only a little time. Already, Kol had nearly reached the gates of the garrison. They swung open as he approached.

Kol's horse reared as orcs, not soldiers, poured from the gates. Perhaps because of his wound, Kol had trouble getting his mount under control. By the time he had Thunder turned around, an orc raced after him. Dar watched as the orc gained on the galloping horse and reached for its rider's ankle. Then, with a show of heart, Thunder pulled away from the pursuer. The city's gate was still closed and Murdant Kol headed his mount southward. Soon horse and rider were a diminishing speck in the distance. "Good riddance," said Sevren, although he looked disappointed.

The orcs moved with amazing speed, and soon they knelt before their queen. Muth Mauk looked like a gnarled tree that had weathered a storm. In the rosy light of dawn she seemed radiant and filled with a strength that rose from a deeper source than her frail body. When she spoke, her voice was neither powerful nor loud, but commanding in its stillness. "I have returned," she said in Orcish. "I fell under evil magic. My mind was clouded and my words were twisted. Dargu-yat saved me." The queen had to pause to catch her breath. "I'm still weak from my ordeal. Dargu-yat will speak for me. Obey her as you would obey me."

Dar gazed at the queen with surprise, but before she could speak, Zna-yat called out. "Dargu-yat, tell us what to do."

Dar's immediate impulse was to take refuge. "Return to walled camp." *There*, she thought, *I can give the queen some proper clothes and free the branded women.* Dar pointed to Sevren. "This washavoki helped save queen. All other soldiers are our foes, but don't kill them if they don't attack."

As the orcs headed back to the garrison, Dar had two of them carry the queen. Sevren asked what had happened. "The queen said I'm to speak for her," said Dar. "I told them not to harm you and return to camp."

"They should na stay there. In a siege, the king will have the advantage."

"We have no desire to fight. All we want is to be left alone."

"The king will give you na choice. Your orcs have rebelled. War has already begun."

Thirty-eight

♛

As Dar walked to the walled garrison, Sevren talked about their situation. "Time is on your side," he said, "but only briefly. The king's a wary man, so he keeps his generals in Taiben, but na his troops. He has his royal guard on hand, plus a few shieldrons of foot. That's na enough to take on your orcs. He needs to summon more troops for that. But he assuredly will."

"Sevren, this isn't your fight."

"There are but two sides, and I can na go back to Taiben."

"You can take neither side and leave."

"On foot? Nay, I've made my choice. I'm yours if you'll have me."

"I could use your advice. I've seen little of war."

Sevren smiled grimly. "And I've seen too much. You should know that the garrison was built as a cage, na as a stronghold. It lacks a well, and little food is stored there. In a siege, thirst and starvation favor the attackers."

"How soon could an attack come?" asked Dar.

"There's a regiment of foot that could reach here by late morning. Horse troops could arrive soon after. They'd suffice to pen you in the garrison until forces gather for a full assault."

"So we should flee."

"The king will na let you go unchallenged. Instead of

running, take a strong position on a hill. Orcs are best in a head-on fight, something simple."

Dar sighed. "I wanted to save the queen, not start a war."

"You can win if the orcs fight to their advantage." Then Sevren launched into an explanation of tactics, waving his hands in the air to represent opposing armies. Dar tried to follow his descriptions as best she could, but found it difficult to think of war abstractly. She was too intimate with its carnage to think of orcs and men as pieces in a game. War might be a game to kings, but they could watch in safety while others fought. Moreover, they had generals to guide their moves. Dar had only a guardsman. The orcs would be even less useful as strategists.

Despite her misgivings, Dar was prepared to give orders by the time the orcs neared the garrison. First, she halted them before the gates. "We will stay here just long enough to prepare for marching. All sons with capes, come speak with me." She turned to Zna-yat. "Get my urkzimmuthi clothes for our queen, then join sons with capes." She turned to Kovok-mah. "I'll need your help also."

Kovok-mah bowed. "Hai, Mother."

Dar was about to enter the gates when Sevren tapped her on the shoulder. "You should post a watch," he said in a low voice.

Dar hastily corrected her oversight. Then she had the queen carried to an empty barracks and ordered a fire to be built. As the room warmed, it began to fill with armored orcs. Garga-tok was among them. He had added many ears to the fringe of his cape since Dar had last seen it. When all the caped orcs had assembled, Dar turned to the queen. "Great Mother, do you have any words for these sons?"

"Listen to Dargu-yat's wisdom," said Muth Mauk.

Then she hobbled over to the fire to warm her shaking hands.

All eyes turned toward Dar. For a moment, she felt overwhelmed. Then the press of circumstance forced her to speak. "Washavokis will fight. This place does not favor us in battle. Hilltop would be better. Tell those sons who follow you to hurry. When we march, washavoki mothers will join us. Honor them."

The caped sons departed, leaving Zna-yat and Kovok-mah. "Zna-yat, watch over Muth Mauk and do whatever she needs. Kovok-mah, come with me."

Dar strode toward the women's building. "Remember how frightened I was when you first saw me?" she asked.

"Hai," said Kovok-mah.

"Mothers here will be equally frightened. Some more so. I want them to see your goodness."

"Do you still think I'm good?" asked Kovok-mah. "Are you not angry?"

"It was proper for you to obey your muthuri. I'm sad, not angry."

"I'm sad also."

Dar stopped before the women's building. "Let's make some mothers happy." Dar unbarred the door and entered. Kovok-mah followed, and his presence hushed all the women inside. Dar addressed them in a loud voice. "All the soldiers are gone. Orcs now possess the camp." A low, frightened murmur arose. "Now you have a choice. Your brands mark you as the king's property. You can flee to him for use as he sees fit, or you can listen to me. I've learned orcs honor women and protect them. Soon, the orcs will leave this camp. If you join them, you'll be safe and free."

The room erupted in a din of voices. One called out, "How do we know the orcs won't eat us?"

Dar shouted back. "Such tales are lies! Who among you survived this summer's fighting?"

"I did," shouted a woman.

"Tell them what happened," shouted Dar.

"The soldiers left us to die. All my friends were slain."

Still, the debate raged on. Finally Dar shouted, "You can wait here for the soldiers or you can leave with me now." Then she led Kovok-mah outside and waited. About a dozen women emerged from the building, including the one who had survived the summer campaign. Dar waited for others to join them, but no more came.

When Dar realized that she could save only the few women before her, she grasped Kovok-mah's hand. "This is Kovok-mah. He is kind and gentle. He speaks our language and will take care of you." She turned to Kovok-mah. "Stay with these mothers and protect them." Then she added, "Kaf tha sat therth, reefat pi Tahwee Ki." *When you see them, think of Little Bird.*

Kovok-mah bowed. "Ma lo." *I will.*

By early morning, Dar led the orcs from the garrison. In choosing their destination, she relied on an odd pair of counselors—Sevren and Garga-tok. Both favored a tall hill that overlooked the road to Taiben. It was sunny, but a chill north wind caused Dar to clutch her cloak about her. The garment was too large for her, having belonged up till that morning to an officer in the garrison. It bore a fresh bloodstain, but it was warm, and the mountain road would be snowy.

Dar marched at the head of the column alongside the queen's litter. Zna-yat, Garga-tok, and Sevren accompanied her, along with two dozen seasoned fighters who served as guards. The remainder of the orcs marched as they had for the king—arranged in orderly shieldrons. The women walked in the middle of the column, wearing soldiers' cloaks and guided by Kovok-mah.

As the orcs headed for high ground, a formation of

foot soldiers appeared on the road to Taiben. The city's gate opened and a mounted contingent of the royal guard, accompanied by two shieldrons of infantry, joined the approaching soldiers. The combined forces didn't seem small to Dar. At first, she thought they would attack immediately, but they seemed reluctant to do so. The soldiers pursued the orcs, but slowly. Meanwhile, Dar quickened the march and the distance from the soldiers increased. This pleased her until she watched the king's men change direction and move off at a forced march. Sevren observed this maneuver also, and his expression worried Dar. "What's the matter?" she asked.

"I've been a fool," said Sevren. "They'll na face us on a hill. They're going to take the pass and block our way home. We should attack before they're in position."

The queen spoke from her litter. "Grunat dati?" *Fight today?*

"Hai, Great Mother," replied Dar in Orcish. "This washavoki son is skilled in battles. He says we'd be wise to kill washavokis while they're unready."

"Sons don't advise mothers," said the queen in her own tongue. "There shall be no more killing today. More important things will happen."

Dar had no choice but to obey her queen, although she questioned Muth Mauk's thinking. *That battle will determine our fate. What could be more important?* Dar could think of nothing. Even if the queen wasn't delusional, her decision was terrible strategy. It caused Dar to recall Murdant Teeg's claim that orcs lost battles because they lacked guile.

"What did the queen just say?" Sevren asked.

"We're going to the hilltop," replied Dar. "There'll be no fighting today."

"That's daft!" said Sevren. "We can overcome that force, but it'll be reinforced soon. The pass is narrow and the enemy will occupy high ground. Remember the Vale of Pines?"

"I remember, but the queen's made up her mind." Dar softened her voice. "It's still not too late to leave."

"I'd rather stay with you."

"Then you're a fool."

Sevren smiled ruefully. "That's been said before."

The orcs reached the hilltop by midmorning. Wind had swept most of the snow from its summit. Using stones, the orcs marked the Embrace of Muth la, then erected their shelters within it. Afterward, the camp grew peaceful. Some sons gathered wood for the women, who began cooking what little food there was. A few orcs stood guard, while the rest retreated to their shelters. Muth Mauk basked in the sun, despite the cold.

But Dar felt far from peaceful. The quietness of the orcs' encampment contrasted with the activity of the king's men. From the hilltop, Dar watched them prepare for battle. First, she observed the enemy troops make their way north to the pass. Before the last of them were hidden from view, cavalry appeared on the road, riding from the south. They headed for the pass also. Dar felt certain they would join the other soldiers soon.

Seeing the royal army's skillful deployment gave Dar a sense of doom—a conviction that their journey home would be bloody and their chances diminished as time passed. Dar felt it was imperative to attack immediately, and she went to convince the queen to act. She found Muth Mauk still seated outside her shelter. The queen was shivering and her breathing was labored, yet she smiled. "Long has it been since I sat under Muth la's golden eye and felt her breath."

"You'll have many days to do that," said Dar. "You should get out of wind and cold."

"Did Muth la send you visions of my many days?"

"Thwa, Auntie."

"I thought not," said the queen, "so I'll enjoy this one."

Dar bowed very low. "Muth Mauk, my thoughts are troubled. May I speak them?"

"Please do."

"I think we should start home today. There are washavokis that will fight us, but fewer now than later."

"That's not important," replied the queen.

"Forgive my rudeness, but how is that not important? You are our great mother. Muth la sent me to bring you home. Those washavokis will try to stop us."

"And why need I go home?"

The question took Dar aback, and it was a moment before she replied. "Poison has made you sick. You need healing magic."

"Dargu, I've received healing magic for many winters." The queen smiled at Dar's puzzlement. "Black Washavoki put it in my food each night."

"Thwa. That was poison."

"Black Washavoki poisoned me long ago. Since then, he has given me magic so I might live. That magic clouded my thoughts, but it kept me alive." Muth Mauk read Dar's stunned expression. "Hai, Dargu, I'll die soon. Today, I think."

Dar felt overwhelmed by guilt and despair. "Then I will have caused your death!" She knelt before the queen as tears welled in her eyes. "My chest bursts! I didn't know. Please forgive me!"

"There's nothing to forgive. I chose to die."

Dar's shock, sadness, and confusion were reduced to a single word—"Why?"

"I'm not important," said the queen. "Before I was Muth Mauk, I was Zeta-yat. When I received Fathma from queen before me, I became Muth Mauk. Fathma is important, not I. It is spirit of urkzimmuthi. I endured living only so Fathma wouldn't be lost, so I could pass it to you."

"Why should I receive it?"

"Because Muth la chose you. Remember your vision of me? When I asked where you were, I was asking for mother to receive Fathma."

"Thwa! Thwa! It can't be me."

"Dargu-yat, it must be you. I'm dying, and you're only urkzimmuthi mother here. This is Muth la's will, your purpose in life." With shaking hands, Muth Mauk gently wiped the tears from Dar's face. "Sit close to me. Let beauty of Muth la's creation calm your chest."

"Muth Mauk, I'm not ready."

"No one is ready for life. We are simply born and start living. When you're Muth Mauk, just follow your chest."

"That was Velasa-pah's guidance."

Muth Mauk smiled. "Muth la's also, I think." Then the queen turned her face toward the sun.

Thirty-nine

♛

When the sun was setting, Muth Mauk requested the orcs to assemble. Sevren and the women were invited to watch, although they couldn't understand what was being said. The orcs sat encircling the queen, who stood gripping Dar to steady herself. Muth Mauk began by recounting how a child possessing Fathma had been born into the Yat clan. She told how that Fathma had been passed on from great mother to great mother, naming each. She ended with her own name.

"Fathma is Muth la's gift to urkzimmuthi," said Muth Mauk. "Mother who receives this spirit is closest to Muth la. Her words are wisdom and must be obeyed."

"Hai, Muth Mauk," said the orcs in unison.

"Soon Muth la will embrace me," said the queen. "She has sent another mother to receive her gift. That mother is Dargu-yat."

Dar expected some expression of surprise or protest, but she detected none in the solemn faces surrounding her. Dar knew what to do next. She cast off her cloak and stood bare-chested before Muth Mauk. Then the queen placed her hands above Dar's breasts. "Let Fathma pass to Dargu-yat."

The queen's hands felt warm against Dar's skin, and when Muth Mauk spoke, that warmth increased. Dar had thought the touching was purely ceremonial, but the sensation it caused was more than tactile. The warmth became transforming energy that spread throughout her body. Dar heard soft voices murmuring like leaves stirred by a gentle breeze. She glanced about, but the assembled orcs were still and silent. The murmuring grew louder, and Dar realized that memories, not sounds, echoed inside her head. Then the memories faded, and the night was quiet again. Dar felt different and knew she was different. The world remained the same, but she saw it through eyes that were both new and ancient. The gift she had received was greater than wisdom or power. It was love. Dar gazed at the orcs around her and knew they were her children. She cherished them as their mother—their great mother.

The former queen removed her crown and placed it on Dar's head. "My time is over," she said, and sank to the ground.

All the orcs rose immediately and bowed low to Dar. "Tava, Muth Mauk!" they said. Then, without further ado, they departed for their shelters. Only Sevren and the women remained, standing apart and confused until Kovok-mah spoke to them in low tones. Then they departed, also. Dar didn't notice. Her sole concern was the former queen.

"Auntie, I'll take you to healer. You'll be well again."

"Someone who's dead cannot be healed."

"Please don't say that. You're alive."

"My spirit departed with Fathma, and spirit is life. There can be only one living Muth Mauk."

"Will someone tell . . ." Dar paused and glanced around. "Where is everyone?"

"They left because it's unnatural to speak to those who are dead."

"You're not dead. And I won't leave you."

"Thwa, Muth Mauk, it is *I* who will leave *you*."

The former queen proved her point by dying before midnight. Dar roused some orcs and told them to prepare a funeral pyre. Afterward, she retreated to her shelter, already feeling the loneliness of sovereignty. All the lives around her depended on her judgments. It was a burden she didn't want but couldn't evade. Dar possessed Fathma and understood her obligations. Still, she didn't want to order her children into battle, knowing that many would perish, even in a victory. Moreover, fighting felt wrong. *Then how will they get home?* Fighting seemed the only answer.

At last, Dar decided to speak to Sevren. *He's fought for the king. He can advise me.* She found him wrapped in his cloak, asleep by the embers of a cooking fire. Dar shook him awake. He blinked and rubbed his eyes. "What do you want, Your Majesty?" he asked without a trace of irony.

"So you know I'm queen."

"Aye, that green-eyed fellow told us. Congratulations."

"I didn't want this. It was a complete surprise." Dar sighed heavily. "I need to know how to fight the king."

"That's a tricky problem. Numbers and terrain will favor the king's men. Orcs are best in a straight-on fight where their strength gives them an edge."

"So what should I do?"

"Bull your way through the pass and take your losses."

"And why is that best?"

"Your soldiers are orcs. You must employ their strengths."

"And what are the king's strengths?" asked Dar.

"They'll fight cleverly. They use the terrain to dart in and out, avoiding a single battle. If you can na crush them, they'll hit you again and again."

"So I should try for a big battle?"

"Aye."

"That doesn't make sense," said Dar. "You're only a

guardsman, and you understand strategy. Why would the king's generals be different? If we do what's expected, we're doomed."

"You can na change the nature of an orc."

Dar stared into the starry sky, lost in thought. A long time passed before she spoke. "You're right, Sevren. You can't change the nature of an orc." Then Dar smiled for the first time since she was crowned. "But the nature of their queen has changed."

Dar slept, and by some special grace, awoke refreshed. When she left her shelter, she knew her most difficult task would probably be the first one. Dar summoned the orcs to address them. "I've pondered why Muth la made me queen. Now I know. It's because I understand minds of washavokis. They're different from ours."

The orcs gestured their agreement.

Dar continued. "When we speak, our words have meaning and reflect what we know. Yet washavokis often say words without meaning, words they call 'lies.' They know urkzimmuthi do not speak lies."

Dar prepared herself for the hard part. "Today, you must do something that makes little sense, something that goes against your natures. Today, we'll forgo ancient customs. We won't place our dead mother on pyre. We'll carry her body to washavokis and say she lives."

An agitated murmur arose from the orcs. Dar heard shock, puzzlement, and even anger in their voices. *Soon I'll find out if I'm truly queen.* As she waited for the orcs to quiet, she felt strangely calm. Life had become simple. She would explain her plan as best she could and then discover its fate and hers. She could do no more.

King Kregant was pacing in his throne room when the guardsman entered. "What news?" asked the king.

"The orcs have left the hill, sire."

"Are they headed for the pass?"

"No, for the city."

Kregant whirled and glared at the Queen's Man. "General Tarkum, you said they'd flee. Now they're about to attack!"

"Your Majesty, the piss eyes lack the means for an assault."

"Then why are they headed here? Some kind of trick?"

Tarkum remained calm. "They're incapable of tricks."

The mage spoke. "Their queen has sickened without my potion. They realize they need my magic."

"That must be it," said Tarkum. "I know their superstitions. If the queen dies without a piss eye bitch nearby, the royal line is broken."

"That's why we kept her isolated," added the mage. "To keep her in our power."

"Well, we don't have her now," said the king, "so I've lost my piss eye troops!"

"The orcs will return their queen to my care," said Othar, "and obey us as before."

Kregant wanted to ask Othar why his precious bones hadn't warned of the queen's escape, but a glance at the mage froze his courage. Instead he asked, "Who helped the queen flee? She couldn't have done it unaided."

"A branded girl works in your kitchen," said Othar. "I sense something wrong about her."

Kregant turned to a guardsman. "Find out who she is and fetch her."

The guardsman wavered for a moment, then spoke. "Sire, I know who she is. Her name is Dar. A murdant came looking for her just before the piss eye queen vanished."

"Well, find this Dar if she's still here," said the king. "Torture her and bring me her confession."

The guardsman left and the king resumed his pacing. Throughout the morning, reports arrived: No one could find Dar. A guardsman named Sevren had deserted. The orcs were definitely headed for the city.

The king took what actions he could. He decreed the deaths of Dar and Sevren. He sent messengers with orders requiring all the soldiers at the pass to march to Taiben. Having done those things, he waited for better news. By early afternoon he received some: The orcs had returned to their garrison and only a small delegation was headed for the city. The king sent his most sharp-eyed guardsman to observe and report.

The guardsman returned a short while later, out of breath from running. "There are seven unarmed piss eyes outside the gate. Six carry a litter bearing their queen. One holds up a tree branch."

"That's the piss eye sign for truce," said General Tarkum.

The guardsman continued. "The piss eye with the branch has prisoners. A guardsman and a girl. The girl's really carrying on—weeping and pleading with the piss eye."

"What does it want?" asked the king.

"It wants to parley with you."

"With me? Preposterous!" He turned to General Tarkum. "You're the Queen's Man. Go speak with the piss eye, but have soldiers hiding. If anything seems funny, kill the lot and seize the queen."

Forty

♛

General Tarkum watched the gate rise to reveal a small group of orcs standing on the road. He recognized the one waving the tree branch as Garga-tok by his ear-fringed cape. That reassured him, for he recalled the orc's steadfastness during the summer campaign. *That piss eye's loyal.*

Garga-tok's scabbard was empty, as were those of the orcs who bore the litter. Tarkum regarded the queen upon it. *Her Majesty doesn't look well. She needs magic quick.* Tarkum couldn't read the orcs' expressions, but judging from the queen's condition, he assumed they were desperate. *This will make things easy.*

Besides the tree branch, Garga-tok held ropes that tethered the wrists of his captives. Tarkum turned his attention to them. He didn't know the guardsman, who stood silent and defeated. The hysterical girl looked familiar, despite the fact her face was smeared with charcoal. Tarkum thought a moment, trying to place her. Suddenly, it came to him. *The orc wench! The girl Kol spoke about.* Tarkum grew puzzled. *I thought she was dead.*

Garga-tok spoke. "Queen's Man, we have been foolish. These two . . ." He jerked the ropes of his captives. "These two stole Great Mother. Said take home for gift of yellow iron. Now Great Mother sick."

"Hai, you have acted foolishly," replied Tarkum.

"We take Great Mother to Black Washavoki for

magic. We speak good words to Great Washavoki. I show friendship and kill these two."

Tarkum formed his lips in the imitation of an orcish smile. "I know urkzimmuthi are friends, and I will tell this to king. Go back to camp. We will take Great Mother for healing and punish two evil washavokis."

"Thwa," said Garga-tok. "We must carry Great Mother. Honor says this."

Tarkum didn't like the idea, but he knew orcs were touchy about their queen. *They're unarmed, and I have troops hidden.* He put on another smile. "Come. Honor your Great Mother. We will make her well."

Garga-tok bowed. "Shashav, Queen's Man." Then he said something in Orcish, and the procession entered the city.

As the prisoners walked past Tarkum, his curiosity about the girl caused him to approach her. Her face was downcast, so he reached out and turned it toward him. As soon as he touched the girl, the orcs halted. That disturbed him, but something he thought he glimpsed on the girl's smudged face disturbed him more. Tarkum used his free hand to wipe her chin clean. When he saw a clan tattoo, he grew alarmed. "Lower the gate!" he shouted. "Attack!"

Tarkum heard the girl shout in Orcish, and the orcs dropped the litter. As the queen rolled onto the pavement, Tarkum realized she was dead. He also saw that her body covered a cache of weapons. Garga-tok pushed him away from the girl, bounded over to the litter, and grabbed an ax. By the time Tarkum drew his sword, Garga-tok was standing before him, his lips curled back in a black-toothed grin. Tarkum swung his blade and the orc countered the blow, sending the sword clattering on the cobblestones.

Garga-tok grinned again. "Nice ears," he said.

*   *   *

Dar had hoped to reach the palace without opposition and was surprised when her plan unraveled so quickly. Nevertheless, she had prepared the orcs for such a contingency. One cut her bonds and shielded her from arrows with his armored body. Another orc freed Sevren. Meanwhile, Dar shouted orders in Orcish. "Open gate. Signal others. Kill washavoki soldiers."

The last command was hardly necessary, for the orcs had already counterattacked with unrestrained ferocity. As Dar reached the shelter of the gatehouse, which was already littered with the bodies of its defenders, two orcs reached the parapets on the city's walls. Soon it rained archers instead of arrows. The orcs raised the gate and Dar could see their comrades leaving the garrison and running for the city. The king had kept the royal guard at the palace and his best troops were still at the pass. Thus, by the time the orcs arrived from the garrison, the first fighting was over. When all the orcs were within the city, Dar had the gate lowered to lock out King Kregant's army.

Dar gave orders, and the orcs, except for guards left at the gate, headed for the palace. They passed through the city without harming its terrified inhabitants. As Sevren marched with them, he couldn't help contrasting the orcs' behavior with how the king's men treated captured cities. *I chose the right side*, he thought.

The palace gates were shut, but only a few archers defended them, and they soon fled. An oak beam was pulled from a building to serve as a battering ram. Before long, the gates lay shattered on the ground and the orcs poured into the palace courtyard. It was eerily quiet. Dar turned to Sevren for an explanation. "Where are the guardsmen?"

"They'll have retreated to the keep. 'Tis an ancient stronghold, the oldest wing of the palace. The king will take refuge there, for it can be shut off and easily defended."

"So, he'll just sit tight?"

"Aye, and let the common folk fend for themselves until the army retakes the city."

"That won't do," said Dar, fearing that the battle she had hoped to avoid would be merely postponed. "Won't he parley?"

"Nay. The mage holds sway o'er the king, and he favors bloodshed."

Dar recalled how Velasa-pah had warned her about the mage. *He's more my enemy than the king.* She still didn't understand how the bones were a greater enemy, but thinking about them gave her an idea. "The mage's tower doesn't lie within the keep!"

"Aye, 'tis in the new palace. So what?"

"Then maybe I can force the mage to parley."

"Na one can force him to do anything, na even the king. How will you manage such a feat?"

"Come with me and find out."

Dar, in the company of Zna-yat, Kovok-mah, and another orc headed for the palace. Sevren followed, curious what Dar would do. Dar entered the kitchen and peered about. Everyone had fled. Abandoned food cluttered the tables, meat charred on unturned spits, and pots boiled over. Dar headed for the servant passageway.

After a long climb, the five stood inside the dark corridor that led to the mage's tower. "Will you tell me why we're here?" asked Sevren.

"The mage may have left something behind, something precious to him."

"If it's precious, why would he leave it?"

"Maybe he didn't," conceded Dar. "But I'm hoping he thought it would be safe. After all, who would want to pass that door?"

Na I, thought Sevren. Yet he followed Dar into the tower. As he climbed its spiral stairs, he felt that his reticence had been well founded, for he had never encountered a more evil place. The cold and darkness had a foul, unnatural quality that made Sevren's skin crawl. Even the orcs looked frightened. The stairs ended at a second door, its rusted surface covered with strange runes. Dar pushed it open and stepped into the room beyond.

A single candle burned in the chamber, casting no more light than a crescent moon on a foggy night. Dar used it to light more candles, but the room grew only marginally brighter. An evil presence was so strong that Sevren expected the mage to step out of the shadows.

While the orcs stood guard, Dar passed into another chamber. Sevren gathered his courage and trailed after her. He found Dar standing before a black stone pedestal with a black cloth bag upon it. Sevren drew closer. "Are those the bones?" he whispered.

"I think so," said Dar. She lifted the sack. It was abnormally heavy, but its contents felt like bones.

"Open it," whispered Sevren.

Dar reached for the drawstrings, then drew back her hand. "No. That's what they want."

"Who?"

"The bones. I think those stitches on the bag are spells to contain evil."

"Why do you think that?"

"A feeling. Also something the mage said about what happened to his face." Dar seized the bag. "Let's get out of here."

The orcs had stayed in the outer room, but they were as anxious to leave as Sevren. By the time the five emerged into the kitchen, Dar's fingers stung from the cold emanating from the bag and her arms ached from the effort of carrying its unnatural weight. Also, nightmarish images flickered through her mind, visions of slaughter so real that they made her tremble. She felt that the contents of the bag were resisting her and she wasn't holding inanimate objects, but something possessing a malign will.

Regardless, Dar held on to the bones, for she needed them to carry out her plan. It was a simple one, based on her assumption that the mage was the true power behind the throne. Dar would return the sorcerer's magic bones only if the king made peace. Facing Kregant and his mage would be dangerous, but Dar felt peace was worth the risk, especially since the negotiations wouldn't endanger the orcs. The peril would be hers alone. If her plan worked, bloodshed would be avoided and the orcs would be left alone. Yet Dar was already worried. She distrusted both the king and the mage. Insuring that they kept their word would be tricky. Moreover, the bones are not mere valuables to be traded. *They're my enemy too.* Having sensed their evil nature, Dar knew they would work to betray her.

Forty-one

♛

The keep was a formidable structure. The huge stone tower thrust from the ground like a cross between a tree trunk and a small mountain. Its single entrance was midway up its side and reachable only by a slender stone bridge. The keep was built to meet military needs, not human comfort. Its windows were slits for archers, and its thick walls were cold and dank, even in the summer. It had its own well and storerooms filled with food. Within its walls, the king, his court, and his guard could live for many months.

Sevren thought of all those things as he stepped onto the narrow bridge, flanked by two orcs bearing signs of truce. The gate was closed, but Sevren knew someone was listening. He also knew that behind each slit in the wall stood an archer with his bowstring drawn. Very likely, most of the arrows were aimed at him.

"I have a message for the king and his mage!" shouted Sevren.

"Let's hear it, traitor."

"Know that the orcs have a new queen. She wishes to speak with your king and his dark counselor."

Sevren waited a long time for a reply. "The king has no desire to speak."

"Would he rather watch this city burn around him? Does he wish to be sovereign over corpses and ashes?"

Again Sevren had a lengthy wait for a response. "Tell your queen that whatever harms she visits on our kingdom, will be returned tenfold. The orcish halls will flow with blood."

Sevren thought he heard the mage's counsel in the reply. "Then know that when the destruction begins, *this* will perish first." One of the orcs held up the bag of magic bones. "If the king's sorcerer ever returns to his tower, he'll find the black pedestal empty."

The response came quicker than before. "They will talk."

An iron basket containing a man whom Sevren recognized as the royal steward was lowered over the keep's parapet. He climbed from the basket displaying empty palms. "I'm here to arrange the time, place, and conditions of the parley. To whom am I to speak? To a traitor or piss eye brutes?"

"Speak to me," said Sevren. "My companions are provoked by insolence."

The lengthy time required to arrange the parley was a measure of the distrust between the two sides. The steward made many trips in the iron basket and Sevren spoke with Dar often before an agreement was reached. At Dar's insistence, the talks were to take place that day. The king and his mage would meet with her in a small room off the palace's great hall. All three would be unarmed, but accompanied by armed followers who would wait in the hall. Both sides would inspect the parley room in advance and each would have a key to one of two locks on the room's door. The negotiants would ring a bell when they finished their discussions and wished to leave the room.

When Dar negotiated the terms of the meeting, she relied on her own judgment. The orcs were too straightforward to give useful advice, while Sevren was so suspicious that his conditions would have jeopardized the talks. Zna-yat voiced concerns also. Dar admitted that she was taking a risk, but since the alternative was war, she overruled all objections.

Once the arrangements had been finalized, Dar prepared for the meeting. She bathed and scrubbed the charcoal from her face. Since the former queen was still dressed in Dar's kefs and neva, Sevren found Dar a noblewoman's gown to wear beneath her urkzimmuthi cloak. Dar completed her outfit with the shoes Sevren had given her and the gold band that was her crown. Then she waited for the parley to begin.

Though Dar had been queen for less than a day, she possessed clarity of purpose. She had none of royalty's affectations and was ignorant of courtly manners; she simply was Muth Mauk. Inspired by Fathma, she expressed her new power as naturally as a river or the wind.

At last, Zna-yat appeared to escort her to the negotiations. When Dar reached the hall, the red light of sunset shown through its windows, painting the guardsmen and orcs with bloody hues. Dar hoped it wasn't an omen. The parley room lay at the far end of the hall. When Dar reached it, Zna-yat handed her the bag containing the bones and opened the door. The room beyond was small, and all its furnishing had been removed. The walls bore no tapestries and the limestone floor lacked carpets. The only light came from a large window and the fire in an ornate fireplace. No candlesticks or other objects that could serve as weapons were present.

King Kregant II and Othar, the royal mage, entered the room shortly after Dar. The door closed behind them, and its two locks clicked. Dar looked the two men over. The king was red-faced and moved with the exaggerated care of one wishing to appear sober. The mage's eyes instantly fixed on the bag. He seemed desperate for its return and enraged that Dar had taken it.

While Dar sized up the king and mage, Kregant looked her over. His expression became amused and disdainful. "You bear my brand! Am I to parley with my own chattel?" He laughed. "A mare doesn't bandy with her rider. That's why we have bits."

Dar fixed the king with a cool glance. "I was lowly once," she said. "Yet such is the power of the World's Mother that I've been transformed. I'm Muth Mauk now, reborn to rule a noble race. All their might is my power, and my words are their words. You'd be wise to listen."

Kregant attempted another laugh, but it died in his throat. "I guess it matters not who speaks for the piss eyes. What favor have you come to beg?"

"I'm not here to beg," replied Dar. "This is our due. We are to be left in peace. No more will we fight your wars. Those women who once served us must be rewarded and released from further duty."

"The oaths that bind the orcs to me harken to my great-grandfather's time," answered the king. "I see no cause to set them aside."

"We've long served this kingdom, but you've abused our service. We won't die to enrich you."

"So you'd rather die as rebels? My troops are massing outside the city. I've viewed them from the keep."

"Do you also wish to view your city's destruction and the slaughter of its folk?"

The king returned Dar's gaze. "And you'd command all that death? The hewing of sweet babes? The murder of their weeping mothers?" Kregant waited for an answer, then smiled. "I thought not. Women lack the stomach for war."

"Perhaps I can't kill innocents," replied Dar. Then she held out the black bag. "But *these* I can destroy. If there's no peace, the bones will be lost forever."

The mage, who had been observing silently, suddenly cried out. "Sire!" There was a note of panic in his voice.

"I'll cast them into a fire," said Dar, "and be glad to be rid of them."

"I care not," said the king.

"Sire," said the mage. "Such an act would blind you to the future. Why grope about like ordinary men?"

"And pay this girl's price?" asked Kregant. "It's too dear."

"Too dear!" exclaimed the mage. "For the power the bones bestow?"

Kregant smiled and seemed to enjoy his mage's dismay. "I detest the wretched things. If she wants to burn them, she may."

The mage began to tremble, but Dar was unsure if it was from fear or rage. Then the sorcerer flicked his right arm and something flashed into his palm. Before Dar could see what it was, the mage's hand shot out and crossed the king's throat. It left a bloody line in its wake. For an instant, Kregant gaped in astonishment. Then his hands went to his throat to discover what had been done. They came back covered with blood. The king stared at them in terror, made a gurgling sound, and fell face-down. A crimson pool spread over the white stone floor.

"What have you done?" cried the mage. "Oh false woman, you've killed Our Majesty!"

If Dar hadn't been so horrified, she would have laughed at the mage's accusation. Then she realized it was for the ears outside the door. Dar recalled the frightened queen with her young son and perceived the mage's intention. *He'll "counsel" them and rule in their name. Only one witness stands in his way.* Dar saw the mage touch the object in his hand and its blade retracted into its handle. He touched it again, and out sprang a thin, silvery spike. Dar noted that its tip was discolored greenish-brown. *It's poisoned!*

"So I'm to die, too," said Dar.

"Aye, and much quicker than I'd like."

The mage thrust the spike at Dar, and she jumped to avoid it. She used the bag as a shield, guessing that the sorcerer dared not pierce its fabric. From the cautious way he jabbed at her, she realized that her guess was right. Still, the mage pressed his assault, backing Dar toward the fallen king. Soon she was standing in Kregant's blood.

The bag turned suddenly heavier, pulling Dar's arms downward. Othar saw his opening and thrust at Dar's chest. She twisted sideways, but felt the spike graze her skin. The mage was triumphant. "Ha! You're slain!"

Dar knew it was true. She already felt a pain below her breast. It felt hot and cold at once. Dar recalled the vision she had in the darkness with Muth-pah, and finally understood its true meaning. That spot of pain would become a hole through which her life would drain away. *I've lost the battle*, she thought. Then Dar saw how she could make the mage lose also. With all her strength, she threw the bag at the fireplace. It landed in the flames.

Othar's triumph instantly became horror, and he rushed to the fireplace. He thrust his hands into the fire to pull out the bag. As he did so, its bottom gave way and the bones tumbled into the flames. The mage screamed, and the scream rose in pitch until it became an unearthly screech, horrible to hear. Othar jerked around as his skin bubbled and blackened. The flesh of his fingers dripped away, exposing charred bones that dropped—joint by joint—to the floor. All the while, the mage screamed and writhed. Dar couldn't imagine how he still lived, but he did. His skin continued to char and shrivel until his wide eyes seemed to gape from a burned corpse. His voice dwindled to a whisper of a shriek, which, for all it faintness, lost none of its power to appall.

Dar looked down. She was standing in a pool of blood, and it was steaming. She realized that if she stepped outside the pool, she would share the mage's fate. All she could do was to stay put until the magic lost its potency. It did when the last bone crumbled into ash.

Then the mage ceased writing and the blood cooled. Dar stepped from her crimson refuge and pulled up her gown to examine her wound. It was a mere scratch that barely broke the skin. "So strange," she said to the still room, "that such a little thing should kill me."

Forty-two

♛

Having foreseen her demise, Dar expected it to happen quickly. Yet the pain from the poisoned wound didn't spread rapidly, and Dar continued to live. It gave her hope that she might still accomplish something. It also made her bold. Dar rang the bell to signal that the talks were over. As she waited for the door to be unlocked, Dar prepared herself for the chance that the king's death would cause fighting to break out.

The two locks clicked, and both the high tolum of the guard and Zna-yat peered past the open door. The high tolum spoke first. "What treachery is this?" He moved to draw his sword, but Zna-yat seized his arm before he could.

"Treachery indeed!" said Dar. "Yet the traitor is already dead, killed by his own sorcery."

"Lies!" said the high tolum, who was still restrained by Zna-yat. Dar could see that the orcs and men behind the two were growing restive.

"Before you call for revenge, look around," said Dar. "Does this look like my handiwork?"

The crumpled figure of the mage was so blasted that it barely looked human. The king's death looked equally unnatural. The pool of blood had evaporated and the gash in his neck was so scorched and blackened that it seemed he had been struck by lightning. Dar spoke to Zna-yat in Orcish, and he released the guardsman's arm, permitting him to walk freely about the room. The high tolum inspected the two bodies and shook his head. "This was foul magic indeed." He spit on the mage's charred body. "Blood Crow was a fitting name for him."

"Does Kregant's queen now rule?" asked Dar.

"Aye, Girta will be regent until her son's of age. May Karm protect him."

"The mage wanted war, but peace is all I desire," said Dar. "Perhaps Queen Girta will be of like mind."

"Perhaps."

"I would fain parley with her," said Dar. As she spoke the pain in her chest grew stronger. "There is urgency in this matter."

"I will speak to her and bring you her reply."

After the guardsman left, Zna-yat cast Dar a concerned look. *He smells my pain.* Dar couldn't bring herself to tell him of her wound or to lie about it, so she remained silent and waited for the queen's reply. She was surprised when the guardsman didn't return with a message, but with the queen. Girta went straight to her fallen husband. If she felt any grief, she didn't show it. Rather, she looked at his corpse dispassionately, as if it were some curiosity. Her reaction to the mage's body was undisguised satisfaction. Then she turned to Dar. "Tell me what happened."

Dar recounted everything except that the mage had wounded her. When she was done, Girta seemed satisfied, "I'd like to finish what the mage interrupted," said Dar, "and bring peace to our realms. May we speak in private as queen to queen?"

"Tomorrow, perhaps. So much has happened."

Dar grasped Girta's hand firmly. "The chance for peace is slipping away faster than you know. We *must* speak now and away from other ears!"

Dar's intensity made Girta acquiesce. She had the others leave the room and shut the door. Then she turned to Dar. "Well?"

"I omitted something from my account," said Dar. "The mage has stabbed me with a poisoned blade." She handed Girta the mage's weapon, which she had retrieved and hidden in her gown.

"Why tell me this?"

"Because I'll die soon. If I do before peace is made, I dread what will follow. Wars are easy to start, but hard to end. The orcs are already inside the palace, if they're provoked . . . Well, I've seen firsthand what they can do. Pray you're spared the sight."

Girta looked shaken. "So you asked for this private talk to threaten me?"

"No. I'm here to offer you strength to do what's right, something the mage would have never done. I think he killed the king and poisoned me so he could rule through you. You know the man. Do you agree?"

"Aye. Already, he was more the king than my husband."

"I was an ordinary woman once. I know men. They think our sex is weak. Other men will attempt to do by force what the mage would have done by magic. You'll be queen in name only, and your son will always be in peril."

Girta looked on the verge of weeping, causing Dar to soften her voice. "There's a way to avoid that fate. Orcs honor mothers. They'll protect you. With them by your side, who'd dare oppose you?"

"Why would they do such a thing?"

"Because I would command them, and because it's their nature. Soon I'll walk the Dark Path. I wish peace to be my legacy."

Still, Girta hesitated, and there was fear in her eyes. "Orcs? Live surrounded by orcs?"

"When I was freshly branded, I thought the orcs would eat me. Yet the only kindness I received came from them. Learn to see them as I do, and you won't be afraid."

"I don't know if that's possible."

"Among the orcs is the one who first befriended me. His name is Kovok-mah. He speaks your tongue and will show you the gentleness of his kind. Meet with him." Dar moaned. "But hurry! My pains are growing stronger."

When Girta saw that Dar's lips had grown as pale as her face, she was gripped by a sense of urgency. "My heart tells me that you speak true. I'll see this Kovok-mah later tonight. For now, tell me what we must do."

"Let us make a treaty. The orcs will form a guard to protect you and your son. In return, you swear to use them only for defense, never for conquest or pillage. Also, their accommodations in your court must conform to orcish customs, so that mothers may visit to give them food and guidance. Finally, promise to honor and reward the branded women for their service and release them from further duties."

"Those are easy terms," said Girta. "Why so generous?"

"Those terms will secure peace, and peace is priceless."

Girta kissed Dar's clammy forehead. "Then let us announce this treaty together."

Dar addressed the orcs first and described the agreement in their own tongue. She didn't mention her fatal wound. Instead, she attempted to appear perfectly well, although the effort strained her. Girta spoke next. By then, courtiers had mingled with the guardsmen and many of them scoffed at their fledgling ruler's plans. As soon as Girta finished speaking, the orcs thundered their allegiance to the "Washavoki Great Mother," demonstrating that the new queen had formidable allies. Those men who responded to power instantly changed their attitude, and those who valued peace saw cause for hope.

Next, the treaty was committed to parchment, and

heralds were dispatched to announce the news. By the time those formalities were accomplished, Dar was feeling dizzy and the pain in her chest had intensified. Exhausted, she ceased to struggle against the poison. Dar slumped into a chair. Her eyes closed, and she thought she was in the cave with Muth-pah. She envisioned a hole growing in her chest from which her essence streamed into the void. As in the cave, she perceived there was something else within her—something precious. *Fathma!* Dar's eyes shot open. *If I die here, Fathma will be lost again!*

Dar struggled to her feet, found Queen Girta, and pulled her aside. "I can't die here!" she whispered. "I must return home."

"I'll have you escorted in honor."

"There's no time for honor. A fast horse is what I need. That, and a fast rider." Dar gasped from a stab of pain. "Sevren. The guardsman who helped me. Get him. Please hurry."

Dar experienced the succeeding events as if drifting in and out of a dream. Moments of clarity were followed by stretches of vagueness. She found herself lying on a bed. People were talking in low voices. She saw Girta and Sevren. Then they faded. Next, she realized Zna-yat was bent over her. "Muth Mauk, atham dava-dovak?" *Great Mother, what has happened?*

Dar replied in Orcish. "Black Washavoki made evil magic. Tell no one yet. I must go home and see matriarch."

"I will take you."

"Thwa. Horse is faster." Dar groaned. "Stay here and see my will is done."

Zna-yat bowed deeply. "I will."

Dar tried to curl her lips into a smile, but her face was too tight with pain. Her vision blurred, so she couldn't see the grief on Zna-yat's face. People gathered round. Hands lifted Dar and carried her to the stables. There, someone wrapped her in a thick cloak. She was hoisted up to a waiting horseman. Dar felt his arm grasp her waist. "Sevren?" she whispered.

"Aye, 'tis me."

"Must . . . ride . . . fast."

"I know," said Sevren, his voice tender and anguished. "If the road's clear, you'll be home by morning."

Dar wanted to say something else, but the world was slipping away. She scarcely noticed when Skymere began galloping.

In a room made bright by candles, young Kregant III stared at the huge orc seated on the floor. Queen Girta stroked the prince's hair, attempting to calm him. She noted that he was sucking his thumb for the first time in years. "Darling," said Girta, fighting the tremor in her voice, "this is Kovok-mah. He's our friend."

The prince remained silent.

"I must seem very big to one so little," said Kovok-mah.

Queen Girta felt as frightened as her son. Already, she was having misgivings about the treaty. *Are these orcs any better than the mage?* she wondered. Nevertheless, Girta put on a brave front for her son's sake. "You seem big to me, also. I've never seen your kind close up." She recalled hearing somewhere that orcs could smell fear and thought it prudent to speak honestly. "I'm a bit frightened."

"Dargu was also frightened when we first met," said Kovok-mah. "Then she became angry."

"Dargu?"

"She is Great Mother, now. Back then, she was only Dargu. Word means 'weasel' in your tongue." Kovok-mah curled back his lips.

Girta had no idea what that disturbing expression meant. "I can see how one would call her weasel," she said, thinking the name was an ill omen. "I wish I could speak to her now."

"I think she will visit often."

"How can she? I doubt she'll even make it home before . . ." Girta's voice trailed off.

"Before what?" asked Kovok-mah.

"Before the poison kills her."

"Poison! What poison?"

When Girta saw the orc was agitated, and her fear increased. "I thought you knew that the mage stabbed her with a poisoned blade."

"Can I see this blade?" asked Kovok-mah.

Girta sent a servant to fetch it. Then she turned to Kovok-mah. "Didn't she tell you?"

Kovok-mah shook his head. "Dargu always hid her pain."

When Girta perceived the anguish in Kovok-mah's eyes, she had a startling insight. "You have feelings for her!"

"Hai, she fills my chest, even though . . ." The servant returned bearing the mage's weapon. Its poisoned spike was still extended. Kovok-mah sniffed it. "I know this herb. Its magic is strong and evil," he said. "Now I understand Dargu's haste. Did you see her wound?"

"No," said Girta.

"I have little hope, but little is better than none." Kovok-mah bowed low. "Forgive me, Great Washavoki Mother, but I must find Dargu."

"Will she live?"

"Long enough, perhaps."

"Long enough for what?"

Kovok-mah rose, his thoughts already elsewhere. "Perhaps. Perhaps. But only if I hurry."

Forty-three

♛

Sevren pushed Skymere as fast as he dared. Although he believed only speed could save Dar, he knew a lame horse would doom her. Trained to bear wounded from battle, Sevren rode holding Dar in front of him, her cheek resting against his chest. Only her body was close; her mind was distant as she mumbled. Usually, she spoke in Orcish. She kept repeating "Fathma," but Sevren didn't understand why.

Sometimes Sevren spoke to Dar. He said "Hold on" and "We'll be there soon." But he didn't speak his heart. *How can I tell a queen I love her? She's risen above me.* Dar had become like the farm in the hills of Averen—a lovely dream, and even less obtainable. Sevren feared the dream would soon die. It made him more reckless in urging his mount.

Sevren had never traveled the road between Taiben and the Yat clan hall, but it was easy to follow even at night and dusted with snow. He made good time at first, considering his burden. Soon he was in the hills. They were lovely in the moonlight, glistening silver against the starry sky. Their beauty was lost on Dar, who stared without seeming to see. She appeared neither awake nor asleep. Sevren grew more worried.

As Skymere climbed higher into the hills, the snow grew deeper on the road. Sevren was forced to proceed more slowly. Soon the snowdrifts rose above Skymere's knees, and Sevren was forced to dismount. Dar was unable to sit in the saddle, so he laid her across it like a sack of grain. Then he took the reins and broke a path for his horse to follow. It was slow going, and Sevren hoped the drifts would soon diminish. Instead, they grew higher. Time was working against him, and the cold was also. Sevren began to fear that Dar would perish on the road and tears flowed down his frigid face. Despite cold and fatigue, he pushed on, stopping only to check that Dar still lived.

As the night grew old, Sevren began to despair. He had spent far more time struggling in the snowdrifts than reaching them. Despite all his efforts, the pass was distant. He raged against the elements and reproached himself for letting them defeat him.

When a hint of dawn lightened the sky, Sevren spied a dark shape on the road. It seemed to be a man on foot. He was running. Sevren watched him come closer. Soon he realized the runner was an orc. Sevren grew nervous, wondering if he had committed some offense by taking Dar away. If he had, Dar was in no condition to explain his actions. Sevren waited. At the rate the orc was moving, he would catch him soon.

When the orc arrived, all he said was "Follow me." He took the lead, easily pushing his way through the drifts. Sevren meekly trailed behind. The orc walked down the road a distance, then veered toward a sheltered spot. He cleared a space in the snow, lifted Dar from the horse, and placed her on his lap as he sat down. Sevren watched, feeling excluded, as the orc sniffed Dar's breath, then pulled up her gown to examine her chest. A dark spot the size of Sevren's fist was revealed. In the dim light, it resembled a hole beneath Dar's breast. The orc looked up. "Break branches from tree," he said, pointing to a bare pine. "She needs fire."

Sevren did as he was told. When he returned, the orc was cradling Dar so she faced toward him. He was chewing something, and as Sevren watched, he took out a dagger and pulled up Dar's gown to expose her wound again. Sevren grew alarmed. "What are you doing?"

The orc looked up, his blade poised over Dar's discolored flesh. "I make magic," he mumbled, his mouth full. He drew the blade three times over the dark spot, creating a star-shaped incision. As blood welled up, he bent over and spat into the new wound.

"Can you save her?"

"This is small magic," said the orc, his mouth still stuffed. "It will give her time, nothing more." The orc continued spitting until the bloody star was completely covered. Then he spat out a wad of chewed herbs, pulled down Dar's gown, and wrapped her in the cloak. He handed Sevren a bag containing tinder, a flint, and an iron. "Will you make fire? She should be warm."

"Hai," said Sevren, using the little Orcish he knew. As he worked, he couldn't help but notice the tenderness with which the orc held Dar. It made him uncomfortable. Sevren realized he was jealous. At last, he felt compelled to speak. "Are you the orc that sheltered her in the army camp?"

"Hai. I am Kovok-mah."

"Do you love her?"

"I do not know that word."

Sevren pointed to his heart. "Big feeling. Here."

"Hai, Dargu-yat fills my chest." Kovok-mah sniffed the air. "Like she fills yours."

Sevren realized that the orc had smelled his atur. Then, knowing that his feelings were already exposed, he asked the question that bared them even further. "And what of Dargu-yat's chest. Do you fill hers?"

"It matters not."

"Because she's going to die?"

"Even if she lived, we could never be blessed."

"Does that mean 'married'?"

"I think so."

Sevren regarded Kovok-mah, who looked so alien to him, and marveled that such a creature could think of marrying Dar. Yet he felt certain that the orc had. *Had Dar similar thoughts?* Sevren realized he'd never know. *That's one thing we have in common—we both love a woman who's about to die.* Then sympathy made Kovok-mah seem less alien. "She's Great Mother now," said Sevren, "so, like yours, my feelings matter not."

"I understand your sadness," said Kovok-mah. He studied Sevren awhile. "I think you are not like most washavokis. Let us care for Dargu-yat together while she lives."

Sevren moved to where Kovok-mah cradled Dar, and held her hands to warm them. Whether it was the warmth of the fire, the healing magic, the attention of the two who loved her most, or a combination of these things, the pain left Dar's face. After the sun rose, she opened her eyes and smiled weakly. "Sevren," she whispered. "Kovok."

"Kovok-mah gave you healing magic," said Sevren. "You'll be home soon."

"Hurry," whispered Dar.

Sevren mounted Skymere, then grasped Dar when Kovok-mah lifted her up. Afterward, the orc strode to the snow-choked road, clearing a path for the horse and its two riders. In this manner, the three wound their way toward the pass. The sun shone in a clear sky, but the air was crisp and a wind made it bite. Dar slumped against Sevren and appeared oblivious of everything.

Dar didn't see the mountains or feel the wind on her face. She existed in the twilight world of her visions, which she observed through closed eyes. It had become more real to her than waking life, a misty landscape where most features were indistinct. Yet some things were clear to her. Without moving her head, she glanced downward and saw Skymere's heart pulsing in his chest. It was large and glowed with every beat. Dar understood that the horse would gladly run for Sevren until that great heart burst. *It's a form of love*, she realized. Dar perceived Kovok-mah's heart in the same way and viewed Sevren's also. Although their feelings were more complex than the horse's, she understood them. *Is this how Muth la sees her world?*

Dar's view of her own body conjured up memories of her vision with Muth-pah. The hole in her chest was distinct, its edges glowing faintly red. Her skin appeared as a translucent shell. It seemed to be growing thinner as the hole grew larger. Inside her skin, Fathma fluttered like a bird within a jar. *If my skin breaks, Fathma will fly away. Then it will be lost to the urkzimmuthi.*

Through a force of will, Dar returned to the world of wind and mountains. She opened her eyes and saw the snowy road glow in the morning sunlight. She felt Sevren's arm around her and saw his hand grasping the reins. "Hurry," she whispered.

Beyond the pass, the road headed downward and the snow became less deep. After a while, Kovok-mah was no longer needed to break a trail. "You should ride ahead," he said to Sevren. "When you get to hall, say this—'Dargu-yat nak Muth Mauk. Fer thayak.' It means 'Dargu-yat is Great Mother. She is dying.' They will do what is necessary."

"But you gave her healing magic."

"That was only small magic. I have little skill." Kovok-mah reached into his cloak, pulled out an object, and showed it to Sevren. It resembled a handle from a small knife until Kovok-mah pressed a button on its side. Out sprang a wicked-looking spike. Kovok-mah pointed to its discolored end. "This is poison. Say 'Gatav ma muth thusi.' It means 'Bring me healing mother.' Show her this." Kovok-mah pressed the button again, and the spike retracted. Then he handed the weapon to Sevren. "Go now. Ride quickly."

Sevren spurred Skymere onward, and as the road became less treacherous, the horse ran ever faster without urging. It was as if Skymere understood the importance of getting Dar home. They sped down the road and entered a twisting valley. Sevren noted small huts in the empty meadows and guessed they were close to their destination. Since Dar was unconscious, he couldn't ask. Without any command from Sevren, Skymere broke into a gallop. The road turned, and the Yat clan hall was visible for the first time.

When Sevren reached the hall's gates, he spoke the words he had memorized to the two orcs who flanked the door. They reacted immediately, lifting Dar down and carrying her into the hall. Sevren followed behind them. There, he saw many orcs who were different from any he had seen before. Their proportions were similar to those of humans and their faces were similar also. Sevren knew they were females, for most wore no covering over their breasts. It was obvious that they, not the males, were in charge.

The guards took Dar into a circular room and laid her on a mat close to a hearth. Several orc females were there, and Dar's arrival stirred them into action. Sevren saw grief but no hysteria. One of the orcs rushed over to Sevren. "I am Zor-yat. Queen was my sister. Dargu-yat is my daughter. Tell me what happened to her."

Sevren was so relieved that the orc spoke in the human tongue that he didn't question her assertion that Dar was her child. "The mage has poisoned Dar," he said, producing the weapon. "It's still on the blade." He made the spike appear. "Can you bring a healing mother?"

Of all the orcs in the room, Zor-yat displayed the least

emotion. That surprised Sevren when he considered that Zor-yat had just learned she had lost a sister and was about to lose Dar. With the sangfroid of a hardened veteran, she took the weapon and said something in Orcish. Another female came over to take the poisoned weapon from the room. Zor-yat turned back to Sevren. "Tell me how Dargu-yat became Great Mother."

Sevren briefly described Dar's rescue of the queen and the ceremony that soon followed. When he finished, Zor-yat asked. "Did you see Great Mother touch Dargu-yat's chest?"

"I did."

Zor-yat appeared pleased. "That is good. Very good."

Another orc female arrived in the room, and Zor-yat went over to talk to her. Not understanding what was being said, Sevren could only watch. A young female kneeled beside Dar. She gently stroked Dar's face. Dar didn't respond. Her eyes were open, but seemingly blind.

An orc female arrived with a flask of liquid. She made the other orcs stand apart before she undressed Dar and examined her chest. The ugly purple mark beneath Dar's breast was larger than when Sevren last saw it, and the star-shaped cuts that Kovok-mah had made no longer reached its edges. The orc bent down and sniffed the mark. Then she lifted Dar's head and slowly poured liquid from the flask into her mouth. When the flask was empty, she lowered Dar's head to the mat.

Zor-yat and another orc crouched by Dar's side. Everyone seemed to be waiting; yet the liquid appeared to have no effect. Dar lay motionless, staring blankly at the ceiling. Time passed without any change. Then Dar suddenly tried to rise.

Dar was aware that she had returned home, but she was unable to leave the world of mist. She heard voices, but they sounded distant. She felt the touch of hands.

Though motionless, she was aware of everything, perceiving the world through an inner eye. She saw forms around her and knew they were urkzimmuthi. Their faces were unrecognizable, but their spirits were exposed. One glowed. It possessed qualities that were visible to Dar's new sight: compassion, wisdom, and fortitude.

Fathma burned brightly within the fading shell of Dar's body. *It's time to pass it on.* Dar knew exactly where it must go—to the glowing spirit before her. *If I only had the strength.* Then a hand lifted her head, and strength poured down her throat. Eventually, Dar felt able to bestow Fathma. She marshaled all her strength and rose up to grasp the bright spirit.

The spirit wasn't there! The faceless forms before Dar were not worthy to receive Muth la's gift. Dar cried out. "Naug . . ." *Where . . .* Before she could say more, the forms darkened and expanded, becoming a void that encompassed everything. Dar's strength dissipated. As she sank down, all she could perceive was Fathma glowing in the dark.

Forty-four

♛

Muth-yat and Zor-yat sat in the Great Chamber. The sun's last rays streamed through the windows, illuminating the throne with golden hues. Zor-yat gazed at the royal seat and sighed. "I was certain either you or I would sit there."

"Instead, your daughter will," said Muth-yat.

"My *daughter*." Zor-yat pronounced the word with a bitter twist. "You said she'd die."

"Didn't you also think so? You heard her vision. She had hole in chest. Her spirit was pouring out of it."

Zor-yat nodded. "Indeed, it seemed she had foretold her death. What happened?"

"Who knows? Perhaps healing magic saved her. Perhaps Muth la."

"Why would Muth la spare Dargu and not our sister?" asked Zor-yat. "Zeta was queen, and Dargu was just some washavoki."

"Don't you believe she was reborn?"

"I don't understand magic, and I can't see another's spirit. Dargu may be urkzimmuthi inside, but all I see is washavoki."

"She has clan tattoo," said Muth-yat.

"Hai. Otherwise, she looks same." Zor-yat wrinkled her nose. "Smells same, too."

"Since you knew magic would only change her spirit, why did you agree to become her muthuri?"

"It seemed wise plan when you asked me," said Zor-yat. "And I thought things would turn out differently."

"My plan didn't entirely lack wisdom," said Muth-yat. "I spoke with washavoki that brought Dargu here."

Zor-yat wrinkled her nose again. "One who smelled of atur?"

"Hai. Just like your brother's son. I spoke with him also. Both had interesting news. Dargu was busy in Taiben. Mother rules washavokis now. Urkzimmuthi sons will no longer kill for them. King is dead. So is Black Washavoki. He wasn't just Dargu's enemy. He threatened all urkzimmuthi."

"Hai. Hai. But what do those things matter compared to Velasa-pah's prophecy?" said Zor-yat. "Admit it, Sister, we've been fools!"

"Things have gone ill, but how could we have foreseen it? Velasa-pah's prophecy didn't seem to apply. He spoke of queen, not some wandering washavoki."

"But Dargu's queen now, so doom approaches." Zor-yat sighed. "If only we hadn't made that magic."

"Don't despair," said Muth-yat. "There's hope yet."

"Could her wound still kill her?"

"Healer says she'll recover. But new-crowned queens can perish for other reasons. Custom is unforgiving, and Dargu is newly born. In some ways, she's as naive as an infant."

"As in her feelings for my brother's son?"

"Hai. Dargu is unaware how close disaster looms."

"Well, she's great mother now," said Zor-yat, smiling for the first time. "It's not *our* place to tell her."

In Taiben, Valamar and a new recruit entered the great hall, bearing a stretcher. "A word of advice, lad," said the seasoned guardsman. "Never cross your murdant."

"Is that why you pulled this duty?" asked the recruit.

"Aye. All because of a tavern wench." Valamar grinned. "But she's worth it. Come on, let's get this foul task over."

The two guardsmen crossed the hall and unlocked the room where the parley had taken place. The light was fading, and the bloodstain on the floor resembled a shadow creeping toward the mage. His body still lay where it had fallen.

The recruit shivered. "It's freezing in here!"

"Aye, it's unnatural cold," said Valamar, his breath visible in the frigid air. "They say Black Crow's tower was the same."

The younger guardsman peered at the mage. "You sure he's dead?"

"Look at him! He's burned to a cinder."

"But his robe isn't even singed. And his eyes! I swear he's staring at me!"

"You've had no dealings with the slain," said Valamar. "I've seen whole towns full." He casually leaned down and closed the mage's eyelids. "There. Does that suit you better? Now give me a hand."

The two guardsmen lifted Othar's body onto the stretcher. When they did, the mage's boots remained on the floor. Like his robe, they were unaffected by whatever had ravaged him. Valamar picked up one and upended it. Ash poured out, mingled with charred bone. "Fancy a pair of boots? They're almost new."

The recruit shrank back. Valamar laughed and tossed the boots on the stretcher.

"Where are we taking him?" asked the recruit.

"We're to dump him in the pit. He killed our king, so he can rot with criminals and vagrants." Valamar smiled. "Our new queen's gentle. I'd have dumped him in a cesspool."

The two men carried their gruesome burden out to the courtyard where a horse and cart were waiting. They put

Othar in the back and drove off hurriedly in order to return before the city gate closed for the night. The pit lay outside the city walls, just far enough away so its stench didn't bother Taiben's inhabitants. The royal mage's funeral ceremony consisted of a quick toss into the hole followed by the guardsmen's hasty departure.

Night fell. Thick clouds obscured the moon and stars. Inside the burial pit, Othar opened his eyes.

END OF BOOK TWO

Glossary of
Orcish Terms
♛

armor Warfare was unknown to the orcs before they encountered humans, and their armor is based on human designs. It is strictly functional, being devoid of ornamentation, and more massive than its human counterpart. Orcs call armor *loukap*, which translates as "hard clothes." The basic item consists of a long, sleeveless tunic made from heavy cloth reinforced with leather and covered with overlapping steel plates. The plates are small and rounded at the lower end to permit ease of movement. The effect is that of fish scales. This tunic is worn most of the time in the orc regiments. Its protection is supplemented by additional armor strapped to the arms and legs. These pieces tend to be worn only while marching or in combat. A rounded helmet completes an orc's armor. Simple in design, it encloses much of the head. There are small holes opposite the ears, and the area about the face is open to permit good vision and communication. Some helmets have nose guards.

Orcs regard their armor as a tool necessary for distasteful work. They take no pride in its appearance, allowing it to rust.

atur noun—The scent indicating love. Also see "sexual practices."

bah noun—Eye.

Bah Niti proper noun—The night of the new moon. *(Hidden Eye)*

Bah Simi proper name—Orcish name for Murdant Kol. *(Blue Eye)*

bakt noun—Orcish tool for working stone. It is similar to a hammer.

bathing As opposed to humans, orcs bathe frequently. If given the opportunity, they will do so daily. This fondness for cleanliness is probably related to their keen sense of smell. Orc settlements have communal baths where both sexes often bathe together.

biting of neck A practice where one orc voluntarily and permanently submits to another. The relationship is similar to that of a mistress or master and her or his disciple, although strict obedience is expected from the bitten individual.

Blath Urkmuthi proper noun—Orcish name for Urkheit Mountains. *(cloak [of] mothers)*

blessed adjective—Human translation for *vashi*, the Orcish word for "married." The term refers to the fact that an orc couple's union must be approved by both their respective muthuris. In practice, a muthuri will seldom reject her daughter's choice of husband. A son's muthuri is more likely to oppose a marriage. Also see "sexual practices."

blooded mother noun—An orc female who has received the Gift, or monthly period, and is thus considered an adult. Some clan lore is revealed only to blooded mothers.

brak noun—A tuber with crunchy yellow flesh that has a nutty flavor. Called "groundnut" by humans.

cape, as a sign of leadership. See "military ranks and units—orc leaders."

chest Orcs consider the chest, not the heart, to be the site of emotion. Their expression "to have big chest" means one is brave. A lover would say that his or her beloved "fills my chest."

clan noun—Related orc families that form the principal social unit of orcish society. A mother's offspring belong to her clan, and her daughters will spend their lives in her household. When sons marry, they move into their wife's household, but retain their clan affiliation. Each clan is headed by a matriarch who assumes the name "Muth" upon her election. The matriarchs are subordinate only to the orc queen, and they form a council that occasionally meets to advise her. Every clan has a distinctive tattoo that is marked on the chins of its members when they reach adulthood.

cursed one The human term for an individual afflicted by the "rotting curse," or leprosy. The cursed are feared and shunned, but the belief that their affliction passes to another upon death insures they are not slain. The cursed carry bells to warn of their approach and live off the offerings given to speed their departure.

dargu noun—Weasel.

Dark Path proper noun—The human term for the afterlife. Also known as the Sunless Way, it is conceived as a plane of existence that parallels the living world. Spirits of the dead travel the path on a westward journey to the goddess Karm, leaving their memories behind in the process.

death song The human term for the *thathyatai*, a song sung by orc males prior to going to war. Though mournful, it is not principally about death. Its purpose is to cleanse the spirit and beseech Muth la's comfort. The origins of the song are lost, though it undoubtedly dates from the beginning of the washavoki invasions.

deception Orcs do not have words for any form of deception, such as "trickery," "lying," "betrayal," etc. Sometimes lying is called "speaking words without meaning," but the understanding of this expression comes closer to "speaking nonsense" than to "lying."

depyata noun—Orcish soap that is used in a paste form. It is unknown to humans, who use herbs or flower petals in bathwater on those rare occasions when they wash. *(dirt go)*

falf noun—Water.

falfhissi noun—A potent distilled spirit flavored with washuthahi seeds and honey. It is often drunk at the conclusion of a feast. *(laughing water)*

fath noun—Spirit or soul.

Fathma proper noun—Muth la's gift to the orcs, it is a unique spirit that confers sovereignty. Passed from one queen to the next, Fathma transforms its recipient's spirit by mingling with it. The queen comes to regard all orcs as her children and becomes dedicated to their welfare. She also receives part of the essences of all the past queens. As a queen approaches death, her ability to perceive the inner qualities of others becomes enhanced. This allows her to choose a worthy successor. Because the queen's spirit and Fathma are intermingled, once she transfers this gift to another, the orcs consider her deceased. Henceforth, they will not openly acknowledge her existence.

Fathma was lost to the orcs when their queen was slain during the fall of Tarathank. For several generations, there was no queen, and the orcs suffered a period of chaos. Fathma returned to the orcs when a child who possessed it was born in the easternmost settlement. She was a member of the Yat clan, and afterward, that clan became the Queen Clan.

Flis Muthi proper noun—Orcish name for the bridge over the Turgen River. *(leap [of] mother)*

funeral practices Orcs send the bodies of their dead to Muth la in the same state they entered the world—naked. Corpses are cremated or left upon the ground (*Te far Muthz la*—On Muth la's breast). In the latter case, the body is placed within Muth la's Embrace (see separate entry), preferably under a tree.

Gift noun—Orcish term for a mother's monthly period. A mother receives the clan tattoo after her first period, for she is considered to have reached adulthood.

goblin noun—Another human word for "orc." This term is mainly used in the western kingdom.

Goblin Wars proper noun—The human name for the orcs' attempts to retake their lands after the washavoki invasion. Savagely fought by both sides, this conflict lasted several generations. Most of the fighting was in the form of raids. When it ended, no orc settlements remained south of the Urkheit Mountains.

goldenroot noun—A root, tawny in color, that is a staple crop among humans. It resembles a turnip, is filling, and can be eaten raw.

great mother noun—The orc queen. Also see "Muth Mauk."

hai adverb—Yes.

hanmuthi noun—A circular room with a central hearth that is the heart of orc family life. Meals are eaten there, and sleeping chambers adjoin it. Its outer walls constitute the Embrace of Muth la. The ranking muthuri heads the hanmuthi and commands the obedience of all its members. *(hearth [of] mother)*

hard milk noun—Orcish term for cheese.

healer noun—An orc who practices healing magic. This "magic" is based on an understanding of the medicinal properties of herbs and other practical therapies. It does not involve sorcery. Both sexes may be healers, though the most skilled healers are mothers.

high murdant—See "military ranks and units."

high tolum—See "military ranks and units."

hiss verb root and noun—To laugh, laughter.
human noun—Human word for *washavoki*.

Karm proper noun—Goddess worshipped by humans. Called the Goddess of the Balance, Karm is supposed to weigh one's deeds after death.
kefs noun—A pair of short capes of slightly differing sizes that are worn by orcish mothers. In warm weather, the smaller cape is worn on top of the larger one so that the breasts are exposed. In cold weather, it covers the chest.
kip noun—Orcish tool for working stone. It is similar to a chisel.

latath noun—A clan mother who bestows the clan tattoo.

man noun—There is no equivalent term in Orcish for a human male, although they are sometimes called "hairy-faced washavokis."
military ranks and units Orcs never developed a highly organized military, and all the following terms are of human origin. In the orc regiments, all the officers were human.
  general—The highest-ranking officer. The general for the orc regiments was called the **Queen's Man** because the orcs believed he derived his authority from their queen.
  high murdant—The highest-ranking noncommissioned officer. A high murdant reports directly to a general.
  high tolum—Usually commands a regiment.
  human ranks Ranks in ancient armies were less specific than in contemporary ones, and the modern equivalents are only approximate.
  military units An orc regiment was composed of orc fighters, commanded by human officers. Human

soldiers served support roles, and women served both the orcs and men. A **shieldron** was the basic orc fighting unit. It consisted of thirty-six orcs. The term was also applied to a shieldron of orcs and the humans that commanded and supported them. An orc **regiment** had six shieldrons of orc fighters, accompanied by a human contingent of officers, support troops, and serving women.

murdant—A noncommissioned officer, the equivalent of a sergeant.

orc leaders Orcs had no officers or murdants, but did recognize leaders among their own kind. Such leaders lacked the authority of human officers and led by their example and through the use of persuasion. They wore **capes** as a sign of wisdom. These capes were bestowed by the consensus of their comrades and could be taken away in the same manner. The authority of **Wise Sons** derived from the clan matriachs who appointed them to act in their absence. They guided the orc males in nonmilitary matters. Outside the orc regiments, they had no more authority than ordinary orc males.

sustolum—The lowest-ranking officer, the equivalent of a lieutenant.

tolum—The equivalent of a captain. Usually commands a shieldron (see below).

min noun—A male orc, regardless of age. Usually translated as "son."

minvashi noun—Husband. *(blessed son)*

moon noun—Human word for *bahthithi*, which translates as "silver eye." The eye referred to is Muth la's.

mother noun—The human translation for the Orcish word *muth*, although the two terms are not completely equivalent.

murdant—See "military ranks and units."

muth noun—Often translated as "mother," it is the word for any orc female, regardless of age or whether she has borne children. Orcs occasionally use this word to describe human females. Mothers wield the real authority within orc society because Muth la's guidance always comes through them.

Muth proper noun—This is the name a mother assumes when she becomes matriarch of a clan. Thus the head of the Yat clan is always named Muth-yat. The orc queen also assumes this name. However, she is called *Muth Mauk*, which means "Great Mother."

Muth la proper noun—Orcish word for the divine mother who created the world and all living things. Muth la sends guidance to mothers through visions.

Muth la's Embrace proper noun—Human translation for *Zum Muthz la*. This sacred circle symbolizes the Divine Mother's presence. It may be temporary or permanent. Orcs always sleep and eat within its confines. A wall, upright sticks, stones, or even a line drawn in the dirt can mark the circle. Orc dwellings always incorporate Muth la's Embrace and tend to be circular for this reason. The Embrace is hallowed ground; the dead are placed within it and worship takes place there. It is said that mothers are more likely to receive visions within Muth la's Embrace.

Muth Mauk proper noun—Orc queen. *(Great Mother)* This is both the queen's title and her proper name. The orcs also use *nathmauki* as a word for "queen."

muthuri noun—A mother in the reproductive sense. A muthuri holds strict authority over her offspring. The ranking muthuri heads a hanmuthi. *(giving mother)*

muthtufa noun—A traditional, spicy orcish stew that consists of pashi and other vegetables.

muthvashi noun—Wife. *(blessed mother)*

names Orcish names consist of two parts, the given name and the clan name. Thus, Zna-yat is a member of the Yat clan. In the familiar form of address, the clan part of the name is dropped. This is often done when parents talk to their children, when adult mothers of the same clan converse, or when intimates speak together.

When a mother becomes the clan matriarch, she assumes the given name of "Muth." The orc queen assumes the name "Muth Mauk," *Great Mother*. Her name has no clan part because she is mother to all the clans.

nayimgat noun—A healing herb with large, fuzzy leaves that is also a sedative.

neva noun—An article of clothing worn by orcish mothers that resembles a skirt. It may consist of a length of cloth wrapped around the waist or it may be a tailored garment.

nuf noun—Night.

Nuf Bahi proper noun—Night of the full moon. *(Night [of] Eye)*

orc noun—Human word for *zimmuthi*. The human word derives from the shortening of the orcs' collective name for themselves, *urkzimmuthi*.

orcs noun—Human word for *urkzimmuthi*.

orcish adjective—Human word for *urkzimmuthi*.

Orcish language Orcish is the human word for *Pahmuthi*, which translates as "speech [of] mother." Orcish differs from human speech in several ways: The equivalents of the articles "a" and "the" do no exist. Adjectives follow the noun they modify. All personal pronouns are gender-specific when they refer to orcs, with mixed-gender plurals taking the feminine form. Genderless pronouns are used for things, animals, and humans. Plurals are indicated by the prefix *urk*, which translates as "many." Possession is indicated by the addition of a "z" to the end of a noun. Orcish nouns are often formed by the descriptive combination of other words. Example: "Rain," *hafalf*, combines "sky," *ha*, with "water," *falf*. Verbs are conjugated regularly and their roots often function as nouns. Example: *Ma urav ur*—I give gift. *A more extensive treatment of Orcish grammar and vocabulary can be found in the glossary to* King's Property.

Pahmuthi noun—Orcish language. *(speech [of] mother)*
pashi noun—A bland-flavored root that is a staple in orcish cooking. Called "whiteroot" by humans, it is more flavorful when roasted.

Queen's Man—See "military ranks and units."

rebirth noun—An ancient orcish ritual that allows a washavoki with "mixed spirits" to become urkzimmuthi. Although physically unchanged, a reborn person becomes the child of the muthuri participating in the ritual and receives her clan tattoo. There is controversy over whether rebirth involves actual sorcery.
regiment—See "military ranks and units."

samuth noun—A part of courtship where an unblessed mother travels to the hall of another clan and is visited by its eligible sons. *(see mother)*
sand ice noun—Orcish term for glass. Orcs first discovered the secret of its making.
sapaha noun—A guide.
scabhead noun—Human slang for a newly branded woman serving in the orc regiments.
sexual practices Orcish sexual practices differ markedly from human ones for two reasons: Females are the dominant sex in orcish society, and orcs can detect the

scent of love, which they call "atur." The latter insures that orcish courtship lacks the bumbling and misunderstandings that often characterize its human counterpart. It also means orcs cannot keep their feelings secret.

Intimacy is always initiated by the female. This is usually done by the mother grasping the son's hand and touching it to her breast. This gesture is the socially proper sign that she is receptive to his attentions. Until he receives permission, a son will not express his desire by word or deed. The orcs believe if a son were to make unwanted advances, Muth la would condemn him to eternal punishment. Thus, despite human claims to the contrary, rape is unknown among orcs.

Sexual intercourse between unblessed (i.e., unmarried) couples is forbidden and carries strict sanctions (see "blessed" and "thwada"). However, any intimacy that falls short of intercourse is considered a proper part of courtship. Orcs call such acts "giving love." A son or a mother at this stage of courtship is called a *velazul*, which loosely translates as "lover." It is not uncommon for mothers to have several velazuls before becoming blessed.

A muthuri will commonly ignore a relationship until it becomes serious. When she shows awareness of a couple's attachment, the muthuri is said to have a "wise nose." Then she is expected to act in the couple's best interests by either facilitating or preventing their permanent union. If a muthuri disapproves of the relationship, she will end it by forbidding her child to see his or her velazul.

shash verb root and noun—To thank, thanks. *Shashav* translates as "thank you."

shieldron—See "military ranks and units."

sleep Orcs sleep sitting upright in a cross-legged position, with only a mat as a cushion. Only babies and the extremely ill rest lying down.

smell Orcs have an especially keen sense of smell, and their language contains many terms for scents that humans cannot distinguish. They are also capable of smelling emotional states and physical conditions. They can detect anger, fear, love, pain, and some forms of sickness. This ability has affected their culture in fundamental ways and may partly explain why orcs do not easily grasp deception. Orcs usually do not speak about those emotions they detect by smell. This is particularly true of the males.

spirit noun—The human word for *fath*. An equivalent term would be "soul." The orcs hold that one's spirit defines one's being. That is why they believe rebirth is possible, since the ritual alters the spirit. Fathma is an additional spirit that passes from orc queen to orc queen. It mingles with the queen's original spirit and transforms it. In the process, it instills aspects of the queen's predecessors.

sun noun—Human word for *bahriti*, which translates as "golden eye." The eye referred to is Muth la's.

sustolum—See "military ranks and units."

tabuc noun—Root crop grown by humans. It must be cooked before it is edible.

tahwee noun—Bird.

Tarathank proper noun—An ancient orcish city destroyed during the washavoki invasion. It was the queen's city in the time when the monarch always came from the Pah clan. Other clans also had their halls in Tarathank. For this reason, it was called the City of Matriarchs. Tarathank was the center of the orcish civilization at its greatest height, and its grace and splendor were never matched. Since orcs of that era were ignorant of warfare, the city lacked defenses.

tava interjection—Hello.

thrim verb root—To have sexual intercourse.

thung noun—A succulent leaf grown by orcs. Its thick sap tastes similar to broth.

thwa adverb—No, not.

thwada noun—A condition that renders an orcish mother untouchable. There are two kinds of thwada and they are very different in their cause and nature. The ceremonial thwada is temporary and pertains to mothers about to undergo certain serious spiritual rituals, such as Entering Darkness. Contact with that mother is considered dangerous to all involved. In this state of thwada, the mother cannot eat or associate with sons.

The second form of thwada is a punishment imposed on a mother for having intercourse before she is blessed or continuing in a forbidden relationship. The mother is considered dead, and no member of orc society will have open dealings with her. This form of thwada is permanent. A mother who is thwada leads a ghostlike existence on the outskirts of society, seen but ignored. Though she sometimes dies of hunger and exposure, orcs usually sustain her by "losing" necessities in her vicinity.

It is interesting to note that this punishment is inflicted only on mothers. Offending sons are permanently disgraced, but permitted to remain within society.

tiv noun—An orcish digging tool with a short handle and narrow flat blade affixed to its end at a right angle. It is used for planting root cuttings.

tolum—See "military ranks and units."

Tree Because trees bridge the earth and sky, orcs consider them a manifestation of Muth la. They make a sign for Muth la by pressing a palm upright against the chest and splaying the fingers like branches. This sign is usually made to acknowledge Muth la's presence in an event or deed.

tul adjective—Real, having a verifiable existence. This word approaches the meaning of the human expression "true," although the orcs have no term for its opposite.

urkzimmuthi noun and adjective—The orc race, also the plural of orc. As an adjective it means "orcish." *(children [of] mother)*

urkzimdi noun—An ancient orcish term for humans. It translates as "second children" and is based on the orcs' belief that Muth la created humans after she created them. The word fell into disuse after the washavoki invasion.

vash verb root and noun—1. To bless, blessing. 2. To marry, marriage.

vata interjection—Good-bye.

vathem noun—A stone retaining wall used to create a terraced field. After the orcs occupied the Urkheit Mountains, such fields were used extensively.

Velasa-pah proper noun—The name of a human who was reborn before the washavoki invasion and became a great urkzimmuthi wizard. He tried to warn the orc queen of the invasion, but she failed to comprehend the danger or act upon his advice. He was residing in Tarathank when it fell. The orcs tell differing tales about his fate and the nature of his prophecies

velazul noun—Lover. Unlike the human term, it is used only in the chaste sense. *(give love)*

wash noun—Tooth.

washavoki noun and adjective—Human, either male or female. The word translates as "teeth of dog" and refers to the whiteness of human teeth.

washavoki invasion The first contacts between humans and orcs were peaceful, but that era was ended by the onslaught of human invaders from the east. At that time, orcs were ignorant of warfare and they were easily overwhelmed despite their superior size and strength. Although orcs quickly learned how to make arms and became ferocious fighters, they never acquired the strategic skills required for victory. They were driven from their lands and survived only in the inhospitable Urkheit Mountains, which they named *Blath Urkmuthi* because they sheltered fleeing mothers.

washuthahi noun—A black, pea-shaped seed that is mildly narcotic and stains the teeth black when chewed. *(teethpretty)*

weapons Orcs did not make weapon before the washavoki invasion, and their arms are adapted from human designs. Swords, axes, and maces are primarily used for combat, but orcs also carry daggers and sometimes hatchets. All their weapons are strictly utilitarian in design. They reflect the orcs' strength, being larger and more massive than those humans carry. Spears and pikes are not unknown to orcs, but they are rarely used. Although orcs use bows and arrows for hunting, they do not employ them in combat.

wind noun—Human word for *foof Muthz la*, which translates as "Muth la's breath."

wife noun—Human word for *muthvashi.*

Wise Sons—See "military ranks and units—orc leaders."

Wise Woman noun—A human woman skilled in the healing arts. Wise Women also practiced midwifery.

woman noun—An orc female is called a *muth*, but the term is not commonly applied to human females. There is no specific term for them in Orcish, although "woe man," a corrupted pronunciation of "woman," is occasionally employed.

yes adverb—Hai.

zim noun—Child.
zimmuthi noun—The singular form of "orc." *(child [of]
    mother)*
zul verb root and noun—To love, love.

Read on for an excerpt from the final book in
the Queen of the Orcs trilogy

Royal Destiny

♛

Morgan Howell

On sale September 25, 2007

♛

Dar awoke, both surprised and puzzled. "Mer lav?" *I
live?*

A mother knelt before her. She bowed her head and
replied in Orcish. "Muth la has preserved your life."

Why? thought Dar. She had returned to pass on
Fathma, the Divine Mother's gift that bestowed sovereignty over the orcs. In her near-death state, she had been
able to see it fluttering within the shell of her body, a
thing of spirit like a second soul. That vision had departed. Dar could no longer see her spirit or any other's.
The world was solid again. It was also unfamiliar.
"Where am I?" she asked in Orcish.

"Your hanmuthi, Muth Mauk."

Dar realized that she was still queen. Muth Mauk—
Great Mother—was not only her title; it had become her
name. Dar tried to raise her head and look about, but
found she couldn't. She recalled the mother's face, but not
her name. After Dar had been reborn, every Yat clan

member had formally introduced him or herself, and the parade of visitors had lasted days. "I know you," said Dar, "but I forget your name."

"I'm Deen-yat, clan healer."

"I thought I was dying."

"You were," said the healer.

Dar thought she should be relieved and joyful. Instead, she felt daunted. *I returned to pass on the crown, not rule!* In her still-fragile state, that task seemed overwhelming. *I don't know what to do!*

Deen-yat smelled Dar's anxiety, but mistook its reason. "You'll live, Muth Mauk."

"Then I have your skill to thank."

"Your recovery is not my deed. That herb's magic is deadly."

"I was only scratched by blade."

"Such scratches have slain sons, and quickly too. Your life is Muth la's gift."

Dar knew Deen-yat's words were meant to comfort, but they didn't. *Muth la has her own purposes.* While Dar thought she understood why she had become queen, she couldn't understand why she remained so.

"How long have I been here?"

"Sun has risen thrice since your return."

"I wish to see my muthuri and my sisters."

"And you will when you're better." Deen-yat smiled. "Even queens must obey healers."

The healer stayed by Dar's side and tended her throughout the day. Toward evening, Dar found the strength to sit up and gaze about. She was in one of the numerous sleeping chambers of the largest hanmuthi she had ever seen. Even the sleeping chambers had adjoining rooms of their own. *Many families could live here,* she thought. She peered through a carved stone archway into the spacious central room. As with all hanmuthis, it was circular and featured a hearth in its center. The room was empty, as were all the other chambers.

Dar's chamber was especially magnificent. There was a huge window glazed with panes of sand ice. The floor was a mosaic of a flowery meadow. The meadow extended to the stone walls, which were carved with a low relief that depicted a landscape. The foreground was filled with delicately rendered wildflowers. In the distance was an orcish city. "It that Tarathank?" asked Dar.

"Hai, Muth Mauk."

"I've visited its ruin," said Dar, recalling her night with Kovok-mah. Deen-yat's expression underwent a subtle change, and Dar realized that the healer had smelled atur—the scent of love. Good manners precluded Deen-yat from mentioning it, but orcs seldom hid their feelings.

"Washavoki brought me here on horse," said Dar, "but there was son who helped him. He gave me healing magic on way." Dar glanced down at the star-shaped incision beneath her breast. It was surrounded by dark, discolored flesh. "Did he come here also?"

"Do you mean your muthuri's brother's son?"

"Hai. Kovok-mah."

"He came here, but he has returned home."

Dar's heart sank. In her weakened state, she feared that she might start weeping. "I wish I could have seen him. He helped save my life."

"His muthuri forbade him to be with you," replied Deen-yat. "Once he learned you would live, he couldn't linger."

Dar's despair deepened. *So the word is out. Even Deen-yat knows.* "What of washavoki who brought me?"

"It has returned to its own kind."

So Sevren's gone too, thought Dar. *At least I have my family.* "I'd like to see my muthuri soon. And my sisters, especially Nir-yat." Dar surveyed the empty rooms about her, already missing the lively atmosphere of Zor-yat's hanmuthi. "It's too quiet here."

"Perhaps tomorrow," said Deen-yat. She felt Dar's brow and sniffed her wound. "Hai, you should be well enough to see them." She gave Dar a sympathetic look. "It would do you good. It's lonely being great mother."

It was long after nightfall when Kovok-mah arrived at the hall where his parents lived. As he shook the snow from his cloak, his aunt greeted him. "Sister's son! I'm surprised to see you. Kath! You son has returned from Taiben."

Kath-mah emerged from a sleeping chamber, still rubbing the drowsiness from her eyes. "Kovok? Why are you here? You were sent to kill for washavoki king."

"King is dead, Muthuri. Another rules washavokis now."

"Doesn't our queen wish you to kill for it also?"

"We have new queen."

"This is news indeed! How is that possible? Our queen lived apart."

"She found someone to receive Fathma. Before she died, queen passed it to that mother."

"But mothers no longer visit Taiben."

"This one did."

Kath-mah regarded her son irritably. "Who is she? Why don't you tell me?"

"She was Dargu-yat. But since Fathma changes spirit, she's Dargu-yat no more."

Kath-mah stared at her son, momentarily dumb-founded. Then her expression hardened. "And because I forbade you to be with Dargu-yat, perhaps you think I'll change my mind."

Kovok-mah bowed humbly to his muthuri. "That's my hope."

"When Dargu was reborn, magic transformed her spirit but not her body. She was still as ugly as any washavoki. Now that she's great mother, has that changed?"

"Thwa."

"Then her body won't bear me granddaughters."

"Although I wish for daughters, I think other things are more important."

"That's because you're young. Daughters give you standing. Look at my sister and me. Who greeted you to her hanmuthi?"

"But Dargu is great mother!"

"And her hanmuthi—however grand—will always lack children."

"Then you won't change your mind?"

"Thwa."

"When I saw Dargu-yat in Taiben, she said you would bless us."

"Where would she get that strange notion?"

"Perhaps from her muthuri. Didn't you two speak together?"

"We did. And Zor-yat knew my mind in this matter. She sympathized and even warned me of Dargu-yat's power."

"What power?"

"Your attraction to her is unnatural. That's magic's doing."

"Dargu knows no magic, though Muth la sends her visions. My feelings come from Muth la."

"Don't speak foolishly. Sons don't understand such matters."

Kovok-mah summoned his courage, and for the first time in his life, he refused to submit passively. "My chest is strong in this."

"I know," said Kath-mah. "Air is heavy with your

atur. Whether it is due to magic or Muth la, I remain firm and withhold my blessing. Do nothing rash. Our laws are strict, and even great mothers must bend to them. Heed my wisdom, or your feelings will destroy our queen."